THE
MURDER
CHILDREN

THE
MURDER
CHILDREN

John Ball

SPEAKING VOLUMES, LLC
NAPLES, FLORIDA
2014

The Murder Children

ISBN 978-1-62815-000-1

For Peter J. Pitchess, Sheriff
Los Angeles County, California—
The best in the business

AUTHOR'S NOTE

This book contains savagery and violence that may be disconcerting to some people. Unfortunately, the conditions described are real, and incidents recounted are based on actual occurrences.

I am most grateful to the people of East Los Angeles who in the great majority are both law abiding and have a strong sense of community responsibility. Brothers Phil and Modesto, who represent two different religious orders, have given me great assistance, as have the members of the Citizens' Council, who meet so faithfully at the East Los Angeles Sheriff's Station.

My sincere thanks are tendered to all of the deputies with whom I rode in the field. In particular, Deputy James Vetrovec and his partner, Deputy Richard Valdemar, put in uncounted hours of their own time supplying essential material and expertise.

The faculty of the Los Angeles Sheriff's Academy, surely one of the finest police training schools in the country, was of immense help. In particular I would like to acknowledge the assistance of Sergeant Dave Crisp and Deputy IV John Fernandez in giving me expert instruction in the use of the PR-24 baton.

Captain (now Chief) Jerry Harper and all of the members of the Sheriff's Information Bureau literally made this book possible.

Lieutenant Barry King and Sergeant Dick Rogers knew no limitations in meeting sometimes very difficult requirements.

I am grateful also to Captain Rudy De Leon, Commander, Hollenbeck Division, Los Angeles Police Department, and to Sergeant Raul Vega of the CRASH unit (Concerned Residents Against Street Hooligans) for unstinting help. Investigator William Miller of Southwest Division CRASH also made a major contribution.

Finally, I offer my warmest thanks to Sheriff Peter J. Pitchess for his great support and help. He arranged personally for me to receive that academy training and field activity that I needed to understand more fully the responsibilities borne by the more than 7500 dedicated men and women of the Los Angeles County Sheriff's Department who serve under his direction. He then paid me the very high honor of permitting me, as a reservist, to become one of them.

I trust he will never have cause to regret that decision.

John Ball

THE
MURDER
CHILDREN

CHAPTER ONE

THE ROOM was small and very plain. The bed that it held had been defeated by time—the mattress was worn and lumpy, the blankets thin and tattered. What passed for a dresser had been purchased long ago for a few dollars in a thrift shop. The floor was bare cracked linoleum.

Spread out on the bed there was a black silk taffeta dress that had been carefully prepared and preened. When new it had cost a considerable amount of money because, like a wedding dress, it had been bought for a very special purpose where appearance was paramount and cost, therefore, had to be secondary. It too was a ceremonial garment—one reserved exclusively for funeral occasions. Its purpose was to show the ultimate respect traditionally due to the deceased.

It had last been worn by Mrs. Consuelo Fernandez two years previously, when Reubin had been killed. It had been tight even then and now, despite its billowing size, she was concerned that she could not get into it without disaster. She was enormously heavy and the carbohydrate-filled diet that she loved had been adding to her already massive figure with steady implacability. It could not be let out any more, there was no material left, and no time remained. She would have to squeeze into it somehow. Maria was waiting to help her—Maria who had the curved girlish figure she herself had once possessed many years and thousands of generous plates of rich Mexican food ago.

Painfully, because of her much too ample body, she began to remove her outer clothing. When she was down to her slip, she called for assistance. Her seldom-worn corset would have to be fitted around her body and then tightened until her very flesh protested, but there was no other way. Maria came, and with her her sister Dolores. Together the two girls went to work. It was a mighty struggle for which they had been prepared. Already Dolores was refusing desserts when she was out with her boy friend, and she was eating less and less refried beans. She was a pretty girl with a spectacular bustline that was to her both an asset and a warning.

After the painful preliminary work had been done, the precious dress was lifted over Mrs. Hernandez's head. Dolores guided it while Maria undertook the process of fitting it over her mother's body. It went a little better than had been expected, due to the severe corseting, so that presently Mrs. Hernandez could look at herself in the narrow, wavy mirror mounted flush on the wall and see that she was properly attired for the evening ceremony. Maria fitted on the black shoes which badly cramped her splayed feet. It would all have to be done again in the morning for the actual funeral service, but the wake was very important, and therefore even acute physical discomfort had to be endured. Mrs. Hernandez patted her hair to assure herself that it was in place and then declared that she was ready.

A few steps took her from the bedroom into the small, crowded living room where her husband awaited her. In almost violent contrast to herself, he was a slender man; no one could remember when he had ever had an extra ounce of weight on his body. His gnarled hands hung out of the sleeves of his stiff coat as though they were embarrassed to find themselves in such a situation. Nineteen-year-old Pepe was already outside in the car, an ancient machine that had traveled over a hundred and fifty thousand miles, but which somehow managed to keep on running.

Step by painful step in her tight shoes, Mrs. Hernandez was guided across the sidewalk and then maneuvered backwards into

4

the front seat of the car. Sitting down was painful and hazardous, but she managed it finally, because it had to be done. She was already short of breath, and her face was flushed with the burden of her discomfort.

It was not quite two miles to the church of St. Ynez; during the short ride she sat as close to immobile as she could. If any of the seams of her dress, ample as it was, were to let go, she would be faced with unforgettable disgrace. She could feel the fabric straining against the huge bulges of her body. When the car at last pulled up in front of the church door, she did not attempt to move until her husband had opened the door for her and both he and Pepe had positioned themselves to help her out in as dignified a manner as possible.

With their assistance she got to her feet and climbed the concrete steps up to the door of the sanctuary. Once inside she forgot her suffering body for a few moments as she looked down the nave and once again felt herself to be in the house of the Almighty. Then she made her way on the arm of her husband slowly down the center aisle—toward the altar and toward the casket that rested on a carefully draped stand before it.

She paused for a moment, closed her eyes, and remembered Jesus Manuel when she had last seen him: dressed in an old t-shirt and worn blue jeans, but alive and still in school. Then had come the will of God, and now he awaited her in silent death.

Her mind fortified for what she now faced, tears struggling to escape from her eyes, she approached the coffin and looked down at the peaceful face of her sixteen-year-old son. His eyes were closed, of course, and he lay in a suit he had never worn during his short lifetime. She crossed herself and wiped away the tears that were running down her cheeks. As she did so, she forced herself to remember that he was now in Heaven and with his brother Reubin. How happy they would be to see each other again, even though they had not been that close at home.

When she felt that she could, Mrs. Hernandez bent over the coffin, and looked with close care at the silent face of her departed son. When she straightened up once more, she was grateful and satisfied. They had done a wonderful job; the ugly bullet hole on one side of his forehead hardly showed at all.

* * *

5

Toward the back of the sanctuary Brother Julio sat very quietly in one of the pews. His plain black garments marked him as a servant of the Church, but everyone knew he was not a priest. It was understood that he had taken vows, as indeed he had, and it was conceded that he knew the East Los Angeles barrio as well as any man alive.

Physically he was not especially impressive. He was a thin, almost lean man in his early thirties, of only average height, and with a certain narrowness of face that suggested a distaste for violent action. He did not have the gaunt look that might have made him an El Greco type of religious figure, but at the East Los Angeles Sheriff's Station he was highly respected. A handful of the men there knew that he had already twice been forced to fight for his life, once after he had been badly knifed. Following his recovery from that incident he had declined to press charges, and at his request the matter had been dropped.

Brother Julio had known both of the Hernandez boys before they had been killed; he was present in God's house to add his petition for grace and mercy so that Jesus Manuel's entrance into Heaven would be prompt and abundantly happy. But he was also infused with a cold fear that made him want almost desperately to be out on the streets instead.

The death of Jesus Hernandez had been a gang killing. When he had dropped with a bullet in his brain, it had put up a bitter score, one that would never be forgotten until it had been erased by vengeance. Jesus, like his brother, had been a member of the powerful Chicano gang Los Counts. Now, in the continuing warfare that raged between Los Counts and the even larger gang from the section known as the Heights, there was a deadly imbalance. As of that dangerous moment, according to the implacable rules of gangdom, Los Counts owed two murders to their deadly rivals, Montaña Mara. That price would have to be extracted, clearly and visibly, or Los Counts would lose position and influence. The gang's macho would be devastated, and it would be known throughout the barrio that it could not control its own turf.

The church of St. Ynez was on Third Street, the traditional dividing line between the territory of Los Counts and the gang to the south, the Sixth Street Lobos. Between those two there had

6

been an uneasy peace that had lasted several weeks; how much longer it would last no one could say.

Brother Julio knew all this. The cold facts marched inexorably through his mind, and he grew more and more disturbed. He disliked intensely to think of such things in God's house, but most of the members of Los Counts would be coming to the wake, and therefore a time of violence might be close at hand.

He thought it possible that if he were to show himself outside the church, right up to the last moment, it might prevent an incident. He knew many of the gang youths—he had talked with most of them—and they knew him for a man of peace. He fervently hoped that he had at least a small measure of their respect. If that were so, they might think enough of him to forestall any provocative actions.

As soon as he was sure where his duty lay, Brother Julio moved almost silently to the aisle and slipped out the front door. The evening was warm; there was no wind, not even a mild one, to make it unpleasant outside. The moon hung high in the sky.

As he stood on the steps, a white car drew up just past the church and stopped at the curb. It was several years old, but it shone with almost pristine splendor. Its bright surfaces were hardly touched by dust, and the chrome trimming was brilliant, even at night. Brother Julio knew the vehicle at once. It belonged to Jambo, one of the leaders of Los Counts. Why he had chosen that street name no one knew.

The seats inside had been lowered so that only the heads of the four occupants could be seen. Brother Julio knew that it was fitted with a set of illegal power lifters that allowed the driver to make it go up or down, front or rear, to suit his pleasure. When the front was far down and the rear lifted high, it had extra maneuverability on city streets to help it elude pursuit. It was Jambo's great pride and joy, proof of high status attained in his seventeen years.

As the four teenagers that it held got out and gathered on the sidewalk, Brother Julio was not the only one who saw them—the area had been quietly staked out by sheriff's deputies as a precaution. Wakes were usually respected, but when rival gangs got themselves jacked up, there was no telling what they might do.

As Jambo bent over to lock the door of his car, another with much the same configuration came up the street. The moment

Brother Julio saw it he began to run down the steps. Sharp concern tightened his chest. When he reached the sidewalk he ran forward toward the four youths as fast as the dignity of the occasion would allow. If he could just stand with them . . .

By only a few seconds he was not in time. As the other car went past, its windows open, a few words were flung out in Spanish. Although he spoke English and Spanish with equal fluency, he was not close enough to catch the words. He had no need to—the moving car had held five members of Montaña Mara; from that moment anything could happen.

Three or four quick strides took Brother Julio to the place where Jambo and his friends were still standing together. He drew a quick breath and said, "Welcome in the name of God."

With those words he extended the aura of the sanctuary to the spot where they were. He tried to suggest that he had seen and heard nothing, because he had long since learned to leave no straw ungrasped. It sometimes pleased the Almighty to perform miracles. In gang-ridden East Los Angeles insults were never ignored and could be purged only by violence. But someday that might change, and Brother Julio was tireless in his search for the way to make it happen.

Because things had been irrevocably altered, when he returned to the church he moved forward and seated himself opposite Mrs. Hernandez, the mother of the murdered boy. His quick eye told him that she was breathing with difficulty. For a moment he wondered if she needed assistance, then he saw her protesting feet rubbing together and he understood. He hoped sincerely for her sake that her corset would not burst. Then all secular thoughts were banished from his mind as the service began.

CHAPTER TWO

LIEUTENANT RALPH MOTT guided his small dark green Buick down the Atlantic Avenue off-ramp from the Pomona Freeway and turned right toward Third Street. He was in plain clothes, and there was little about him that would have suggested a police officer to any casual observer. In slightly more than an hour he was due to check in at the East Los Angeles Sheriff's Station for his new assignment; he had deliberately come early because he was totally unfamiliar with the barrio and he wanted to look it over first. Later, he knew, he would see it *ad nauseam,* but for the moment it was all new.

He turned right on Third and easily located the sheriff's station. It was a low, reasonably modern building set well back, with an entrance for the official cars and patrol units, and another one for the use of the public. Just beyond the station, to the west, there was an attractive and well-kept little park. Its principal feature was a small lake that, despite the very early hour, had already attracted a few visitors. Mott could not remember another police station that was in such an agreeable setting, and it gave him a momentary lift.

An intricate freeway intersection on four levels directly ahead of him caused him to turn left toward Whittier Boulevard, a street named for the city that had given Richard Nixon to the nation. Since the barrio was obviously to the east, he turned left again onto Whittier and began to drive as slowly as he could, studying all that he saw. He took in the people, who were already much in evidence, the types of businesses, and the general feeling of the area. He saw few black faces—most of the people were brown, and if they themselves had not given clear evidence of Mexican origin, a majority of the business signs would have told anyone that this was largely a Spanish-speaking community. The fast food stands advertised tacos, burritos, and other Mexican specialties.

He passed a corner where a large shop had a lavish display of wedding finery. A series of mannequins was dressed in garments full of ruffles and elaborate decoration. The bride in the group wore a gown that was a cascade of lace and virgin white satin. The whole ensemble was like something from Neverneverland, over-done until it touched the edge of unreality. It was a dream world that could come true for the ordinary-appearing people walking past the shop only if they had however much money it would take to buy or rent the dramatic costumes on display.

For another forty minutes Mott drove slowly up and down the streets of the barrio, seeing and observing much. There were many murals—almost every available flat surface of any size had been elaborately painted. There was a variety of scenes: some religious, some composites, some political. On one a gang of bloodthirsty white men in deputies' uniforms were depicted assaulting a de-fenseless, but heroic Chicano. Mott wondered at the sort of dis-torted racial hatred that had created the unrealistic scene and hoped that not too many would believe it.

He also noted a large number of black spray-painted symbols almost everywhere there was a flat surface: on retaining walls, on the sides of buildings, even on windows. Some were just initials, some fanciful names such as Snoopy and Flaco. A few of them had been crossed out by X's and other symbols had been painted above and below. Everything badly needed cleaning up, Mott decided. He had no idea at all what the various symbols meant.

Deputy James Rose dropped a coin into the coffee machine that occupied wall space in the day room and accepted the plastic cup of hot brew that it dispensed. Another coin bought another cup. Armed with the two portions, he sat down with his partner to enjoy a few minutes of relaxation before going out on patrol. "What do you think?" he asked.

Deputy Willis Rodzinski was inclined to take things calmly. He tried the coffee, knowing that its quality was totally predictable, and then answered without emphasis. "I guess we can use all the help we can get."

"True, but have you got the word?"

"Fill me in."

Rose leaned forward and rested his elbows on the plain bare table. "He's a lieutenant, to start with."

Rodzinski nodded his understanding. "A little heavy, I'd think."

"Most of the guys I know feel that way. His name's Mott— Ralph Mott. Do you know him?"

"I never even heard of him. But there're more than five thousand—"

Rose unintentionally cut him off. "And he's been working detectives for the past few years, out of Malibu."

"Jesus, as a lieutenant?"

"As a sergeant. He just got promoted."

"Then he must be good to get assigned out here."

"I'm not denying that, but what the hell does he know about—"

He stopped because Captain Miguel Gutierrez had come into the room. The captain was easy to get along with if everything was going well; this morning he seemed relatively happy. But that could be deceptive. He had a square, handsome, rugged face that could produce as many different expressions as a fall sky. He was dressed, as usual, in a well-fitted sports outfit of obvious quality; people who came to see him were usually impressed. What didn't show was the load of responsibility that he carried; it was always heavy and sometimes explosive. Obviously he knew a lot more than the working troops, whose job it was to keep the peace whenever there was any worth preserving.

The captain took his coffee, glanced around, and then sat down with studied casualness with two of his best gang control specialists. There was clearly a purpose in this, and Rose didn't hesitate. "Morning, Captain," he said. "We hear that the new gang sector commander is coming in today."

11

The captain put on one of his amiable expressions, which gave an immediate clue. "That's right, I'm glad that you mentioned it."

He paused, but neither of his listeners made the mistake of commenting.

"You know the amount of heat that's been put on the sheriff himself to do something about this gang business." Gutierrez gulped a swallow of coffee almost as though it were a distasteful task. "Mott is going to need help—all he can get. He's a good man. I've been over his personnel file, and it's outstanding. You can take my word for that."

Rodzinski knew the captain well enough to inject something at that point. "The word we get, sir, is that he's a burglary detective."

"He was; now he's been reassigned to something else. You know that that's standard procedure."

Obviously the captain didn't want to go into that any further, but Rose risked a question anyway. "How good is his Spanish? Can he get by?"

Gutierrez, who was fully bilingual, pretended to consider that for a moment before he answered. "I haven't met him yet."

Both deputies knew that every man's personnel folder showed any language skills that he might have. There wasn't a ghost of a chance that Mott knew any Spanish at all, and to head up a new gang control section that was almost an essential requirement.

In a completely casual manner Los Counts were gathering for a meeting. Jambo had put out the word that he wanted to see everyone, and nothing more had been necessary. In Mexican-American East Los Angeles, traditional family ties deeply rooted in the old country were preserved and upheld, but gang affiliations were even stronger and more immediate. Because the outside world seemed to offer only rejection and no hope of anything better to come, the gang members found their strength in close companionship, mutual trust, and a feeling of belonging that could take fierce possession of the senses. Los Counts was a well integrated, closely knit unit—everyone who was a member took an almost savage pride in being among the chosen.

As they met on a bare piece of ground on their turf, most of them in various stages of puberty. There were a few twelve- and thirteen-year-olds who were anxious to earn themselves a place in the sun. Most were the more experienced members of seventeen and eighteen, who planned and carried out many of the gang's activities. A few older members—*veteranos*—had come largely to display themselves to the envious youngsters.

As Los Counts stood and sat together, Jambo talked to them with no pretense of formality. He used a mixture of Spanish and English, flavored with a number of local words that had meaning only in the narrow environment in which he lived.

"Ya know what happen," he said. "The fuckin' Montañas made fun of us. At the wake, when we had to go in the church. We'll fix 'em for that quick and good. An' last week them shitheads painted three of their signs on our turf."

That was important news. His lieutenants shifted, uneasy and expectant.

"They think we can't protect what's ours. They're gonna learn different—we make 'em shit right in their pants."

Jambo, who was less than medium height, wore only a t-shirt, jeans, and a pair of broken-down canvas shoes. As he spoke, he let his weight shift from one foot to the other and then back, a slight rocking that betrayed his nervous temperament. He was a warrior who was never off the field of combat. He had been arrested several times and convicted twice, qualifications that helped him maintain his position.

"Now," he continued, "we're goin' after Montaña Mara and fix them cocksuckers good. But before we hit 'em, we gonna show 'em —an' everybody else—how tough we are. Tougher than they ever knew before. Then we're goin' up on the hill and shoot some balls off."

It was what they had all wanted to hear. They lived for macho —to be known as the toughest gang; the one everyone else had to fear and no one dared to challenge. When everyone was terrified of them, then and only then would they be big and important, and their turf would become sacred territory.

Jambo paused and, like a skilled lecturer, felt out his audience. He sensed that they were with him and that his leadership wasn't challenged. He had told them what they wanted to hear.

"One more thing," he went on, while he had them. "Benjie Morales wants to join up. He's big enough and ready. We're gonna jump him in tomorrow. Nine o'clock. Here. You tell him."

13

Most of them knew the thirteen-year-old Morales boy and agreed that he was ready for initiation. How good he was, the traditional procedure would tell.

Word would get to Benjie, and he would come. It would be the only chance he would get, and if he ducked it, his life in the barrio after that would be a continuous hell. He would show up and on time.

Then Jambo got down to business, laying out exactly what was going to be done during the next few hours.

Mike Wickman, the operations sergeant who kept the paper work moving, looked in on the captain. When he had Gutierrez's attention he passed the word. "Lieutenant Mott is here."

The captain waved an arm in invitation; seeing it, Ralph Mott walked in to meet his new boss.

As Gutierrez stood up to shake hands, he took in his new man with a careful appraisal. Mott was just under six feet, in good physical condition by all appearances, and well-dressed for the occasion. He had an average Anglo face that might have belonged to a thousand other policemen, but he looked capable.

Mott took the captain's hand firmly, then on invitation sat down with a good air of waiting to hear what would be expected of him.

"This is your first assignment in East Los Angeles." Gutierrez made it a factual statement.

"Right." Mott responded, confirming what the captain already knew.

"Have you worked with ethnic communities before?"

"No, I haven't."

"How much do you know about the gang problem in this area?"

"Just what I've seen in print," Mott admitted. "I'll have to start from square one."

Gutierrez liked that. Obviously Mott wasn't the kind of man who would offer excuses later on if he ran into trouble, as he almost certainly would. It came down to a basic question: how fast and how well would he learn to handle his new job? He had a very long road to go.

"We've had gang problems for forty years," the captain said. "It's a deep tradition in the barrios. A lot of the heavy gang activity all over the country had its origins right here. As of now our gang situation is the worst that it's ever been. We're averaging more than one gang murder a week. Your name's Ralph, isn't it?"

"Yes."

"Ralph, I want you to look at this. Now." Gutierrez handed over a stapled report several pages long; then he watched Mott's face as his new man began to read.

For several minutes it was silent and still in the office, the only movement a quiet one as Mott turned the pages. When he at last got to the end, he studied the recap and then looked up. "My God!" he said.

"That's a summary of one month's gang violence in our area," the captain said in his calmest voice. "Three homicides, four rapes, thirty-one incidents involving guns, fifteen more with knives, nineteen known injuries, five cases of arson, sixteen armed robberies, and thirty-eight instances of beatings. Of those, more than twenty involved mayhem and mutilation. That doesn't include incidents that weren't reported or that we don't know about. There's at least one gang rape—eleven guys and one girl. But she won't talk."

"Was this an unusually bad month, Captain?"

"Average. It's getting worse."

"The courts?"

"Lenient. Not quite so much so lately, but we've got a seventeen-year-old kid on the streets right now who admits to five homicides—he was just released after firing shots into a shopping center. The judge didn't see enough hard evidence to bind him over for trial."

"Is the kid a gang member?"

"Yes, Montaña Mara. That's the bunch up on the Heights."

"Are they all Mexicans?" Mott wondered if he'd used the right term.

"They're Americans, and that's a big thing with them. In some instances they despise Mexicans from Mexico. But about ninety-nine point five percent of them are of Mexican descent."

"English-speaking?"

"Partly. They mix English and Spanish, and they have a lot of words of their own that don't belong to either language."

15

Mott's facial muscles tightened a little. "How many of your people speak Spanish—fluently?"

"About twenty percent. You'll hear a lot of radio calls asking for a Spanish-speaking deputy."

"I've got a strike against me there." Mott knew he was at a disadvantage and didn't like it; for a moment he wished he were back at Malibu.

Gutierrez approved his new man's attitude and lack of pretense. "Don't worry about that right now, Ralph. Just remember that we're going to give you all the help that we can."

As the top half of the sun began to slide down below the horizon, the remaining daylight was still crisp and sharp. Distant outlines had a stark clarity that challenged the encroachment of night. The air, which had been driven by a westerly wind all day, had a slight tang of ocean freshness that ignored the existence of the nature-murdering city. It seemed to be aware that in centuries yet to come the city would someday be gone, but the winds would still blow.

None of this entered the consciousness of Jambo as he drove with his three companions through the barrio, scanning everything in his line of vision along the way. Beside him he had Flaco, who was normally quiet-looking and inobtrusive. But that was deceptive. Flaco was immune to fear and already expert in the use of a switchblade knife. He was thin, hence his name, but he was taller than average and exceptionally quick for his fifteen years.

In the back seat Apache and Angel were maintaining a careful lookout as well. Apache was eighteen and had had more than four years experience in the gang wars; that made him a known factor who could be depended upon however hot the action might become. Angel was less reliable, because of his use of PCP, but when he was feeling right he had a certain savagery that contributed to the reputation of Los Counts. He had done most of the house shootings for the gang and was known to be good with a shotgun.

Jambo drove south toward Whittier Boulevard, the nerve center of the sensitive East Los Angeles area, keeping under the speed limit and doing nothing to attract attention. It was part of the plan. Surprise was an element he understood very well, and he was going to make it work for him again. Inside the car the atmosphere was tense and tight, even though what had been planned was not very dangerous, or even exciting. It would be one small step in a much larger, all-out campaign.

Still driving carefully, Jambo turned onto the turf of the small but very tough gang, La Calle Verona. Boxed in by the Santa Ana Freeway on the south and the territory of the Sixth Street Lobos on the north, Calle Verona had less than a quarter of the turf of Los Counts. Because of that, the members lived in a constant state of frustration. The freeway had robbed them of most of their jurisdiction years ago, and what was on the other side of that great artery could never be reclaimed. Every few months there were sharp rumblings that the Veronas were about to burst out of their boundaries, but Whittier Boulevard to the north had never been successfully crossed by any gang. Their only hope was to raid the equally confined Laguna Mara to the east. That possibility could explode at any time, and since the Lagunas, too, were violent, it could be in either direction.

Jambo pulled to the curb and stopped. Looking up and down the street, he got out of the car holding a can of black spray paint in his right hand. He saw no one for a block in either direction. Safe for the moment, he ran to a wooden detached garage that had once been painted white but was now liberally covered with painted symbols and carelessly written street names. Scanning the display, Jambo selected the largest and clearest of several "CV" symbols that declared which gang had sovereignty over the turf, aimed his spray can, and painted a bold X across it. The quick work done, he ran back to his car and was gone from the area in seconds.

In the car expectation grew higher and the tingling sensation of combat charged all four of the occupants. The supreme insult had been offered. The Veronas would see it within the hour and would know who was responsible. Almost before morning the whole barrio gang world would be aware that Los Counts were on the warpath, because only one gang had suffered a recent loss of macho and was out to get it back. Also, a Verona car, some weeks before, had jumped a member of the Counts. That insult still waited to be avenged.

"Are we ready?" Jambo asked in Spanish.

Three quick responses gave him an extra charge of excitement. Everything was right—he could feel it as though it were a living thing. He pulled his car up to the curb and stopped.

As the four Counts got out they were acutely aware that they were on foreign turf, forbidden land behind the enemy's lines. They walked carefully, two and two, with an affected carelessness, as though they were on their own turf, where they were in absolute control. On this hostile terrain Jambo felt again the savage thrill of danger and the acrid sensitivity of warfare that could erupt at any moment. If he needed it, his path of retreat was open for the moment. On the dead run he and his companions could be back in his car and gone in seconds. But there was no thought of retreat in his mind, only a plan for successful escape after a daring action had been completed.

Although on the ordinary-looking sidewalk of an undistinguished street, he knew that he was on a battlefield with the enemy in possible ambush all about him. He told himself that like his hero, James Bond, he was without fear and that no power of destruction could overcome him. And he had three able troops with him who were proven good fighters. He reached the corner, turned it, and was abruptly confronted by another teenager very like himself.

Almost instantly he knew that he was facing a hostile gang member—he could sense it as smoke indicates fire. For three seconds it was an impasse, then for a bare moment a look of fear flicked in the eyes of the one who was alone. It came only when he saw the other three appear and quietly surround him. Then the fear was gone, in its place the look of a cornered animal prepared to fight to the death.

"What gang you from?" Jambo asked.

All five members of the tense tableau knew that there was no right answer to that question, no possible response that could avert disaster.

The surprised youngster had his macho back. "La Calle Verona!" he threw into Jambo's face. He took one step backward, to give himself more room, and from somewhere a knife flashed into his hand.

Jambo took one moment to make sure that no more of the enemy were in sight to surprise him, then he lunged into combat. He was not foolhardy—Flaco was his knife man, and Flaco was on the victim's left. As the four Counts closed in like a thunderclap, Angel grabbed the right wrist of the Verona while Apache, with his greater age and size, jumped on his back.

With the knife immobilized Jambo delivered a hard driving kick into the other's stomach and knew that he had forced most of the wind from his opponent's body. In four more seconds they had him on the ground. The victim's knife fell from his fingers as he fought desperately to free himself. Flaco picked the knife up, balanced it in his hand, and then thrust it forward and down, into the upper abdomen.

That was it, and there was no need for Jambo to give an order. The four Counts ran madly back to their car, jumped inside with practiced speed, and were off almost before blood had begun to stain the sidewalk.

CHAPTER THREE

IT WAS four minutes before word of the attack reached the sheriff's station; when it did come in it was reported as a 415 fight, so only one car responded. When Deputies Sanchez and Morse saw what they had, they almost literally snatched the victim off the sidewalk and without wasting precious minutes waiting for an ambulance rushed him in their patrol unit with flashing lights and siren to the USC Medical Center, the huge complex once known as Los Angeles County Hospital.

Deputy Morse carried the unconscious victim through the emergency entrance and laid him carefully on a Gurney. He did not offer any explanation—the emergency room personnel had seen this type of injury far too often. As the victim was swiftly wheeled into a treatment room, Morse went to the head to sponge some of the blood off his uniform.

He glanced at his watch and saw that it was barely ten minutes since the radio call had come in. He knew that the very fast action he and Sanchez had provided might well have saved the victim's life, and he was professionally gratified. He joined Sanchez to have a quick cup of waiting coffee before they went back on patrol.

At the scene of the stabbing, the sheriff's detectives rang all of the doorbells in the vicinity, but they did not turn up a single witness who was helpful. Someone had seen the body of the victim lying on the sidewalk and had called the station; that was all. No one admitted having seen a strange vehicle of any kind in the area.

Four of the homes were known to house members of La Calle Verona. If anything, there was less help available there than in the nongang houses. It was a gang matter, and the gang would settle it in its own way.

It was not until almost an hour later that the identity of the victim was learned, and then almost accidentally. The hospital had found no ID on his person. He had been in surgery for some time when his mother phoned the station to check a rumor that he was in custody.

In the day room Sergeant McBride, a gang expert, passed the word as he saw it. "It was the Counts. They owe two up on the Heights, but that's a tough place to invade—it's like a fortress. So they're building up their macho first; then they'll go after the big hit."

He was stating what they all knew, but at times blowing off steam was necessary. Sergeant McBride had seen murder victims many times, but he had never gotten used to them.

He checked out a car and went up onto the Heights to see what his trained instincts would tell him. He knew that deputies were sporadically ambushed and felt a tinge of danger, because the only sure thing was that there was no sure thing. It was part of being a deputy in East Los Angeles, and it made his job a different one every day he reported in.

As he drove the crooked, confusing streets of the Heights he had the window open beside him, as was standard patrol procedure. He could clearly hear the whistles that echoed from point to point, warning of the coming of the police car.

He spent several minutes cruising very slowly through the labyrinthine streets that overlooked so much of the city, and saw virtually nothing. The stillness became unnatural. And with the stillness came a sensation he had experienced many times before: an awareness of coming violence. He could not escape the feeling that the breath of death itself was in the air.

*   *   *

At eight the following morning Mott arrived for work and changed into uniform. He didn't do so in order to display the neat gold bars that were pinned on each side of his collar—he had no desire to flaunt his promotion. He put on his uniform because he wanted to make it clear that he was one of the working troops, that he didn't intend to sit in his office all day and read reports on gang activity. When the action came, it would be on the streets, and it was there he would have to learn his new responsibilities.

He checked in with the watch commander and said that he wanted to go out on patrol with one of the more experienced gang control deputies. As far as the watch commander was concerned, he could not have made a happier suggestion. A call was put out for Rodzinski, and when the tall, dark-haired deputy responded, he was told what was wanted. His option was to say that he would be happy to oblige, and that he did. Ten minutes later, with Mott sitting at his right hand, he rolled one of the black and white Novas out of the parking lot and down onto Third Street.

"How long have you been working gangs?" Mott asked.

"A couple of years." That was an understatement, deliberately made to fit the circumstances.

"Then how about starting from the beginning and filling me in."

Rodzinski felt a touch of pride in that. He was one of the best in the gang control section, he knew it, and he was more than willing to share his knowhow. Furthermore, he was in a position to do it on a man-to-man basis, without having to kowtow to rank. He turned south toward Whittier and began in a quiet, conversational tone.

"The whole of East Los Angeles is divided up into roughly fifteen to seventeen gang areas. The number shifts from time to time, usually because of heavy construction, such as freeways, that change the geography. Each gang has its own specific area or barrio—commonly it's called turf. A member of one gang can't go onto the turf of another, and he can't ask a girl who lives in another gang's area for a date."

"Is it ever tried?"

"Yes, sometimes. A few weeks ago a girl who lives in Los Sapos turf was seen with a member of Los Magnolias. A week later she was gang raped, to impress on her the importance of the gang she had offended."

22

"Were any arrests made?"

Rodzinski shook his head. "There wasn't even a formal complaint. It was a gang matter, and it stopped there." He slowed the patrol car and waited for a light to change.

"What about the girl—what did she do?"

"Nothing. She still lives where she did. It's the way that it is: the people here almost all want to stay in the Mexican-American community. They won't split, no matter what."

Mott discovered that he was unconsciously working the muscles of his jaw trying to digest that idea, but he kept silent and listened.

Rodzinski turned into a side street and pointed out a house. "Three gang members live there," he said. "We respond to that location at least once a week. Look at the right-hand side of the doorway and you will see bullet holes—the place gets shot up all the time."

When he had covered another half block in the bright and peaceful sunlight, he returned to the topic. "Understand this, Lieutenant: when a gang commits a murder—or one member does —they don't think of it as a crime at all. They're at war, so the killing is part of their military campaign. They talk about it the way that a fighter pilot might talk about an enemy plane he had shot down."

"How much of it is an education problem?" Mott asked.

Rodzinski bumped across an intersection with low gutters and resumed his patrol pattern. The radio was putting out a steady series of calls, but he appeared to be ignoring them. Mott knew that he wasn't. Even though the volume was low, if their unit were to be called, Rodzinski would be aware of it immediately.

"I don't think you'll find the answer there, Lieutenant. For one thing, education is a sore point in the barrio. A lot of the residents claim that the teachers assigned here are substandard—that the good ones won't come into this area. Then the gangs get in the way, too. The Spiders don't go to high school. They can't, because to get to the school they would have to cross the turf of Los Magnolias, and there's no way they're going to be allowed to do that."

"But dammit," Mott protested, "that's something specific we ought to be able to handle."

"We've tried and it didn't work—take my word for it. Until you get the full feel of gang macho, all this may sound pretty wild to you, but it isn't to them. The whole thing gets into their blood; they like the danger and the excitement."

"Are all the kids here gang members?"

"No, not at all. A lot of kids grow up here without becoming gang-involved at all. Some join but don't take any part in the rough stuff. It's a fairly small, hard-core nucleus that raises all the hell. A lot of fine people here in East L.A. haven't been able to stop the gangs. So far we've failed too."

Mott made a frank admission as the car crossed Whittier Boulevard once more. "It scares me to death—What it can lead to, I mean."

"It scares us all," Rodzinski responded. "If you can find the answer, they'll make this a separate city, and name it after you."

That stopped the conversation for the next several blocks. They rolled on silently, each man involved in his own thoughts. Mott again remembered the report he had read in the captain's office. For a few seconds he was almost physically sick.

Benjie Morales was fighting hard against the rising fear that was taking hold of him—his hands were wet and unwanted perspiration stood out on his forehead. He was only thirteen years old, and the adolescent processes that had taken hold of his body had not yet reached his mind. As he walked fatefully down the street, he thought of his mother and wondered desperately if there wasn't some way that even at that late moment she could come to his rescue. He knew that was impossible—she didn't know where he was going, and he had obeyed the rules in not telling her.

Bitter regret began to set in, but he fought against it with all his strength. He had to keep his macho up—it was the only thing on earth that could save him. He had asked to join the gang, and they had set the time to jump him in, a time that would arrive in twelve short minutes. He tried to work up enthusiasm for the excitement ahead, but it was hopelessly beyond him. Suddenly, and fearfully, he wanted to cry.

Jambo and a group of the others were waiting for him when he arrived. One of the members who owned a cheap watch looked at it and nodded—at least Benjie was on time.

With his hands casually hooked in the front of his low-slung jeans, Jambo ambled forward. That simple action terrified Benjie even more. It was as though a steel door had clanged shut behind him.

"Ya know all about the Counts," Jambo said.

Benjie swallowed hard and then nodded.

"We're the toughest, man. Every other fuckin' gang shits in their pants when we're around."

"Ain't nobody like the Counts," Benjie managed. He would have kept on talking if he could, it would have gained him a few seconds respite. But he knew enough not to—it would only make things worse.

"Ya wanna' join us, ya gotta' be tough," Jambo continued in a mixture of Spanish and English. "So we gotta' see how tough you are."

In five seconds of stupefying silence Benjie saw six of the gang members step forward. Six! He doubled his fists and forced the paralyzing thought out of his mind. He had known what to expect. At that last moment he tried his pitiful best to look brave and tough.

They came at him in a wave: faces, arms, bodies all out to knock him senseless. He saw a body, and with all the power he could muster, he drove his right fist into it. At the same moment something exploded against the side of his head; for a second his vision failed and a sickening pain almost paralyzed his body. He kicked, fighting wildly and without aim, and caught one of his opponents squarely in the groin. He heard a yell, and at that desperate moment he knew that he hadn't yet screamed himself. Perhaps he had courage after all.

He flailed out with all his might, punching anywhere and everywhere that he could. A frightful pain seized hold of his abdomen as his wind was all but slammed out of his body. To keep from falling he whirled around, saw one of his tormentors with his guard down, and thrust the first and second fingers of his left hand out into his opponent's eyes.

A kick in the small of his back sent him sprawling. As the ground came up he turned his face away, doubled his body up into fetal position, and then kicked out with both legs, fighting not against his attackers but against the pain that filled his insides with more agony than he had ever known.

He caught the ankles of an unseen foe. A seventeen-year-old fell hard.

That was all that Benjie had left. He was struggling to get up when a solid, well-directed kick just below his ribs finished him off. His mouth opened and the contents of his stomach came out, some of it through his nostrils. He knew that he had been killed, and he did the only thing that he could: he shut his eyes and asked death to come quickly. A vicious kick at the base of his spine hardly hurt him at all. Unconsciousness was swirling up, and he wanted God to come and get him—he couldn't stand any more.

His body jerked as his already empty stomach tried to void itself once more. Then, dimly, he became aware that he had emptied his bladder and his bowels into his hand-me-down pants. It did not matter—Jesus would forgive him. He forgave everything. Brother Julio had told him . . .

When he came to, his body was on fire. A spear seemed to have been thrust into his abdomen, his back blazed with pain, and his breath came in little jerks in and out of his body.

He felt himself being lifted onto his feet. He tried to stand, but they had to help him. His nose was streaming blood, but he was unaware of it; his body had become something he could no longer control. All he knew was horrible, sickening pain.

"Ya did all right," he heard Jambo saying. "That was to find out how good you are when you *know* you're gonna' get the shit beat out of you. O.K., you joined—now you're a Count. An' you're gonna be one until you get jumped out. That'll be the same thing, only worse. A lot worse. Now go home and clean up your pants."

Even though he smelled, two of the gang members took Benjie home in their car and dumped him off on the sidewalk in front of his house. He was still lying there when they left, but that was no worry—his family would come out and get him.

The call came at 11:07 for Lieutenant Mott to return to the station. Six minutes later he found one of his detectives waiting for him in his office.

The man, whom he hardly knew yet, gave him the word. "You remember the kid that was knifed last night. The one in the USC Medical Center."

"I remember."

"O.K., some info. His name is Marcellino Acosta, and he's a member of La Calle Verona. He's a real tough kid—we have him down for two attempted homicides, several armed robberies, and ADW. The word just came in from the hospital. He's regained consciousness, and the doctor looking after him thinks he might be willing to talk."

Mott knew at once that he was expected to handle it. "I'm on my way," he said.

"Good. Here's the keys to one of the plain units. It's ready for you."

Mott went outside wondering what in hell he was going to say to the gang kid in the hospital. He had interrogated hundreds of victims of burglaries and almost as many suspects, but this was a different matter altogether. As he fitted himself into the driver's seat, he had the sudden thought that perhaps young Acosta couldn't, or wouldn't, speak English.

It took Mott a considerable time to find a place to park at the immense hospital complex. He finally solved his problem by stopping in front of a patrolling guard and asking him. The guard sent him to the area for official cars and told him where to go inside.

After getting directions a half dozen times, he finally found himself in a large ward where there could have been as many as twenty beds. He blocked all but one out of his mind and looked down at the 245 victim he had come to see.

It was the first time that he had actually seen a gang member who had been involved in violence, and for a few seconds he had to reassess his thinking. Lying on the bed was an adolescent boy—he could not use any other word for it. He had a thin, pinched face and eyes that were sunk deep almost inside his skull. His body, outlined underneath the sheet that covered him, was thin and, apparently, undernourished. It was hard to tell when he was lying down, but Mott estimated that he could not have been more than five feet five inches tall. One arm, laid on top of the cover, had a tattoo of woven flowers with some words in Spanish.

Mott found a chair and pulled it up beside the bed. That got his own head lower and in a more comfortable position for communication. He tried to put out of his head the long rap sheet that the

27

boy in the bed had run up and concentrated instead on the fact that he was a victim of 245, felonious assault. He had been knifed, and that had to be extremely painful as well as dangerous.

When several seconds had passed and the patient had given no indication that he was even aware anyone was there, Mott spoke the boy's name softly. "Marcellino."

The thin head with the straight black hair turned toward him and two very dark eyes looked at him. "I'm Chino, man. Don't you know that?"

Mott picked up on that without hesitation. "How are you feeling, Chino?"

"I got my guts sewed up—how do you think I feel?"

"Pretty damn tough."

"You ever had a knife stuck in you, man?"

"Not yet."

"Don't go lookin' for it."

So far so good, Mott decided. He was over the language hurdle, and he had let the boy tell him something. That would make him feel a little superior, perhaps start him talking more.

"My name's Mott." He kept the same quiet tone.

"Big deal."

That was the end of that; he reached for a new tack. "How many guys hit you, Chino? I don't think one could do it."

It worked; he got a response. "Damn fuckin' right! There was four of 'em. They came around the corner and jumped me."

"What kind of a car did they have?"

"How should I know? I seen four guys and that was all."

Sensing a hint of hostility, Mott abruptly changed the subject. "How's the food here?"

"Good enough, if you're a pig."

That could be taken two ways, and Mott knew it. He also realized that if the victim before him had just regained consciousness a short while ago, he probably hadn't had any hospital food at all. "You've been here before," he said, making it a statement.

"Ya."

"What happened last time?"

"I got shot. In the leg."

"How did it happen?"

Mott waited fifteen seconds until he knew there would be no

reply to that. He tried something else. "Chino, you know what a victim is?"

"You think I'm stupid, man?"

"O.K., you're a victim. We call it ADW—Assault with a Deadly Weapon. That means the joint for the guys who did it to you."

"You won't find 'em."

"There are a lot of guys in Q that were sure we wouldn't find them."

After another long period of silence, Mott put another question. "How old are you, Chino?"

"Sixteen."

"How many times have you been hit?"

"I don' remember."

"Was this the worst?"

"I guess maybe."

"All right, Chino, we're going after the guy who hit you—the guys. With luck we'll have them in the can by the time you're ready to go home."

"Forget it, man."

"It's my job not to forget it. So tell me about it. How many of them did you know?"

The black eyes of the boy in the bed flashed with anger, and Mott saw it. "I said forget it, man. Go back to writin' traffic tickets. I can take care of myself."

"Chino, hitting you was a crime—a felony. I told you—it's good for a term in the joint. Whether you know it or not, right now I'm working for you."

The boy gave him one last statement. "Listen, I don' want no help, man. So leave me alone."

After that he turned over, showing part of his too slender back, and pretended to go to sleep. Mott sat still for a few more moments, then he left.

CHAPTER FOUR

THE BOARD ROOM of Morrison and Hale, Inc., was not lavish, but it had been designed for atmosphere. The wood-paneled walls, the large table that filled the center of the room, and the plush executive chairs that surrounded it all testified to the substantial nature of the corporation. There was a concealed bar, a hidden projection facility that could handle most types of audio-visual material, and an adjacent small kitchen equipped to provide suitable luncheon menus.

Almost every day the room was used for some sort of meeting, including gatherings of top management personnel whenever there was a matter that called for serious discussion. At a little after ten, on a fine spring Monday morning, Brother Julio was ushered into the room by invitation. Within two or three minutes, four of the five ranking executives of the corporation had come in, seated themselves, and prepared to give him their attention. The Brother tried almost desperately to convince himself that these were ordinary men and easy to address.

"Gentlemen," he began, "despite the fact that I'm in holy orders, what I want to discuss with you is a hundred percent practical. For an opener, I'm not here to solicit any funds."

He stopped, waiting for some response to that. He got none. He tried to remain calm. If he couldn't remain factual and businesslike now, the hopes that he had been building up for months would go right down the drain. He began to perspire—that he couldn't control.

"Excuse me." One of his listeners interrupted the silence. "I didn't entirely get your name, Father."

"I'm not a priest, sir. I'm Brother Julio, and that's how everyone addresses me."

"I see. Thank you."

"Gentlemen, my work is in the East Los Angeles area, which is widely known as the barrio. Its population is almost entirely Mexican-American. Let me say right here that, contrary to what you may have heard, most of the people living there are American citizens who are honest and reliable. I could give you quite a long list of outstanding Mexican-Americans, but I won't take your time for that. The point I want to make is that the great majority of the people of East Los Angeles would be desirable, trustworthy employees for anyone who would hire them."

He paused for a bare moment and sensed that he was still being heard. That gave him new hope. He decided instantly to get a bad problem out of the way.

"I'm perfectly aware, gentlemen—as you are too—that many lending institutions redline the barrio, which is to say that they don't want to make loans in that area and charge maximum interest rates when they do. But that's not because the people are unreliable—it's because of the very high level of unemployment. East Los Angeles is filled with good people who are eager to work and work well. All they ask for is the chance."

Brother Julio stopped and took time to set an enlarged photograph up on an easel that had been provided for him. As he did so he could sense the lag in interest, but he had had to dispose of the idea that his people were not dependable. At least that was behind him, and the knowledge of that fact gave him a little additional hope.

When he had his photograph positioned, he stood beside it and waited for a moment. It showed a one-story industrial building surrounded by a chain link fence. It was not an impressive structure, but it had clearly been designed for utility. That meant to the

31

assembled men that it would have adequate fire protection systems, the proper wiring, loading docks, and, somewhere up front, offices.

Brother Julio took a deep breath and continued. "This facility was built eleven years ago as a furniture warehouse and manufacturing plant. I've checked with the county, and they've told me that the building is fully up to code and that there's nothing wrong with it whatever, to their knowledge. I inspected it last a few days ago, and as far as I could see, it doesn't need any repairs at all. The company that built it went out of business before they could put it into operation—something about their stock and the way that it was sold. I don't know any of the details."

One of his listeners came to his rescue. "We're familiar with that situation, I believe."

"Thank you, sir. Then you probably know also that this facility was put in East Los Angeles for two reasons: there was a good site available, and the company wanted to take advantage of our good labor supply. We have many willing workers, and their salary demands are moderate. They speak English."

He instantly knew that had been a mistake. He determined not to let it throw him off—he was in the heart of his presentation now, and he had to keep going. In spite of all his careful rehearsing, that had slipped out, and he hadn't been able to stop it in time.

"I'd like to point out to you, gentlemen," he went on, trying to recapture his confidence, "that there are some strong economic advantages in making use of our labor supply. Our people are intelligent and capable. And this building that you see before you is available right now."

One of his listeners, a man who wore rimless glasses and looked like the fiscal officer that he was, put a question. "Do you know the price of the facility, including the real estate?"

"Yes, sir, I do. That brings up one of my main points." It was that moment or never—Brother Julio knew it and hoped to his merciful Lord that he would sound convincing. "Right now this whole plant, just as you see it, can be bought at way under the market. I don't need to tell you how rare a genuine real estate bargain is now. I came to you, gentlemen, because the *Times* reported that you are planning an expansion in your light manufacturing division."

He meant to say more, but the next sentence refused to shape itself in his mind. He was, for a brief moment, tongue-tied.

The man who sat opposite him at the far end of the table spoke for the first time. "Your points, Brother Julio, are well taken, but let me be frank with you. It's unfortunately well known in the business community that East Los Angeles is a trouble area. What I mean is, any substantial investment there might be in greater jeopardy than if it were in some other place."

Brother Julio did not need to be told that this was the man he had to sell. The chair he occupied established his position. More than that, the tone of his voice, and the basic underlying concern that it revealed, proved that he was the chief decision maker. The others were all important, but if this man did not agree, the cause would be lost.

"Sir," the Brother answered carefully, "ninety percent of our trouble, as you put it, springs from one cause: unemployment. For some time it's been dangerously high. I work with the community all the time—it's my calling. I can tell you honestly that if the people had the opportunity to earn a decent living and support their families properly, our problems would begin to disappear right from that moment. One plant alone won't do it, but it can be a major step in the right direction."

For fifteen minutes more he addressed his listeners, supplying the facts, figures, and other data he had so carefully assembled. He had made one mistake by calling attention to possible language problems; he was most careful not to make another. Finally the man at the head of the table got to his feet; the others followed.

"Brother Julio," the chairman said, "thank you for coming and giving us this presentation. I will have the matter looked into and we will contact the owners of the building. Beyond that I won't commit myself, but we will consider your thoughts carefully."

That was the most that the good Brother could possibly have hoped for, and he knew it. He shook hands briefly with each of the company officers, then deliberately left the expensive photograph behind him as he went. The real estate company concerned had contributed it, which was fortunate because Brother Julio had no funds whatever of his own.

On his way back to East Los Angeles he drove very carefully, his eyes on the road, but his lips moving silently in prayer.

* * *

Ralph Mott actually regretted that his working day was officially over. He could not escape the feeling that so far he had not been effective in his new assignment. It was much too soon for anyone else to have noticed it, but he did not intend to let it go on for even one more day. He called Nancy and told her that he would be working late. She was upset—she had been waiting for him and his dinner was ready.

He went to the dining room of the Holiday Inn, where two cocktails helped put him in a better frame of mind. After that he had a quick meal and then returned to the station. He told the watch commander that he wanted to go out on patrol.

Sergeant Fred d'Amico was already in one of the gang control units. A 1019 call was put out to him; within ten minutes he rolled into the station yard to find out what was wanted.

Mott met him for the first time in the watch commander's office. The sergeant gave him a quick policeman's glance that took in almost everything that was externally visible, then held out his hand. "The word is that you're here to give us some more muscle in handling the gangs," he said. "Welcome aboard."

Mott shook hands and then said, "I'd like to come along with you for a while tonight. I know that most of the gang activity is in the early evening."

"Right. Glad to have you, Lieutenant. Any particular place you want to go?"

"I'll leave that to you."

"Good enough.

"How about grabbing a coffee before we roll?"

A few minutes later the gang control car left the lot with d'Amico driving and Mott beside him in the front seat. "What are the odds on any serious trouble tonight?" Mott asked.

"We'll probably see some action before the shift is over. It's coming up full moon, and there's a war on between Montaña Mara and Los Counts that can erupt anytime. How about checking out the Heights to see what's going on up there?"

"I'd like that," Mott answered.

D'Amico turned on the blinker, but before he could make the corner the steady prattle of the radio caught his full attention.

"Twenty-three Adam four."

"Twenty-three Adam four, by."

"Twenty-three Adam four, a two-eleven just occurred—Yasuda Grocery, Floral and Cordova. Two suspects last seen running west."

D'Amico flipped his overhead lights on and waited, listening.

"Suspect number one: a male Mexican, sixteen to eighteen, armed with a handgun. No further description. Suspect number two: also a male Mexican, fifteen to eighteen, dark trousers, white t-shirt, long hair, armed with a knife. Twenty-three Adam assist."

"That's us," d'Amico said. He U-turned expertly and floored the gas pedal. The car jumped forward and swung around a corner at close to skidding speed, straightened out, and then accelerated rapidly down the wide, clear street. Seconds later it touched sixty; the wind whipped in through the open windows as the tires dug hard against the pavement. D'Amico braked sharply as an intersection neared, cleared it visually, and then spurted ahead once more. After another minute of expert, high performance driving, he braked hard once more and turned down a narrow alley.

"It'll be the Machetes that pulled it," he said. "This is their favorite escape route." He pulled the car in front of a row of garages and cut the lights.

Seconds later headlights showed as another car turned down the alley, coming from the opposite direction. Then it suddenly stopped—the driver had seen something. He rammed into reverse and began to back up as fast as he could.

D'Amico hit his lights and spurted forward, closing the gap rapidly between the two cars. Mott grabbed the mike, then realized he couldn't give the location. He didn't need to: just before the rapidly backing car reached the street another patrol unit, coming fast, jerked to a stop, blocking its way. A third car appeared in the alley behind Mott and d'Amico, its roof lights on.

Two deputies were already out, approaching the trapped car from the rear, one on each side. Inside the vehicle, two juvenile subjects could be seen, for the moment motionless.

"Put your hands on the dashboard, where I can see them!" one of the deputies barked. As soon as he was obeyed, he gave further orders. "Rider in the right hand seat, open your door slowly and get out. Keep your hands where I can see them every moment."

The door of the suspect car opened, and a thin teenager got out, his hands in view as directed.

"Turn and face the car. Spread your feet apart and lean against it, your hands on the roof." As the youth did as he was told, Mott noted at once that he had undoubtedly done the same thing many times before.

"Driver, get out the same way. Slowly—do it now!"

The driver complied. As he did so d'Amico picked up the mike, gave the location, and put out a Code Four—no further assistance needed. Then he got out and Mott, following his lead, did the same.

The deputy who had been giving the orders held his position while his partner patted down both suspects for possible weapons. From the driver he took a clasp knife that was in a holder suspended from his belt. When he opened it, the light caught the long blade that had been whetted until it was lethal.

There being no question of probable cause, another deputy was carefully searching the car. From under the front seat he recovered a four-inch, .38 calibre handgun. He held it by the trigger guard, displaying it long enough so that the other deputies present could witness his find. Then he took it to his own car, put it into an evidence bag, and used the radio to advise that the subjects were in custody.

The two arrestees were cuffed and told where to stand. They obeyed indifferently, almost as though their thoughts were at some other time and place. A small group of onlookers had gathered, and from it came voices of protest.

"Hey, man, whatcha doin' that to them for? Why you hate us?"

"You're just down on us, man. You hate our guts!"

One of the subjects claimed that he was in pain and demanded that his cuffs be loosened. Mott checked them himself and was satisfied that, if anything, they were a trifle slack.

He was greeted by a voice from the growing crowd. "Hey, lieutenant, help that man out! Hey, fuck you!"

The deputy who had been on the radio passed the word. "They're bringing the victims here—ETA five minutes."

Mott looked again at the subjects, studied their faces, and knew that they were almost certainly guilty. He had handled too many burglary cases not to be able to recognize the signs.

It was quiet then, more or less. A few more remarks came from the crowd, but there was no thrust behind them. The onlookers, too, were waiting.

"It's a good bust," d'Amico said. "The gun in the car is enough."

"I'm sure they're good for the felony, too," Mott added. "Two-eleven will put them away for a while."

Another black-and-white rolled up, this time with appropriate dignity. The deputy riding on the right-hand side got out and opened the back door that could not be operated from the inside. A middle-aged Japanese-American couple got out and were led to the place where the subjects were being held.

"Do not be influenced by the fact that these subjects are in custody," the deputy warned. "They could both be entirely innocent."

The man heard but nodded at once. "That's them," he declared. "No doubt whatever. I recognize them both."

"Are you absolutely certain, Mr. Yasuda?"

The store owner was clearly unafraid. He nodded vigorously. "Absolutely," he repeated.

For the first time the subjects showed emotion. Apparently they had expected the store owner to be too fearful of gang reprisals to identify them.

"How about you, Mrs. Yasuda?" the arresting deputy asked.

"My husband is right—it is them."

D'Amico touched Mott on the shoulder. "Let's go," he said.

Mott got back into the car and, with d'Amico again driving, left the scene. The sergeant headed north once more, toward the Heights and the potentially very dangerous situation that might be developing there.

The cool of the evening had settled in, and the freshened air that now flowed easily through the open windows was welcome. Despite the still early hour, the north-south streets were relatively quiet, and few pedestrians appeared on the sidewalks.

"You know about the situation between Montaña Mara—the gang on the Heights—and Los Counts, don't you?" d'Amico asked.

"I know that there's trouble between them."

"It's the worst situation that we have going right now. Over the past few weeks it's been building up, largely because the Counts owe two murders to Montaña Mara. The knifing of the Verona kid was part of it."

"What do you think is the best way to attack the problem?" Mott asked.

D'Amico was not too quick to reply. He cleared the area where the Long Beach and Pomona freeways intersect and then headed north on Eastern before he spoke. "A lot of good people, in and out of the barrio, have tried to figure out the answer to that. Jobs would help; so would stricter law enforcement. We do our part, but the courts don't always back us up. We've gone in sometimes with what we thought was conclusive evidence and have been turned down. Take those kids who were busted tonight: I know them both and they both have records that are pretty heavy. But they're still juveniles, and our only chance for getting them off the street for a while is to have them declared unfit to stand trial in juvenile court. We may make it this time, because of their records. If we do, then they'll be tried as adults. They could be looking at five to ten years, but parole would cut that way down, of course."

"Somewhere," Mott said, "there's got to be a point of attack. Something that can be done to cut down on this violence."

"I'll tell you one thing," d'Amico responded. "You won't do it by organizing basketball teams. It's been tried. There was even a project to start some hydroponic gardens and use the gang kids to tend them. It might work, but right now I doubt it."

The level street gave way to a fairly sharp incline; after two or three hundred feet it began to twist to conform to the rising terrain. As the patrol car climbed steadily, d'Amico said, "Listen —you can hear the whistles. They're to warn that we're coming."

When the car reached the top of the Heights, four or five hundred feet above the level of the city, d'Amico was forced to slow almost to a crawl. A web of twisting streets, apparently without names, turned in every direction. Built along them, in almost helter-skelter fashion, were houses, some old and tiny, some fairly new and moderately impressive. Most of them were covered by graffiti. Mott looked at them as the headlights of the car picked them out and saw the symbol of the two interlocking M's in almost every instance. There were also spray-painted names like Dopey, Rabbit, Piggy, Draco, and Flaco. This was gang territory all right—he had learned to recognize that very quickly.

He also noted something else: the limited area that comprised the Heights was a rabbit warren of passageways between houses, hillside trails, and hopelessly twisted streets. Trying to catch a fleeing suspect who knew the geography would be an exercise in futility. And no suspect in that area would be likely to stand peacefully and wait if he thought the deputies in any particular prowl car were looking for him.

As d'Amico drove, ferreting his way through the maze of tiny streets, every half minute or so there would be a panoramic view of the city below: a studded carpet of lights that went on for mile after apparently endless mile. Although Mott had lived in the Los Angeles area for many years, the spectacle of the city seen from such a vantage point had never ceased to move him. As a policemen he knew how many tens of thousand of things were hidden behind the visible lights, and also how many good people there were who lived like human beings and not animals. They were the public that made it all worthwhile.

He forgot his daydreaming and jerked himself back to reality. "I don't see a thing," he commented.

"Me neither," d'Amico answered, "and that's what's got me worried."

"It's too quiet."

"Exactly. Usually there are some of the kids around, hanging by their cars, keeping a visible image. But tonight there's nobody, and the weather isn't that bad."

After another ten minutes they left the Heights and came down a series of short, steep streets until they were on the level once more. D'Amico drove back and forth through the turf of Los Counts and found the same thing: no evidence of any activity at all. When he had completed that sweep he asked, "How about Code Seven?"

"Good," Mott concurred. "You pick the place."

The stand where they stopped for a brief meal was much like any other—it had hamburgers, hot dogs, and a selection of Mexican delicacies, if the short order items on the menu could be called that. Mott and d'Amico ate off the hood of their car so they could hear the radio, but they were not called during the brief ten minutes they took for their meal. After that they got back in the car and patrolled until long past midnight, but the streets of East Los

Angeles remained quiet, and only the painted graffiti throughout the area gave any indication that such things as youth gangs existed.

Mott attended the weekly community meeting the following morning. By ten o'clock some twenty people had gathered to hear what they had heard too often before: a summary of the week's gang-related violence and a discussion of what might be done at least to decrease it in the future.

The room set aside for the conference was just large enough to hold the people who came. There was a senior sergeant in uniform from the Park Patrol, Brother Julio, perhaps fifteen people representing various community organizations, and a sprinkling of sheriff's personnel. Coffee was passed around in plastic cups; when everyone had settled down after that, Lieutenant Hayden Finley stood up. He was a medium-built man, broad in the shoulders, casually dressed, and with a quiet, almost self-effacing manner. He held three typewritten pages in his hand.

It took him five minutes to get through the summary; there were two or three interruptions for questions, which he answered casually before continuing. The attack on the Yasuda grocery was included, together with the other incidents that Mott had already encountered. When Finley was finished, there were a few seconds of quiet. "As you can see," he told the group, "this past week has been a very little above average. We have a fairly good chance to put away the two gang members who hit the Yasudas and get them off the street for a while. The victims will testify, and that's extremely important. You may have noticed that the Japanese are like that: they won't be pushed around. I've got to admire them for it."

"Will they be tried as adults?" The woman who asked the question was heavy-set. She was halfway down the table and had been taking careful notes.

"We certainly hope so. Of course, that's up to the court, but both suspects have heavy records, and there is a good chance that the judge may declare them unfit to stand trial as juveniles. I don't like to add this, but I'd better so that you know. The new law on retroactive sentencing is going to dump forty-four convicted gang members back on the street during the next two weeks."

A broad-faced man of about thirty-five, wearing an inexpensive suit that had been freshly cleaned and pressed, and shoes that had been neatly shined, raised a hand halfway. "Does that include Luis Cabrera?" he asked.

Finley nodded. "Yes," he answered simply.

"I hear that he has done three murders."

"He has that reputation." Finley was careful with his words. "We had him in for two-eleven—armed robbery with violence— but he is being released. We have no control over that, of course. The next time that we get him, if we do, perhaps we will be able to keep him a little longer."

The heavy-set woman had another question. "What chance is there that he will keep out of trouble this time? In your opinion?"

Finley stood with one foot resting on his chair, thinking that one over. He passed a hand across his face and came to a decision. "It's impossible to predict what anyone is going to do in the future, Mrs. Zapeta," he answered. "I can give you the facts, that's all. He's eighteen years old, possibly nineteen by now—I'd have to look that up. He was sentenced last time as an adult for armed robbery, which normally is good for ten-to-life, since he used a gun. Prior to that he had thirteen other arrests."

"Fifteen," a deputy at his side corrected quietly.

"Fifteen," Finley acknowledged.

"But isn't it true that he was released or found innocent most of those times?"

"Most of the time, yes."

"Then why was he arrested in the first place?"

"We don't arrest anyone, Mrs. Zapeta, unless we believe that they are guilty. As you know, the courts decide on the question of guilt. About three years ago we arrested Luis running from the scene of a stabbing. He had a knife on him when we arrested him. There was blood on the knife. The weapon fitted the victim's wound and the blood on the knife was fresh. It was typed and it matched the victim's blood. That looked pretty good to us when we went to court, but he was found not guilty."

"Why?" the broad-faced man asked.

"I'd say because the juvenile court judge didn't believe the evidence. He's a great admirer of Father Flanagan and often quotes his famous statement that there's no such thing as a bad boy."

41

A thin-faced man with a mass of black hair bunched on top of his head raised a pencil. "Lieutenant, is it true that there's a war on between Los Counts and Montaña Mara?"

"Yes, it is."

"I know that Luis is a member of Montaña Mara. When he's released, what do you expect? He is violent—we know that, too. Can he make it much worse?"

Once more Finley was cautious in what he said. "It's a bad situation, and we're watching it carefully. In all honesty, I've got to say that his being out may aggravate things. But he may stay out of the barrio—sometimes these young gunmen are recruited into gangs like the Mexican Mafia while they're still in prison."

"Do we have any information about that in Luis's case?" Mrs. Zapeta made another note as she spoke.

"Nothing I can discuss at this time."

"But you consider it possible."

"It's definitely possible—yes."

Mott shifted slightly in his chair, and the movement caught Finley's attention. Glad of the chance to get off the topic of Luis Cabrera, he made a little speech. "You all know how concerned the sheriff himself is about the gang situation here in East Los Angeles. To help us in controlling it, he has appointed one of the most capable people in our whole department to head up a new unit that will be concerned only with gang problems—Lieutenant Ralph Mott."

Mott wondered if he should stand up and decided against it. The lack of his own knowledge of the barrio would be very apparent to these community leaders if he gave them half a chance. Since he was required to say something, he made it as brief as he could.

"We will have a reenforced unit in operation as soon as we're able," he said. "Meanwhile, I'm interested in everything that you have to say. I want to get to know each of you personally as soon as possible."

Captain Gutierrez, who had stopped in the doorway for a moment, heard that and approved. Mott was no fool, that was evident, and it was already clear that he intended to give his new job his best effort. Gutierrez turned away, satisfied that the meeting was going as well as could be expected.

An hour later it broke up, following a discussion of the hydroponics project that was still under consideration. A possible location had been found and the Parks Department was going to be asked to cooperate.

Brother Julio had a few words with the captain behind a closed door. The subject again was Luis Cabrera, who was expected back on the street within the next few days. Waiting for him would be his wife and an infant daughter that Luis had never seen. Since a child had been born, the Brother was going to urge him to make it a legal marriage. That would give him a good excuse to evaluate Luis and, if possible, persuade him to accept employment in some other part of the city. There was a car wash on West Pico that would take him—they were short of help.

They did not discuss the possibility of opening the new plant at all. The captain knew about it, and there was nothing definite to add. Brother Julio had already made several presentations to various firms; he had no real reason to believe that he would be any more successful with Morrison and Hale. He continued to hope, but if he had failed there, he would try again. And keep on trying until he succeeded.

CHAPTER FIVE

AS BROTHER JULIO drove, his hands were locked around the steering wheel as though at any moment it might be snatched from him. His heart was pounding, the result of additional adrenalin that had been released into his bloodstream, but his vision was sharp on the roadway because he could not at that moment afford an accident.

 Once more he repeated to himself an obvious and desperately hopeful deduction: he would not have been summoned back to see the chairman of Morrison and Hale in order to be told that his suggestion had been rejected. That could have been done on the telephone or by brief note, and they had his address. It had to be good news, and so good that the Brother did not even dare to contemplate it until it had been confirmed.

It was not easy for him to appear both relaxed and businesslike when he entered the important corner office, but he had asked God for strength, and at that moment he had no doubt whatsoever that the Almighty was solidly in his corner. With the strength of that knowledge he presented himself to the secretary, was ushered in, and sat down as invited.

He was asked what he would like and declined anything at all, afraid that his digestive apparatus might refuse to function. He did his desperate best to relax, and also tried to prepare himself for possible disappointment. They could be trying to let him down gently; perhaps they had called him in so that they could give him the reasons for their refusal.

"Brother Julio," the chairman began, "we were all impressed by your presentation a few days ago, particularly by your obvious dedication, and also by your assurances that East Los Angeles offers a good reliable working force looking for opportunity. You realize that we are in business to make money, but we also feel that we have a certain community responsibility, both as a company and as individuals."

He waited, but the Brother didn't move a muscle. He didn't dare.

"I promised you that we would look into the plant you proposed for us. That's been done, and we also surveyed the neighborhood where it is located. It's quite close to the freeway and, as you said, it's in good repair."

The chairman paused, then went on. "The basic question was how well it would fit our specific needs." He touched a folder on his desk. "I have the feasibility report here, and I've been over it quite carefully. It's not wholly favorable, but that would be asking too much. It does say that it wouldn't involve a great deal of time or cost to fit it reasonably well to our purposes. And the county verified your statement, which I didn't question, that it is fully up to code and legally ready for occupancy and use."

The chairman mercifully paused, knowing perfectly well that his listener had to be emotionally involved, despite the fact that he was concealing it well. Brother Julio was a man to be reckoned with; he had recognized that promptly at their first meeting, and that factor alone had weighed in his decision.

"I won't keep you in suspense any longer," he continued. "We've made an offer for the property, and while it's under the asking price, I expect that it may be accepted. If it is, we will start the moving-in process almost immediately. We have enough reserve equipment to set up operations and we have good delivery positions on the other things we will need."

He stopped and his tone changed.

"Brother Julio, you impressed us all very much and to some

45

degree we are counting on your assurances. We will be hiring people from your parish, perhaps quite soon if our offer for the property is acceptable. We do have some reservations, and you know what they are. It has nothing to do with the ethnic background of our potential employees—we accept your statement that there are good and reliable people who would like to work for us. That's fine. But there is a very high crime level in your area, and this does concern us."

"I might point out," Brother Julio interjected, "that that building has stood there for some time, unoccupied, and that it has not suffered any damage."

"True, but of course everyone knew that it was empty. It is well fenced, which is a plus, and we are also counting on the fact that the people there wouldn't want to see anything adverse happen to the place where they were employed."

"I'll make a particular effort to get that point across," the Brother said.

The chairman nodded. "We were to some extent counting on you to do that. We recognize that you must have considerable influence in the community—in fact we've been told so. Captain Gutierrez, at the sheriff's station, has promised us good police protection, and at the same time, he spoke very highly of you."

Inspiration hit Brother Julio as he recognized a hot iron. "I'd like to offer a suggestion," he said.

"Go ahead, by all means." The chairman leaned back to symbolize that he was listening.

"Assuming that you will get the building, I'd like to mention that the west side is flat and windowless. Among our people there is a strong tradition of mural painting—you will find them all over the barrio. And they are respected—even when they're on the open street, they are almost always left intact."

"I was down there and saw some of them," the chairman commented.

"I have a young man who's only nineteen years old," Brother Julio continued, again being careful with his words. "I am not an artist myself, but I know people who are, and they agree with me that he has a great native talent. I arranged two years ago for him to get some instruction, and his teachers are also sure that he has a great gift from God."

"And you would like to have him do a mural on the side of the building."

"It would be tasteful—I can promise you that—and it will help the whole community to take pride in your facility. It would make it something in which they would have an additional interest. It can be designed on paper and then presented first for your approval."

"If it's suitable, we might even consider it for the cover of our annual report. We always spend some money to make it attractive."

"Would you like to meet the artist?"

"No, you take care of everything. I would like to see the sketches before any of the painting begins, but we might find a few dollars in the budget for the mural. I rather like the idea."

Brother Julio stood up. "If I may be excused," he said, "I have a pressing appointment at my church. God is expecting me."

The chairman smiled. "I understand—don't keep Him waiting. Call me whenever you have anything to discuss."

As Brother Julio left the building, it seemed to him that his spirit was overflowing his body. A strange peace came over him, and he felt very humble in the role he was being allowed to play.

"Twenty-three Adam seventeen.

Deputy Sanchez, who was driving, had the mike in his hand almost at once. His partner, Deputy Rose, had picked that moment to untwist his seat belt, and his hands were for a few seconds occupied.

"Twenty-three Adam seventeen, by."

"Twenty-three Adam seventeen, a four-fifteen J, parking lot, Fifty-two-hundred East Whittier."

Deputy Sanchez reversed direction expertly and gave a two-minute ETA. A 415-J meant a juvenile disturbance. It could be a small matter that could be disposed of in two minutes, or it could be a major incident. But if it was that, more information would have been put out. No other unit had been called to back up, so it was in all probability another fight.

"There it is," Morse said, and pointed. With a policeman's sure instinct he had identified a knot of teenagers gathered together as the almost certain source of the call. Sanchez turned into one of

47

the driveways and cut on the diagonal toward the point where the group was standing.

He pulled to a stop forty feet away and got out of his car. As he did so, Morse exited from the other side. Together they walked up to the small gathering that was intensely aware of their presence.

"Evening," Morse said. "Anything we can do for you?"

A fifteen-year-old replied in Spanish. Morse did not understand that and looked toward his partner, who was bilingual. Sanchez replied in Spanish and then told Morse, "The kid in the blue shirt says that the one in the old shoes threatened him with a knife."

Morse did not need to ask if the complainant was a gang member—obviously he was not. He listened while Sanchez spoke again in Spanish and quickly questioned one of the girls in the group. While doing so, he positioned himself so that he had the suspect in front of him and a little to one side.

Sanchez nodded and then switched to English. "Shake him down," he said.

Morse did, and from the youth's right-hand pants pocket he took out a switchblade knife that was almost six inches long. He opened it and looked at the blade. "That's a helluva lot more than two inches," he said. He put the knife that exceeded the legal limit into his own pocket and reached for his handcuffs. As he did so, a touch of fresher air brushed his face. It was near twilight and some cooling from the unusually hot day could be expected. His mind was on that pleasant thought but half a second before he was jolted by someone jumping onto his back. As he staggered forward, his cuffs were snatched out of his hand.

Someone else rammed him in the back of his knees, and he was forced to go down—there were four or five of them on him by that time. His right arm was pinned behind him so that he could not reach either his weapon or his baton.

He tried to yell a warning to Sanchez, but the one quick look he managed showed him that his partner was being swarmed over as well. And, frighteningly, he saw a knife.

He did not know who held it, or where it was, but he knew that he had seen it. Morse was a man of only average build, but he gulped air and with his total strength made one supreme effort. He succeeded: he rolled away from his attackers and got to his feet, off balance, but at that moment free. And he knew what to do. Someone tackled him about the legs, but he kicked free and ran with bursting lungs to his car. They were so close behind him he could hear their breath, but his determination was total. He reached inside the car, grabbed the mike, and despite the crash of other bodies into his own, he put out his message.

"Twenty-three Adam seventeen; nine ninety-nine, request immediate assistance. Fifty-two hundred East Whittier. Partner down."

He still held the button depressed when he felt a sudden intense pain in his upper arm. He looked and saw blood all over that part of his uniform. Apparently he had been hit even before he had put out his call, and he had not felt it. Not then.

His arm was suddenly useless, and he dropped the mike. Despite that, he pulled out his baton with his left hand and lurched forward to help his partner. He heard a surge of running feet and in bitter disappointment saw fifteen or twenty youths escaping on the dead run. He heard a siren coming and dropped to his knees, totally grateful for the help that was coming.

It had been quiet in the sheriff's station just before he had gone on the air. In the report room four deputies had been doing paper work. In the day room three more deputies had been discussing the merits of an eighteen-foot sailboat.

When the words "nine ninety-nine" came in, the reaction was drastic: every deputy who was free headed for the outside doors and the parking lot on the dead run. Only the watch commander, the duty sergeant, and the jailer remained. As the watch commander stood by the radio, the men outside jumped into the black-and-whites almost as fast as humanly possible. Roof lights on, the cars burst out of the driveway and turned west on Third. The lead car went Code Three, using both lights and siren to clear the way.

At maximum safe speed the patrol units sped down Atlantic Avenue. When they came within a block of their destination, the three lead cars went straight in; the four others that remained split off to set up a tight perimeter.

The first car to arrive stopped with the smell of hot rubber. It was still settling on its springs when the three men it was carrying jumped out toward the place where Morse was being helped to his feet. Sanchez still lay sprawled on his back.

49

Cars were pouring in from everywhere—those from the station joined the five or six already on the scene. A frightened girl pointed silently in the direction that the attackers had fled. On foot and in cars, a group of deputies set off in pursuit as others attended to Sanchez and Morse. Overhead, from an altitude of three hundred feet, the brilliant spotlight of the ARGUS* helicopter bit through the first traces of twilight.

More cars bounced onto the parking lot; more deputies jumped out, two sergeants among them. Morse had known that help would come fast. The first unit had responded to his location in less than fifty seconds. After that, the avalanche.

Anxious, careful hands put both Sanchez and Morse in the front seats of patrol cars—with stab wounds they wouldn't wait for an ambulance. Although there was a closer hospital, the two cars sped away in Code Three condition toward the USC Medical Center, where the highly qualified emergency room would already be alerted to receive them. It would be a five-minute run, and if anyone got in the way of the speeding cars, that would be his problem.

For twenty minutes an intensive search of the vicinity was conducted, with no conclusive result. The helicopter orbited, checking for any traffic over backyard fences or any other evidence of suspicious conduct, and came up empty. A sergeant had already put out a Code Four—no further assistance required. As he got back into his car to return to the station, he could not help wondering, a little bitterly, how the new lieutenant from Malibu was going to deal with this one.

Seven minutes later he was closeted with the watch commander. "I've got most of it," he reported. "We have four witnesses who substantially agree. Sanchez and Morse were taking a subject into custody, a gang kid, when they were both jumped by a small army. According to the best I could get, about eighteen other juveniles attacked our guys, knifed Morse, and beat up Sanchez—he may have been cut too. Somehow Morse got back to his car and called in; at that point the kids fled."

"We got two other calls from storekeepers who saw the trouble," the watch commander said. "Is there any doubt who did it?"

*Aerial Reconnaissance, Ground Unit Support.

"None. It was Los Sapos—it had to be. They fled back onto their own turf, but at the moment we can't prove a thing against any one of them."

"God damn!"

"Get the word from the hospital as soon as you can, will you?"

"Count on it," the watch commander said, and reached for his phone.

Ralph Mott had been home for a little more than an hour when he took the call. He was out of his apartment and in his car in a matter of seconds. He opened up on the freeway, weaving through what traffic there was, at times close to eighty miles an hour. For a miracle he was not stopped; in less than twenty-five minutes he burst up the ramp at the East Los Angeles station and swung his car into the first vacant spot along the wall.

Ever since he had taken on his new assignment he had been careful to keep a low profile. The time for that was past—two of his men were in the hospital, and the subject they had been taking into custody was still at large.

He went directly to the watch commander's office. "What's the latest from the hospital?" he asked. He bit the words off tight; the other lieutenant instantly noted the change.

"I just called, less than five minutes ago. They're both still in S-three condition. Morse is being stitched up; Sanchez has broken ribs—probably kicked. Both conscious."

"How many of my unit are in right now?"

"Six—seven, counting you."

"Call the hospital, see if Sanchez has the name of the subject who was being busted when the four-fifteen went down."

"Right."

Mott did not wait for the call to be made, he went to the duty sergeant and issued orders. "I want a ten-nineteen on every man I have on duty. Also, any backup you can spare. I'm going after that Adam Henry who escaped."

The sergeant was right with him. "Take Vetrovec and Valdemar with you—they've been working the Los Sapos gang turf and know the gang well."

"Where are they now?"

"Probably down there. I'll give them a ten-nineteen call."

51

Mott turned around to find Brother Julio there. It was a surprise, but he had already learned that the Brother was likely to turn up anywhere at any time. "Have you got anything on this?" he asked.

"Only I can confirm that it was Los Sapos. I do not tell tales, but I cannot condone what was done this evening."

Mott would have liked to have invited him to have a cup of coffee, but there was no time for that. He excused himself and went back to see the watch commander.

Lieutenant James handed him a slip of paper. "The subject is Edward Horcasitas, a member of Los Sapos. His street name is Piggy—because he looks like one. He's seventeen and one of the prize hit men for his gang. Vetrovec knows where he lives."

"Thanks." With that Mott went back into his own section and dug out the card for Horcasitas. At first glance his picture looked like all of the other gang kids, then his semiflat, upturned nose made him more easily identifiable. Mott read all the the data and was grateful to whatever deputy had put it down. When he had finished he slipped the card into his pocket, probably against regulations, and made himself a promise that before the night was over that young man was going to be in custody, no matter what it took.

He had just finished when Vetrovec and Valdemar came in. It took him less than half a minute to brief them—they both knew the subject and had arrested him before.

"If you want," Valdemar said, "we can go right down the line and bust every member of the gang we can find."

"I don't think so," Mott responded. "If we herd them all in here, question them, and then have to let the majority go, we won't do ourselves any good. Let's do F.I.'s instead."

"Why field interviews?" Valdemar asked.

"Principally to get a look at them. Morse and Sanchez are both good men—"

"Damn right," Valdemar cut in.

Mott overlooked it. "—so there's a good chance that some of the gang members are marked. Those guys didn't go down without a fight. As soon as we spot any of the Sapos who show signs of recent injury, those we'll collect."

With Vetrovec and Valdemar in the car with him, Mott led a small procession of patrol units into Los Sapos territory. He was determined to bust Horcasitas himself. If the gang wanted to make a war of it, he had plenty of help. If it went the other way, the additional deputies could start in immediately on the field interviews.

Valdemar, who was driving, pulled up before a small frame house that had once been painted white. A tiny starved lawn was visible in the moonlight, decorated with an overturned, rusty tricycle. As Vetrovec covered the back, Mott walked with Valdemar up to the front door and knocked.

After a minute it was opened by a flat-faced Mexican woman in a tattered dress that was utterly lifeless. The sizing was long gone from the fabric; it hung on her because it was powerless to do anything else. She took one look and then began to talk rapidly, and with gestures, in Spanish.

"Do you understand English?" Mott interrupted.

The woman ignored him, pouring out her native tongue with the obvious attitude that if he couldn't understand her, he had to be some kind of an imbecile. Valdemar resolved the matter by interrupting her with one or two short sentences in slightly jerky Spanish. In response to that she retreated and returned in half a minute with a typical gang youth. Already Mott was beginning to recognize them.

"Are you Edward Horcasitas?" he asked sharply.

"What about it, man?"

As he was being cuffed, the teenager seemed almost disinterested. He paid no attention at all when Vetrovec came around the side of the house and got into the patrol car without any kind of protest.

Mott put out the Code Ten-fifteen, signaling that he had the subject in custody; the other cars were released to beginning collecting field interviews.

An hour later things were in good shape as far as Mott was concerned. Piggy had been put into a cell, there to sit and reflect on his sins. Five other members of the Sapos gang had been rounded up, all of them bearing marks of having been in a considerable fight. They all had explanations to offer, but Mott ignored them. The hospital had advised that both Morse and Sanchez might be able to look at the subjects within twenty-four hours, and that was all that he needed.

He allowed himself a few minute to have one cup of machine-made coffee before he started back home again; he was seated in the day room when Brother Julio, still at the station, came in. "I have been speaking with one of the boys you have in custody," he said. "He is now convinced that it would be in his best interests to talk with you."

Mott had already put in more than a full day, but the prospect of getting further definite results spurred him on. In three quarters of an hour he had a more or less full statement, highly equivocated but still usable, from one of the gang members who had taken part in the melee. The detectives could take it from there—that was their job. He got into his car to go home, still in a savage mood.

When he returned to his apartment, Nancy's first words were, "Why didn't you call me?"

He knew in his heart she was justified, but he had no desire to discuss the matter. He said something, enough to get past her, and went into the bathroom, where he took a Valium. He didn't do that very often, but he recognized the need.

Nancy failed to take the hint and pressed him again. "If you could just take a minute to call me and tell me that you're all right, or when you'll be home—"

He cut her off abruptly. "I've not been where I could—most of the time. It's been a helluva night, and I want to get some sleep. So lay off, will you?"

She clearly didn't like that. She had expressed concern for him and that had been her reward. A dozen suitable responses came to her, and she avoided them only with difficulty. She was a person also, entitled to his full consideration, and this time she knew unmistakably that she was in the right.

Mott went to bed without saying anything further. He tossed for some time before the pill took effect and gave him the blessing of sleep.

Nancy was awake for almost a full hour after that. The thoughts churning in her mind refused to let go.

CHAPTER SIX

IN THE MORNING Mott found McBride waiting to see him. The sergeant led him down a corridor into the room where most of the gang control efforts were concentrated. "We've fixed up an office for you," he said, and pointed out a cubicle with glass side panels that effectively destroyed any hope of privacy. "Mike Wickham has stocked it with all of the usual supplies."

He continued on inside, where a standard police desk and a pair of straight-backed chairs occupied most of the available space. "Also, we've moved the set of gang books so that they're just outside your door. They may be of help to you. You'll find detailed maps of each gang's turf, and a roster of the members. They aren't complete, but they're pretty good and include most of the details you'll want. We keep them all up-to-date. There are mug shots of the gang members, F.I. cards, and a summary of their rap sheets, if any. Most of them have records of one kind or another."

Mott knew then that he was not going to be up against any internal problems. Despite his inexperience in the barrio, the rest of the gang control personnel wanted him to do a good job, and they were ready to back him up. It gave him a good feeling, the same one he had experienced the first time he had discovered the police fraternity and its international ramifications.

"Also," McBride went on, "there's a year's file of the monthly gang violence reports. You'll find a lot of information in there. Other reports that bear directly on gang activity will be routed to you as soon as they're available."

"I couldn't ask for more," Mott said and meant it.

"You know Brother Julio. He's in the day room and would like to see you when it's convenient."

"He's certainly around a lot," Mott commented.

"Yes, and we're grateful for it. He's a major asset and completely dependable."

It wasn't often that a police officer would give an outsider a recommendation like that, and Mott knew it. Taking it at full value, he went to the day room, where he found the Brother patiently waiting. He bought two coffees, knowing that Julio was without funds, and then sat down to listen.

Brother Julio revealed an unexpected gift for concise narration: within two minutes he outlined fully the more than two years of work he had put in trying to get a responsible company interested in the unused building that offered a potential for three or four hundred jobs. "I am explaining this," he concluded, "first because I happen to know that the offer for the building is going to be accepted. This will be the biggest step forward for the whole barrio in a very long time. But there is a problem."

"The building is on the turf of one of the gangs."

Brother Julio nodded. "Yes, Los Magnolias. There aren't enough of them to control the plant, but even if there were, I could not permit it. The plant must be open to all qualified applicants, and it must succeed, to show that businesses operated here are a good investment—that our labor supply is plentiful and dependable. What we must do, you and I, is to go and see the Magnolias and convince them that the building must be declared neutral territory. This will include the right of others to cross their turf to get to and from work."

"That won't be easy," Mott said.

Brother Julio finished his coffee, holding the cup in both hands as he tilted it back to get the last few drops. "It will be very difficult," he agreed, "but we must succeed. I will explain to the Magnolias that they will not lose macho, but will gain it, by allowing this. At least they must be made to see it that way."

"Are the Magnolias at war with anyone?"

"At the moment no, but the gang had a small run-in with the Machetes a few weeks ago that could flare up into something serious."

"What caused it?"

"A girl. She is thirteen and pregnant. One of the Roses swears that a member of Los Magnolias is the father."

A surge of frustration rose in Mott. He leaned forward, suddenly intense. "Julio," he asked, "is this ever going to stop?"

The Brother crushed his empty coffee cup and tossed it into a trash container. "We must have jobs—enough jobs to keep everyone working. Then it will be different. People will be able to live decently, to buy the things they need, and to be proud of themselves. Solve unemployment and the barrio will rise. When it does, the gangs will diminish, because there will be other things to do. That is why the new plant is so vital. It must, absolutely must, succeed."

Mott spent the rest of the morning on essential paper work. He made out a requisition for replacements to cover for Morse and Sanchez while they were out, but the budget was very tight since the property tax limitation had been passed, and he could only hope.

When it was close to noon he walked through the station to the locker room in the back and splashed cold water over his face. It was time to eat, but he had no appetite. He felt instead that he would like to go somewhere, by himself, to do some hard thinking.

He went out the front door of the station and found himself looking at the little park and the small lake that adjoined the building. Without making a conscious decision, he started out to walk around the lake, not at the shore line, but back far enough where he could be alone with his own thoughts. He felt the grass underfoot, and the fragile illusion came that he was not close to the heart of one of the world's great cities, but somewhere at a place where the things of nature grew of their own volition, where he could be in communication with them through the senses of feel, of smell, and even of hearing if the wind would just blow enough.

He lifted his head, ignoring the cluster of signs that surrounded the park, and looked up into the open sky. It was very clear, and its blue vastness told him that infinity was there above him and that he could see hundreds of light years into nothingness. Even the hot, burning sun was ninety-three million miles away.

As he began walking again, he organized his thoughts into a conscious stream. For the past three years he had been working burglary. He had visited hundreds of homes where things had been taken, where precious possessions had been smashed in the search for money or other valuables that could quickly be exchanged for narcotics, or sometimes other things. He had caught many suspects, some of whom had been convicted. Occasionally a confession would clear up a number of cases, but often the suspects in custody couldn't tell how many jobs they had pulled or where. Sometimes they confessed to things they hadn't done, because they thought they might have been responsible.

Many of his best burglary suspects, men he knew to be hardcore professionals, had been released on one technicality after another. He believed in the law he had sworn to uphold; he only wished it were a little less complex and less subject to so many, to him, distorted interpretations.

But another thought demanded his mind's attention as he walked slowly northward toward the freeway and the Special Enforcement Bureau, which was two or three hundred feet behind the East Los Angeles station. The gang kids of the barrio carried and used deadly weapons—in the detectives' room there was a whole display board of some that had been confiscated. Everything was there, from brass knuckles to zip guns that fired real bullets, from Saturday night specials to sawed-off shotguns intended for mayhem and death. And all of them had been in the possession of minors.

And that brought up the question. As a burglary detective he had not drawn his gun in the field for years; could he do it now? Could he take aim with deadly intent at a seventeen-year-old boy? That was what was bothering him, and it would not go away.

He knew that the gang members were not normal youths. He knew they ruthlessly killed each other—he had read the reports. Two of them had attacked and killed a harmless ice cream vendor who had only been trying to earn his living. The man had been murdered for the small amount of change he had had on his person. The suspects had been convicted, but that did not bring their victim back or wipe out the unspeakable injustice that had been done to him.

If he saw one of those murder children pointing a gun at him, he would have to draw to protect himself. But once a loaded gun was pointed, time after that was measured in microseconds.

Somehow their weapons would have to be taken away. But there was that damnable matter of the right to bear arms. The founding fathers had not foreseen the fourteen-year-old hitman, the crazed hophead, the organized crime enforcer—they had been thinking about the frontiersmen who had to protect their homes and families from Indian attacks or from greedy white men who wanted to take their few possessions from them by force.

He came back to Third Street and realized that he had walked as far around the lake as he could. He had not found any answers; he had not expected to. But at least he had thought about some things, and that was, if nothing else, a significant start.

That afternoon he talked at length with Danny Torres.

The captain set it up for him. Gutierrez came into his new office, looked around, and asked, "Have you got everything you need?"

"For the moment, yes," Mott answered. "Now I'll try to make good use of it."

"I know you will. One thing you may want to do is to get to know some of the gang kids. We've got one in the cells right now, and he'll be here at least a couple of more hours. His name is Danny Torres, and he's a member of Montaña Mara."

"The gang up on the Heights."

"Right. There is a war on between Los Counts and the gang Danny is in, and he's very much aware of it. Also, he's a little more inclined to talk than some of the other kids."

"Do you mind if I bring him in here?"

"No, but he's a rabbit—watch him. He knows that the present beef that has him inside is a nothing and that he'll be out quickly —unless he starts something. So he should be cooperative."

"I'll go and get him."

Within five minutes Mott was back at his desk with the youthful prisoner in his custody. He took Danny into his office, put him in a chair, and sized him up. He was Mexican-American—that was

59

written all over his features. He was fairly thin, but solid. Despite the starchy nature of much Mexican food, Danny had a flat abdomen and narrow hips that supported his close-fitting blue jeans. He wore a white t-shirt with a bunch of roses stenciled on the front. His raven black hair was of medium length and amateurishly cut. His lips were somewhat full, his nose a little small for his face.

"What are you in for this time, Danny?" Mott asked. He made the question mild, almost suggesting that the arrest didn't really matter.

Danny answered without hesitation. "Nothin'. Some of us was fooling around. Among ourselves. Then some shithead thinks it's a riot and yells for the cops. Shit."

Mott nodded as though he agreed, then he picked up the Montaña Mara gang book and looked up his young charge. His was the fifteenth face in the manual: a Polaroid shot taken against a plain background with an unflattering light. It was a little lopsided, and Danny looked as though the whole thing were some kind of mistake.

The information on the opposite page was, at that moment, highly interesting:

> TORRES, Daniel. "Poochie." Age 18. Education: grade school only, although reported as a "gifted and promising student." Member of Montaña Mara for four years. Car: a brilliant blue Chevrolet, 1964. Lifters installed and other racing equipment. Employment: none.
>
> "Arrested 415 9 instances, no convictions. Arrested for burglary—case thrown out for lack of evidence. Involved in several shootings at houses; believed to be in possession of a sawed-off shotgun. A hard-core warrior, possibly responsible for two 187 shootings, but no adequate evidence. Often talkative.

"Why do they call you Poochie?"

"Cause they think I look like one of those little French dogs, a peke something.

"Are you happy in Montaña Mara?"

"Hell yes, man. They all real good friends of mine. We got the best turf in the barrio—you go up there, you'll see. There ain't no other gang anywhere as good as we are: we got more guys and we got more of everything. It's something makes us proud, man."

"Are you worried about Los Counts?"

"Those mothers? Man, I'm laughing. They ain't nothin'."

"What do you do in your gang?"

"Oh, we have fun. Play basketball sometimes."

"Against other gangs?"

"Man, you're funny."

"How often are you getting laid, Poochie?"

"All I want. There's a lot o' girls around."

"And they're all willing?"

"Man when they know I'm from Montaña Mara, that gets the pants off 'em real fast. We're tops, man, I tol' you that."

Carefully, expertly, Mott led him on, pretending to be impressed with the status of the Heights gang and with his subject as an active member of that group. After some twenty minutes he brought Danny around to the house shootings, and encountered some glib lying. Crimes of that kind went on all the time, but Danny claimed never to have taken part in such a thing himself. "It don' make no real sense, man," he said. "Maybe for the gangs down below, but we don' have to do that kin' of stuff."

"No names, Poochie, but how many of your guys use the stuff?"

"You mean weed? Shit, everybody does that. It's tradition, man. You ever tried it?"

"No."

"Maybe if the cops learned to use weed, it would cool everything. Then you'd know where we're comin' from. 'Course some of the guys use the hard stuff, but I don' want none of that. I don't like needles, man—I'm scared of them."

"You drink beer?"

"Hell, man, what you think! Everybody drinks beer. It's nice, man, and it don' cost too much."

"Some of your guys have guns, I hear."

"Jus' for protection. If we didn't, those mothers from Los Counts, they'd come up and shoot our balls off."

"How about the war?"

"Don' worry about it. We ain't gonna start nothin', so whatever happens will be their fault."

"The way I hear it, you're two up on them."

"That's right: they got shootin' at us and they oughta know better. We're too tough for them. So when they tried, we protected ourselves. Fernandez, I don' know who shot him, but he had it comin'. He asked for it hard. You ask anybody. An' it was self-defense."

"If you don't know who shot him, how do you know it was self-defense?"

Danny Torres shrugged. "We all know, that's all. We stick together. The other guys, they're closer to me than brothers."

"Have you ever had to do any protecting, Danny?"

"Sometimes, sure. You'd do the same thing if somebody that didn't belong came on your turf."

Mott tried another tack, feeling his subject out, trying to get behind and underneath his stock answers. "When you were in school, you did well—better than most."

"I'm good at everything, man."

"Sure, but this was something different, something that called for a lot of things to make it possible. Tell me, Danny, what were you thinking about in those days?"

"You mean in school?"

"I mean at that time. In school you didn't have much time to think for yourself. But outside of school, what was on your mind then?"

"I dunno—a lot of crazy ideas, I guess. I was just a kid. For a while I had the idea that I was gonna be a doctor."

Mott deliberately reacted to that. "Danny, that's a fine profession. It takes a lot of hard work to make it, but if you do, then you're set for life."

"You crazy, man—they won't take no Mex like me."

"Oh yes, they will. There are special programs almost everywhere to give some added help to minority students. How much high school have you had?"

"Not much."

"Danny, it isn't too late. You could get your diploma, and from your record I know you could do it, and with good grades. What kind of a doctor did you want to become?" He asked that to find out just how much Danny had thought about his intended profession, whether or not he had had any conception of the various fields of specialization.

Danny shrugged, reluctant to exhume the dead thoughts. "Take care of kids, maybe. We got a big family and I got used to taking care of lots of kids."

That simple statement was almost electrifying to Mott. It told him that the idea of becoming a physician had not been a casual thing or something thought up on the spur of the moment to answer the question he had put. And it *was* possible. The boy was only eighteen: he could take his high school work in three years if he applied himself and got one of the lost years back. As a Chicano he would benefit from the preferences being given to minorities. God, if he could only be motivated!

In Mott's mind the thought forced itself that possibly, just possibly, he could help. In was conceivable that this gang-oriented youth could be reshaped into a potentially valuable member of society. He tried to imagine what it would be like to walk past a door with a small sign on it reading:

Daniel Torres, M.D.
Pediatrics

At that moment a certain enthusiasm for his new job began to make itself felt, and for the first time he was genuinely glad he had drawn the assignment.

"Danny," he said. "I want you to think hard about the idea of becoming a doctor. According to your school grades, you might make it."

"I got a record, man."

"Yes, but as a juvenile, and there is a difference. If you show some of the promise you have, you can forget the record. You're still young enough. Remember: a doctor is a very important man."

Danny did not appear impressed, possibly, Mott thought, because he couldn't bring himself to believe in his own potential. As Mott took him back to his cell, he looked for any kind of hopeful sign. There were accelerated courses that might help Danny to complete his high school preparation. After that—

"I hate the can," Danny said suddenly. "You can't fuck no broads."

* * *

63

Just after five Mott called home to give Nancy the familiar news that once again he wouldn't be home for dinner. He felt a flush of guilt as he did so. For a moment he wanted to forget his damn job and give a little more attention to his home life. But it was too late for that. He had accepted the assignment to East Los Angeles, and there was no way he could back out of it short of quitting the department and giving up his career. As he hung up he made a mental appointment with himself to take her out for a fine dinner on Friday. It took him a moment to realize that it was already Thursday, so he would have to ask her as soon as he got home. If she were asleep, the first thing in the morning.

He ate at a place that looked fairly good from the outside and was precisely that inside. The food he was served was adequate and the one drink that he allowed himself loosened him up a little and made things seem a bit less harrowing. As he ate he watched the time so that he would be back at the station by seven to meet Brother Julio.

He was there with five minutes to spare; when he came in the back door he found the Brother there already waiting for him in his office. He sat down behind his desk and felt a sense of his own tiredness. A better dinner would have helped, but he had felt that way many times before. Detectives didn't punch time clocks, and there was no real quitting bell. Crime was a twenty-four-hour-a-day affair, and there was no period of even five minutes that the police could safely take off.

Brother Julio got up and held out his hand as though it were an offering. "I'm sorry to have to ask you to do this," he said.

Mott forced himself to smile. "I don't mind, it's part of my job. What kind of car shall we take—marked or unmarked?"

"It makes no difference; they know the unmarked ones as well as you do. But perhaps a plain one would help a little."

As they started eastward, toward the turf of Los Magnolias, Brother Julio began to talk, quietly and in a conversational tone. "When we get to the place where the Magnolias hang out, it might be a good idea if I did the talking. I know all of them by name, and they know me."

"Of course," Mott agreed.

"Understand, Lieutenant, they have already heard of you, but you have no reputation as yet with them, one way or the other. That means they will be very doubtful—they will automatically assume that you are there to harass them."

"If you want me to say something, give me a clue."

"Fine. One thing, if you'll forgive me: don't talk down to them because of the language problem. They will understand you in English, even though they talk Spanish among themselves."

"I'll be careful," Mott promised.

"That will be good, because in their own minds they absolutely own their turf, and you won't be able to convince them otherwise. So we must get their permission for the plant to be declared neutral territory and for a corridor to be set up, like the one into Berlin, for people to come and go."

Mott listened carefully and filed the information away in his mind. As he drove, he let the sensations of the barrio flow in on him through the open window beside him. Like all policemen, he seldom closed the driver's window when he was in an official vehicle, regardless of the weather. With it open he could see more, hear more, and occasionally smell more than with it closed.

The graffiti everywhere meant something to him now. The air was warm and muggy, saturated with the ambience of the city as though it had never known the freshness of the Pacific or the cleanness of the desert. It was tinged with a certain redolence that belonged only to the barrio—something that could not be defined, but was still there.

The car bumped across the guttered intersections toward the place where a group of young males would be hanging out, spending their youth in that curious form of inaction that could erupt without warning into a peculiarly uninhibited violence.

He looked up through the windshield at the darkening sky and saw that the moon was already poised, like a great yellow Japanese lantern. The full moon always brought trouble with it; every experienced policeman knew it. He remembered something he had heard a New York patrolman assigned to Times Square remark when he had dropped in for a visit. "If you want hell," he had said, "pick a night that's warm, with a full moon, on the day that the welfare checks are distributed. The narcs go out of their minds."

Brother Julio caught his attention. "This is the Magnolias' turf. Turn left at the next corner."

After three short blocks they arrived at a corner where a lone wooden building had apparently been abandoned and boarded up. Its last vestiges of pride were buried under an incredible number of symbols and names that had been painted on it in every imaginable color and at almost every possible angle. Some of the writing was fairly even; other names had been sprayed on with a total disregard for symmetry or alignment. With almost a shock Mott saw that there were lights inside and that the building was occupied. The boarded windows were a final surrender to vandalism.

Loosely gathered at the corner were the members of Los Magnolias. They wore a variety of clothing, all of it of the most casual kind. One youngster was trying to grow a beard, with slight success; several others had the start of mustaches. To Mott they were a motley bunch, but because of the prevailing turf rules, they controlled the territory that included the unused factory building. For the time being he would have to go along with their presumption of authority. He did not recognize it for a moment, but he was willing to give it lip service if it would help to preserve the peace.

He pulled up the car and parked. After locking the car, he played the role he had been assigned. He followed Brother Julio across the street in a casual manner, knowing that he was under intense observation and that his every movement was being analyzed by street-wise eyes looking for all possible flaws.

"Hello, Ernesto," Julio said to the tallest of the assembled Magnolias. "This is Lieutenant Mott."

"Eh."

That was a barely courteous response that Mott understood. He slowly nodded his head in acknowledgment, pretending that he was more or less along for the ride. Then he wandered slightly to one side, so that the conversation, for the time being, would intentionally exclude him.

"How much do you know about the new factory?" Brother Julio asked. His voice implied that most if not all of the gang members would be fully informed.

"We know." Ernesto chewed a toothpick and laughed as though he had suddenly been much amused. The others who loosely surrounded him looked interested, but no more. Ernesto was the gang leader, he would do the talking.

Brother Julio turned and leaned against the building, suggesting that time was immaterial to him. Mott saw something more: he was protecting his back. If things did not go well, the defaced building would be his ally.

"You know what they're going to make?"

"Yeah."

Brother Julio had expected that; he didn't turn a hair. "Do you know how many jobs?"

Ernesto answered with an elaborate shrug.

"Four to six hundred. Production people, office staff, drivers, maintenance men, security, and bosses."

"That's a lot, man." Ernesto offered that like a gambit at chess —a possible opening of his own choosing.

"It's good, but it's only the first plant."

"There ain't no more." It was close to an accurate statement; Mott sensed that without actually knowing it. He saw how Brother Julio was playing the game and thought that he was superb.

"I said, it's only the first plant. They can build more. And they will—if this one works out good for them."

Ernesto sensed that he had had a pawn captured and his defenses rose.

"Of course, a lot of that depends on you," Brother Julio said. He made that a general remark, addressed to all of the gathered Magnolias, who were at least fifteen in number.

"On us, man?"

Julio nodded. "Of course."

He stopped, avoiding the obvious. From where he was listening Mott was fully aware of the tough street knowledge that Brother Julio was up against. But he was also aware that the Brother could handle himself well in that kind of situation. He had just put the ball neatly into Ernesto's lap, and Ernesto would have to play it.

"If anybody comes on our turf, he gets his balls cut off."

That was pure bluster. In response, Brother Julio squatted down, picked up a small stick, and began to draw a pattern in the dirt between the sidewalk and the curb. That had once been intended as a grass area, but cactus could not have survived on it as it was. The Magnolias gathered around to see what was going on.

"Here's the southern boundary of your turf," Brother Julio said, pointing with the stick in his hand. "The Pomona Freeway."

Ernesto suddenly became vocal. "Yeah, and before they built that fuckin' freeway we went all the way down to Third! We got half what we had."

"Want to trade with the Spiders?"

"Them shitheads? They got nothin'!"

"If they had the plant, then they'd have big macho. The most important thing going would be on their turf."

Without warning, Brother Julio switched into Spanish. For the next ten minutes Mott could not understand a thing, but he could see that a considerable and intense argument was going on. It was not the kind that comes to blows; it was the kind that involves raised voices, elaborate gestures, sometimes shouted protests. Mott listened, making himself as invisible as he could, but trying not to reveal that he couldn't understand a word. If that became known, it could seriously damage his as yet unformed reputation in the barrio. In Brother Julio he had a strong ally, and he knew it.

After some minutes things subsided. At that point Mott was called over, not sure what was expected of him. Brother Julio relieved his embarrassment. "We have been discussing the new plant," the Brother said in an astonishingly calm tone of voice. "Since it is on the Magnolias' turf, we have been working out some arrangements. First of all, we have agreed that workers for the plant will be coming from all over the barrio."

Mott nodded his agreement, backing his man without committing himself vocally.

"The plant has its own parking lot, which is part of the fenced area. We have agreed that because of the nature of the plant, and the fact that it is being opened for the benefit of all of the Mexican-Americans in the area, it must be neutral territory in the true sense of the word. In return for this, I have promised to pass the word to all of the other gangs that this is by the special permission of the Magnolias, and that the arrangement will end if anyone tries to take advantage of their generosity."

That very definitely disturbed Mott—no one should be in a position to give permission to drive down public streets. They belonged to the taxpayers. But if expediency was necessary in the opinion of Brother Julio, for the time being he would agree to it out of necessity. The thought crossed his mind that it was a little like certain deals that had been made with informers, letting them off with less than they deserved in return for information that was badly wanted.

"I have also promised the Magnolias that they will have first pick of the available jobs and, secondly, that the Sheriff's Department will see that order is enforced. If some of the other gangs were to get together to try to run things in and around the plant, we will prevent that."

It was Mott's cue and he took it. "We'll certainly give the plant full police protection, and if we hear about trouble brewing anywhere, we'll stop it as fast as we can."

Brother Julio looked his approval of that. "The Magnolias have lost much of their turf due to construction, so they want to protect every bit they have left. During the hours that the plant is closed, no one else can come and go except people who are actually employed as watchmen, janitors, or others on the night shift."

Moot nodded again without speaking. He didn't like that rule either, but he used his rare gift for putting himself in the other man's place and saw it from the gang kids' standpoint. They were making a major concession, not because they wanted to, but because it was being forced on them. They were trying to save as much face as they could, and he couldn't blame them for that.

"If it becomes necessary," he said, "we will remember how we were helped."

Ernesto shifted slightly from one foot to the other. "One of our guys is out on bail," he said. "It's a lousy beef."

"I'll look into it," Mott promised.

"O.K., man."

Brother Julio led the way back to the car, and Mott let him.

CHAPTER SEVEN

ON THE HEIGHTS Montaña Mara was gathering. The members of the gang began to cluster around a crude stone fireplace that was decorated with a black spray-painted MM symbol as bold as the space allowed. Similar symbols were painted all over the turf, where they were left alone—the residents knew that to remove or deface one would be to risk prompt retribution. The gang completely controlled the Heights, which, because of its peculiar geography, was something of a fortress.

Access to the Heights was by a limited number of roads, all of which twisted through several turns before reaching the upper plateau. There the few streets were tangled haphazardly, following no systematic pattern. The houses were often set at odd angles. Between them narrow passageways ran in many different directions, forming a labyrinth that only someone totally familiar with the terrain could know.

Montaña Mara had complete knowledge of every pathway, and the intimate details of every cul-de-sac. Frequently deputies had to pursue gang members through this warren, and they were not always successful. Furthermore, it was a big turf; the gang, therefore, was one of the largest.

The meeting on the hillside was about Los Counts. Cochise, who was one of the leaders of Montaña Mara, was talking. "They beginnin' to get juice back into their balls, so pretty quick they're goin' to come and hit us. They may come pretty fast—might catch somebody. So what we do, we hit them first. Tonight we go down there and we shoot up Jambo's place. He sit out on the porch a lot, so maybe we get him, too. Fix Jambo, and the Counts ain't gonna be nearly so big no more."

"Can't we just go after Jambo?" someone asked. "He ain't too hard to find."

Luis Cabrera spoke up. As he did so there was almost instant silence. He was the experienced man with the added glory of just having come out of prison. "You go just for Jambo and the rest, they come after your ass. You do like he say and you keep 'em all scared." He spoke in Spanish with a heavy infusion of the gang's own words.

After that, all that remained were the logistics. The car to do the job was chosen, and the crew was picked. Only three would go: one to drive, one to keep a lookout, and one to carry the shotgun in the back. Kiko was picked to drive, since he was the best the gang had in high-speed elusive maneuvers, if they became necessary. Indio would serve as lookout; Jin-Jin would handle the shotgun in the back.

It would be dangerous, of course, to go into Los Counts turf, and that added huge macho to the mission. The gang began to break up as it did almost every early evening, giving no indication that anything unusual was afoot. Two of the members decided on their own to go down on Perry Street and rip off a little all-night grocery and beer store that hadn't been touched in almost two weeks. A couple of six packs of beer would be enough, and for that small an amount the owner probably wouldn't even say anything—it would be best for him if he were to pretend not to notice. He knew who ran the territory, and he paid little enough tribute.

The mission car left the Heights after two or three others had preceded it, headed down toward Whittier. They stayed on Eastern Avenue, which was neutral territory, so there was no hint of warning that something had been planned. It was not until it reached Brooklyn Avenue that the mission car turned west, and that still did not prove anything—Brooklyn cut directly through the center of Los Counts turf, but it was a main thoroughfare and therefore normal passage was expected and allowed.

Very calmly and quietly Kiko turned south, only two blocks from the corner where Jambo's home was located. The possibility of discovery was then infinitely greater, but that was part of the mission. The car was in enemy territory, but had the element of surprise completely on its side.

One block went by without incident. In the back seat Jin-Jin had the shotgun out of sight, but ready.

One block to go.

Jambo had not formed any definite plans. He was aimlessly cruising in his car with Jumpy and Jumpy's younger brother, Stick, both of whom were good with the guns they were carrying. Something in the air had warned Jambo that Montaña Mara might be ready to make a move. He was therefore prowling, as were four other cars from the gang, all looking for the first sign that their turf was under attack.

When the mission car from the Heights had turned off Eastern, he had seen it. He had been headed north with the thought in the back of his mind that if things looked right they might make a bold thrust directly into Montaña Mara, shoot up the house where Luis Cabrera lived to prove that they weren't scared even of him, and then get the hell out before anyone really knew what had happened.

If they had great good luck, it was remotely possible that they might get Luis himself, who was known to have killed a member of Los Counts before he had gone inside. That would go a very long way toward setting things right.

The instant that he saw the Montaña Mara car turn west onto Brooklyn, he was alert to the possibilities. He fell in behind it, just another car in the stream of traffic, pretty certain that he would not be spotted.

When the mission car from the Heights turned south onto a forbidden street and headed directly toward Jambo's own house, he cut his lights and followed. He did not need to alert his companions—Stick already had his weapon ready, and Jumpy was betraying the nervous excitement that had earned him his nickname.

It would all be decided within the next half minute.

The car from Montaña Mara began to drift toward the right as it approached the second intersection. On the southwest corner, exposed on two sides, was the modest wooden house that was home to Jambo and his family. The invading car could be planning to turn right, but Jambo didn't think so.

The moment he saw that it was going to cross the intersection, he hit the gas on his own car and felt it leap forward in response. When he saw the snout of a shotgun come out of the right rear window of the car ahead, he knew that he was too late to prevent a blast.

"Driver!" he shouted. "Get the driver!"

The thunder of shotgun split the air as Jambo pulled his car almost alongside the one from Montaña Mara. At that moment Jumpy aimed his forty-five and pulled the trigger.

The windshield of the enemy car burst into a pattern of radial lines. Half a second later, the shotgun in Stick's hands blasted into the back at a sharp angle.

With the presence of mind that street tactics had taught him, Jambo floored his gas pedal and burned rubber on the dry pavement. His car spurted down the block in a burst of high-pitched engine noise. White smoke trailed behind him from the exhaust and mixed with the acrid black fumes coming from the tires. As he fled, he kept his arms up high so they would conceal his face and hunched down low over the wheel so that he could not be seen.

From across the street a frightened woman seized her telephone. When the sheriff's station answered, she shot off a running sentence in frantic Spanish. It was almost half a minute before she was understood.

In the middle of the street, the car from Montaña Mara rolled aimlessly southward, drifting slightly to the left. Almost half way down the block, going no faster than ten miles an hour, it approached the east curb. There it smashed head-on into a parked Chevrolet, and came to a stop with a shudder. A few seconds later steam from the cooling water hitting the hot engine began to float upward from the edges of the hood.

Mott was on the parking lot, walking toward his own car, when he saw the back door of the station burst open and deputies coming out on the run. He had no idea what had happened—for the moment he did not need to know. He burst into a run himself and jumped into the back seat of the nearest patrol car that was being manned. He was barely inside before the deputy driving wheeled sharply and almost shot down the incline that led to Third Street. The car slowed just enough to be sure that it was safe to enter traffic, then, lights and siren on, it accelerated rapidly westward.

"What have we got?" Mott asked.

The deputy on the right-hand side turned and answered. "Gang cars with shotguns. Shots fired."

That was enough: the words *shots fired* would always trigger a full response.

"What turf?"

"Los Counts."

A fast right turn that barely avoided turning into a skid abruptly stopped the talking as Mott, minus a seat belt, braced himself and hung on. The tires screamed; the car lurched as it settled onto its new heading. It was headed up Eastern, the siren clearing the way. A startled pedestrian froze in the middle of an intersection, forcing the patrol car to brake hard almost to a stop. As it spurted forward once more, the deputy riding shotgun waved his arm out the window, signaling the pedestrian back toward the sidewalk.

A high performance left turn took the car onto a residential street where it was forced to go more slowly. After two more blocks it pulled up beside another patrol car that was already stopped in the intersection. At the same time a third responding unit rolled up rapidly from the south. The night was punctuated by the flashing patterns of the revolving roof lights.

Mott took two or three seconds to clip his ID card to the outside of his jacket before he got out of the car. Then he saw that there were two immediate centers of interest: the house across the corner and an apparent traffic accident farther down the block. Because he was on that side of the street, he ran down the sidewalk toward the accident site. He had seen hundreds of traffic collisions, but since shots had been reported fired, the situation could be a great deal more serious than it appeared.

Patrol cars were flooding in from all four directions; several uniformed deputies were already at the accident when he arrived.

The first thought that hit Mott was that with his new rank, he was probably the senior officer on hand, and therefore in command.

When he reached the car that was pointed the wrong way, he braced himself and looked inside. He saw first a pair of staring, sightless eyes and then a mass of bone and blood where a lower face had once been.

He had never gotten used to things like that; his stomach knotted and he had an immediate, desperate urge to be sick. He fought it down, because he had to, leaned over the sill of the car, and surveyed the rest of the interior.

"Paramedics," he barked. "Ambulances—two."

"On the way, Lieutenant." So they knew who he was.

A deputy opened the rear door and scanned the interior. "We'd better get those guys out of there," he advised.

He wouldn't have said that unless he had been trained and experienced in first aid. His partner ran around the car to help from the other side; as he did so Mott carefully opened the driver's door, making sure that the man behind the wheel, whether living or not, couldn't fall out onto the sidewalk. A deputy stepped up to help him; together they maneuvered the driver out of his car. There was a considerable amount of blood, but neither man allowed that to deter him.

There was no opportunity for thought or inner reactions—the job was at hand and time was of the essence. The electronic wail of an approaching siren meant that either the paramedics or an ambulance was arriving.

Mercifully, it was a paramedic team from the county fire department. The men were out of their vehicle with their equipment in seconds and went to work with admirable efficiency, wasting no motions. Mott stood and watched, still not concerned about the blood that was beginning to clot on his clothing. He was concerned almost entirely with the condition of the victims.

One of the paramedics looked up. "This one's still alive," he reported. He might have added more, but a small ring of intense spectators had already formed to stare at the grisly spectacle. There were low murmurs, but no sudden penetrating scream of recognition of a son or close relative lying bloodied on the sidewalk. If that happened, then the distraught parent or family member would have to be restrained so that the paramedics could do their job.

An ambulance arriving Code Three pulled up sharply. The rear doors swung open and two attendants quickly took out a Gurney. Bad as the situation was, it was under control, and Mott knew that there was nothing he could do to help. He crossed the street past the emergency vehicles and walked toward the house on the corner that had been the other center of interest.

There he found Sergeant McBride on the scene. Mott had not known that he was even in the station. "What's the story?" he asked, keeping his voice low.

"The house was hit by a shotgun blast. One casualty: a fourteen-year-old girl who was inside. She caught a pellet in the arm. Otherwise they were lucky."

"Any idea who did it?"

"The Montaña Mara gang." The sergeant gestured down the street, "That's probably the hit car—I haven't been down there yet. Jambo lives here—Vincent Jurado. He's one of the leaders of Los Counts. Shooting up a house this way is pretty common. How about the car?"

"There were three S-fours in the car, apparently all juveniles. At least, I hope they're all still alive. One of them is a mess for sure."*

"Did you obs the license on the car?"

"I was too concerned for the victims."

McBride produced a grim smile, if it could be called that. "I'd have done the same thing. And the car isn't going anyplace."

"Is there anything I can do here?" Mott asked.

McBride pretended to look around for a moment. "I don't think so, Ralph. One of the units has already taken the girl to the hospital."

*The condition of injured victims is normally described by a code to speed radio communications and avoid excess details that are not immediately necessary. The code is:
- S-1, slightly injured;
- S-2, requires medical attention;
- S-3, probable hospital case;
- S-4, in serious or critical condition;
- S-5, dead.

"Then I'll go back as soon as I can get a ride."

"Get you one right away; we've got more help here than we need now." He signaled with his flashlight and caught a deputy's attention. "Can you run the lieutenant back?" he asked.

The deputy nodded. "Sure, we're just going in."

As soon as he arrived back at the sheriff's station, Mott went to the large, clean washroom in the rear, wet some paper towels, and did the best that he could to sponge the blood off his clothing. He made an acceptable job of it and then washed his hands. As he did so he was quite suddenly aware that he was very tired. It had been a hard day, and the conclusion of it had taken out of him about all that he had had left to give.

When he had finished, he went back to his office for a moment to be sure that it was in order. Satisfied, he said good night to the watch commander and went outside to his own car. He wasn't through yet: it was still a long way to Santa Monica where he and Nancy had chosen to live. She in particular liked the cooler temperatures off the ocean and the fresher air, despite the fact that it was often overcast. What she wanted he would give her if he possibly could—she had to put up with far too much as it was.

He drove smoothly to the entrance ramp and up onto the Pomona Freeway. At that hour there was very little traffic, and he could drive at the full legal speed, plus a little more. He settled down and within a few minutes reached the intersection with the Santa Monica Freeway. He turned up the transfer ramp, checked for traffic over his left shoulder, and then pointed his car straight down the smooth concrete that promised a free, comfortable passage westward to the ocean.

With reasonable luck he would be home in thirty or thirty-five minutes.

Nancy was waiting up for him, sitting quietly with a book in her hands. He came in, smiled at her, and tried to turn away before she could see the stains that remained on his clothing. He didn't succeed. She got quickly to her feet and came to him, her eyes wide.

"Are you hurt?" she asked, and seized hold of him.

He put his hands on her shoulders, grateful for that little bit of physical contact. "Not a scratch. Nothing. I helped to pull a traffic victim out of his car."

"Dead?"

He shook his head quickly to banish the image that might be forming in her mind. "No. Banged up, but he'll be all right."

She knew that he could be lying to her, but she was used to that. In fact she preferred it to learning the grimmer realities of his job. "You're very late," she said.

"I know." Mott wished he could come up with something better to say.

He knew that she was not a beautiful girl—that few heads would turn when she walked down next to the ocean. She was quite tall and almost too slender. She did not have very much of a bosom, and her legs were definitely too thin. That meant nothing to him really, because what she had to offer of herself was the kind of stuff he used to dream about so many burglaries ago. And when she lay next to him at night, woman to man, warm flesh against warm flesh, she was a total consummation for him and an integral part of his life.

She sensed his weariness and felt herself soften. "Can I fix something for you?" she asked.

"Can you manage some hot soup?"

"Chicken noodle—out of a can."

"That would be great."

As she went into the kitchen he retreated to their bedroom, where he got out of his clothes. He had a good wash and then put on his robe, the most comfortable thing that he had. He came back and sat down with her, sipping the thin hot soup and eating the crackers she had put on a plate. For ten precious minutes he talked with her, savoring the fact that they were alone together and that the rest of the world was outside on another plane. It was many miles back to the barrio, and he could forget all about it until morning.

When he had finished, he took the dishes back into the kitchen himself to save her the few steps. When he came back she was on her feet, her head slightly tipped to one side, looking at him a little obliquely.

"Are you tired?" he asked.

"Yes, but make me a proposition."

"O.K., I promise no overtime or cop stories all next week."

She came very close to him and rubbed her cheek against the sleeve of his robe. "You've got a deal," she whispered.

CHAPTER EIGHT

AT EIGHT-THIRTY in the morning the East Los Angeles Sheriff's Station was operating smoothly: the scheduled number of units was out on patrol, the essential paper work was moving through the proper channels, and the administrative personnel were ready to deal with the next emergency.

A report was in from the USC Medical Center: one of the victims of the previous night's shooting was dead; the other two were both in intensive care in very critical condition. The car they had been riding in had long since been taken to a sheriff's garage where, roped off, it was being held as evidence. Two teams of detectives were already in the field conducting an investigation.

At a quarter to nine Captain Gutierrez called his new lieutenant on the interoffice telephone. "I hear that you were on hand at the shooting last night," he said.

"I got there shortly after it went down," Mott answered. "Quite a mess."

"More than that, Ralph—one of the victims just died, so its murder. I want you to stay with it and work with homicide. It's their case, but I'm sure they won't mind."

"Yes, sir."

He waited to see if the captain wanted to say anything more, but the line went dead. He put the phone down, reminding himself that he hadn't been assigned to this new job in order to take a free ride. He decided to follow homicide's lead and do whatever he could to help with the gang angle.

He went first to talk with Lieutenant Finley, whose grasp of the whole barrio culture from top to bottom was widely known. "What have we got so far on the shooting last night?" Mott asked.

Hayden Finley, as usual, was in calm possession of himself. "I can give you part of the picture at least," he said. "It's pretty clear that Montaña Mara came down onto the turf of Los Counts to shoot up the house of one of the Counts' leaders—a kid called Vincent Jurado, whose street name is Jambo. The car used for the hit belongs on the Heights, and the three juveniles who were riding in it are all Montaña Mara members. One of them just died, by the way."

Mott knew better than to say he already had that.

"You've been reading the gang violence reports," Finley went on, "so you know that shooting up a house that way happens all the time. We recovered the shotgun from the wrecked car. The way I put it together, Montaña Mara made the attack and then was hit immediately after that. That opens up several possibilities. One of them is that a fringe member of Montaña Mara, or someone else on the Heights, knew what was going to happen and tipped the Counts off. If so, he's dead. They'll find him and kill him—you can depend on that."

"Can't we prevent it?"

Finley shook his head. "They can find him faster than we can, and nothing will stop them from carrying out the execution. Betraying the gang is the worst offense they know. Believe me, they'll make him pay the hard way."

"What other possibilities do you see?"

"Well, if the house wasn't staked out by the Counts, then it's most likely that the hit car was seen coming in and one of the Counts' cars got behind it. Both gangs run up and down Eastern Avenue a lot, so that isn't as far out as it sounds. I'm certain that the Montaña Maras definitely intended to hit Jambo's house, and kill him if they could. They got caught doing it and were hit themselves."

"As I reconstruct it," Mott said. "Montaña Mara fired first."

"Agreed—the shotgun we recovered had just been fired."

"Hayden, I saw the occupants of that car after they had been shot up, and there's no way that any one of them could have fired that shotgun after what they took."

"Which leaves us with two unanswered questions," Finley pointed out. "First, who were the suspects in the car that shot up the attackers? Secondly, how was it possible for them to retaliate so fast—literally within a few seconds?"

"On the first point, I would think it would have to be a Counts' car."

"Granted that, but we don't have a make—so far no description of either the car or its occupants. We know that a forty-five was fired into the Montaña car, and also a shotgun blast. That means two different gunmen, plus the driver."

Mott was thinking. "As I understand it, the gang kids don't normally run around with their guns in their cars—it's too easy for us to get hold of them."

"That's right."

"So, since there were guns in the second car, that means that whoever was in it had something planned of their own."

"I go along with that."

"Hayden, in the area where the shooting went down, how many of the local people speak English?"

"Perhaps fifty-fifty."

Mott made up his mind. "I'm going out to talk to them," he said.

One of the basic techniques of field investigation is meticulously careful and thorough interrogation of witnesses. Like so many aspects of police work, it calls for endless patience coupled with a constant alertness to catch anything that might be revealing. A minute pause, a look away before giving an answer, a too casual attitude—any one of them could be important, and a multitude of other indicators as well. Ralph Mott had conducted thousands of field interviews, and he knew that if he could make himself understood, he would be able to ferret out whatever there was to learn. He got into a plain car, drove to the area of the shooting, and then set out on foot.

Technically he was in charge of the investigation, but the other men in the field knew their jobs thoroughly and would not have to be told what to do. One team was on the Heights; the other was at the hospital keeping watch over the two still living victims from Montaña Mara. If there was a dying statement to be had, they did not intend to miss it.

For almost all of the rest of the morning Mott rang doorbells, showed his white ID card and the plain star that was his badge, and conducted interviews. He was at a severe disadvantage, in that he did not understand Spanish. Most of the people with whom he talked much preferred that language and a few spoke no English at all. He kept on, not allowing himself to become discouraged as he called at every home where there might be a chance that the second car had been seen. Several times he was sure that his interviewee had seen something, but no one would admit to anything. If it was true that the gang ran the turf by rule of terror, he did not blame them too much.

Mrs. Consuelo Espinoza looked though the front window to see who was ringing her doorbell; as she did so Mott held up his identification and badge for her to inspect. A few seconds after that she was framed in her doorway—cautious, suspicious, and alert.

"I'm from the sheriff's department," Mott said, making it an easy, relaxed statement.

He got a swift response in Spanish, and Mrs. Espinoza prepared to shut the door.

The very slight hesitation in her movement telegraphed to Mott that she wanted to be rid of him, but wasn't quite confident that she could escape so easily. That very strongly indicated she knew something she didn't want to tell.

"Madam, I know that you understand English." Mott made his voice a little more firm. If she did understand him, it would have its effect; if she didn't, nothing whatever would be lost.

"Not good, not good," she protested.

"Good enough." Mott pressed his advantage. "May I come in, please." He timed it exactly right, not pushing past her, but making it clear that he expected immediate admission. Hesitantly, and reluctantly, Mrs. Espinoza yielded and stepped aside to let him in.

Without waiting for an invitation Mott perched himself on the front half of a rickety chair to emphasize that he could not be dismissed too easily or too quickly. This witness, he was confident, could tell him something.

If she could, she was determined not to. It took several minutes to get her to admit that she was fluent in English, or at least enough so to understand his questions and to reply to them. As Mott began to talk about the shooting the night before, she became visibly more tense to the point where Mott had no doubts whatever that he had uncovered a key witness. First he would have to get her to talk to him; later it might be necessary to persuade her to appear in court. For the moment, it would be enough to pry out of her whatever it was that she knew.

The small house was on the same north-south street that had been the scene of the shooting the night before. The Espinoza home was well down the block, much below the point where the uncontrolled car from Montaña Mara had drifted slowly head-on into a parked vehicle on the east side of the street. It therefore followed that the witness, if at home at the time, had not seen the actual shooting and probably not the collision either. But she could have seen the second vehicle, the one that had fled after firing into the Montaña Mara car and killing at least one of its occupants.

"Last night about nine o'clock, Mrs. Espinoza, where were you?"

"Casa," she replied. *"Casa."* Then she added some more in Spanish. She had to know that he couldn't understand, therefore it was her way of evading the question while pretending to reply.

"In what part of the house?" Mott did not let up a hair.

"All parts, back and forth."

"Sometimes in the kitchen?"

"In the kitchen—yes."

"In the bedroom?"

"Si—bedroom."

"And sometimes the living room."

The witness stopped dead, but she had been trapped and there was no way she could fend the question off. "Only sometime," she offered. It was weak and lame.

Mott leaned forward and looked judicial. "Now, Mrs. Espinoza,

I want you to tell me what it was that you saw while you were in the living room."

He let the words hang in the air while he waited for his answer. He did not move a muscle or relax the stern expression that was on his face. His body was leaning forward, expectantly.

Clearly his witness was terrified. She paused a few seconds, then, very slowly she began to shake her head from side to side. As she did so, two huge tears appeared and started to run down her cheeks.

Mott hated what he was having to do to her, but somewhere in the hospital morgue a boy lay dead, and two more might join him at any time. This was murder, and where that crime was concerned, no compassion could be shown.

"I don't know," she stammered.

Mott visibly pressed his lips together, rejecting the answer. "No, Mrs. Espinoza, that won't do. You see, I came here because I knew that you could tell me something. And I'm going to stay until you do. Unless, of course, you'd rather have me take you to the sheriff's station in a patrol car and question you there."

The very thought of that made her begin to shake visibly. For some reason that idea redoubled her terror. Then Mott saw it. If she were taken in for questioning, the whole street would know. And rightly or wrongly, she would be branded an informer. Without intending to do so, he had applied the final pressure that she could not resist. She paled before his eyes, and he saw moisture on her brow. More tears came, and his whole compassionate being cried out inwardly to him to cease putting this innocent woman through such an ordeal.

He forced the thought aside and remembered again that he was investigating murder.

Murder. The viciously, deliberate killing of at least one human being—who had been only a boy, perhaps sixteen or seventeen years old.

"Well," Mott said. The word was almost frigid and carried a certain terror of its own.

The witness capitulated. "I see the car," she whispered, as though the very walls had ears.

"And you know whose it is."

With her eyes closed, she nodded a reluctant answer to that.

"Members of Los Counts," Mott prompted.

Again a hesitant, fearful nod.

"You saw who was in the car, didn't you." He stated it as a hammer blow of fact. He did not raise his voice, but he was like an angel of judgment.

The tears were coming faster now, making his witness a pitiful sight. He steeled himself and hung on. Then, as though she were confessing herself a heretic before the Inquisition, Mrs. Espinoza yielded what she knew. "The driver I not see. But in the back I see one person. One person. Arturo Lucero—the boy they call Stick."

The fearful deed done, she dropped her head far down and gave herself up to shaking sobs.

Mott went into the little kitchen, found a clean glass, filled it with water from the tap, and took it to her. He knelt beside her and laid a protective hand across her shoulders. They were big shoulders, but there was no strength in them then. They were like masses of shapeless dough. Through them Mott could feel the anguish he had inflicted on this woman.

She took the water and drank. When she had somewhat recovered herself, Mott spoke to her very carefully and slowly, to be sure that she would understand every word.

"Mrs. Espinoza, I want you to know that I will keep very confidential what you have told me. You won't be called as a witness if there is any way I can prevent it. I will protect you—do you understand?"

She looked at him. "It make no difference now," she said. "They will know."

To cover her Mott continued all the rest of the way down the block, ringing each doorbell, asking to go inside, and putting questions. At no time did he betray the fact that he had found out anything at all. When he finally finished, he went back to the unmarked car and drove to the sheriff's station, reasonably sure that he had protected his informant. No one paid him any apparent attention.

But before he was back in his office it was already known that the new lieutenant from the sheriff's station, the one that was supposed to head the new gang control section, had been to several houses. But he had spent the greatest amount of time by far with old woman Espinoza, the weird one whose husband had been killed in a construction accident.

He had been there too long. She had talked. Within the hour, Los Counts were planning what to do about it.

Sergeant d'Amico was waiting for Mott when he came in. "Lieutenant," he said, "I've got some dope for you on that shooting last night."

"Great, come on in."

In his office Mott seated himself, put a block of paper in position, and picked up a pen. "Let's have it," he invited.

The sergeant put down three completed forms, each with a small picture fastened at the upper left hand corner. "These are the three kids who were shot up. All of them belong to Montaña Mara. This one, Jurado, died in the hospital. The other two are still alive as far as I know, but neither one has been able to say anything."

"Would they if they could?"

"They might—you never know. Two of our guys are staying right with them."

"What's the prognosis?"

"The last I heard, both of them have a chance to pull through. We have a parolee on the Heights, Luis Cabrera. He was interviewed, but he swears by Almighty God that he doesn't know anything at all about the shooting or why it went down. He claims that he would have tried to stop it—which I don't believe. He's too violent himself."

"I may have something, too," Mott said. "But let me ask something first. When the kids take street names, do they ever duplicate each other?"

"Yes, but not in the same gang. There are a lot of Flacos, which means skinny—probably one in every gang. Once in a while brothers will share the same name—in one of the gangs, Los Lobos, there's big and little Dopey. They're both inside right now —armed robbery."

"One of the kids riding in the car that got away last night— probably a member of the Counts—has been ID'ed as Stick."

D'Amico whistled softly. "You've got a snitch?"

"Yes."

"Male or female?"

Mott thought a moment and then realized that the question

would not have been put without good reason.

"Female."

The sergeant suddenly became dead serious. "Lieutenant, you know how dangerous that is—particularly in this area. If the gang kids find out, they'll hit her."

"They never will from me."

"I know that, but you couldn't throw away a gum wrapper up there without them seeing it. They'll know everyone that you talked to—and for how long. I think we'd better take some covering action."

"What do you want to do?" Mott asked.

"Bring in Jambo for questioning. If we keep him here long enough and sweat him hard enough, they may think that we got something from him. At least it may create a doubt."

"That's the leader of the Counts, isn't it?"

"One of them. Also, I want to do something else, if you'll go along. We've got to make it look like we don't know anything. One way is to intensify the patrols past the point where the shooting went down. That will also help to protect your snitch, if she's in that area." The sergeant made no pretext he didn't know it to be a fact.

"What charge do you want to hold Jambo on?"

"For the time being, suspicion of being in the getaway car. As suspicions go, it's not bad."

"Go get him," Mott directed.

The hospital called the East Los Angeles Sheriff's Station shortly after that with a report. The coroner had taken possession of the body of Javier Romero, known as Kiko, for further examination and autopsy. Maximino Gallardo, known as Jin-Jin, had had a complete groin amputation and was still in guarded condition. Victor Burgos, called Indio, had been removed from the critical list, but his condition was still serious. Neither Gallardo or Burgos could talk to anyone, and both remained in intensive care. Father Lopez had given both of them the last rites of the Church.

Sergeant d'Amico conferred briefly with the watch commander. As a result, the conspicuous black and white patrol cars began to run up and down the scene of the shooting with greatly increased frequency. A team of detectives began to ring doorbells in the neighborhood, asking many questions. Then a patrol car pulled up before the Jurado house while another covered the back. Two deputies rang the front door bell, gained admission, and came out shortly thereafter with Vincent, known as Jambo, between them. Jambo put his hands behind him as though he had been cuffed and he held them that way while he was put into the car. He was anxious to gain every bit of glory that he could.

When they brought Jambo in, they didn't take him directly to see the lieutenant. Instead they sat him down in a small office and subjected him to a considerable barrage of questions. Jambo had been in the station many times before, and the environment didn't disturb him in the least. He was totally confident that they were shooting in the dark—unless old woman Espinoza had opened her big fat yap. In that case, steps would be taken promptly to see that she never did it again.

The initial team of interrogators had one job to do, and they did it: they thoroughly convinced Jambo that they were indeed shooting in the dark and hadn't been able to find any kind of witness. Jambo knew, of course, that deputies were still out asking questions all over his neighborhood, but that could be a cover-up. However, he was certain that if the men talking to him did know anything, they would never be able to avoid showing it.

In that he was totally wrong.

After his first interrogation, he was taken to the bathroom and then offered food, which he refused. He had tasted what came out of the vending machines set up for Los Angeles County's finest, and although he was hungry, he knew what he was doing.

After that respite, he was taken to see Sergeant d'Amico, who was even crisper in his questions and more disconcerting in his nonacceptance of the answers he was getting. Jambo grinned; he was getting to the old bastard. Sergeant d'Amico was, in point of fact, thirty-two and a candidate for the police olympics, but to Jambo all men in uniform were on their way downhill.

The interview with the sergeant took more than an hour. Before it was over, Jambo changed his mind and asked for something to eat. The quick, careful, detailed questioning was beginning to get to him; because he had been asked so many things, he was not at all sure he could remember what he had said. Also, he was troubled that they were keeping him so long. Some of his friends and fellow gang members might begin to wonder what he was saying. They should know that he would die before he would tell the pigs a thing, but he should have been back long ago.

Jambo was kept waiting another whole hour before the lieutenant was able to see him. That would be the new guy, the smartass that didn't know a goddamned thing. During the hour Jambo tried to recall some of the answers he had given and discovered, to his chagrin, that he had contradicted himself at least four times. He hoped that the pigs hadn't noticed it. Judging by the way they acted, they hadn't. Pigs were dumb, which was why they were pigs.

When they took him into the lieutenant's office finally, they sat him down and then read his whole rap sheet, even including the time that he had been busted for helping himself to a lousy six-pack of beer. They had let him off, of course, but they had written it down, which was a stinkin', lousy, unfair thing to do. Jambo was hot.

Mott looked him over for almost a full minute, not saying a thing. Then his first question was totally unexpected. "Where did you get the name Jambo?"

"Can't you figure that out, man—it's short for James Bond."

"You think you're James Bond."

Jambo shrugged.

"I don't think Commander Bond would be flattered."

That made Jambo laugh. "Hey man, you're stupid. He ain't a real guy, he's made up."

"Then why do you call yourself by his name?"

Jambo was lost. "Because he's a great guy: he kicks the shit out of anybody that gets in his way."

"How can he if he's made up?"

"Well—hey, man, you know . . ."

"I don't know. Explain it to me."

The phone rang and Mott picked it up. "Yes," he said.

"Ralph, this is Hayden, calling you as you requested. I hope you're making out with your subject."

Mott waited a few seconds before he spoke. "That's extremely interesting," he said. "And you say that all three witnesses agree?"

"For your information, Ralph, the kid has been lying in his teeth ever since we brought him in. He's given four different accounts of his movements at the time of the hit—all wrong."

"I didn't understand which gang these witnesses are from."

"Don't give him a name—we don't want to start another war!"

"Not a chance. Now let me get this straight: the three witnesses all state that it was Jambo driving the car. Good, that will hold up in court."

"They're lying, man, they're lying!" Jambo protested.

"Now I'll tell you what I want done," Mott continued. "Since we know that for sure, I want the deputies to go back and talk to every possible witness to the shooting to see if we can't find *someone* to back that up. Did the witnesses give you any other names?"

Mott listened to the supposed reply and then turned to d'Amico, who was keeping himself in the background. "Sergeant, there are three witnesses who have identified one of the suspects riding in the hit car as 'Stick.' Bring me the card on him."

Ralph Mott was still new to the gang warfare business, but he had had many years of successful interrogation experience, part of what had won him his lieutenant's bars. Therefore he did not miss the slight, but very definite reaction that Jambo gave to that, and he knew that he had scored. Jambo knew who had been in the second car, and the chances were very good that he had been in it himself. Obviously he had had something planned. It began to look more and more likely that his finding the Montaña Mara car had been the result of pure chance.

Mott would have given a lot to know what Jambo's original plan had been. Probably some kind of an attack on the Heights gang with which Los Counts were at war, but it could also have been something else entirely.

When he felt that the role had been played out, he released Jambo and let him go home. He had no hard evidence at all on which to hold him, and even well-founded suspicion was not enough.

As soon as he was once more on his own turf, Jambo headed immediately to the place where Los Counts always congregated. The first thing he had to do was to warn Stick, then the search for the three witnesses would have to go forward without a lost minute. Nothing else would matter until they had been found and silenced.

91

CHAPTER NINE

BROTHER JULIO sat in the temporary employment office of Morrison and Hale, waiting to talk to the man in charge. Outside the normal traffic of Whittier Boulevard was flowing at its usual rate, vehicles and pedestrians all going about their separate businesses. To the Brother all that was incidental. He was an absolute rock of conviction that the new plant was going to be a splendid success and that the people of the barrio would prove themselves once and for all as desirable, capable, and loyal employees.

He had heard that the employment people who had been assigned to the new office were not so sure, and he had come to enlighten them.

A girl came out to speak to him. She had been picked for her job: a fairly short and rather chunky brunette who, perhaps, might be able to relate to the people of East Los Angeles better than one of the more succulent receptionists that might have been chosen. A tall, willowy blond could have caused some of the latinos to feel uncomfortable, so that had been carefully avoided.

"Mr. Cummings can see you now, Father," she said.

Brother Julio got to his feet without bothering to correct her. He had told her once who he was, and there were far more important matters on his mind. He followed her toward the back and down a very short corridor to an office door where he was gestured inside. As he entered, the girl went away.

The man behind the desk was squarely built, perhaps an ex-athlete. His faintly reddish hair was already thinning badly, but he was not the sort of person to let that worry him. His desk was piled with papers, many of which the Brother noted immediately were employment forms of the kind he had already examined at the outside counter.

The man, who was wearing a light brown seersucker suit, came out from behind his desk to shake hands. He made a show of putting his visitor into the best available chair and then took up his place once more behind his desk. He radiated the cordiality and willingness to communicate that was part of his professional equipment. "I'm glad that you came in, Brother Julio," he said. "Please tell me what I can do for you."

That told the Brother two things at once: that the man before him already knew his name and occupation, and that his host was an intelligent person who knew his business. That would save a lot of time.

"I would like to ask first of all, sir—"

The employment manager interrupted him. "I'm sorry. I didn't introduce myself. Roger Cummings. For the moment, at least, I'm in charge of this office."

"Thank you, Mr. Cummings. I was about to ask if you are having any problems interviewing and employing our people."

That touched a tender spot, and Cummings made no attempt to conceal the fact. "As a matter of fact, Brother Julio, we are having some very serious problems. And to be completely truthful with you, I don't know at this moment how to resolve them."

"Perhaps, Mr. Cummings, I may be able to help. It is why I came to see you."

Cummings hitched forward in his chair, reached into a drawer, and pulled out a form. He turned it around so that it was facing his guest and tapped it with his finger. "This is our regular employment questionnaire," he said. "We've been using it for years and find it very effective. Furthermore, we've simplified it as much was we can, so that even applicants of limited comprehension can fill it out. Not all of our jobs call for mental skills or particular knowledge. The help on the loading dock—things like that. We've had a policy for a long time of giving the educationally disadvantaged a break, and on the whole it's paid off. But now . . ."

He paused and considered just how he was going to put his next thought. He decided that there was no easy way and he might as well come out with it. "Brother Julio, we went to the trouble of having some of these forms reprinted in Spanish, but even with that, many applicants don't seem to be able to fill it out. Look here: we're asking for name, address, phone if any, place and date of birth, education, marital status—the usual things that every employer has to know to keep proper records and meet the requirement of the law. About ten percent of the applications filed at the front desk are so illegible we can't make them out at all. We have to discard them because there is no way they can be processed."

Cummings ran a hand across the top of his head and then, sensing that he had a sympathetic audience, unburdened himself further. "Now understand, Brother Julio, I'm not putting down the people of the barrio. We want to hire them—that's definite. Furthermore—and this is confidential—I've been told to try to hire as many of the gang-type kids as I can to get them off the streets. Management knows that they may be underachievers, but among them there may be some genuinely bright boys that we can bring along and help."

Brother Julio nodded his concerned interest, a gesture more eloquent than any phrase he might have spoken.

Cummings dug through the pile before him and extracted a half dozen applications that he sorted out and laid before his guest.

A glance told the Brother what he had already expected to find: in some cases only the name had been put down, and the printing of that simple information wandered all over the paper. One was written diagonally across the form, and underneath it a symbol had been drawn. It was a name the brother knew; he could have supplied the address from memory, and the symbol of gang affiliation was as clear to him as the early Christian drawing of a fish.

"It's quite clear," Brother Julio said calmly, "that many of your applicants are illiterate. This is because some of the gang members cannot go to high school—they must cross the territory of other gangs to do so, and that is not allowed."

"That's cheating both them and the taxpayers who provide the schools," Cummings commented.

"That is absolutely right, sir, and we're working to correct the situation. Your plant will help a very great deal. Already we have arranged to erase the gang boundaries where it is concerned."

"That's good news—I was a little concerned on that point. I don't know too much about this area, of course, but that point was explained to me."

Brother Julio was listening politely, but his attention was still focused on the application forms that were before him. Cummings realized that and remained silent until the Brother finally looked up. "It is entirely obvious," he said, "that you cannot be expected to decipher applications made out like this, and the form is a very simple and good one. There is nothing asked that is not right and proper. So I propose a solution."

"I certainly want to hear it," Cummings said.

"There are some capable ladies at our church who will volunteer. I can arrange to have them here at least two or three hours each day. This will not cost you anything, of course. They will assist the applicants in filling out the forms. I promise you that they will do a superior job."

Cummings thought for only a moment. "The policy is to have each applicant fill out the form in his own handwriting, but that hasn't worked out in this case. So if your ladies can assist us . . ."

"I'll see to it," Brother Julio promised. "They will print very neatly, and those applicants who can fill the forms themselves will, of course, be encouraged to do so."

"That does sound like a solution, Brother Julio. How about these we already have that we can't read?"

"We may be able to read most of them. We will try to find the people and then help them to file a proper form."

"Brother Julio, you're a godsend!" Cummings allowed a look of real relief and appreciation to show on his face. "Let me meet you halfway: we'll pay your ladies the minimum wage, if that's acceptable, while they're working here. On an hourly basis, of course."

Brother Julio, having just gotten what he had come for, rose to his feet with fresh happiness visible in his bearing. "I shall start on it at once," he promised. "You may look for our first volunteer right after lunch."

Cummings came out from behind his desk once more to shake hands. "Should we state in our employment ads that help in filling out the forms is available?"

"That will not be necessary, sir—they will know."

Cummings went back to his work with at least one major problem off his mind. If more of the people of the barrio were like Brother Julio, he decided, things would be much better all the way around.

He reexamined his personnel requirement tables, determining where he might be able to use people who could barely write their own names. Later on, after the plant had begun operations, he would shift people as might be necessary. Hopefully, he would not have to let too many go for total incompetence.

Morrison and Hale had already approved a series of ads that mentioned their decision to open a new plant in a disadvantaged area. It was good public relations that might eventually pay off. But experience told him that there would be some bothersome lumps before everything would be set up and running smoothly.

The next twenty-four hours were a nightmare. For reasons that were buried deep in the culture and traditions of the barrio, the double shooting apparently triggered a new impetus of gang activity. It could have been that Los Counts and Montaña Mara were getting too much attention—building too much macho—but it was more likely that a very miasma of violence permeated the atmosphere and, in turn, spawned more violence. Whatever the reason, the procession of gang-related incidents that never really ended began to pick up in intensity.

Just before closing, a department store on Whittier triggered a burglar alarm. The first unit to respond checked and saw three gang type suspects near the gun display. The clerk behind the counter was clearly on his guard—he knew the potential danger of his merchandise, and his experience told him that the three gang members were very likely to attempt a hit. Deputy Rozinski made an immediate decision, he radioed in and called for the Special Enforcement Bureau SWAT team.

His judgment was sound. As alert store personnel began rapidly and quietly to steer customers away from the area, one of the Chicanos pulled a gun swiftly from inside his shirt and aimed it directly across the counter at the gun clerk. "Don't move," he warned. "Don't move your feet. Put your hands on the counter and leave them there."

The clerk did as he was told, trying not to let his face show that he had already tripped one of the hidden robbery alarm switches. As he held his position, being careful to do nothing else at all, the other two gang members jumped behind the counter and began to seize weapons, stuffing them under their shirts and into their pockets. They ignored the rifles and long-barreled Rugers, seizing instead small, more easily concealed hand guns. Outside, six sheriff's units had the area perimetered while they waited for SWAT.

They did not have to wait long. The Special Enforcement Bureau was only a short distance behind the East Los Angeles Sheriff's Station, and there was no delay whatever from the moment that the call came in. The SEB responded in its own black-and-whites and was pulling into the parking lot by the time that the perimeter had been formed. The whole thing took hardly four minutes.

Normally SEB worked methodically, but this time there were urgent reasons for the fastest possible control of the situation. The plan took less than ten seconds to formulate; then the SEB members, on the run, took up positions at the front, side, and rear of the store. As customers came out, they were quickly and silently waved out of the way. As soon as they obeyed, the perimeter deputies hurried them on out of the danger zone.

When the three young bandits came out of the store, their clothing bulging with the weapons they had taken, they found themselves confronted by SWAT guns pointed directly at them from every direction. The SWAT leader, who was dressed in field combat uniform and wearing body armor, called out an order to freeze. The gang members, aware of what they were up against, surrendered. They were swiftly hooked up and loaded into the waiting cars, one at a time. The guns they had taken were confiscated as evidence, along with the loaded weapons they had brought with them. Not a shot was fired—the presence of the Special Enforcement Team members had been enough to contain the incident and keep all of the many shoppers away from danger. As the area cleared, everyone knew that if the three gang members had tried to resist, they most certainly would have been killed.

They were booked and interrogated. The gang files yielded cards on all three and identified them as members of Los Marengo Chicos. Before they were sent downtown to the central jail, they admitted that they had been attempting to seize guns for the use of their gang. That climaxed an evening that had had three previous theft incidents, all gang-related.

An hour and a half later, two male Caucasians were shot at in their car while driving down Whittier Boulevard. The suspects were described as four Mexican youths in two cars, but neither victim could give any description of the vehicles or their occupants. The windshield of the car was shattered, but there was no other concrete evidence and no bullets were recovered. A report was taken, but there was no point from which to start an investigation.

Deputies Vetrovec and Rose, while on graveyard patrol, observed a suspected gang car slowing before a house that was a known hangout of the Los Sapos gang. When they heard the blast of a shotgun, Vetrovec floored the gas pedal, while Rose rapidly called in. Seconds later, roof lights on, they were in pursuit at speeds in excess of seventy miles an hour.

In less than a minute and a half, two other units joined in the chase, running parallel streets in anticipation of a turnoff. Since the pursuit was westward, the dispatcher alerted the Los Angeles Police Department, whose jurisdiction was less than two miles away.

In a screaming turn the suspect vehicle skidded through a corner and headed north. When it reached Whittier, it crossed at high speed, clearly headed for a freeway on-ramp. As soon as that occurred, Rose called in so that the Highway Patrol could also be alerted. Once again, the persistent jurisdictional problem in the Los Angeles basin reared its head, as it did so often to hamper essential police duties.

The gang car burned around another corner, sliding several feet sideways on the dry pavement. That change of tactic meant that the driver had bluffed the freeway and was headed instead toward Los Angeles. Rose passed on the information. Vetrovec continued the all-out pursuit. He was a graduate of the Pomona high-performance driving school and handled his patrol car with cool precision at the maximum safe edge of performance. That included the safety of citizens who might be on the street and of other traffic that was not involved. The fleeing gang driver had no such scruples—he was anxious only to make his escape. If he could do that, his macho would blow up to the bursting point, and his reputation would be glorious.

Unfortunately, the ARGUS helicopters were not available—one was engaged and the other, on standby at the Long Beach Airport, would not be able to get to the scene in time to help with the pursuit.

The suspect car made another unexpected, screaming turn that took it up on two wheels and held it there for a second or two on the edge of disaster. It came down again just before the driver skidded it into an alley, ran halfway down, and burned rubber in a smoking stop. Three doors opened and three youths hurled themselves out of the car, running in separate directions.

Vetrovec brought the patrol car to a stop close behind the suspect vehicle; Rose was out before it had settled on its springs, in immediate pursuit. He went over a six-foot fence in less than three seconds, plunged down a passageway between buildings, and found that he had taken the wrong path—a pile of debris blocked the exit. He had to turn and run back, wasting several precious seconds.

Five minutes later he gave it up as a bad job: the eel-slippery suspect had somehow escaped, and there would be no finding him now. Discouraged and frustrated, he returned to his car to find Vetrovec with a subject in custody, leaning up against the car and being patted down.

The frisking deputy found a wicked clasp knife in a holder on his belt and evidence of a suspicious package in his right trouser pocket. Acting on that knowledge he removed a plastic bag that contained two and a half to three ounces of low grade marijuana.

"That's against the law," he said mildly.

An assisting deputy, who had been going through the car on a probable cause basis, produced a handgun and a sawed-off shotgun. Both had recently been fired.

Immediately Rose felt much better. He had lost his own suspect, but Vetrovec had his and one look at the red marks on the subject's hands identified him as the driver. They had the vehicle, two firearms had been recovered, and there was the narcotics charge to boot. The only thing that was belittling was the size of the driver —he was only sixteen years old and visibly small for his age. It had taken eight grown men to capture him and, obviously aware that he would be tried in juvenile court, he seemed almost amused by the whole incident. He had seen too many others in similar positions go scot free once they were in court.

A tow truck arrived to take the suspect car away as evidence. The other deputies climbed back into their own vehicles, radioed in, and left the area. Rose put the juvenile subject into the caged back seat of the patrol car, in handcuffs as was required, and then enjoyed the night air as Vetrovec drove calmly back to the sheriff's station.* Once again, by the grace of God, no one had been injured, unless the house that had been shot at held a victim or victims he didn't know about. Fortunately that was not his immediate responsibility.

He turned around. "What gang you belong to" he asked, almost casually.

"No habla Engleesh."

"Yes you do. Now am I going to have to take you out and kick your ass, or are you going to tell me?"

"White Roses," the subject said. *"Mucho macho."*

As the chairman of Morrison and Hale sat down in his usual place in the board room, he gestured that the door was to be closed. It would have been closed anyway, but those who knew him best understood what he meant. Nothing that was about to happen was to be discussed outside the room with anyone.

He nodded agreeably to the young woman on his left, acknowledging her presence, and then addressed the business at hand. Four of his colleagues were present and listening, all of them aware of what the topic was to be.

"I want to talk about the new plant in East Los Angeles," the chairman began. "At the outset it had two main things to recommend it: an existing facility that we could have at a favorable price, and the mileage we can get out of it from a strictly PR viewpoint. We are sticking our necks out in offering employment in a minor-

*In the Los Angeles County Sheriff's Department, juvenile suspects are known as "subjects."

100

ity community that hasn't had too good a reputation as a business investment area. That makes us look damn good and I've told the ad agency to get as much out of it as they can without violating good taste."

Down the table one of his listeners interrupted. "Frank," he said, "I'm not clear on a point: did we buy the building or lease it?"

"We leased it with an option to buy. The owner held out for a straight sale, but I told him it was that or nothing. Also he agreed to a ninety-day cancellation clause. If for any reason the plant doesn't suit our needs, we notify the present owner in writing of that fact and our obligation ceases ninety days later."

"We'd need that much time to move out, in any case."

"That's the way I saw it," the chairman agreed. "Now, some problems. Nothing comes free, you know. I've been shopping for insurance coverage, and the rates I've been quoted are through the roof. Nobody, apparently, wants to underwrite property in that part of town. The plant protection looks good, and certainly the local people should be in favor of it, but the insurance people are worried about all the gang kids that run around that area. Even our regular carrier wanted out. Finally we worked out a deal."

He looked at the financial officer who adjusted his glasses and picked up a paper. "What it comes down to is this," the treasurer said. "The insurance company is willing to write a policy, but at a red-line rate reflecting what they see as a high-risk situation. We've agreed to pay this rate for the time being, the reason being that we can't get a better deal anywhere else, and we can't operate without insurance. Now here's the kicker: if at the end of three years there hasn't been any bad experience or a claim problem based on the nature of the neighborhood, they will refund the additional premium and rebill us at a standard rate."

The operations manager offered an opinion. "Under the circumstances, that looks good to me. Of course, if we sustain a major loss . . ." He stopped right there because that same thought was already in everyone else's mind.

The chairman kept things moving. "There are other minor problems, but we're dealing with them. One of the social service organizations in the barrio is making waves because we aren't accepting applications from 'undocumented workers.' That's a euphemism for illegal immigrants."

He stopped and glanced at his operations manager, because the Immigration Service had given him a senselessly hard time when he had tried to bring in a Philippine house boy through the proper legal channels. His associate chose to remain quiet.

"Anyway, we're staying out of that one until the federal government sorts it out—one way or the other. Our temporary employment office on Whittier Boulevard is having some headaches, but Cummings, who's down there, feels that he's on top of it now."

"I don't envy him his job," someone said.

The chairman did not consider that worthy of comment. "If there's nothing else . . ." he began, and let the words die in the air.

On the Heights Montaña Mara had gathered, as it did daily, at the open hillside spot the gang considered to be its own by right of occupation. Since Luis Cabrera had come out of the joint, the other members had accepted him at once as a restored leader, now much enhanced with fresh prestige. He was a general escaped from enemy captivity, and they were all immensely proud of him.

"It ain' so good," Luis told them in the curious language that was part English, part Spanish, and part street patois. "We gotta do somethin' about it."

Gaucho, who had been Kiko's brother, scrubbed his shoe backwards through the dirt and then tried to kick a tiny pebble down the hillside. It flew off instead at a different angle, refusing to obey him. He was just getting used to the idea that he wouldn't see his brother anymore, not for the rest of his life. He didn't like that— he didn't like it at all, and the more he thought about it, the more he was obsessed with the blinding determination to somehow reverse what had taken place. He wanted to kill somebody and get Kiko back.

Cochise was watching him to see if Gaucho might suddenly spring on him for having sent his brother on the fatal mission, but that thought didn't even seem to have entered his mind.

Luis continued. "Jin-Jin, he got his balls shot off, I just heard."

They hadn't known that, and it hit them all hard. Most of them thought that he would have been better off dead, because what woman anywhere would go with a guy who didn't have any balls?

"What's he got left?" Cochise asked.

"His sister say he got nothin'—his pecker's gone, too."

"Does that make him a woman?" Luis turned to see a thirteen-year-old who still ought to have known better.

"It makes him a nothin'," Luis answered. "He can become a priest, maybe."

Luis looked around to be sure that no one who did not belong was possibly within earshot. Then he spoke. "Now, we gonna find out who did it; then we fix it they get what."

As he continued, a hard intensity came into his voice and his eyes were almost reptilian. He had just been in the joint and he was never going back, no way, but this time no one was going to get caught.

On Whittier Boulevard, Dolores Fernandez, she of the spectacular bust, was sitting in the temporary employment office of Morrison and Hale helping a member of Laguna Mara fill out an application form. The eighteen-year-old was close enough to sense the warmth of her body, and he kept hitching up closer to the small table to conceal the fact that he had an erection.

On the turf of Los Counts Mrs. Espinoza saw two or three cars drive past her house slowly; the boys inside looked into her windows. She went into her bedroom, took her crucifix in her splayed fingers, and knelt beside her bed in tearful prayer.

CHAPTER TEN

AS BROTHER JULIO drove at legal speed toward the turf of Laguna Mara, he was fighting a small battle within himself. In his mind nothing would be more splendid than to have a moving religious mural on the side of the new factory building—something with the Virgin in it and with the Christ Child in her arms. But much as he wanted to add to the glory of God, he had to face the fact that an industrial motif would be much more suitable.

There was no doubt whatever who should do the painting. He had known for more than three years that Lorenzo Archuleta was enormously talented, and now that he was nineteen, he was ready to undertake a major project. That was why the Brother was on his way. It never occurred to him to question that the responsibility for the mural was his.

He pulled his car up before a very modest house, went to the door, and knocked. The woman who answered looked at him for a brief moment and then quickly crossed herself. "You have bad news?" she asked in Spanish.

Julio quickly smiled and shook his head. "Good news," he responded.

Still doubtful, the woman let him in. The dress she had on was damp and water stained—obviously she had been working in the kitchen. The Brother seated himself on a broken chair. "Is Lorenzo home?" he asked. Then he added an afterthought. "That's a wonderful name for an artist."

"An artist, yes, but he should get a job."

"I have one for him," Julio said.

The woman looked at him in disbelief. "A job? Something for the Church, or does it pay real money?"

"Real money, Mrs. Archuleta. That's why I'm here."

The woman was suddenly decisive. "I'll get him!" She left in a pathetic waddle that was a faint attempt to run. Brother Julio relaxed and wondered why there were no religious pictures on the walls.

Lorenzo came in. He was a tall youth, verging on manhood. His arms were loose and dangling, and he held his head slightly to one side as if he were curious about something. Like so many others in the barrio, he wore blue jeans and a white t-shirt, nothing more. "You talk about a job?" he asked.

Julio nodded, slowly and with import—it was a glorious moment for him. "Right here in the barrio," he began, "there is a fine factory building that has never been used." He spoke formally to impress how important the matter was.

Lorenzo brushed a hand through the air. "I know. The Magnolias got it on their turf."

"Yes, that's the place." The Brother looked at Lorenzo's mother and showed her a confident face. "It's going to be opened by a fine company that will offer many jobs."

"But not to me, man," Lorenzo was quick with his retort. "I can't go on that turf; you know that."

Brother Julio continued in unconscious imitation of St. Paul. "Yes you can. I have met with the Magnolias and they have agreed that the plant will be neutral territory. Also, employees may cross the turf to go to and from their jobs."

Lorenzo shook his head. "I don't believe it," he said flatly.

His mother was quick in answering that. "Lorenzo, he speaks for the Church. He does not lie."

Lorenzo sat down and put his hands along the sides of his head. "It won't work," he said. "The Magnolias, they're tough. They never do this."

105

"I think they will." Brother Julio spoke quietly, but with authority. "They have agreed with me and they have agreed with the police. A very important officer, Lieutenant Mott, went with me and also received their promise. If they do not keep it, they will be in great trouble."

The Brother waited silently for his words to sink in and to be believed. He was breaking new ground, and that did not come easily in the barrio, where tradition was a semipermanent obstacle in every direction.

"What kind of a job?" Lorenzo asked.

Brother Julio came alive. "The most wonderful job—for you. There is a large, smooth blank wall that is perfect for a fine mural. I have talked to the management of the company, and they want to have it done. You, my son, have been selected to do the job."

Lorenzo looked up and studied the Brother's features. "Have they seen the one that I did in the park? Inside the meeting room?"

"They are about to inspect it, but it does not matter. The choice has fallen on you, and it is final. You will paint the mural, and you will be paid for your work. All of the supplies will be donated. When you have finished, it will be photographed and used for national publicity by the company—that is their own idea. After the work is done, there may be more murals inside—I do not know about that yet. And I will see that you are given a good job in the plant itself until there is more mural work to be done."

Lorenzo Archuleta took his hands down from his face, clasped and unclasped them, and then allowed himself to imagine the promised land. "How big is the wall?" he asked.

Captain Rudy De Leon, who commanded the Los Angeles Police Department's Hollenbeck station, was not a big man, but he had about him an aura of competence that was unmistakable. When he spoke, his voice was agreeable and friendly, but it also carried weight, not only of his command, but also of his vast knowledge of the Mexican-American barrio and of the people who lived in it. He was one of the best known officials of LAPD and deservedly so. As both policeman and humanitarian he had earned his considerable reputation and also a very large measure of respect.

In the conference room of the East Los Angeles Sheriff's Station he sat at the head of the table at the invitation of his old friend

Captain Miguel Gutierrez, whose command bordered on his own. Seated around the table were representatives of law enforcement agencies from Montebello, Monterey Park, Lakewood, and, somewhat surprisingly, Beverly Hills. Mike Gutierrez was the host, but it was Rudy De Leon who presided by invitation.

"Let's get right down to it," De Leon began. "According to our intelligence—and it's good—eight new gangs have formed within the last ninety days in nearby jurisdictions, and they have already had some serious incidents." He squared a pile of papers before him with the palms of his hands. "I've been collecting reports from New York, Chicago, Detroit, and a number of other major jurisdictions around the country, and the picture they paint is pretty damn grim. Gang activity is spreading, far and fast, and it's now getting to the point where you practically have to live in Burning Stump, Oklahoma, or Yellow Dog, Wyoming, to escape it. And the violence level is increasing."

The man from Monterey Park spoke briefly. "Our intelligence bears that out," he said.

His colleague from Montebello was even briefer. "Ours too," he added.

Mike Gutierrez was specific. "In the Casablanca area, which is about four or five square miles, eight new gangs formed in four months in direct imitation of what we've got here in East L.A. And here's a new one for you: we had a gang member killed in his car when he pulled over for a fake funeral procession."

The man from Beverly Hills leaned forward and folded his hands on the table before him. "You know our profile: we have a quiet, very wealthy, largely Jewish community. During the past six weeks we have had four incidents of citizens being jumped on the street by juveniles who obviously don't belong in our area. Their descriptions, and their vehicles, fit the pictures of your gang people. I've been getting a lot of phone calls, and right now I've got the wife of a prominent philanthropist in the hospital. She was knocked down and injured when her purse was snatched. I've seen similar reports from Malibu, Westwood, and other affluent areas. We're very seriously concerned."

Captain De Leon took over the meeting once more. "Let me add some of the things I've been getting from other parts of the country, starting with New York. Most of the gangs there are Puerto

Rican or Irish. They have a good many neighborhoods terrorized; there have been several reports of their burning down the houses of potential witnesses against them. The situation there is very bad and deteriorating.

"In Chicago at present there are approximately a hundred and fifty gang murders per year—one every other day, or close to it. The problem areas there are largely black, and the same holds true in Detroit." He did not need to add that he was not being ethnic in his comments—the Watts riots were still fresh in the minds of everyone present.

"What it amounts to, gentlemen, is that you can hardly live in an American city today without facing a real or potential gang problem of serious dimensions. And much of it started right here in our own barrio."

"What hope have you got for improving conditions in Hollenbeck?" The man from Beverly Hills pressed his lips together, his mind on his own community only a few minutes away from the barrio.

"I'll give you the word, straight and with the bark off. First of all, the new sentencing law is going to dump seventy-eight convicted gang members back into the community during the next four months. Under the present law, we nail someone for murder one and we're lucky if he does three years. We've had instances of parolees committing another felony on the day they were put back on the streets. But that's in the political area, and I'm not supposed to talk about that.

"Now as to Hollenbeck itself. At present we've got thirteen active gangs with a total of about three thousand members—this is the highest gang density in the United States. Our human congestion is tremendous. In some cases we have up to four hundred people living in one apartment house. In Boyle Heights, which is part of our jurisdiction, the best estimate I can give you is that seventy percent of the population is made up of illegals. The average family income in our area is less than five thousand dollars and the education level is less than seven years per adult. Over fifty percent of the families don't own or have a car. And, so that you get the whole picture, ninety percent of the buildings are fifty years old or older.

"In case you don't already have this information, a lot of the illegals pay for their trip from Mexico by committing burglaries. Resta, for instance, is a gang trained in Tiajuana to do just that.

"Before you ask me what we're doing about it, we have about twenty-five hundred gang members identified and on file. As of now, I have twenty-three men assigned exclusively to working gangs. The latest development is that some gangs are coming into our area from outside to get into fights. Some of them are the black gangs that formed in the fifties; others could be anything. But the gang kids have learned one thing: when a citizen is walking down the street, or shopping in a small store, or visiting a park, and ten or fifteen gang members surround him, there's damned little he can do but give them whatever he's got. And that's no guarantee that they'll let him off just to walk away. They may beat him, knife him, or you name it."

"How can we help?" the Montebello representative asked.

Rudy De Leon shifted in his chair to a fresh position. "We can all help each other if we can do something about the jurisdictional divisions that we all have to deal with. This is a first class headache for us—and for you. If we could get rid of this, we'll be a lot better off than we are."

The man from Monterey Park nodded his agreement; a lieutenant from Glendale spoke for the first time. "We'll do all we can," he said.

"We're getting some place," De Leon responded. "Now let's get down to some specifics. I've got a set of fresh intelligence reports here. You won't like them, but they're damn interesting."

Sergeant Mike Wickman looked in the door and got a wave-off from Captain Gutierrez. He withdrew and passed the word that the meeting was not to be disturbed. When he returned to his office, two units were in pursuit of three juveniles in a stolen car. They were believed to be members of Los Magnolias.

Mott worked late that night. He was out on the streets in a black and white cruiser, and he did not bring it back in until after eleven. Nancy had gone with friends to hear the concert at the Hollywood Bowl, which took a little pressure off him. Nothing of any importance had gone down while he was out, but as he got into his own car for the long drive home, he felt for the first time that he knew the area as he should. Every street and byway was firmly in his mind, and he could respond to any given location in minimum time.

As he took the now familiar route to the freeway entrance, the classical music station provided a background of stark, evocative, and compelling Sibelius. He thought it was the First Symphony, but he was not sure.

The traffic was light—it was still too early for the through trucks to be pounding into the city. He let himself relax so that he almost didn't see the black object on the line that separated the third and fourth lanes. He could have ignored it, because it was the Highway Patrol's job to take care of things like that, but his policeman's reflexes were too strong. He pulled off to the side and, taking a flashlight in his hands, walked back the short distance to where the object was lying in the road. It appeared to be a dead dog.

That made it unpleasant, but he had no police radio in his own car and it was a potential hazard. At the first traffic lull he went on the roadway, protected by his flashlight, to remove it.

It was a medium-sized black dog of no certain breed, and it wasn't quite dead. That made it just a little easier. He picked it up and carried it to the side. Unfortunately, he couldn't leave it there. No one would have criticized him if he had, but the body that he had cradled in his arms was still warm and breathing.

He thought of the animal shelter, but he didn't know of one nearby. He paused, debating, when the creature made a faint sound. Mott looked down and in the imperfect light saw a pair of large luminous eyes looking up at him. Silently the animal was pleading for its life.

"Oh hell," he said to himself. Then, before he thought about it any more, he collected the miserable dog, and took back to his car.

Nancy opened the door for him, took one look, and asked, "Where did it happen? You must feel awful!"

"I didn't do it," he answered. "I found the poor thing this way. On the freeway, near the station."

"Put it on the kitchen table," Nancy said. "That's easy to clean up."

"Its rear leg is crushed," Mott said. "I don't think we can do much for it. I'll take it to the hospital; they can put it to sleep."

Obviously she heard that, but she ignored it. Instead she ran her hands gently down the animal's body. "I bet it's starved," she said.

It was almost as if the dog understood her. It tried to raise its head and looked from one of them to the other.

Nancy drew a dish of water and brought it over. "Let's see if it's thirsty first," she proposed. She put the dish down, and Mott lifted the dog and held it so it could drink. In response the dog thrust its muzzle into the bowl and in seconds drank every drop. Then it attempted to lick the bowl with its tongue.

"Poor thing!" Nancy said. "Wait, I've got some hamburger." She took the meat out of the refrigerator and crumpled it into small chunks on a glass pie plate. When it was offered the injured dog, the creature wolfed it down with small whining noises that were edged with pain.

"All right," Mott said. "I'll take the beast over to the all-night vet and see if anything can be done for it. If not . . ."

"Do the best that you can," Nancy urged.

At the pet hospital he had to ring the bell four times before he roused a bearded young man clad in some kind of outrageous clothing. Mott glanced at his feet and noted tennis shoes. "I've got an injured dog here," he said, stating the obvious. "I'd like to see if the doctor can do anything for it."

"Come in."

The animal was put on a metal-topped table and the young man, without bothering to introduce himself, began to check the dog's eyes and mouth. "It's right rear leg is crushed," Mott said.

"I know that."

The young veterinarian bent down and looked carefully into the dog's eyes. Then he opened a drawer and took out a packaged hypodermic kit.

"Are you going to destroy it?" Mott asked sharply.

The young man paused a bare moment to look at him. "Not unless I have to. What's your pet's name?"

"It isn't my pet—I found it. On the freeway."

The doctor administered the injection, then waited. In less than a minute the dog closed its eyes and lay totally still. "What do you do?" the young man asked.

"Police officer—deputy sheriff."

"Then you can stay if you want to. I've got to do some surgery."

Despite the dubious first impression he had had, Mott was forced to admire the deft skill of the veterinarian as he worked on the mangled leg. He laid it open neatly, removed some tiny splinters of bone, and then literally cemented the major fragments back together. "I can't do much about the joint," he said. "It may or may not be all right. The tissue is in rough shape, but it should heal. The dog may end up with a completely stiff leg. In that case, you'll have to make a decision."

"I understand. Do you want a deposit?"

"That's all right. If you'll do this for a stray, you won't clip me. It isn't really a stray, incidentally. I think someone threw it out of a car. A lot of people do that: get rid of their pets when they move some other place. A lot of them get dumped in the desert to die. This is a good animal. It's starved—probably been wandering for a couple of days."

The young doctor was filling out a card. "Dog's name?" he asked.

"Gringo," Mott said. "I found him in the barrio, but he didn't belong there."

"Good choice."

"My name's Mott—Ralph Mott."

"Epstein."

When Mott again reached the door of his home, he slipped his key into the lock so as not to disturb Nancy if she were asleep. She wasn't. She was standing there waiting for him. The lights had been turned low and she was leaning gently against a door jamb, beautifully nude and with a flower tucked in her hair.

He looked at her, as he had so many times before, as she stood motionless, inviting him to do just that.

He was tired, very tired, and the muscles in his legs ached, but none of that mattered. "Let me wash first," he asked. "Then . . ."

When he finally went to sleep, she remained curled next to him. His last thought was that he didn't care if he never got up again.

At the East Los Angeles Sheriff's Station it was not that peaceful. In fact the watch commander had seriously thought of calling Mott at his home, but he held off because there was nothing his lieutenant could really do until morning. Also, the watch commander remembered that Mott lived in Santa Monica, which was a long way.

Deputy Dick Valdemar and his partner had answered the call of a concerned neighbor who knew that Mrs. Espinoza never stayed up late or kept a light burning after midnight. They had gone to the front door, had knocked, and then had stepped to one side, just in case. When Valdemar got no response to his third knock, he called out "Deputy sheriffs" and tried the door. It swung back from a broken lock that had recently been forced.

Valdemar had been a deputy for some time and was thoroughly experienced. That still didn't help him much when he saw the heavy body lying on the floor, the nightgown pulled up to expose the bloodstains of at least eight stab wounds, most of them intentionally nonlethal.

The victim was dead—there was no doubt of that. Valdemar wanted to pull the gown down to cover her decently, but he could not in any way interfere with the crime scene. He stepped to the side and saw the wad of cloth stuffed into her mouth and taped there. Post mortem expressions weren't reliable, but there was no doubt that the victim had been tortured. And he also knew from bitter experience that undoubtedly she had been viciously gang raped as well, despite her advanced age.

Above her sprawled body, a Spanish word he did not know had been spray painted on the wall.

CHAPTER ELEVEN

MOTT got up on Saturday morning at a fairly early hour simply because he had lost the knack of sleeping late. He took a small portable radio with him into the bathroom and tuned it to the all news station. When he was ready to shave he turned up the volume so that he could hear it over the steady noise of his electric razor. The usual parade of information that flowed out of the speaker told of abnormally low rainfall, of another lower opening on the stock market, and a pending bill in the state legislature. Mott listened with the half attention that the routine news justified and then began to shave under his chin.

"... Late last evening sheriff's deputies were called to the scene of a homicide in East Los Angeles. Shortly before midnight an elderly woman was found fatally stabbed with multiple wounds. First reports indicated that she may have been sexually assaulted. Her name is being withheld until next of kin. . . ."

Nancy was at the door, frightened. "Do you hear that?" she asked.

"Yes," he answered, "Excuse me." He brushed past her and punched numbers rapidly on his telephone. As soon as he had an answer he spoke with swift precision. "This is Lieutenant Mott. Give me the watch commander, please."

It took only a few seconds to put him through. "I just got the word over the radio that we had a homicide last night. What was the victim's name?"

As Nancy watched, his face went abruptly pale. She had never seen that happen before, and she clutched her small hands into fists in support of him.

"Is Hayden Finley in? . . . Good, let me talk to him."

Unwanted seconds marched implacably by while he waited. "Hayden? Ralph Mott. I've just learned about the homicide—Mrs. Consuelo Espinoza. How much do you know about it?"

Nancy watched him as he listened and could not read a thing in his features except that he was terribly upset.

"Listen, Hayden, I'm coming right in. Forty or forty-five minutes, give or take a few . . . Right."

He hung up.

Nancy hurried to him. "I'll get you some breakfast right away."

He shook his head, already on his way back to the bathroom. "No time. Coffee, if it's ready. And don't say a word to anyone."

"No, of course not."

He had almost finished dressing when she took his coffee to him, fixed the way he liked it. He drank it hurriedly as he laced his shoes. "I don't know how long I'll be," he said. "I'll call you if I get the chance.

"How about tonight? The Bartons . . ."

"Cancel. They'll understand."

He got into his car, hit the freeway, and drove faster than he should—he realized that when he saw the red lights behind him on the roof on a Highway Patrol cruiser. He pulled over and got out his license.

The patrolman was very young but well trained. He parked his own vehicle exactly as he should behind the car he was stopping and walked up just to the edge of the driver's door. When he saw that Mott had laid his hands on the top of the instrument panel, he was alerted.

"I'm a deputy—can I get my badge?" Mott asked.

"Go ahead."

Mott pulled out the folder and displayed the bronze-colored star. "I'm trying to get to the East Los Angeles Station as soon as I can."

"O.K., be my guest."

"Right. Thank you. Good luck."

"Same to you."

Mott was off again, and while he knew that he should drive more slowly, traffic was light and every minute was an agony to him. When at last he reached the Atlantic Avenue turnoff from the Pomona Freeway he was as tense as he had ever been in his life. He kept seeing in front of him the pleading face of the elderly woman begging him to leave her alone—not to make her talk. But he had kept on, he had made her talk and give him a name, and the price of that name, he was sure now, had been her life.

Blind rage swept over him until it was all he could do to get out of his car calmly at the station and walk to the door that was frequently used to take prisoners into the station. He located Finley in the watch commander's office. "The Espinoza killing," he said, making an effort to keep his voice normal. "What's the latest?"

Finley sensed his mood and fitted his own words to it. "The detectives working it have come up with quite a bit. The motive seems clear: there was a colloquial Spanish word painted on the wall where she was found. A loose translation would be 'blabbermouth.' Do you know anything about that?"

"Yes," Mott admitted, and bitter frustration filled him. "When I canvassed the neighborhood, she gave me a make on one of the kids in the Counts' car. I had to pry it out of her, and it took a while." He paused a moment and tasted the bitter bile of what he had done. "I haven't given her name to anyone," he added.

Finley was sympathetic. "I think I know how you feel, but don't blame yourself too much. Here's some more. She had multiple stab wounds, not all made by the same instrument. At least four different knives were used, possibly as many as eight."

Mott stated the obvious. "A gang job."

"No doubt. And she was gang raped. She was sixty-six years old."

"Any suspects?" He spoke automatically, without consciously forming the words. The additional information hit him hard, because he knew that he was responsible for the innocent woman's death.

Lieutenant Finley continued as calmly as before. "We're rounding up every member of Los Counts we can lay our hands on. One of them, a kid they call Flaco, had some small blood stains on his clothing. He's in custody—suspicion of murder—but so far we haven't been able to get a thing out of him. He claims he was in a fight and got a nosebleed."

"What can I do?"

"Relax, Ralph, until we have some more to go on. Homicide is on it right now, and they're very competent."

"We have this Flaco here?"

"Yes, but he won't see anyone without a lawyer, and he's a juvenile to boot. Fifteen, and as tough as they come. Right now we can't go near him."

"You said that you were rounding up all of the Counts."

"In the field, yes, and we're talking to them all. And six of our best are combing the neighborhood. They're not getting much cooperation."

For a moment Mott was silent and still. "No, I don't suppose they would. What's the next step?"

"We're keeping a very close watch on Montaña Mara. You can see why. There's going to be a lot of interrogating to do, and I know you're good at that."

Throughout the rest of the day Mott talked with members of Los Counts as they were brought in for questioning. In each case he had a card in front of him with a summary of the gang member's police record, if any. Only a small lad called Benjie Morales, who insisted that he was a full member of the gang, was clean of any previous arrests. He had nothing to contribute, so Mott let him go with a word of caution.

On Monday morning, at a little after eight-thirty, a long flatbed truck backed up to the loading dock of the vacant East Los Angeles plant that had been taken over by Morrison and Hale, maneuvered into position, and settled to a stop. Steel plates were run over from the dock to the truckbed and a small group of waiting workmen prepared to unload the equipment that the truck had brought. Four of them were newly hired Mexican-Americans who lived in

117

the barrio: brawny middle-aged men who were still trying to grasp the reality of gainful employment. They waited together, asking to be told what to do.

The foreman who had been assigned to the job knew his business and how to utilize the help he had been given; within a few minutes had the process going smoothly. By the time of the lunch break several trucks had been unloaded, and a number of pieces of equipment had been placed on top of waiting chalk marks. To the men who lived in the area a small miracle was coming to pass.

During the early afternoon some members of Los Magnolias who had nothing better to do came by to see how the work was progressing. They did not attract very much attention and did nothing whatever to make their presence more evident. They talked among themselves from time to time, and that was all.

At the sheriff's station less than a mile away, the investigation into the murder of Consuelo Espinoza was well into its third day. Ceaseless questioning of Los Counts members continued to be fruitless, and an exhaustive recheck of all local residents in the area of the attack produced nothing.

The coroner's report confirmed the information that was already available concerning the victim's death and added a little more. She had been brutally handled, beaten, repeatedly raped, and stabbed a total of eleven times. There was no doubt whatever that a group of several attackers had been responsible for her death. To the experienced gang control deputies, that admitted only one possibility, but hard evidence against any individual members of Los Counts was close to impossible to obtain. The one suspect in custody remained sullen and uncooperative, while his attorney raised legal questions about the evidence already obtained from his person.

In the early afternoon Mott called in Sergeant d'Amico for a conference. The sergeant had been working almost continuously, and his whole body drooped with fatigue. His hair was no longer as neatly arranged as usual, and his clothes suggested that he had slept in them for at least two nights. That was nothing new to Mott. He knew as well as anyone the amount of unrelieved time that had to be put in on police work.

"Chris," Mott asked, "are we going to get anywhere with this one?"

The sergeant slumped into a chair and covered his forehead with his right hand. "That's a good question, and as of this moment I don't have an answer for you. A gang isn't a corporation, and we can't indict it for what we know it did. The kid we have in custody isn't going to do us any real good. He won't talk—one reason being that if he did, the other members of Los Counts would eat him alive and he knows it."

"Are we going to file against him?" Mott's voice was hopeful, as though he were trying by his tone to change the odds a little in their favor.

D'Amico shook his head. "He's guilty; there isn't the slightest doubt of that. The blood type on his clothes matches the victim's and it doesn't match his, so that's the end of his nosebleed story. But the D.A. wants more to file, and in a way I can't blame him, because we don't have enough hard evidence to get around the presumption of innocence. He's about as innocent as Jack the Ripper, but we won't be able to hold him much longer."

Mott did not prolong the agony. He knew as well as d'Amico did that the gang members had closed ranks, that not one of them would say a thing. After the death of the Espinoza woman, no possible witness would talk. It was a dead end unless they got a break, something that Mott wanted with something close to desperation.

He went out and checked with the patrol desk for any reports from the new plant site. Several units had driven past, and everything seemed to be going well. Trucks were unloaded, and there was no evidence of any gang activity.

Brother Julio was waiting for him in his office. Mott greeted him as well as he could with his own feelings under tight control. "What can I do for you?" he asked.

"I wish to tell you," Julio said, "that I understand what is in your mind and heart. You questioned Consuelo Espinoza—everyone knows that. Now you are blaming yourself for what was done to her."

"I talked to her, yes," Mott admitted. "I leaned on her pretty hard. So I have to assume that I was the direct cause of her death." He surprised himself that he had confided so freely. It was not like him.

"That is not so," Julio retorted. "You did not raise your hand

119

and strike her down. You are not responsible for this gang thing that is the poison of the barrio. Mrs. Espinoza—God rest her soul —did as I would have done. If I had seen what she saw, I would have come here and told you about it, because I cannot condone murder."

"But you would not have to pay the price she did."

Julio silently shook his head. "My service for the Church sometimes serves as a shield for me, but not always. If I were to betray a gang's secrets or put one of the members on trial for murdeer, I would receive the same treatment—possibly even worse. To the gang member, the gang and its reputation are supreme—everything else must give way before the welfare of the gang. It is an intoxication."

"I think I understand that," Mott said.

Brother Julio stood up. "I just wished to tell you not to blame yourself. You did what was right. And what you have told me, I will never speak of to anyone."

"Thank you,"

As the Brother left, Mott considered the idea of talking with some members of Montaña Mara. Since they were at war with Los Counts, they might know a great deal and be more willing to talk. It was an outside chance, but he decided to take it.

Los Lagunos were having a council, as they did every day. Much reduced since freeway construction had taken two thirds of their turf, they had to find more. The only possible direction for expansion was toward the west, but that territory belonged to La Calle Verona, one of the toughest small gangs of the barrio. Taking over that turf would mean a fierce war to the finish. The odds, however, had recently shifted.

Chino, one of the best fighters in La Calle Verona, was in the hospital and would be out of action for some time. In a big gang that would have meant very little, but the turf of the Veronas was also very small, and their membership was therefore limited.

Also, the Veronas now owed one to Los Counts, and despite the size of the big gang to the north of them, they would have to extract vengeance or accept permanent disgrace. The Counts would understand that, so a single act of retribution might not start a war. Or it could. Whichever way it went, the Veronas

120

would have something heavy on their minds, and that could help, too.

Perhaps the time to strike had at last come.

Any thought of a meeting to join forces was ruled out—new territory had to be seized by force and held against all counterattacks. In that way the new turf would be earned, and the gang that had taken it would be feared—one of the ultimate objectives to be gained. When that had been done, the gang would probably call itself Laguna Mara once more, its defeat by the freeway permanently avenged.

The Lagunos had talked about this same thing over and over again, each time inching closer to an all-out war against La Calle Verona. Every member knew that the topic would never be resolved until some kind of action had been taken, either by themselves or by the sworn enemy that stood squarely in their path.

The leader of the Lagunos, Antonio Mendoza, was called Bobo for no reason that anyone knew. The name had come to him, and he had adopted it. He had been in juvenile hall several times, which gave him a position of strength and importance. He was also a deadly street fighter whom no one was anxious to challenge to an intergang contest—he was much too good with a knife. Bobo was secure and to a large extent what he said would be done.

"If we don' go get them mothers, they come get us," he declared in the half Spanish patois that was the language of his world. "They not wait forever. When they hit, they get maybe one or two of us, so we then handicap. If we hit first, we get maybe two of them. And we can pick who we take. That make it look good for us."

He had said all that before many times, but he knew the value of repetition.

One of the middle rank members, Gabriel Dominguez, decided that the moment had come for him to reveal a big surprise. "I got somethin' in my car," he announced.

That was of immediate interest—any additional weapons would be important factors toward a positive decision. The gang drifted over to the curb and surrounded a low-slung vehicle. Opening the rear door, Gabriel drew back a tattered piece of carpeting that covered the rear floor space and revealed an awesome prize: a high velocity combat rifle with an eight-power scope aligned in posi-

121

tion above the barrel. "That help, heh?" he asked.

Bobo bent in and examined the gun with interest, but he did not offer to pick it up. "It ain't no good," he said.

Gabriel looked at him in disbelief. "Man, that's a real good gun. I never tell nobody where I stole it."

"It ain't no good," Bobo repeated. "You kill someone with that, nobody know who hit him; you get no credit. You can be a block away, and he never know what hit him. He got to see, man, got to fear, got to know it's us, man, that's hittin' him. A shotgun is O.K.—maybe you can trade for one."

Gabriel knew all that, but he was not finished. "The Lobos, they got a semiautomatic. A chopper, man."

Bobo was unimpressed. "I know. Hold it sideways and it's full automatic. That's O.K. sometimes, but this here you gotta trade for somethin' else."

Somewhat disappointed, Gabriel covered up his prize and, because he had lost face for the moment, he drove his car away. He had hoped that the mighty power of his fine rifle would have overcome the objections, but he acknowledged to himself that there was no macho in shooting someone from a safe distance, particularly when the enemy had no weapon able to shoot back. He did know where he could exchange it for a good solid shotgun. The Lagunas had only one, and a shotgun was a real handy thing.

Without him, the gang was once more going over possible battle plans for an attack on La Calle Verona. No firm decision had been made to launch the campaign, but it was a hairbreadth thing—any new element, even a very small one, would make the difference. If Gabriel came back with a good workable shotgun and some ammo for it, that would be close to decisive.

At eight the following morning the barrio was bathed in fresh new sunlight. The already bright sky was a light blue, patterned with a few thin cumulus clouds that gave promise of a beautiful day. The air, which was fresh off the ocean, was close to crystal clear, untainted by its night passage over the sleeping bulk of Los Angeles. Hope and renewed aspiration seemed to have come with the dawn of the newly born day. Just briefly the Creator seemed to have blessed the land and given it a renewed opportunity to find peace and happiness.

In his very modest home Lorenzo Archuleta, already up and dressed, sat before a window adding finishing touches to his design for the mural he was to paint on the new factory. This was the most important project that he had ever been allowed to attempt, and he was inspired to do much better than he ever had before. The miasma of the virgin morning added to his mood, and his fingers almost shook as he sketched in the details he had conceived even before the sun had risen. One corner of his design had never really satisfied him; now he was doing it over and with every stroke of his pencil he knew that this time he had it right. It all fitted, it all flowed, and the whole concept took on a better life because of what he was doing.

On the Pomona Freeway a heavy flow of traffic was already moving toward the city. From multiple thousands of exhaust pipes a flood of pollutants combined to form a semi-invisible cloud that spead in the atmosphere, poisoning its freshness.

At the watch commander's office Deputy Alvarez reported for duty, replacing Deputy Morse who was on sick leave to recuperate from his injuries.

Ralph Mott was not aware of that; he was trying to find some way of using the information he had about the Counts' gunman Stick. His one witness to the subject having been in the car from which the fatal shots had come was dead, and he could not clear from his mind the picture of her pleading with him to leave her alone. He had forced her to talk, and he knew that he would have to live with that knowledge for the rest of his life.

The one suspect for her murder did not have enough evidence against him to make a convincing case; in all probability he would not even be bound over for trial. A sense of helplessness and strong frustration was building within Mott, and he could not control it. The only cure for him would be to find enough new evidence against the murderers of Mrs. Espinoza to take them off the street and put them where they belonged. If they were adults, he would not be satisfied with anything less than the gas chamber, which they had richly earned.

He looked up to see a uniformed female deputy standing in his doorway. She was a decidedly attractive young woman, but he was in no mood to take particular notice. "Yes?" he asked and waited to see what she wanted.

123

"Lieutenant Mott?"

"That's right."

"I'm Deputy Alvarez. I've just been assigned to your unit."

That news was enough to arrest his attention. "Sit down," he invited. "What's your first name?"

"Elena."

"What have you been doing?"

"After I came out of the academy, I did my three years in custody. That's just over. This is my first patrol assignment."

"Have you been briefed on this unit?" he asked. In the back of his mind he was wondering what he was going to do with her.

"Not directly," she answered. "But I picked up quite a bit while I was at SBI.* I know how the hypes behave, and things like that. I don't know too much about gangs—not yet."

Mott did not know what to say; he thought so long it became embarrassing. "We're glad to have you, of course," he told her finally. "I wasn't expecting you, and I don't have a schedule worked out for you yet."

"I understood, sir, that you had requested a replacement for an injured deputy."

It was time to get down to hard facts. "That's right, but he is an experienced man. And this is a very specialized unit."

Deputy Alvarez smoothed her skirt and obviously decided to avoid the challenge. "I'll try my best to learn," she said. "One thing might help: I speak Spanish fluently."

"That certainly will help," Mott admitted. "How much background do you have in East Los Angeles? Do you come from here?"

Deputy Alvarez straightened in her chair, making herself a little taller in the process. "No, my father is Professor Alvarez—you may have heard of him. I grew up in Pasadena."

Mott had an irrational urge to do something with his hands. He did not think he could send a female deputy out on patrol in the gang control cars—she would get her butt blown off. He could probably use her in community contact work—her knowledge of Spanish might be useful in talking with community leaders and other residents. He was in urgent need of another competent,

*Sybil Brand Institute, the Los Angeles County women's jail facility.

experienced patrol officer able to handle himself in emergency situations. He had already put in his request, but Alvarez was not the answer. He would use her, of course, but not on the firing line or in high-speed pursuits through the streets of the barrio.

She interrupted his thoughts. "You understand, sir, that I've been sent to you for patrol duty."

"Yes, of course." He made a mental note to call the academy and ask about her. With that information, he would have a better idea how to proceed.

His new deputy stood up. She wore the regulation Sam Browne belt over her uniform. Her Manodnock baton was in place, with the short handle turned the right way. She was properly armed with her reserve rounds correctly positioned. She could shoot, or she would never have gotten out of the academy. And she could drive: she had been through the high-performance and pursuit school—it was part of the course. But he could not see her hassling a tough gang kid she was trying to take into custody; he would have a knife in her before she could put a decent chancery hold on him.

She stood about five-feet-six, he estimated. Also, she could run five miles up and down hill and go over a six-foot concrete block wall, because that was part of the course too.

"To save you some trouble," she said. "I was third in my class at the academy."

"How did you do in PT?"

"I hacked it. And I did my pushups all the way, not from the knees."

He decided to probe further. "Sometimes the gang kids get pretty tough with us, because they see us as a gang, too. When we're forced to, we take physical measures."

Alvarez shifted her position slightly so that most of her weight was on one foot. Although she had not intended it, the result was to emphasize the female structure of her body. "There are several hundred inmates at Sybil Brand, lieutenant," she said. "Officially we call them ladies, but most of them aren't. We have our little disturbances too."

"I'll bet you do," Mott agreed, and made a swift decision. He picked up his phone and called the patrol desk. "Is anyone working alone right now?" he asked.

125

"Jim Vetrovec."

"Call him in. I've got a new partner for him to ride with."

He knew it would be all right. With the opening of the new plant, things had suddenly quieted down in several parts of the barrio. There had been rumors of a peace treaty between the Magnolias, the Spiders, and the White Roses, all of whom were located near the new facility. Members of all three gangs had been hired for work as soon as it became available.

If his new recruit had been a male deputy, he might have gone out with him himself for the first day or two, but Alvarez was attractive and he didn't want to be accused of taking advantage of his position. If he put her on patrol in the northeast sector of the barrio, where for the time being there was peace, there was limited risk and it was possible that she might make a place for herself. There were already two female detectives in burglary.

Deputy James Vetrovec, who had the biceps to strangle a python, learned in the first two minutes that they were in a car together that his temporary new partner wanted her full share of the action, whatever it might be. To find out how good she was, he put her behind the wheel and then directed her toward the Heights. He was absolutely confident that if anything broke loose he could handle it and backup, if needed, would be close at hand.

His reasoning was sound. Elena Alvarez was a dish; the uniform made no difference in that. The gang kids would know all about her in a matter of minutes. Therefore he decided to display her first in one of the most powerful gang strongholds and let it filter down from there. That would give her more macho; she was a deputy and they would have to understand that.

Elena drove as she was directed, up the twisting streets to the Heights. When the car reached the top, Vetrovec took her up and down the short, winding, confusing streets and then suddenly told her to stop. Obediently, she pulled to the curb and waited. On the sidewalk, apparently idly watching them, was a young Latino whose face betrayed none of his inner feelings.

Vetrovec got out, leaving his door open, and sauntered over. Behind him, his new partner followed suit. "How's things?" he asked casually.

The Latino shrugged. "You bring your piece of ass on the job now, man?"

Vetrovec lifted his hands to belt level and rested them there. "This is Deputy Alvarez," he said. "You call her 'officer' or 'ma'am'."

The Latino shrugged, vastly unimpressed.

"This is Luis Cabrera," Vetrovec said, "He's just out of the joint. Member of Montaña Mara."

"What was he in for?" Alvarez asked.

"Two-eleven among other things." He turned to the Latino. "How's Jin-Jin?" he asked.

"He ain't got no fuckin' balls no more. He's like her."

Too late Vetrovec realized he had let himself in for that one. He countered by taking the offensive calmly. "I'm looking for Indio. I want to talk to him."

"He don't feel like talkin'."

"He'll talk. I want him to tell me who was in the car that hit him and Jin-Jin and Kiko."

Luis reached out his arms and stretched. "Don' worry about that. We know who it was, an' we'll take care of it."

"No you won't," Alvarez said suddenly. "We'll do that."

"Like shit, lady."

Vetrovec gestured toward the car. He had planted the seeds he had intended. Elena took her cue from him and got once more behind the wheel. As she was starting the engine Luis Cabrera came casually over. "Hey," he said, "What's your name?"

"Alvarez—he told you."

"Latina, hey?"

"Deputy sheriff. Got that? Deputy sheriff."

Vetrovec leaned forward slightly in his seat, a clue that he was backing up what his partner said.

Luis saw it, but gave no reaction. As the car began to roll he called out. "Hey, lady, you know what?"

As Vetrovec started to look back he yelled again. "I'm gonna fuck you. You watch. See if I don't."

"Try it," Vetrovec said, "and you won't have any balls either."

Mott had been thinking more and more about Daniel Torres. To accomplish the job he had been given, he would have to establish a rapport with the gang kids, no matter who they were. He needed

127

an entering wedge, and in Torres he thought he saw the opportunity.

He spoke to a judge on the telephone and got an opinion that gave him a little encouragement. After that he contacted the training unit for the paramedics and got some further information. He had been a policeman too long not to make sure of himself every step of the way.

When he had enough data assembled, he looked up Danny Torres' address on the Heights and then reread his gang card file. He was a member of Montaña Mara, all right, and he had an impressive record despite the lack of convictions. Mott was troubled most by two possible cases of 187, which was murder, but in neither instance did the evidence seem clear that Danny Torres, known on the street as Poochie, had been directly involved. Once again Mott noted that while he had been in grade school, Danny had been a superior student and had shown much promise.

Danny Torres had two things about him that interested Mott: he was more talkative than most of the gang kids, and he had said that he wanted to become a doctor. The seeds of potential might lie there.

Mott checked out a plain car, which was as conspicuous as a black-and-white in the barrio, and headed toward the Heights. He drove through the intricate, short, winding streets and pulled up before a frame house that might have been adequate for three people and actually was home for ten, including two infants. Mott locked his car, walked up to the door and knocked. There was no evidence of a doorbell.

When the door opened, the woman who stood there was, a little to his surprise, slender and shapely. She was no longer young, but she had taken care of herself and she did not seem to belong in the house where she apparently lived.

"Good afternoon," Mott said. "Are you Mrs. Torres?"

"What is happen now?" the woman asked quickly, only a slight accent suggesting that she primarily spoke Spanish.

"Nothing at all. "I'm Lieutenant Mott from the Sheriff's Department. I came to talk to Danny if he's at home."

"Danny," the woman repeated. Her eyes seemed to glaze a little, as though she were trying to build a defensive barrier between herself and whatever was threatening.

"Are you Mrs. Torres?" Mott asked gently.

"Yes, I am."

"Then you're Danny's mother."

"Si." The use of the Spanish was purely defensive.

"May I come in?"

"Reluctantly she stood aside to let him in. He walked in as a guest, not a policeman, and hoped that his hostess was aware of the subtle difference. As he entered the tiny living room, Danny came out from what appeared to be the kitchen, ready, apparently, to face whatever the problem was this time. His movements were slow and he kept his eyes on the floor.

Mrs. Torres sat down on the edge of a threadbare davenport. "Yes?" she asked.

"Mrs. Torres, is your husband here?"

"No, he's got a job—at the new factory. He just started yesterday."

"Good, I'm glad to hear he's working. That plant should be a great help to everyone."

"It is a blessing from heaven," she answered and looked up at a brightly colored religious picture that was on the wall.

"Mrs. Torres," Mott made his voice as calm and relaxed as he could, "a little while ago I talked to your son at some length at the sheriff's station."

"I know."

"Now, to be frank with you, he's been in trouble from time to time, and some of the charges were very serious. However, he's still a juvenile, so in time that record can be set aside—if what he does from now on justifies it."

"You mean, you're not here to arrest him?"

"Not at all, Mrs. Torres. Let me put it to you very plainly. Danny told me that he had ambitions to become a doctor. Has he ever talked to you about that?"

"Sometimes. He watches all the doctor shows on TV. Anything about a hospital and he's interested."

Danny himself, after standing almost perfectly still, came farther into the room and sat down beside his mother. He said nothing.

Mott waited a moment and noticed that three more faces were looking at him through the two doorways that let into the rest of the house. That was all right; let them hear.

"Mrs. Torres, let me explain why I'm here. When Danny was in school, he made a very good record. His teachers said he had unusual promise. Now I know he hasn't completed high school, but I'm confident that if he went, he would do well there too."

Danny himself responded to that. "I can't go, man, there ain't no school on our turf. And if I go on any other turf, they kick my ass."

"I understand that," Mott told him. "But here's something for you to consider. You're almost eighteen—you will be shortly. If you'd like, I think I can get you a job as the USC Medical Center —the county hospital. As an orderly. It's only a few minutes from here, and you can make good money. But that isn't all. You can enroll in adult night school and catch up on your education at the same time."

He stopped to let that much sink in.

"Now, Danny, listen closely. This means you're going to have to keep your nose clean all the way—do you understand what I'm saying?"

"I know, man."

"Now, if you do well on that job, you'll learn a lot about hospital work. When you've done your high school work—and if you've kept completely out of trouble—there's two possibilities. I might be able to get you a chance at the paramedics. I've talked to a judge, and he told me that if you go ahead and complete your high school without any more trouble, he'll seal the record of your juvenile history, You don't have a felony conviction against you, and that's your big break. Now the other possibility. This isn't an easy road, Danny, but if you can show four years of good work on the job, and your high school diploma with satisfactory grades or better, then it may just be possible we will be able to get you admitted to medical school. Understand, that's not a promise— we're talking about something four years ahead of us, but there is that chance. Now think about it."

Mrs. Torres was confused. Finally she looked up and Mott was surprised to see that her eyes were moist. "Why do you do this for my son?" she asked.

"I'll be absolutely honest," Mott replied. "He seems to show promise. I don't want to see it wasted. Good doctors are needed,

130

and if Danny has enough stuff in him to make the grade, then I'd like to give him some help. If he becomes a paramedic, then he will make a career of saving lives. It's highly skilled work, well paid, and a job with a tremendous amount of pride."

"I told you, man, I'm a Mex," Danny said.

"What the hell difference does that make?" Mott came back.

"I'll think about it," Danny said.

CHAPTER TWELVE

ANTONIO MENDOZA, who gloried in the street name of Bobo, had been away from his turf for most of the day. He had had business of his own that he confided to no one. When he returned he ate his supper before he went out to gather with the other members of Los Lagunos, who were, as far as he was concerned, his true family. His whole life revolved around the gang, and every decision he made was predicated on his membership.

As he walked the short distance to the place where the gang hung out, he looked from side to side, missing nothing that was within his field of vision. He never for a moment forgot that he was a warrior and that the very ground under his feet could erupt at any moment into a battlefield. A car coming down the street riveted his attention until he was satisfied that it was an innocent passerby. He watched the car so intently as he walked that he almost missed the one thing he was expected to see. He had almost passed the tiny white house before he saw that someone had altered one of the symbols that had been spray painted on the side wall. The house had once been close to immaculate, but the gang graffiti that had been relentlessly added had destroyed its last pretentions to attractiveness. The owner might have repainted if he had wanted to, but it would not have lasted. And the gang might resent his destruction of their claim marks and shoot up his house in retaliation. It had happened many times before.

Now Bobo saw that the lapped LL that stood for Los Lagunos and defined the house as standing on their turf had been X'ed out and a linked CV had been boldly painted above it.

It was war!

La Calle Verona had offered a prime insult, one that it was impossible to ignore. Bobo knew that the painting had been very recent or he would have seen it before he had left on his errand. It was just barely possible that he was the first member of Los Lagunos to spot it. All that, however, was immaterial. What did count was his getting to his gang as fast as he could. Fortunately, they had almost all of their plans worked out in advance. And now they had the new shotgun that Gabriel Dominguez had managed to secure in exchange for the all-but-worthless rifle.

Bobo took to the back alleys where he could not be surprised in the open until he had covered the two remaining blocks to the Lagunos' hangout. The street corner, however, was deserted; the gang had gathered in back. So they knew all about the defaced symbol of their strength and were ready for what would have to follow. As soon as he joined them, the other members gathered around him, because he was their acknowledged leader and he would take them into battle.

"Have we got the guns?" he asked, a touch of urgency in his voice.

Gabriel nodded that they did. "Them mothers! They know where we are, so we gotta get 'em real quick."

"How long that sign been up?" Bobo asked.

"There's four of 'em," he was told. "Maybe more. All over our turf."

One defacement had been enough, but four was a monumental challenge. The only thing that would account for it was a sudden increase in strength on the part of La Calle Verona. That meant more guns.

"We gotta shoot up Sniffy's house," Bobo said. "We use the shotgun for that. We take two cars—go together. If the cops come, then we split up, otherwise we stick together."

As if to echo his words, a sheriff's black and white patrol unit

133

went slowly past their corner, then continued on up the street. Deputy Alvarez was driving and the man with her was pointing out the geographic details of the immediate area. For that reason, he failed to see the slight alteration in the graffiti that might have caught his eyes had he been less preoccupied with breaking in a new patrol officer. The fact that Deputy Alvarez was a female did not upset him unduly. All he wanted to know was how well she could perform in the street.

Within two minutes specific assignments had been given, and the members of Los Lagunos climbed into their cars. They knew that they faced something that might cost at least one of them his life, but that consideration was totally thrust aside in the tension of the moment. The thought of backing down did not for a moment enter into consideration. War had been declared, and their response was automatic.

Bobo did not know what plans La Calle Verona had laid, but his strong street sense told him that the rival gang would never have given such a bold challenge if it had not known itself to be in a position of strength. Los Lagunos could not afford to lose even a tiny bit of its remaining turf; therefore the war would have to be fought to its conclusion, with the victor taking over the combined turf of the two gangs. The survivors of the defeated gang might be given the choice of joining the victors, but that would mean accepting total humiliation and loss of macho. The once powerful and feared Lagunos might be permanently erased.

Bobo gave final instructions to his troops. "Don' forget, them mothers know we comin' for them, so they ready for us. We can't surprise 'em. So they think, maybe, we go for their meetin' place. Instead we go for Sniffy's house. That's the other side of the turf. Then maybe they don't know where to go, an' we got 'em split. Let's go."

The eight chosen soldiers climbed into the two waiting gang cars, their guns in their hands but out of sight. It would only be a very short ride to their chosen target. While they were on the enemy turf they would not be able to relax for a moment.

One complication they had to watch out for was the sheriff's patrol. There were many black and white units in the barrio, plus the gang control cars and the umarked detectives' units. Only in a great emergency would they fire on a sheriff's car, so without direction everyone maintained an innocent appearance. Gang members rode all over the barrio almost continuously, so the sight of the cars themselves would mean little. But many of the deputies knew the individual cars and which turfs they belonged on. If Lagunos cars were spotted on Verona turf, then the deputies would know and the whole war would be compromised for the moment.

Bobo drove, hanging tightly onto the miniature steering wheel that was barely eight inches in diameter. It was harder to take a sharp corner with the small wheel, but it was a macho symbol and almost all of the cars had one.

Good fortune was with them: Bobo cleared his own turf and was on Dennison Street in enemy territory in four minutes, and not a black-and-white was anywhere around. He knew where Sniffy, one of the Veronas' principal agitators to take over the precious turf of Los Lagunos, lived. He might not be at home, but that did not matter. He would get the message almost immediately, and so would every member of La Calle Verona.

Acutely alert for the first hint of an ambush, Bobo drove sedately down the street until it was time to turn a half block north. Up to that time he might have been headed into Los Angeles, since there was an entrance to the Santa Ana Freeway off Dennison. With the turn north the battle was on.

It went almost too smoothly. As Bobo's lead car drove slowly past Sniffy's house the blast of the shotgun peppered the small porch and took out the single front window. "Lagunos, Lagunos!" the gunman shouted, knowing that someone would hear. It made no real difference, but it showed total courage and added a bit of macho.

It was only a short distance to Whittier Boulevard where a right turn would take them out of Verona territory and back to their own turf within four or five minutes. Bobo added speed as he drove north, keeping alert. In the rear seat the shotgun was being reloaded, which was a wise precaution.

The blast that hit his car came apparently from nowhere. One moment he was driving up the street, then something seemed to explode and his machine took a mighty jolt. In the back seat Blinky Herrara screamed and blood burst from his face.

Almost instantly Bobo floored the gas pedal; the engine responded and his car surged forward. As long as his vehicle was all right, he had a good chance to get out of trouble. He still didn't know where the attack had come from, but for the moment he didn't care. He did know that he had been ambushed; too late he saw that his strategy in hitting Sniffy's house had been too simple. It was just what he might been expected to do, and he had walked into the trap. In the back seat Blinky continued to scream, so something had to have hurt him real bad.

At that instant he made a decision. As he reached Whittier Boulevard he turned left, away from his own turf, toward the USC Medical Center. There were hospitals in the barrio, but the huge complex that was in fact the county hospital was free, and the doctors there were experts in knifings and gunshot wounds. In five or six minutes, Bobo estimated, he would have Blinky under medical care. The way that he continued screaming left no doubt that he needed it, because Blinky wasn't a bellyacher.

He had been so intent on what he was doing, he had for a few seconds missed the fact that an enemy car had turned in behind him and was in pursuit. He heard two sharp clear shots and for the first instant thought that he had been fired on again. Then, when nothing indicated that the shots had hit, he looked in the mirror. The enemy car was weaving—either it was out of control or the driver was taking evasive action. At that moment he remembered his own second car, the one being driven by Gabriel Dominguez, and the whole thing was clear in his mind—his car had been hit, and the enemy had fallen in behind to finish him off. But the Veronas had failed to realize that there was a backup car behind them. Someone in Gabriel's car had fired, and it was the Veronas that had been hit.

He had no more time to think about it. He was on Whittier now and headed as fast as he dared toward the hospital. If the sheriffs tried to stop him, they would quickly see that he had a wounded man in the car and, if anything, they would help him to get to the hospital faster. As he drove he hoped that Blinky would make it —he was still crying out, but it was not as loud anymore. Maybe he was dying. Anyhow, the best he could do would be to get to the hospital as soon as he possibly could.

For a wonder no traffic unit stopped him, even when he ran two red lights after making sure that he could get across the intersection. He drove as fast as he dared up the ramps to the emergency entrance and blew his horn in short sharp blasts. They ought to understand that.

Darkness was settling fast, so that the lights of the hospital were bright and promising. If anything could be done for Blinky, this was the place. Bobo burned rubber as he pulled to a stop as close to the emergency entrance as he could get. His horn signals had been understood; two men were coming on the run bringing a cart of some kind. Now Blinky had his best chance.

Blinky was taken out, sobbing now and holding his hands across his face. He was laid on the cart and taken rapidly inside. The two men who had come running to help were still at the car. They were busy in the back seat, and for the first time Bobo realized that Chico Trujillo had been hit, too. He was glassy-eyed and his lips were moving, but he made no sound. Another cart came and took him away.

Suddenly Bobo's arm was grabbed by Rudy Diaz, who was sitting beside him. Another gang car was coming on fast, and it wasn't Gabriel. Bobo rapidly figured it out: the other car had to be La Calle Verona. He remembered instantly that two shots had been fired, so he knew that someone of the enemy had been hit. He reached under his seat and grabbed his hand gun. Rudy jumped out and started running toward the cover offered by the official vehicles that were parked close by. Bobo saw the wisdom of that and yanked his own door open to make his escape. Even before the Verona car had stopped, he and Rudy were under cover where they were for the moment safe.

He watched as the men came out once more and took someone out of the Verona car. Bobo could not be sure who it was, but he was so limp he was at least out cold and maybe dead. The third victim was taken inside. As he disappeared, two riders jumped out of the Verona car and took shelter on the opposite side of the parking lot.

Carefully Rudy raised his head and looked, exposing himself as little as possible. Bobo held his own gun at the ready; when he saw one of the Veronas running from one position to another, he fired.

The moment the shot rang out he knew that he had only seconds before security people and deputies would descend on them all. He did not dare get rid of his gun, without it he would be helpless. The only hope he and Rudy had was to make it to their car and get away before the exit ramp could be blocked.

"We go!" he almost yelled and grabbed Rudy's arm to emphasize his decision. Without a second's delay Rudy ran with him, firing as he did so at the point where the two Veronas were taking cover. He did not expect to hit them, but the shots would keep them down and prevent their interfering.

An answering burst of three shots came back, and Bobo fell to the ground. Mercifully, he did not even known he had been hit, the .45 slug that slammed through his abdomen and into his spine rendered him senseless almost at once.

Rudy knew that Bob had been hit, but he was a warrior who stood his ground. He aimed carefully and saw a Verona go down. Ignoring the bullet that bit into his own arm, he fired once more, and the second of his mortal enemies spun around before he collapsed.

Perhaps a minute or two later he was being led into the emergency ward. The thought that was in his mind was that they must be as busy as hell in there. The place was swarming with deputies, but he didn't care. His arm was beginning to hurt like fire, but he tried to pretend that he was in no pain whatever. Los Lagunos were small, but they were the toughest and proudest gang. He was a Laguna, therefore they would never see him give in.

As he sat and waited, he saw someone wheeled out covered with a sheet, including his face. Rudy hoped that it wasn't Blinky.

CHAPTER THIRTEEN

MONTAÑA MARA was meeting, as it did every night, at its hillside sanctum. The news of the fight between La Calle Verona and Los Lagunos had just come in, and the report said that there had been heavy casualties. That did not greatly concern the mighty Montaña Mara gang. Both the Lagunos and the Veronas were small, relatively weak gangs that had very limited turf south of Whittier Boulevard. When the time came for Montaña Mara to take over the whole barrio, they would be a minor obstacle easily overcome if necessary.

Luis Cabrera was listening to Poochie, who was telling him about the offer the new lieutenant at the sheriff's station had made to him. When the account was finished, Luis was ready to give his opinion. "You ain't gonna fall for that, are ya?" he asked. "That shithead. You think he cares for you, man? He's usin' you for somethin'—he wants to make you into a snitch. It's a pile o' crap. You a Montaña Mara, man—that's all the macho you ever need. Tell him to go fuck himself."

That was powerful advice from one who should know. Luis had been in prison, and there wasn't much about cops that he didn't know. Once again Danny remembered that he was a Mex and because of that the sheriffs would as soon clap him inside as spit on the sidewalk.

Danny was on his way home when he saw a sheriff's car starting to come up to the Heights, as one did every little while. Without even thinking he put his fingers between his lips and let out a shrill warning whistle. After all, his duty to the gang came ahead of everything else. Shit, no Mex ever got to be a doctor—he was sure of that.

Just after nine in the morning, while the air was still tinged with the freshness that had come with the dawn, Lorenzo Archuleta stood facing the long blank wall of the newly opened plant facility and in his mind's eye saw his creation complete. It was a magnificant mural that he visualized, one that would been seen and admired for years to come.

The design he held in his left hand was now complete, and every bit of it was just the way that he wanted it to be. It was right. It had a sense of balance, an internal richness, a thrust and sense of movement that Lorenzo knew instinctively was the key to the whole thing. No artist of stature, let alone a muralist had seen his design, but it had been approved by Brother Julio, and the Brother, in turn, had shown it to the people who owned the new factory and they had also given it their blessing.

Lorenzo was still only nineteen, and while he knew he could paint to a degree, he did not overrate his own ability. He looked on it rather as a kind of work he could do satisfactorily, as his father was able to install plumbing—when he could find a job.

Consequently there was no one, not even Brother Julio, who was aware that he was a genius. The Brother thought that Lorenzo had a gift of talent from God, but the true extent of that gift had escaped him.

The mural, when finished, could be a sensation.

All of the paint that he would need had been provided, as well as the other necessary materials. There were even ladders and planks to put between them. Behind him, there was a small grassy area that was beginning to come to life since someone had started to water it. Ten feet farther there was a high, strong chain link fence that surrounded the plant and would protect the mural when it was completed. That was not too vital, as the barrio tended to respect its murals and few of them were ever defaced, but to Lorenzo this would be the first really great effort of his life, and he wanted it to be preserved from someone who might choose to make some additions or changes.

An hour later he was hard at work, chalking out his reference lines and beginning to lay out his design on the surface of the wall. He was at that moment happier than he had ever been before in his life. Several people had offered to help him with the painting, but this one he wanted to do all by himself. He was being paid four dollars an hour for his efforts. Morrison and Hale were not being parsimonious with him—Brother Julio had suggested that he be employed at their minimum wage, with a possible bonus for a satisfactorily completed job. If he were paid too much, there would be resentment from those who were doing real work for their money. As it was, there were those who saw no reason to pay him at all.

As he faced the wall that was his to paint, Lorenzo had no thought of compensation in his mind. Instead he had a vision of the completed work to be and as he uncapped the first can of paint that he was about to use, an almost holy fervor inspired him. The conception that he had filled his mind completely and left no room for anything else. Least of all did he concern himself with the fact that he was technically on the turf of a possibly hostile gang.

Ralph Mott sat in stricken silence staring at the reports in front of him. He had just been reading about the worse incident of gang violence that had happened in East Los Angeles for months— possibly years.

Massacre would be a better word. While he had been concentrating his attention on the potentially explosive situation between Los Counts and Montaña Mara, two very much smaller gangs that he had hardly noticed had had a shoot-out right on the grounds of the USC Medical Center. There had been seven casualties among the gang members, and two more were wounded when their home had been raked by a shotgun blast.

He still didn't know how many would live or die or how many might be left crippled for life. It was no excuse that he had not been on duty at the time or that the gangs involved had been very quiet and had given no indication of pending hostilities. It was a minor detail, but he hadn't been told about the defacing of the gang symbols on the turf of Los Lagunos.

In bitter disappointment at his failure, he thought of the capable people who were under his command and to whom he had not given the kind of leadership they had a right to expect from him.

The phone rang and he was summoned to the booking area.

When he got there a gang kid was standing against the wall, his hands behind him in cuffs, an expression of almost total disregard and contempt on his face. He wore the standard uniform of a white t-shirt, blue jeans slit to indicate his membership, and battered tennis shoes. He could have been seventeen or eighteen and was obviously small for his age. Deputy Alvarez was booking him in.

As soon as he appeared she took him aside. "I thought you might like to know about this, Lieutenant," she said.

"What is it, Elena?"

"The charge is carrying a concealed weapon—he had a thirty-eight revolver on him and a switchblade in a holder on his belt."

"How long is the blade?"

"Six or seven inches, so it's illegal. We stopped him for questioning when he started to run as soon as he saw us."

"How did you make the capture?"

"We pursued him on foot. We had to go over a few fences, but he got into a corner where he couldn't get out."

"Did he fight?"

"He tried to, but Jerry and I had him under control pretty quickly. The point is, Ralph, he's a member of Los Lagunos. He's admitted that La Calle Verona killed at least two of his fellow gang members, and he's determined on vengeance. He was on his way to the gang meeting when we took him."

Mott reacted swiftly to that. "We'd better get some cars down there fast. Where's Wes McBride?"

"That's all done. As soon as we learned what this kid was up to, we radioed in immediately. Wes is on the scene. He knows most of the kids by name, and he'll cool it if anyone can."

"Thanks, Elena." He said that automatically. He knew that he was going to go down there himself, although he also knew that he would be like a fire captain arriving in a blaze of red lights in time to see the hoses being coiled up. Unless, of course, he got a break that he had no reason to expect.

As he had anticipated, the area was already well saturated with sheriff's units, and Sergeant McBride had everything under control—for the moment. As Mott joined the center of the action, he found Wes talking to a small group of gang kids. There was a number of other deputies surrounding them, lending weight to whatever McBride was saying. At one side Brother Julio stood quietly, listening and apparently approving.

Mott had not expected to find the Brother there and wondered if this was the break he had hoped for. It might be that Julio could give him some additional information. McBride finished what he was saying and then gave some directions. Reluctantly the gang kids lined up against a fence, spread their feet, and waited while the other deputies patted them down for weapons or other contraband. The three gang cars that were parked next to the meeting place were shaken down. Presently two handguns, a quantity of marijuana, and three packets of PCP ("Angel Dust") were recovered. Since no one was taken into custody, Mott surmised immediately that McBride had made a deal—and a very good one.

When it was all over he spoke quietly to his most experienced sergeant. "What next?" he asked.

"We're going to pay a visit to La Calle Verona—they may not be expecting us."

"Good," Mott commented. He walked a few steps over to where Brother Julio was standing and asked, "Have you any plans for lunch?"

"I am expected at our school, but that can be deferred."

"I'd like a conference with you—how about the Holiday Inn?"

"That would be fine—they have a nice dining room there." The Brother did not add that he ate there very seldom and only when he had been invited. Brother Julio had been riding in one of the black-and-whites, so Mott took him into his own car and drove the comparatively short distance to the motel. There he parked and took his guest inside.

When they had been seated and their order had been taken, he got to the point. "Julio, I assume that you know all about the shoot-out last night on the parking lot of the Medical Center."

The Brother nodded. "Very sadly I tell you that I do."

143

"I find the reports that I read hard to believe. I don't see how such a thing could ever happen."

"I understand, Ralph. It was incredible, but it was the will of God that it happen, and it did. The rosaries for the dead boys will be tomorrow night. The one for the Lagunos members will be recited at St. Ynez; I am honored to invite you to attend."

"By which I take it that the La Calle Verona victims will have a different service."

"That is right, of course. It would be impossible to hold them together. The other gang members will attend, and if they were to come to the same service, not even the sanctity of the church would keep them from fighting. I am distressed to tell you this, but at one wake, during the time that the holy service was being read, a rival gang burst into the church, created a major disturbance, and ended by upsetting the coffin and dumping the body out onto the floor."

"Oh, my God!" Mott said.

"It was a dreadful thing," Julio echoed. "I myself helped replace the body, and I needed the strength of God to do it. This gang thing, it is spreading now everywhere."

Mott waited while their food was served, then he asked the question that had been gnawing at his mind. "Julio, as you know, I was assigned here to take effective action against gang violence. I know that I'm a good policeman. Also, I have my master's degree in the humanities and a good deal of experience in the suppression of violent crime. But I admit to you that so far I haven't been able to do anything that's likely to be effective in solving this gang problem—I don't even know where to begin.

"And the answer isn't to go out and arrest every gang member we can find on some suitable charge. If we did that, the D.A. wouldn't file in support of us, and the whole community would probably be up in arms. They would claim that we were overreacting, and they would be right. But four young men, the sons of four families, are lying dead in mortuaries right now because two gangs fought last night. I've got to face the fact that I did nothing whatever to prevent it."

For a few moments Julio did not respond, allowing Mott time to compose himself after his declaration. When he did speak, he kept his voice low and conversational. "Ralph, are you a Catholic?"

"No."

"But you are a Christian."

"Yes."

"Then let me point out that in the whole history of this world only one Man was ever able to take all of the sins of creation onto his shoulders. And He did it for all of us. The most important thing now is that you are truly concerned, that you do not think of those who were killed simply as Mexican street kids, but as the sons of families who had looked to their boys with hope and aspiration."

He paused and ate a mouthful of his food. He had ordered very simply, and his meal was a light one.

"You said to me a moment ago that you had done nothing. I ask you, is it nothing that you offered to one of the street kids the chance possibly to go to medical school? Do not be surprised that I know this—a great many people already do, and it has given you a reputation. It has also done much for the image of the Sheriff's Department. In that single act you accomplished a great deal."

"You're overstating it grossly," Mott said.

"No, I am not. The thing that keeps people going, that gives them the strength to face adversity, is hope. In the barrio there is very little hope. The new plant has supplied about all that we have. Now you have shown that there is even hope for someone like Daniel Torres, who has a fine mind and a good, well-formed body. He should become a doctor, and I have advised him to accept your offer of work at the county hospital."

"I can't guarantee it—I said I would try," Mott qualified.

"Of course, that is understood. But he does have a chance. Now I must point out something else to you. There are many very fine people at the sheriff's station, from the captain himself on down. They work hard at their jobs, and there is very little that they do that can be criticized. We have also here many citizens' groups and welfare agencies who are trying to help the people of barrio. All of these people combined have not yet been able to stop the gang activity—it is very doubtful if they have even slowed it down."

A quick question came into Mott's mind. "Tell me, Julio, do

they have these same sort of gangs in Mexico? What do they do about them there?"

"The gangs, Lieutenant, are not so much in Mexico. The gangs are here in East Los Angeles, and from here they have spread throughout the area and on into other cities. There is much publicity of what goes on here, and others read about it and decide to do the same thing. In the last ninety days, eleven new gangs have been reported in cities surrounding East Los Angeles. Already there have been killings and other forms of crime that are gang-inspired."

Mott ate carefully for a brief interval while he thought and digested what he had just heard. "Julio," he asked, "In your judgment—and I respect it—what are we doing wrong?"

The Brother was not a man to sidestep a question like that. He drank a little milk and then replied. "The thing that is wrong right now is that the kids know they can do almost anything and not be punished—at least not enough that they will be made unhappy. Some of them have been arrested many times and then promptly released. If they are convicted, they are given only short terms and long before they have served them they are released by the parole people. Part of this is because of the juvenile laws—that is why they use little boys as gunmen—so that if they are caught and convicted, they will only serve a short term. When they come back, they will be covered with glory and will have much macho. They do not care that they are building records that will ruin their adult lives. Many people are afraid to testify against them. Only last week a small store, the Yasuda Grocery, was almost destroyed because the owners testified against some gang kids that had robbed them at gunpoint."

Mott felt his temper beginning to rise. The unrelenting frustrations that were part of his job forced themselves into his mind. He remembered the Yasudas and the night they had identified the armed juveniles who had robbed them. It was impossible for the sheriff's deputies to give permanent protection to everyone who testified in court, and the gangs knew this. They would wait, every time, until protection was withdrawn, and then strike—because the gangs never forgave, or forgot.

"What is the best thing that I can do right now?" Mott asked.

"I can give you an answer to that," Brother Julio responded.

"The hope of the barrio right now is the new plant. If it is a success, and profitable to its owners, then we may get many more. We have the labor, we have sites available, and the wage scale is reasonable. Once there are enough jobs and enough income for our families, then things will change. This can become a wonderful place to live. Remember, Ralph, that only a small proportion of the youth of the barrio are hard-core gang members. Many do not belong at all. A few, like a very gifted young man I have at work painting a mural on the new plant, take no part in gang activities and do not wish to do so. He will never cause any trouble; someday he may be a famous artist."

Mott paid for the lunch and then dropped his guest off at his modest facility and school. As he drove back to the station, he made a firm decision to keep a constant watchful patrol over the new plant and its surrounding neighborhood. That was something concrete that he could do, and the sense of it was obvious.

147

CHAPTER FOURTEEN

GEORGE WILKINSON looked carefully at the most recent daily report that had been put on his desk and then sat back in his chair, letting a warm sense of relief run through him for a few seconds. He was a large man, made larger by an expanding waistline that he was fighting to control, and rather too aware that the remaining hair on his head was falling out with relentless regularity. He was not vain, but he had been a notable athlete, and it was hard to erase the memory of the rich, full head of hair that had been one of his assets on campus. He had not been so heavy then, and the combination of his impressive size, his athletic reputation, and his acceptable appearance had made him a highly popular figure, especially with the college women. He had married one of the choicest of them. He had no complaints about that, but he wanted to do something to arrest the too rapid deterioration of his physical assets. He belonged to a health club and he exercised regularly, but the results were not matching his hopes.

The report, at least, was good. Every one like that was money in the bank, and for the moment he was operating from day to day. He had started with Morrison and Hale as a production worker despite his degree, because at that time it had been the company policy to put all executive trainees through a factory experience before moving them on to other assignments. He had shown a quick, firm grasp of production techniques and an aptitude for overcoming the occasional problems that arose. He had done so well that in the opinion of top management he had been the logical man to put in charge of the new plant being opened in East Los Angeles.

He had not been enthusiastic about the assignment, not because he shunned responsibility, but because he honestly questioned his own ability to deal successfully with an almost entirely ethnic labor force. He spoke no Spanish and had no background whatever in the culture of the community. In addition, like many others, he had heard that there were serious problems in the barrio, most of them stemming from juvenile delinquency. When he had been offered the job, however, he had taken it with the determination that he would make the new plant succeed, one way or the other. To date the progress of the new facility had been better than he had either expected or hoped. There had been some minor language problems, but enough of the new employees were bilingual to resolve most of them on the spot. The only real potential problem he had, in his judgment, was with the teenagers he had taken on because he had been told to do so. Most of the kids had never worked before, and their educational levels were way below normal. He had had the work assignments laid out to meet those limitations and apparently that solution was working.

His secretary, a lovely dark-eyed girl who spoke both Spanish and English fluently, appeared in the doorway of his office. "Lieutenant Mott is here, sir," she reported. He didn't require the "sir," but she was new and he did appreciate her good training.

"Ask him to come in."

George Wilkinson had known enough cops to be a little surprised by the man who walked into his office. He was neatly and very tastefully dressed in civilian clothes—that was his first impression. He estimated that Mott was just under six feet, well-built, and more relaxed than he had expected. The lieutenant had blue eyes, and somehow their deceptive mildness made Wilkinson like the man. This was a superior individual, one he might enjoy cultivating as a friend.

"Mr. Wilkinson?"

The plant manager was already on his feet. He shook hands and invited his guest to sit down.

"Would you like some coffee, Lieutenant?"

"Don't go to any trouble."

"It's none at all—we keep a pot going." He raised his voice slightly. "Dolores."

His secretary reappeared and took the coffee order. Almost at once she was back with a small tray and served the two men. As she bent over the desk Mott could not help noticing her exceptional bust line: it was striking without being overblown. When she had left and shut the door behind her, Mott stated the reason for his call. "Mr. Wilkinson, you know that this new plant is a major contribution to the economy of East Los Angeles. The Sheriff's Department is as anxious as anyone else to see it an unqualified success."

Wilkinson moved his considerable bulk into a more informal position. It was a trick he had learned some time ago and it worked very well for him. "Thank you. I do understand about the barrio, and all good wishes are very much appreciated."

Mott tried his coffee before he continued the conversation. "Mr. Wilkinson, you're certainly well aware that we have a street gang problem here—this is, in fact, a fountainhead of such activity."

"I do know that, Lieutenant; my secretary has lost two brothers to street gang warfare. Before I came down here, I got a pretty thorough briefing from a priest who obviously knew what he was talking about."

"Brother Julio?"

"Yes, that's the man. I'm aware, Lieutenant, that we have some younger employees here who are gang members. And they belong to different gangs. I've been told that there is a general truce as far as this plant is concerned, and so far we've had no trouble of that kind at all. But until we have a little more experience in dealing with these youngsters, I'm having a very close watch kept. This is not for publication, but I have two or three security people out on the floor in the guise of timekeepers."

Mott nodded. "That's probably a good idea. Now, I came by to tell you that for the time being, we are going to give your facility somewhat more than normal police protection. We don't expect that anything will happen, but we don't want to take any chances."

"Very much appreciated."

"I'd like to meet your chief of security, if you have one."

"For the time being, that's me."

"All right, since you're handling that personally, I'd like to give you this number." He passed over a card. "That's a direct line to our special gang control unit. It also feeds into the dispatcher's desk, so if you ever need us in a hurry, we'll be here very promptly."

Wilkinson thought. "Lieutenant, we're operating now with a burglar alarm system that only works during the hours that the plant is closed. But I do have the option of installing some immediate alarm buttons. Should I do that?"

"That's up to you, but if you use the direct line to call us, it will probably be, if anything, a little faster."

"Thank you. Naturally I don't anticipate any problems, but at the same time, I'm aware that this is generally regarded as a problem area."

Mott stood up to go, but he had one more thing to say. "I know what you mean, but you have something going for you that may help a lot. The jobs you are offering are desperately needed here. Everyone knows that, the gang kids included. Consequently, nobody wants to do anything to rock the boat. Even the gang that normally controls this turf has agreed that the plant is permanently off limits."

"So I've heard."

"One suggestion, if you haven't had it already: as far as is practical, keeps the kids from different gangs in different work areas. That's an added inconvenience, I know, but it might forestall any possible incidents."

"We're already doing that. There's one gang kid, who belongs to the Magnolias, that I'm going to have to let go. He's nowhere near earning his keep, and he's setting a bad example for the other young help. One of our security people found him smoking marijuana in the latrine."

"Let him go by all means," Mott agreed. He did not add that Los Magnolias controlled the turf on which the plant stood. If Wilkin-

151

son didn't know that, he would very shortly. It was too bad, but unquestionably it was the kid's own fault. He hoped that the rest of the gang would understand that.

He left the building by the front door and turned right toward the parking lot. As he did so, a black and white unit rolled past. He didn't know the deputy driving it, but the man raised a hand in greeting anyway—obviously he knew Mott. That slight incident reenforced what he had said—that the police protection of the plant would be maintained at an above average level until it became apparent that no additional precautions were necessary.

At the side of the building his attention was caught by a single workman doing something at the far corner of the building. He was up on a simple scaffolding; as Mott walked toward his car he saw that the man was painting a design—obviously a mural. The barrio was covered with them, and together they constituted one of the principal cultural aspects of the Mexican-American community.

Mott walked over and watched for a few moments. The artist was quite a young man, but he had a face that commanded attention. It was open and friendly, but there was something else, something that Mott could not define, that made him stand out. The painter was working very carefully in a limited area, and his concentration on what he was doing was total. When he at last paused and looked down for a moment, Mott spoke to him.

"Good morning."

"Good morning, sir."

"I'm Lieutenant Mott—from the Sheriff's Department."

"I am Lorenzo Archuleta." He reached down to the plank he was standing on and stirred a small can of paint.

"Are you going to paint the whole mural?"

"Oh yes, sir—I hope so!"

"I've never seen a mural painted before. How long will it take you?"

"Many weeks to do it as I want to, but I have not been told when I must stop."

"What is the design?"

The painter picked up a roll of paper and climbed down to ground level. When he was beside Mott, he carefully spread out his drawing and waited for Mott's reaction.

Ralph Mott stared at the conception for almost a full minute before he spoke. "Lorenzo, did you do this?"

"Yes, it is my work."

"Did anyone help you?"

"No, I did it alone."

"It's remarkable," Mott said. "I'm not an artist and I don't know much about art, but that's good—better than good. Are you a professional?"

"I am being paid for my work. I receive four dollars an hour, and the paint is given me free."

Mott continued to study the drawing; then he looked up at the wall where Lorenzo had been working. A face was emerging. It was not yet finished, but the features had been drawn in, and they were magnetic. He had seen many murals in various places, and the one thing they all seemed to have in common was stylized faces—classically pure but entirely devoid of life. They were symbols rather than people. The half-finished face that Lorenzo had painted seemed to live and breathe. He looked again at the young artist and made an immediate decision.

"Lorenzo, when you finish this mural I want you to come and see me." He handed over his card. "Call and let me know when you will be in. I have a close friend who I think will be very interested in your work. I want you to meet him."

"May I ask who he is, sir?"

"One of the greatest artists in America," Mott answered. "We've played golf together, among other things. Will you promise me that you'll do that?"

"Of course, sir. Yes, I will."

"Are you in a gang?"

"No. I live on the turf of Laguna Mara, but I have never joined. They sometimes consider me a member because of a mural I painted for them."

"Where is it? I'd like to go and see it."

"Please wait and see this one, sir. I was only fifteen when I did that one, and it isn't very good."

Mott said something appropriate and walked away, his mind suddenly full of a surging new idea. Anyone who could paint a mural at fifteen, no matter how bad, had to have an extraordinary talent. And he had seen that face on the wall, that living, almost

153

three-dimensional face, and he did not need to be told more. He repeated the name to himself—Lorenzo Archuleta.

When he was back in his own office his first act was to check the gang files and arrest records for his discovery's name. To his deep-felt gratitude, the young man had no arrest record at all. He was totally clean, and before him he had to have a future that was almost literally unlimited.

CHAPTER FIFTEEN

NANCY MOTT sat on one of the benches that overlooked the water and allowed the unfailing magic of the Pacific Ocean to take possession of her emotions. She loved Santa Monica Beach State Park and came to enjoy it as often as she could. By profession she was a teacher, but the many changes in the school system had made it difficult for her to find a suitable job. An opening in Watts had been offered her, but it would have been a very long drive each day and she was not sure of her ability to communicate well in the all-black area. The kids there spoke a different language, and there were those who didn't want any white teachers coming in while there were still black teachers who were without assignments.

As it was, she was content to be a housewife, despite the fact that the "house" was a fairly small apartment that didn't require much care. The man who lived in it with her was what counted.

There was a tug on the leash in her hand. She looked down to see Gringo, in his peculiar little stiff-legged way, asking for her attention. As she watched he rose up on his hind quarters and sat contemplating her, his tongue out, his life apparently complete. The dog didn't seem aware that he could not walk normally. He did the best that he could and appeared satisfied. Nancy had been watching him very carefully, because the vet had said that he might improve in time, and she had detected that he was indeed a little better. He favored the leg a little less and he seemed to be able to bend it a bit more at times.

She patted her knee and the dog came at once to rest his fore-paws against her, his tail wagging furiously. They had decided to keep the dog, because the alternative would have been to allow him to be destroyed or else used for medical research. The law allowed animals to be taken from the pounds for that, and she hated the thought with all her being. Someday, she hoped, people would become more civilized.

Which reminded her of the barrio where Ralph worked. She had never been there. A community affair was coming up they would be expected to attend, and she was not looking forward to it. She knew no Spanish, and she had the impression that most of the people in East Los Angeles preferred that language. If she were to be confronted with people who could not speak the only language she knew, the results could be awkward for them both.

Gringo, after having considered the matter for some time, took his courage in paw and jumped up onto the bench beside her. With that accomplishment safely behind him, he stretched out his head and put it into her lap. Then he looked up at her with large hopeful eyes and asked for approval.

She didn't have the heart to put him down again, and he was doing no harm on the bench. She stroked his head and sent him into a paroxysm of ecstacy. It seemed to her that the little dog knew that it had been given a second chance at life and was determined to make the most of it. And, mercifully, he was house-broken.

When Ralph came home he kissed her warmly and in so doing told her that he had had an easier day. "I had everything cleaned up, so I left a little early," he told her. "How about going out for dinner?"

She had her meal already started, but a swift calculation told her that it could be stopped and the food saved for later. "Let's," she agreed. Happy because he was happy, she sat down with him and told him about her little outing with the dog.

"I guess that we can consider him a permanent member of the

156

family," he said, fondling the animal with his right hand.

"I haven't said anything to the apartment manager," Nancy said. "But there are other pets in the building."

"If he makes any fuss, let me know. I'll start finding violations of the building and safety code."

She knew that he didn't really mean that, but there were times when it was nice to have a policeman for a husband.

"About next Friday," he began once more. "Do you want to go with me to that affair in East L.A.?"

She had been afraid of that. "If you want me to, of course I will. I'm not nuts on Mexican food, and I don't know what I'd talk about—"

He interrupted her deliberately. "You're afraid that you might not fit in."

"Well, I can't speak any Spanish, you see." She hoped he would understand.

"That wouldn't be any problem—these are educated, cultured people that I think you'd like. But this particular occasion is going to include some speeches, and some of them may be in Spanish. I'll ask Deputy Alvarez to go with me—that will take care of it."

"Alvarez—he speaks Spanish?"

"She. Yes, she does. She's only been working for me a little while, but she's all right. She knows how to do her job."

"How about her husband? Won't he feel . . ."

"I doubt if she's married."

Nancy paused. "Good-looking?"

"Very—quite a figure, too."

Another pause. "You didn't tell me about her before."

"A long time ago," Ralph said, "you asked me to stop bringing too many details of my work home with me. O.K., Elena Alvarez is on my staff as a patrol officer. She's been through the academy, of course, and she's just finished three years at S.B.I. They sent her to me and, frankly, she's an asset."

"I'll bet."

Mott stopped it right there. He got to his feet and looked again at the dog who was poised like a spring, waiting to learn his master's pleasure. "Where would you like to go?" he asked.

"Let's go to Lawry's."

"All right." He glanced at his watch. "Suppose we leave in about forty-five minutes."

"That's fine."

While she was applying her make-up, Nancy wondered if the plain name Nancy Mott could match the romantic glamour of Elena Alvarez. She pronounced them both silently to herself and knew at once that in that small matter she was already defeated —even though her plain last name was the one that her husband had given her.

Danny Torres sat at the dinner table, eating his food as though each mouthful that he consumed were a reprieve. He said nothing and hoped fervently that he would be ignored.

It was not to be. His mother looked up and asked, "What was that that came in the mail today?"

"Nothin'." Danny pushed another forkful of food into his mouth so that he might not have to discuss the matter any more.

"It couldn't be nothing. No tell me what it was."

"It was nothin' important, I tell ya."

"Then why are you afraid to tell me what it was?" His mother paused and added a clincher. "I saw the return address."

"All right. The County Hospital sent me a lot of forms to fill out about getting a job."

"Danny, did you send for them?"

Anger flared in Danny's face. "Course I didn't!"

"And you didn't go down to see those people?"

"No!"

Mrs. Torres was an intelligent woman. She had known almost from that first day that Danny had thought of it that he was interested in becoming a doctor. He never missed a hospital show on TV—she had told the sheriff's lieutenant that. At that moment the pieces all came together.

"Danny, you remember the man who came to see you from the sheriff's—Lieutenant Mott?"

"Yeah."

"He said that he would try to help you get a job at the hospital —as an orderly. I remember. I think he's done this for you."

"I know that." Danny went back to his food, hoping that by a miracle his mother would drop the matter. There were others at the table, and other things to talk about.

His mother had no intention of letting the matter drop; Danny could see that the coming of the impersonal letter and the enclosed forms had made her suddenly very happy.

"Danny, it's wonderful! He's kept his word, that policeman. After dinner I'll help you fill out the forms they sent. I know you can write, but I might be able to make them look a little better."

Danny declared himself—there was no use ducking it any longer. "I ain't gonna fill 'em out." He took refuge after that once more in his food.

His mother was watching him. "Danny, I don't understand. You've wanted this for years. You've told me so dozens of times. Now you've got your chance—a real chance at last. I know that Lieutenant Mott has talked to those people; he's told them about you."

"Sure—big deal."

His father spoke for the first time, and in Spanish. "It is the way to become a doctor," he said.

Danny had no more answers to give. He pressed his lips hard together and focused his mind on what was the most important thing in his life.

Instead of getting mad at him, which would have helped, his mother stayed very calm and much too logical. "Danny, I don't think you quite understand what this means. It's obvious that Lieutenant Mott has been to see the hospital people—or he has at least talked to them by phone. And they've sent you an application. As soon as they have it back, I think you are going to be given a job. In the hospital, Danny, a real hospital, and you'll be a member of the staff."

Danny didn't know how to avoid the issue again—he had known it would be this way from the moment that his mother had handed him the envelope. All right, he would tell them. "The gang doesn't think it's a good idea," he said.

His mother stopped eating and put down her fork. "Danny, which is more important—the gang or your future?"

Danny could not understand the question—she had to know that whatever the gang wanted, whatever the gang thought, that was all that mattered. "I tol' you, the gang don't like it. So I ain't gonna do it."

159

His mother knew that there was no use speaking against the gang—she had tried ever since the day he had come home horribly beaten up and so bloody she had thought that he was going to die in her arms. She had to face the fact that Danny was a member of Montaña Mara and that to him that was a supreme consideration. Disloyalty to the gang could literally mean death. She decided to probe carefully, a small step at at a time.

"Danny, did the gang forbid you to take this job?"

"Naw."

"Then who was it that told you it wasn't a good idea?" The gang as a whole she could not defeat, but perhaps if she contested one member at a time . . .

"Luis Cabrera—he didn't like it. An' he's the big man."

"Because he was in prison?"

"That's one reason. But he's got macho, man, he's made of it."

One of Danny's sisters spoke up. "Luis ain't been around lately. I know, because he's always trying to get inside my pants."

Mrs. Torres drew breath to protest that, then realized in time that she had an ally.

"Yeah, I know. He's been gone about a week."

His mother wanted to ask, "Has he been arrested again?" Before she spoke, however, she saw the fatal error in that and simply asked, "What happened?"

"Well, some guys came to see him, and they offered him a job, I guess."

"What kind of fellows? Businessmen?"

"I guess—maybe."

Mrs. Torres knew very little about Luis Cabrera, but she did know that he had been arrested several times and had just come out of prison a short time ago. And instinctively she knew that a person like that wouldn't be looked up to be offered employment —unless, of course, it was some sort of community welfare agency that helped people who had been in trouble. In fact, that was the probable explanation. "Where is he going to work?" she asked. "Do you know?"

Danny shuffled his feet, something he rarely did. It was a kind of last resort resistance, a fighting against being forced into a corner. "I don't know what he's gonna do!" he snapped and went back to his food.

It was, of course, a lie. Luis had gotten the job because he was smart, because he was good with a gun, and because he had proved in the joint that he could keep his mouth shut. They came to the barrio, once in a while, looking for the kind of talent that Luis had to offer. Actually the whole thing had been concluded very quickly, and Luis had left the gang without being jumped out. That was a serious infraction of the normal rules, but there was no use trying to beat him up. He would probably kill somebody in the fight if they tried it. So Luis had left, and not even the gang knew exactly where he had gone. Only that he had graduated into the big leagues and where before he had much macho, now he was regarded with awe.

If he made good—and they knew that he would—they might read about him sometime. Or he would come back to the barrio and tell them.

Luis was now a *veterano,* the most important one the gang had. And his last words to Danny had been not to take the fuckin' job at the hospital.

At the new Morrison and Hale plant Raul Ochoa took hold of a hand truck and started down a work aisle. He had had three beers with his lunch, and he was thinking of quitting time. There was a woman he had just met who was not only willing, but eager. Raul was looking forward to a very good time.

He was on such a mental high he hardly noticed it when he ran his hand truck into the legs of Jesse Calderon. The sharp edge of the lip cracked hard against the bone. Raul jerked his truck back, but he was too late—the damage had been done.

He might have saved it with a fast full apology, but he could not do that—he was a *veterano* of Montaña Mara and Calderon had been very active in Los Lobos when the two gangs had been at war.

Despite his injury and considerable pain, Calderon grabbed hold of a large wrench that was on a work table beside him. Seeing that, Ochoa thrust his truck in front of him and looked desperately for a weapon of his own.

Several men saw the incident, including Reuben Estrada, who had been active for some time in community welfare programs. He was a big, powerful man who combined a massive body with the ability to think very fast on his feet. At considerable risk to himself he jumped at once between the two combatants and burst into a flood of Spanish.

The supervisor who was nearby did not understand a word, but he grasped what was going on. It was his duty to control things on the working floor, but Estrada was obviously doing that effectively, so he left him alone.

Estrada knew that the supervisor could not understand Spanish, so he did not hold back his words. "Imbeciles!" he shouted enough to be heard by all of those nearby. "Stop for the sake of God! An accident they can understand, but if blood flows, we will all lose our jobs. Raul, you were wrong—you hurt Jesse badly. It was your fault."

Then he looked at the injured man whose macho he had just saved. "Jesse, put down the wrench—you don't need it." When there was no response to that, he added. "Do it, or I will cut off your balls and feed them to dogs."

With a dozen pairs of eyes on him, Jesse put the wrench down. The crisis was over. Estrada said a few more things in Spanish, then he went to the supervisor and spoke in English. "We have had a slight accident," he said. "It is nothing serious, but a man's leg has been cut. It should be fixed."

The supervisor had a brain as well. "Of course," he agreed at once. "Perhaps he should take the rest of the day off to go home and rest."

Time off with pay was an unexpected bonus. The cut leg still hurt ferociously, but more important to Jesse was the fact that he had been made a hero. He had saved many jobs, and everyone knew it. He limped to the first aid station pretending that he felt no pain at all.

The plant manager was informed that there had been a flare-up but that the workers had settled it themselves almost immediately. The supervisor did not add that if Estrada had not been there, it could have been very serious. In turn the plant manager decided to report the incident as a slight industrial accident that would have no serious consequences.

He hoped to God that his prognosis was accurate.

At 15:14 that afternoon Deputies Sloan and Agrivar received a call of shots fired at a location a block and a half from the new Morrison and Hale facility. They responded immediately, knowing that backup would be right behind them. A call like that got action and a great deal of it, fast.

When they arrived less than a minute later, they found a member of Los Magnolias down on the sidewalk. They pulled up sharply, roof lights on, and rushed to the victim. One fast look told them both that he had taken at least part of a shotgun blast in the legs. He was bleeding in several places. Two additional units screamed to a halt; while deputies poured out to check the area, Sloan radioed in for paramedics and an ambulance.

Mott was in the fifth car to reach the scene—he had been in the station only a short distance away. Less than two minutes later, the paramedics rolled up in their red County Fire Department unit and went immediately to work. As they did, Mott tried to talk to the victim. He recognized him as one of the three or four gang members he remembered from the evening he had gone with Brother Julio to negotiate a truce for the factory area.

The victim could not talk—he was in acute pain and making animal noises in his throat in a hopeless attempt to overcome his agony.

One of the paramedics slid a needle into his arm and started an IV. It was hard to do, because the patient, who was lying on his back, was continuously rolling from side to side, trying to find a position that would pain him less. The paramedics loaded him onto a cot and took him away, lights and siren clearing the way.

After that the investigative work began. Every doorbell in the vicinity was rung, and each of the people who had gathered at the scene was questioned. Gradually a picture emerged. A low-slung car had come past with two riders aboard. They had shouted "La Calle Verona" according to one witness, another swore that it had been simply "Veronas." Whichever it was, it identified the same gang, which was a minor miracle in itself.

Mott radioed early to try and locate Brother Julio; after forty minutes word came back that he had been reached and would be at the scene shortly.

Informed now in the ways of gang shootings, Mott took the leader of the Magnolias in his car with him and drove around slowly, emphasizing that no one was overhearing and that the meeting was entirely private between the two of them.

163

"Ernesto," he said, "you know more than anybody. What happened?"

"I dunno, man, we just got shot at, that's all."

Mott had expected that, but he was patient. "The Veronas—they're on the other side of town."

"Yeah, I know."

"They pushing your turf?"

"No, course not." It was the expected answer, but Mott knew how to keep his man talking.

"You've got big macho because of the factory. Are they jealous?"

"They no got enough brains for that."

"The Magnolias, they're pretty tough."

"Right on, man, we plenty tough!"

"Then why did they come looking for trouble with you?"

"I tol' you man, I dunno." It was the same response, but it came slower this time. Mott knew that the answer would come. He continued to drive slowly, to let the idea sink in that the ride would continue until the facts were out in the open.

"The Veronas, they're having trouble with Laguna Mara."

Ernesto laughed. "That ain't nothin' new, man. They always at it."

"Why?" Mott knew perfectly well, but he was keeping the conversation going.

"They both got fucked when the freeway went in—both of 'em lost a whole lotta turf. So now they got blood over the little bit that's left."

"Who's going to win?"

"I dunno, man, an' I not much care."

"But the Veronas just hit you."

"We take care of it, man, you don' worry."

"No, Ernesto, we're going to take care of it."

"It ain't your fight, man."

"Why not?"

"Well, you ain't involved."

"Look, Ernesto, I know you didn't hit the Veronas—you've been leaving them alone. Now all of a sudden they hit you. You're a tough gang. Why would they take a big chance like that?"

The praise soaked into Ernesto until he developed an appetite for more. "We got a little dispute, that's all."

"A little dispute. That sounds like a girl."

"Somethin' like that."

"Let me put it together," Mott suggested. He drove easily, taking a corner at just enough speed to keep the car in high gear, then setting up a slow pace in the new direction. "The Magnolias get around a lot. They've got big macho, so they can. Maybe one of the Verona girls decided that she wanted some of that. So, naturally, she didn't get turned down. How's that?"

Ernesto slumped down a little more in his seat so he would be less easy to see from the outside. "Hey, you pretty smart, man."

"Was she some old girl?"

"Naw, she's only been fuckin' about a year."

"How old?"

"That's the law, man."

"We're not talking about that now. I didn't ask who she was."

"O.K., she's fourteen. But she's piled up—pair 'a knockers knock your eye out if you get too close. Swell piece of ass."

"You have her?"

"Not this time. I smart man. One of our guys, he go down there screw her. He fuck her good. Veronas, they don' like, so they come gunnin' for us."

"Thanks, Ernesto. You don't talk, I don't talk—O.K.?"

"O.K., but somethin' else. You know that guy, he's paintin' the mural?"

"Yes, I know."

"Well he's a fuckin' Verona, man, and next time he comes around here, I tell you now, we blow his fuckin' ass off."

CHAPTER SIXTEEN

WHILE the field investigation was still in progress, Mott took Brother Julio with him in his car to a coffee shop where the manager would seat them, if asked, in the closed section. On the way he briefed the Brother on the cause of the incident.

"I have been expecting this," Julio said. "I know who the girl is, and it is true that she already has the body of a mature woman." He changed his tone slightly. "I hope you understand that most of the young women of the barrio are what we call 'old country girls.' They stay close to the teachings of the Church and keep their virginity until they are married. The small number that associate with the gangs are sexually very active, sometimes from a very early age."

The topic was allowed to rest until Mott had parked his car and they had been seated inside the restaurant. Then he came right to the point. "Julio, I've been warned that Lorenzo, the muralist, is a Verona and that the Magnolias are going to take violent action if he shows up on their turf any more."

"That idea must be stopped at once," the Brother declared. He was interrupted by a waitress who set down two cups of coffee without having waited for an order. "What else?" she asked.

Mott was about to say "Nothing, thank you," when he remembered Julio's financial condition and ordered a sandwich. An example having been set, Brother Julio placed an order also. Mott was sure from the way he made his choice that he had probably missed his lunch.

When they were again alone, Mott said, "I agree we must do something immediately. So I'm going to use every man I've got to try and take the gunmen into custody as fast as possible. As soon as we do that, I'm going to tell Ernesto of the Magnolias two things: that we have busted the gunman for attempted murder and that Lorenzo isn't a member of the Veronas. He told me that himself."

Julio was not satisfied. "If you try to tell the Magnolias that Lorenzo isn't a Verona, they won't believe you. I will try to convince them that he is interested only in mural work and that his new masterpiece, on their turf, will be the envy of the whole barrio. That will give them a reason of their own to want to see it finished."

"That's sound," Mott agreed. "If it doesn't work, you can add that if the mural isn't finished, everyone will consider it their fault."

"Let us agree on what we are to do," Julio said. He picked up a spoon and with its edge traced a pattern on the paper napkin before him. "It will be very good indeed if you and your people could identify and arrest the two gunmen. Once they are in custody it is quite possible that they will cop out and no one will have to be put on the stand. You must convince them that this time there are witnesses who are willing and eager to testify against them. La Calle Verona is a small gang, and they know that they cannot intimidate people as, say, Montaña Mara can."

"What do you think our chances are?"

"Very good, I would think. I know now who made the attack, but I am unable to tell you. I believe that you will find out anyway."

That was certainly all of the information that Mott could hope for under the circumstances. He ate his sandwich in relative silence, thinking as he did so. He considered it quite possible that Brother Julio might get to the attackers before he did and advise them to plead guilty. The more he saw of the Brother, the more he was aware of the man's capabilities. He would have made a damn good cop.

Back at his office, Mott put all of the machinery at his disposal into operation. He phoned Nancy and told her not to expect him for dinner, that something had gone down.

Nancy asked about Deputy Alvarez, inquiring if she were in any danger.

"It's her day off," Mott responded; then he said something appropriate and got off the line. He had too much else on his mind at the moment to do more than let his wife know that he would be late. He always tried to do that whenever he could.

There was a very good roster of the Verona members on file; he took the cards with him as he drove southwest to the gang's territory. By radio he passed the word that he wanted every known member of the gang rounded up for interrogation. As many black-and-whites as possible were to be seen saturating the gang's limited turf. It was his intention to put the fear of God into every member of the Veronas and, by osmosis, into the Lagunas and the Sixth Street Lobos as well. The turf of the Veronas was so small he was able to saturate it easily.

As he drove up and down the few blocks that the Veronas controlled, he could see that his orders were being carried out effectively. A half dozen units had made stops of gang cars, and at least thirty suspects had been interrogated. The radio carried frequent reports of cars returning to the station with suspects in custody.

Hardly two hours later Sergeant McBride reported that the roundup had been a notable success; only two known members of the Veronas were not in custody or in the hospital. The two missing suspects, who were brothers, were reported by their parents to be in San Diego visiting friends. Since the father of the family was a man of good reputation, the deputies who had talked to him had accepted his explanation.

As added confirmation, he had supplied an address where they might be located if needed. The two deputies thanked him, returned to the station, and called San Diego promptly. The father's story checked out.

There were two ways to play it, Mott recognized at once: he could try to establish a rapport with the gang kids, or he could come down hard. His experience told him exactly how he wanted to proceed—for the time being it would have to be the hard line. As soon as he had the suspects identified, then he could and would deal differently with the others. Undoubtedly they all knew who had been the hit men, but it was a foregone conclusion that none of them would breathe a word. To do that would be the equivalent of suicide. The Veronas were a small gang, but they were intense and deadly. They could not be treated as children.

Mott and the deputies working with him started in on alibis. Several of the kids were able to establish where they had been when the attack had taken place; as soon as their stories were verified, they were driven back to their homes. At Mott's instruction a marijuana cigarette or two was overlooked, and only one gang member was detained on a concealed weapons charge—he had been found in possession of an illegal switchblade knife of dangerous size.

When all that had been done, eight gang members were left. With any luck, the actual gunmen would be in that group. Two refused to talk at all, two others claimed alibis that could not be checked out. Mott had them all booked on suspicion of murder and then, in their hearing, he announced that he was going to have them all given tests to determine if they had recently discharged firearms. That immediately generated loud protests and calls for lawyers.

Mott knew that that was their right, and he was careful not to violate it. He told them that they could have all the lawyers that they wanted, but that the fastest way for any of them to prove his innocence would be to submit to the test.

There was much talking after that in Spanish, the gang members knowing that he could not understand what they were saying. Others who were present did, but concealed the fact. One tall black deputy who was apparently completely occupied in making out forms missed nothing.

Two phone calls came in from Chicano organizations protesting violently about harassment of the suspects and violations of their civil rights.

Under careful questioning, three of the suspects were identified as illegal aliens. As soon as their status became known, some desperate bargaining began. None of the three would have dared to name the two Veronas who had made the attack, but they were suddenly willing to own up to minor infractions in order to clear themselves of the main charge. Mott listened to what they had to say and then had them returned to the holding area.

That left five possibles, and if no mistakes had been made, the actual hit man and his driver would be in the group. Mott was on familiar ground now: he had cracked scores of burglaries by skillful questioning, cajoling, offering tidbits of praise, and whetting appetites for more. These were all familiar techniques to him, and he knew how to employ them efficiently.

He had the five suspects separated and then interviewed them again, one at a time. He got back in return a full crop of evasions, but he had an answer to that. From the cards on file he knew each of the gang member's personal record—all five of them had been arrested several times before. That gave Mott a good foundation from which to work. To it he added a number of recent unsolved incidents that might possibly have been the work of one or more of the Veronas. Each of the suspects, on being shown into his presence, found that he had to contend not only with the incident earlier in the day, but also with his own past record and other gang-related cases that had not yet been pinned down.

By a little after two in the morning Mott had pinpointed the two suspects that he wanted. Neither of them had admitted a thing, but he knew from experience that he was on safe ground. At ten minute intervals he released the three suspects he did not want and had them driven back home. As the ranks of the accused thinned, one at a time, the psychological pressure on the two that Mott had identified built up steadily.

When the third released gang member was put into a patrol car to be returned to his home, Mott stood by, patiently waiting. Then he gave directions that the bus was to be called to take the two remaining suspects to Central Jail.

That they did not want. They had both been there before and knew that it would not be a pleasant experience. There was a compulsory admission blood test, for example, that one of them particularly dreaded. As soon as that had sunk in, Mott conferred with the watch commander for the benefit of the suspects. It was concluded that the hour was far to late to bring the witnesses in, but they would be able to make a positive identification later.

Mott successfully conveyed the impression that he was completely satisfied and sure of himself.

The tall black deputy appeared once more and whispered into Mott's ear. Mott nodded and issued another order. "Hold the jail transportation for a few minutes. A witness is willing to come here now."

"I'll send a car right away," the watch commander said. He called two of the duty deputies in, apparently wrote an address on a slip of paper, and then gave instructions in a voice too low for the suspects to hear.

The deputies departed. After that it was completely quiet. Mott very visibly relaxed and drank a cup of coffee.

"I gotta go piss," one of the suspects said.

Mott nodded casually to the black deputy to attend to it. The suspect was taken to the large wash and shower room at the back of the station. Presently another deputy appeared and said, "Lieutenant, you're wanted in the main washroom."

The remaining suspect shifted uncomfortably in his chair. Mott went out and came back eight minutes later, looking relaxed. He even appeared to be in a good mood. "As soon as the statement has been signed, let me know," he said. Then he sat down and picked up a stack of reports. He did not appear to have any further interest in the remaining suspect. The one who had asked to go to the washroom did not reappear.

The suspect broke the silence. "Hey, man."

"What is it?" Mott asked.

"You give me a deal if I cop?"

Mott appeared indifferent. "It might help you some. Judge Ramos puts more weight than I think he should on confessions. But if you want to cop, you'll have to do it before the witness gets here."

"I might get probation?"

"That's up to the judge."

After ninety seconds of silence, the suspect said, "All right."

That broke it. The youth admitted to having driven the car from which the attack had been made. Assuming that his companion had already looked after himself first, he did not hesitate to implicate him. The evidence seemed clear to him: his companion had asked to be taken out of the room, then the lieutenant had been

171

sent for. That only added up one way.

The sky was beginning to show the first evidence of dawn by the time that Mott parked his car and went up to his apartment. He let himself in as quietly as he could, undressed swiftly in the dark, and got gratefully into bed. He had left word that he would not be in until afternoon.

As soon as he left the six o'clock mass, Brother Julio hurried to the home of Lorenzo Archuleta. He would have liked to stopped for breakfast, but vastly more important considerations were on his mind. When he arrived, he found that the young muralist was just about to sit down to his own breakfast. A chair was quickly placed for the Brother and he was offered what was available.

As he ate, Brother Julio talked with his protege about the mural he was doing and the supply of materials on hand for the work. When that subject had been fully covered, he asked several careful questions about Lorenzo's relations with the Veronas gang. Lorenzo stuck to the same story that he had told before: he had never joined the gang and most certainly he had never been "jumped in." At one time, just after he had finished the much-admired mural on the wall of the meeting room at one of the public parks, the Veronas had put out the word that he was a member and that the macho for the new mural therefore belonged to them.

Because it would have been dangerous to do so, Lorenzo had never denied it. He had followed what had seemed a safe course and had kept his mouth shut. He had no interest whatever in the gang or in its activities; he wanted to paint.

Brother Julio listened as carefully as he had put his questions and was completely satisfied. He finished the food that had been given him and then advised the young artist that certain immediate steps would have to be taken. Inviting Lorenzo to go with him, he drove first to the Morrison and Hale plant where he had a short interview with the manager. "Lorenzo is reporting for work," he explained, "but it will be necessary for me to pay a call with him. It has to do with the mural. I ask that you excuse him while this business is arranged."

"No problem," the manager assured him. "Rembrandt didn't work by the hour, and I happen to know that management is very pleased with the job Lorenzo is doing. Take as long as you need. Just bring him back when you can."

That detail arranged, Brother Julio drove the short distance to the place where the Magnolias invariably hung out. "I know that this may not be comfortable for you," he told his charge, "but it is very necessary that we do it. I hope that you understand this."

"I think so," Lorenzo answered.

Brother Julio did not suffer from the delusion that his mission and his holy orders would protect him at all times in the barrio, despite his own great respect for the absolute authority of the Church. However, at this time of day, and under the circumstances as he understood them, he was confident that he would be able to bring Lorenzo and the Magnolias together without having to fear any repercussions.

He got out of his car, told Lorenzo to come with him, and walked across the street with the calm confidence of Daniel entering the lions' den. To Lorenzo's credit, he trusted the Brother enough to go with him. Even then, it was an ordeal.

The Magnolias had been watching intently. Although they did not appear to pay very much attention, not a single thing was missed. And Brother Julio did not need to say who it was that he had had the temerity to bring onto their turf. The plant was, by their generosity, neutral turf during business hours, but the street corner where they met was not.

Brother Julio spoke in Spanish, a language that came to him even more easily than English. "I have come to give you some information," he said. "The Veronas have been telling a lie."

The Magnolias did not appear to be the least concerned. They listened but did not react.

"This is Lorenzo. I want you to know him, because he is bringing great macho to your turf." He did not need to add that he was the mural painter, they would all know that.

Lorenzo himself very wisely kept still and did nothing at all.

"It would give the Veronas much glory if he were a member of their gang, but he is not. Tell them, Lorenzo."

"I don't belong to the Veronas," he said. "I don't have anything to do with them."

That simple statement was very important, because it was unheard of in the barrio for any gang member to deny his affiliation.

Gang membership was regarded as a precious privilege, but to deny it could be extremely dangerous. Therefore when Lorenzo stated flatly that he was not a member of the Veronas, it had all the impact of a medieval blood oath. If he were lying and the Veronas heard about it, he would have to pay a severe price.

"The Veronas want him," Brother Julio continued, "but he is not a gang person. He is an artist. He is now making his masterpiece on your turf. It will be the best mural in the whole barrio; many people will come to see it."

In true gang tradition the Magnolias appeared not to care very much one way or the other—they were masters at concealing their real feelings. They laughed, shrugged, and drew lines with the edges of their shoes in the dry dust. All of that did not deceive Julio for a moment. He had worked with this type of teenager for some time and he understood them far better than they imagined.

Among other things, he knew that he had made his point. And he had done it without causing Lorenzo Archuleta any loss of face. He had initiated the call, he had brought the young painter along, so the loss of face, had there been any, would have been his alone. He had known that, and it had not disconcerted him in the least.

"I want you to know him," Brother Julio continued, "because without you, this great new mural would not be."

"It will be the best work I can do," Lorenzo volunteered.

That was another important statement. It implied that although he lived on the Veronas' turf, he intended to give of his best to glorify the territory of the Magnolias.

"That's O.K.," Ernesto said.

Once the gang leader had pronounced judgment, no further discussion was in order. Brother Julio knew that it had been Ernesto who had warned Lorenzo Archuleta off the Magnolias' turf. Now that he had been called on and the authority of the gang had been acknowledged by implication, he was willing to relent. He did so because he also knew that he had to. If Lorenzo was not a member of the Veronas—and he believed that now—then the turf rules did not apply to him. Trying to enforce them on a nonmember would have risked a loss of macho, and even ridicule.

For another few minutes Brother Julio talked with the Magnolias, asking about their brothers and sisters and letting them get used to the presence of Lorenzo. The corner where the Magnolias met was taken up by an old wooden building, still in use and relatively sound, despite the fact that it was almost totally defaced by gang graffiti over its surfaces and across its windows. Lorenzo was studying it. The south face was hopeless, but the west side had a reasonably large flat area that the builder had not bothered to break up with any windows. It was a motley of distorted designs in many colors that had been sprayed indiscriminately, but that did not matter. Lorenzo was still thinking about it when the Brother indicated to him that it was time to go.

Despite his good intentions to get some much-needed rest, Mott showed up at his office before noon. He found a note on his desk that Captain Gutierrez would like to see him sometime during the day, whenever he came in. He picked up his phone, called the captain's office, and reported that he was available. The sergeant who took the call advised that the captain was free.

Miguel Gutierrez had not lost his considerable gift for putting people at ease. He waved Mott to a seat, completed a small matter that he was engaged in, and then gave his newest lieutenant his full attention.

"Ralph," he began, "I hear that you did a good piece of work last night in tying up the shooting on the Magnolias' turf. I've been talking to Rudy De Leon over at Hollenbeck, and he tells me that their policy of putting the more violent gang kids inside has been paying off. Of course that's what we're supposed to do, but as you know coming down hard almost always stirs up community resentment—I've had several calls this morning. But don't let that bug you. None of those kids like jail, and they like the joint even less. I think you handled it the right way."

"Thank you," Mott said.

"Now, I think it would be a good idea if you were to go across the lake personally and talk to the D.A.'s about this case. As I hear it, they copped out after questioning and that's it. No one has accused us of brutality—at least not yet. And they were given their rights and all that. So it should stick, and since both of the suspects have priors, you may be able to get them declared incompetent to stand trial as juveniles."

"I'll be glad to do that," Mott said, "and while we're at it, I'd like to ask something else. It might be a good idea for me to get together with Judge Ramos. Not on this case, of course, but on the general situation that I'm trying to deal with. But I don't want to call him on my own. What do you recommend?"

Gutierrez thought for a moment or two. "I know him pretty well, and it might be constructive for you to have a talk with him. He's an honorable guy, but he has a strong feeling that all of the gang kids are the way they are simply because they're disadvantaged. Consequently he has a tendency to be pretty lenient with them, and they all know it, of course."

"Would you care to set it up?"

"All right, Ralph, I'll do that. Be sure that you don't take up any specific cases unless the judge asks you to. It wouldn't do any harm if you were to emphasize that you aren't doing any strong-arm stuff over here and that the suspects we arrest are being given their Miranda rights without fail—in Spanish if they request. The judge came up out of the barrio himself, so he's concerned about the conditions here and the limited opportunities. Talk about the new plant and how we're cooperating to insure its success."

"I want to tell him, too, how well the Crash program is working out for LAPD. There's a sergeant over there, Raul Vega, who's given me a lot of help."

"How about tomorrow if the judge is free?"

"Fine," Mott agreed. Normally the captain himself would make any such contacts. It was a vote of confidence that he was being allowed to represent the station and its policies.

From the captain's office he went straight across to the other side of the lake and laid out the case he had in hand for the deputy D.A. who would handle it. His name was Mendoza, and he had all of the usual hangups of a man in his position.

"From the top it looks as if you have a fairly good case here," he conceded when it had all been laid out for him.

"It's a damn good case," Mott retorted. He knew the pattern that was in Mendoza's mind: at election time the D.A. liked to be able to show the highest possible percentage of convictions. One of the best ways of doing that was to refuse to file on anything approaching a marginal case. Every case tried without a conviction would damage the D.A.'s track record, therefore many that might hold up were not filed on. It was pure politics, but the D.A. was an elected official, and the office could very well lead to bigger and better things.

"However," Mendoza qualified, "I don't see it as attempted murder. The victim was shot in the legs; anyone can aim better than that if he really wants to kill. At least the defense is going to claim that."

"File it as ADW and attempted murder," Mott suggested. "Then let them spin their wheels trying to kill the murder part. The attack with a deadly weapon can't be denied. And you can make a good argument that people don't shoot other people with shotguns simply to wound them a little. A shotgun does heavy damage, and everyone familiar with them knows it."

Mendoza was not wholly convinced. "I'll think about it," he said. "It might stick. I'll grant you that there's grounds for making the charge, but it depends on the judge. If we get Garcia, she'll probably bind them over for trial on that charge. On the other hand, Ramos would probably dismiss on the grounds that the kids are always shooting up houses without really trying to kill anyone."

"The hell they aren't," Mott disagreed.

"You say so; I say so. But we aren't the judge."

"Agreed. But this time we have it all in line: rights were read, of course. I personally questioned the suspects, and after a while they copped out. We took down their statements and they signed them. There was no rough stuff of any kind, and no one has suggested that there was. That isn't the way we do things, and you know it."

"I've heard otherwise."

"You heard about an adult who was stoned on angel dust. He became violent and we had to use five men to put him into a cell. You know what PCP does to people."

"He showed up in court with a black eye."

"He assaulted one of the arresting deputies. There was a fight, which is nothing new. The deputy had to go to the emergency room at the hospital for treatment."

"The judge still dismissed."

"Don't remind me," Mott said.

Mendoza seemed to agree, at least for the moment, and made a major concession. "All right, I'll file," he said.

"Attempted murder."

"If you say so." It wasn't usual for a lieutenant to come across the park to talk about a case, and something told him that this one might be significant in his career. The ADW—Attack with a Deadly Weapon—he was almost sure would stick, so he couldn't get hurt too badly.

"Thanks a lot," Mott concluded. "See you in court."

On the turf of the Lagunas a great deal of heavy discussion was going on. Blinky Herrara was blinded, and it was still a question whether or not he would ever get out of the hospital. Bobo, the strongest leader of Los Lagunas, had taken a bullet in the spine. He was in the hospital strapped onto a board, and he was due to have another operation as soon as he was strong enough to live through it. Rudy Dias had not been seriously wounded, but Chico Trujillo was dead. It was a terrible toll.

Two of the Veronas had been killed and two more wounded, so the battle stood about even. Also, two of the Veronas had been busted for taking on the Magnolias, and they were still inside, charged with attempted murder. That reduced their total strength by six, a good percentage of their warriors.

Rudy Dias had taken over the leadership of the Lagunas. He was out on the street once more over the strong objections of the D.A.'s office. His arm was still in a sling, so the judge had been lenient.

"We ain't in no shape to go after the Veronas right now," he declared. "Too much heat. An' we can't afford t' get any more guys hurt right now. The Veronas, maybe they quit now. They lost six guys, and maybe the best six they got. So they not come lookin' for us."

That was discussed and generally agreed to. A lot of the gang macho had been destroyed by the disasterous attack on the Veronas. None of the gang members dared to show it, but morale had slipped badly. Dead was dead, but lying like a vegetable strapped to a board might even be worse. And Blinky was blind. Even if he recovered and got out of the hospital eventually, he still would have to be led around all of his life. That they could visualize and understand, and the remaining gang members wanted none of it for themselves. The Veronas had fallen onto hard times, too, but no one had much heart to stage another attack. The war was, for the moment, over.

"I think of something," Rudy said.

The others listened a little fearfully, acutely aware of their loss of stature and strength. That meant that at any time some more powerful gang might move in, seize their turf, and it would be all over.

"We don't wanna get hit no more, but if we don't do somethin', somebody come down here and cut our balls off. We gotta show we still rule this turf."

He waited until that had been agreed upon. He was leading a sick and weary army that desperately needed a boost in its macho.

"You know that Verona kid, he paint a new mural at the factory. We hit him right now, the cops they give us hell. The heat's on hard. So we do something else. Nobody get hurt."

If that were possible, what remained of the Lagunas were all for it.

Rudy produced a can of black paint and two thick brushes. "I think maybe we go sign that mural, heh?"

The mural was on the Magnolias' turf, of course, so there would be danger. But the Magnolias stayed pretty well away from the factory, and that made things look better.

"How about it?" Rudy asked. He could have given the order, but he wanted more spirit in the troops. Within a few minutes they agreed. There would be no guns, and since the mural didn't belong to the Magnolias anyway, they shouldn't be too much concerned. But it sure would piss off the Veronas.

They left in two cars and drove north on Eastern Avenue. They went down Whittier so as to avoid the sheriff's station on Third, then turned north again into the Magnolias' turf. They were only there a very short while. They had to go over a wire fence twice, but they had done that before, and there was nothing to it if you knew how. When they were back on their own turf they broke up and went to their separate homes. They were badly weakened, and their spirits still sagged from the heavy loses they had taken, but in a very short time the whole barrio would know that the Lagunas had big macho and everyone else had damn well stay off their turf.

* * *

A patrol car saw it first in the early light of dawn and radioed in. When the watch commander received the news, he considered it a serious enough matter to go out himself, and he did. Although he knew what to expect, he was all but speechless when he saw the gross vandalism with his own eyes.

The mural had only been about one-third finished, but already the whole barrio knew that it would be superior to any similar work in the whole of East Los Angeles. The faces especially were close to wonderful.

Or they had been. The watch commander was on duty and in the sight of other deputies, consequently he held himself in check and tried not to let the extent of his feelings show. But the suppressed rage that was within him kept growing until he clenched his fists and wished to Almighty God that he could take some kind of drastic action. He was in a mood to strangle someone with his bare hands.

Across the entire completed span of the mural a huge, wide LM had been painted in heavy black. It effectively destroyed all but one of the matchless faces that Lorenzo Archuleta had so carefully painted and told the world that Laguna Mara was desperate for attention and revenge.

CHAPTER SEVENTEEN

THE TRAFFIC was unusually heavy on the Santa Monica Free-way, despite the very early hour. As he drove, slowing and stopping from time to time, Ralph Mott had plenty of opportunity to reflect on his relatively new job. It was a good time to do it, because a fresh sense of satisfaction was still with him.

At first he had been almost staggered by the amount he would have to learn; now that part was behind him and it had not been nearly as bad as he had expected. He had a quick mind, and it had not taken him very long to master the geography of East Los Angeles and the locations of even the very small and out-of-the-way streets. He now had a full grasp of the gang structure; he could draw a detailed map of the various gang territories. He knew every gang by name and was familiar with who was fighting who at the moment and what the recent past histories had been. He knew an impressive number of the gang kids by name and reputation.

Now that he was on top of his job, he had a sense of confidence and of his own worth. He had been handed an acute problem; he was now prepared to deal with it. He had acquired the necessary background expertise and knowledge of the culture within which it operated.

181

Nancy was unhappy with what he was doing, and in a way he could not blame her. She had known that she was marrying a policeman, but she had not expected the barrio. She knew, of course, that without policemen civilization would be close to an impossibility. There was too much savagery, too much desire to take what belonged to others, too much misapplied sexual drive, too much ambition to live high by ripping off others who had worked for what they had.

For the time being Nancy would have to adjust to where he worked and the hours he was required to put in. They had talked about it, without rancor, and he had made it clear that the barrio would be part of their lives until he was transferred. He was not anxious for that. The simple, honest people, like the Yasudas with their little grocery store, had the inalienable right to live in peace and to earn their living if they could. More than ever he knew that he was a policeman because he had never wanted to be anything else—because helping to make society work and keeping the predators at bay were essential to human survival.

He was still in that lofty mood when he parked his car on the station lot and went in through the rear door past the watch desk. Once more the giant jug that the station kept on hand was standing on the counter. It had not been there the day before, but it was already almost a quarter full of bills. On the side was the same kind of label that was used each time that it appeared. This one carried the printed legend *For the family of Deputy Craig Russell.*

A hard cold knot gripped Mott in the pit of his stomach. He looked at the duty sergeant and asked, "What happened?"

The sergeant looked up. "Lakewood Station," he said tersely, as though he were trying to block the meaning of the words out of his mind. "It was a routine traffic stop—two young blacks in a white Cadillac. He had an academy cadet with him, a kid who was due to graduate next week. Russell was walking up to the car when the blacks opened fire. The cadet jumped out and returned the fire. He hit both of the suspects—wounded them slightly. Russell was dead where he fell. The kid took a slug in the abdomen."

"How is he?"

"We don't know yet; he was still alive the last I heard." He stopped to answer a phone. "Yes, ma'am, we'll see to it. I'll send a car over." He hung up. "Barking dog," he said.

A surge of white-hot rage took possession of Mott and he was not himself. "If I'd been that kid, I'd have blown them both up right now!" he said, knowing as he did so that he was out of line.

The sergeant looked at him. "You knew Russell?" he asked.

Mott struggled to get control of himself. He didn't apologize for what he had just said—he couldn't. "Russell was in my academy class. We ran together."

Then they were silent, because more could be said that way than with any words. Mott opened his wallet and extracted two ten dollar bills. It was most of what he had with him. He put the money quietly into the huge jug, knowing that one like it would be out in every station in the Los Angeles County Sheriff's Department.

"Are they in custody?" he asked.

"Yes, in the jail ward." The sergeant took a deep breath, held it, and then let it out very slowly. "At least we've got capital punishment back."

"You know what will happen," Mott said, bitterness tinging his voice. "They'll claim that the suspects are being unfairly dealt with because they're black. They'll milk that one to the bottom in court."

"Oh, sure, but those two"—the sergeant lost control for a bare moment—"goddamned bastards can lie there and at least think about the gas chamber."

A casual memory flashed into Mott's mind, something that had been mentioned to him once. He didn't believe in coincidences— no policeman did—but the odds were only about fifty to one. That wasn't too far out. The sergeant's reaction, like his own, had been too intense. And his son was in the academy.

Compassion filled Mott, a compassion of human empathy that exists between men who devote themselves to at least trying to maintain law and order.

"The cadet," he asked, "was it . . . ?"

The sergeant lifted his shoulders and squared them. "Yes, it happened to work out that way. The last I heard, they think he may be all right."

"Why in hell . . ." Mott asked.

183

"Because I wanted to. I can't help him in the hospital, but maybe I can here. I wanted to come to work."

The sergeant reached for a pile of booking forms.

"Keep me informed," Mott said, and then left as quietly as he could. He knew what was in the sergeant's mind: he was fighting back, staying on the job to help grab the assholes that were still out there and who still believed that power came from the end of a gun.

Ralph went directly to Mike Wickman's office, where he knew he could get the latest word. "How's the cadet?" he asked.

Mike looked up and saw immediately that Mott knew who the cadet was. "As of ten minutes ago, he's in intensive care with a fifty-fifty chance. But I can tell you this: he's getting the best that the whole damn town can offer. A specialist from UCLA is there —he's got a brother in the Glendale department."

"That helps."

"It sure does. It hits hard that it's Mike Cook's boy, but it had to be somebody's son—or daughter."

"Where's Deputy Alvarez?" He asked that without thinking.

"On patrol. With Vetrovec."

"How about Mike?"

"The captain told him to get the hell out of here, but he wanted to stay on the job. I know how he feels."

"So do I," Mott agreed.

"Incidentally, the sheriff himself went to the hospital this morning to see Mike's boy. He called Mike later to express his personal feelings. It's a good thing that the suspects are in custody; otherwise there wouldn't be anyone left to answer the phones."

"There's no question of their guilt, I take it."

"None whatsoever. After they dropped Russell, Mike's boy shot one of them, took a slug in the gut himself, and then had enough left to shoot the other. Unfortunately, both of the suspects were only lightly wounded. I know I shouldn't say that, but that's how I feel."

"They killed a deputy," Mott said with careful precision. "There's no question as to their identity—they're the assholes who did it. We have them in custody charged with one eighty-seven, so there's no bail. How do you think that should add up?"

"The gas chamber, but the governor may go soft. You know

the pressure that will be put on him."

"Yes, but in the latest statewide referendum on the issue of capital punishment, the vote went more than seventy percent in favor. He'll be reminded of that—depend on it."

There being nothing more to say on that subject, Mott returned to his office and began to read reports. One of them interested him very much, although it was not his direct concern. It suggested a line of action open to him, something he could do almost immediately if he wanted to.

He gave it half a minute of careful thought, then he checked his county telephone directory and dialed the hospital.

George Wilkinson was furious to the point where he did not trust himself to do anything at all until he cooled down. There had been problems, of course, but in the main the new plant it was his responsibility to manage was doing as well as he could reasonably hope. There had been no further incidents to cause him concern or to force him to tone down his reports to the main offices. He was a conscientious, capable man and normally also a compassionate one. But the outrage that had just occurred threw everything back to square one, and he could hardly contain himself.

The new mural that was being painted on the side of the building had been a showpiece of a very important kind. It was a product of East Los Angeles, something that the residents of the area could enjoy, and something that revealed their exceptional gifts in that form of artwork. Murals, he had been told, were almost always respected in the barrio, and the gang kids with their spray cans of paint left them alone. The vandals who had ruined the fine piece of work in progress had done so viciously, and as far as he was concerned, the whole project was beyond repair.

The first incident, the one involving the hand truck, he had chosen to see as an accident, and he had reported it that way. He had been supported in that by the men themselves, who had quickly taken care of the matter in their own way. All in all, he had regarded that as a good sign. But for blatant vandalism there was no possible excuse, and he would have to report it just as it had occurred. What made matters even worse, the chairman of the board had been down himself to see the work in progress and had been enthusiastic about it.

185

Dolores Fernandez, his neat, efficient secretary, appeared in the doorway of his office. "Brother Julio is here to see you," she reported.

Wilkinson wanted to bark at her just to vent some of the rage in his system; with a major effort he controlled himself. "Tell him that I'm sorry; I can't see anyone right now."

"Yes, sir." Her eyes told him that she understood, and that simple act mollified him a little; reminded him that most of the people of East Los Angeles were fine people and that he was giving a lot of them an opportunity they desperately needed.

Presently Dolores came back, bringing him a cup of coffee the way he normally liked it. "The Brother said to tell you that he understood." she said.

That angered him a bit more. He did not want to be understood; he wanted to wring somebody's neck.

Outside, at what had been the mural, a conference was being held. Of the persons present, Lorenzo Archuleta seemed to be the calmest. Even Brother Julio had abandoned his usual placid exterior and was visibly both angry and concerned. Two deputies who were standing by had their portable radios in their hands.

Another unit rolled up from the station, a black-and-white, and Mott got out. He took a long look at what had been the distinguished start of a truly great mural, and his already badly damaged disposition approached the danger point.

With a maturity far beyond his years, Lorenzo was making an evaluation and laying out a plan of action. "I think that we can get the black paint off," he said as calmly as though he were reciting a proposition in geometry. "If we leave it there and paint over it, sooner or later it will strike through. It's best, then, to take it off. If it is done carefully, there will not be much additional damage to the mural. Also it is still fresh, and that may make it easier."

He soaked a rag in paint thinner and tried its effectiveness out on a small area of the black. He rubbed a few times, and the rag turned black in his hands. "It will come off," he declared. "It would be best to have some help, but a few gallons of thinner and enough rags are all that I really need."

Brother Julio slipped away without being noticed. George Wilkinson had joined the little group in time to hear Lorenzo's pronouncement. He said nothing—he still did not want to commit himself in speech. At the same time he had to admire the young Chicano for taking the whole thing so calmly. Some very careful and painstakingly detailed work had been utterly ruined, but he seemed to be able to take that in his stride. George Wilkinson tried to let a little of that composure rub off on him.

"You want some paint thinner, right?" he asked, forcing himself to be as calm as he could.

"Two or three gallons should do it," Lorenzo replied. "And rags —we'll need lots of rags."

Wilkinson went back inside the plant and called his assistant to the lobby on the double. As soon as the young man appeared, he issued orders. "Go down to Whittier Boulevard and get me three cans of paint thinner. Then hit the two thrift shops and get as many rags suitable for a cleaning job as you can. Take what you need out of petty cash, and for God's sake hurry!"

Having done something, he went back to see if there was anything else required.

Mott was busy on one of the hand radios. With a few words he put out a full dragnet to cover the turf of the Lagunas, just as he had done when the Veronas had fired shots in this same area. Several cars rolled out in response within the next five minutes; those on patrol in the Laguna area immediately began to carry out his instructions.

One of the deputies was trying his hand at cleaning the black paint off and reported his results with concern. "I can get the black off all right," he said. "But it takes off the painting underneath."

"That doesn't matter," Lorenzo told him. "I can redo it easily. Some of the faces will take a little longer, but as long as the black is off, it will be no problem."

"Can we get you someone to help you repaint?" Wilkinson asked.

For the first time Lorenzo showed some visible emotion. "No, thank you," he answered with an unexpected hardness in his voice. "I will paint the mural myself, and it will be my work."

A small procession was approaching the work site. Brother Julio was coming with eight or ten others; it took Mott only a few seconds to realize that the Brother had a good representation of Los Magnolias in tow.

By common consent it was quiet until the Brother reached the

187

place where the others were standing. "I have very good news for you," he reported. "These young men are members of Los Magnolias. They have offered their help to remove the black paint that was smeared across their mural. They have much more macho than the other gangs in this area, and they are proving it now."

Wilkinson had long experience in handling people. "I can't tell you how much I appreciate this," he said. "I will see that lunch is served to them all."

The assistant manager came around the corner of the plant, walking as rapidly as he could. He had a gallon can of paint thinner in each hand. "This was close by, so I brought it," he said. "I phoned for the rags, and the thrift shops are getting some ready for us. We will have them in a few minutes."

"Good," Wilkinson said. "Meanwhile, there's some waste in the plant. Have what there is brought out."

Mott took three pictures of the damaged mural and then went back to his car. As far as he was concerned, Brother Julio and the plant manager appeared to have everything under control.

Back at the sheriff's station he asked Sergeant McBride to handle the search for the vandals that was being conducted on the Lagunas' turf. He had something else that was pressing, and he did not want to lose any more time.

He took a plain car off the lot and headed toward the Heights. As he drove, going slowly through the barrio streets, he thought again about Lorenzo Archuleta, the young muralist, and decided once more that he was a find of the first order. There was no question as to his talent, and the way he had conducted himself after seeing the damage done to his work demanded respect.

Obviously Archuleta should go to art school, but it would have to be a very good one so that well-meaning, but uninspired instructors wouldn't take away from him some of what he already had. Art was not something that could be done by formula—it was all a matter of taste, talent, and perhaps most of all, feeling. And technique, of course. He was still pondering the matter when his car began to climb the grades that led up to the turf of Montaña Mara. He heard the warning whistles, but he did not care. The Veronas had been taught a very hard lesson, and he knew that the word would spread.

He drove to the home of Danny Torres and carefully parked

directly in front. When he reached the front door, Mrs. Torres opened it for him before he had a chance to knock.

"Good morning, Lieutenant Mott," she said. "Is there trouble?"

Mott remembered her good breeding and smiled disarmingly at her. "No, Mrs. Torres, no trouble at all. But I do want to see Danny."

"Lieutenant, please, what has he done this time?"

"He hasn't done anything to my knowledge, Mrs. Torres. I want to talk with him and take him out for a little while, but I'm not here to arrest him."

Still not entirely convinced, Mrs. Torres ushered him in. She offered him a place to sit, then stood nervously by as Danny came into the room. There had been no need to tell him that he had a visitor—he had known that from the moment that Mott had pulled his car up to the curb. In Danny's world, a constant watch had to be kept for the coming of the heat. And it was always and implacably, the enemy. "What you want?" Danny asked.

"I'd like you to come with me," Mott said. He put no emphasis at all into the words—he spoke them calmly and flatly.

"Man, I ain't done nothin'!"

"I didn't say you had. I'm not arresting you."

"Ya mean I don't have t' come?"

"That's right, but you'd better."

Danny was in uniform: white t-shirt, blue jeans, and broken-down tennis shoes. He was a gang kid from the word *go,* and that fact determined everything he did. Mott took him out to the car, then turned and told his anxious mother. "We'll be gone for an hour or two, but don't worry. I'll bring Danny back."

That seemed to reassure her. If Danny was being taken to jail, she couldn't believe that the lieutenant would have made such a promise. She saw her son driven away. For the first time that she could remember he was being taken in a police car without having been handcuffed first. That was the rule: all persons in custody had to be cuffed before being transported.

Mott drove away from the curb and started down the hill. Danny, sitting unaccustomedly in the front seat, waited in stony silence until Mott turned north on Eastern, away from the sheriff's station and toward the San Bernardino Freeway. That was not according to plan, and Danny didn't like it. "Man, you take me to

189

Hall of Justice?" he asked. If that were true, it could be very heavy, and Danny couldn't think of anything he had done recently that would deserve it.

"No, Danny, I'm taking you to the USC Medical Center."

"I'm not sick, man!"

"I know, but I sent you some forms to fill out for a job there. You didn't complete them."

For a few seconds Danny was speechless. What was happening was completely outside his experience and therefore totally suspect. "I can't go there," he said finally.

"Why not, Danny? Give me one good reason."

"There's lots of reasons."

This was the kind of byplay that most of the gang kids used, and Mott knew it thoroughly. He had run into much the same thing when he had been working burglary.

He turned onto the freeway entrance ramp and down onto the multilaned throughway. "You see, Danny," he explained quite calmly, "you told me that you were interested in perhaps becoming a doctor some day."

"I know, but that ain't for me, man."

"Why not?"

"They don't want no Mex—you know that."

"No, Danny, I don't know it, and I don't think that Dr. Sanchez does either. He's the man who's been helping me on this. You're going to meet him in a few minutes."

Danny was suddenly in a position of very mixed emotions. He squirmed in his seat and then looked ahead at the immense hospital complex that was only a short distance ahead. In his mind it was a Mecca, a promised land, but there were insurmountable obstacles.

He turned in his seat and half faced Mott. "Look, man, I can't go there."

"Yes you can, Danny, there's no reason why not. And if you get a job, you've got a car that will take you there and back."

It was a desperate situation and one that was getting steadily worse every second that they drove. In less than five minutes they would be there, and then big trouble would follow. Danny knew that he had to talk—to explain—even though doing so to the fuzz was automatically disaster. No one talked to the fuzz if they could avoid it. Kid around a little, yes, but not tell them anything really important.

Danny grabbed Mott's arm. "I can't go there, I tell ya. Don't make me."

"Danny, didn't you used to watch all of the hospital shows on TV?"

"Yeh, sure, but—"

"And didn't you tell me once that you were thinking about becoming a doctor?"

That's what came from telling the cops anything!

"Yeah, but I changed my mind."

"Danny, I don't believe that. Now tell me the real reason."

He was trapped; he could not see any way out. "Well, my gang, they don't think it's a good idea. So I can't do it. That's all."

"By your gang you mean Luis Cabrera, isn't that right?"

That threw Danny a heavy curve, because he couldn't see how the cops could possibly know that—unless Luis had talked, and he would never do that. He'd been in the joint, where you learned to keep your mouth shut.

He had to say something, but a direct denial would be dangerous. Luis was too prominent in the gang.

"Luis, he says it stinks," he admitted. "Course—"

Mott cut him off. "You don't need to concern yourself about what Luis thinks."

Up to that moment Danny had thought that Mott was smart. But to tell a Montaña Mara member not to pay any attention to Luis Cabrera was idiocy. He sneered a little, because he was suddenly in the driver's seat, and knowledge of that fact surged through him. "Luis, he important guy," he said, and waited for Mott's response to that challenge.

"No, Danny, he isn't. Luis Cabrera's dead."

That was a bomb out of the blue. It almost literally jammed Danny back in his seat. Then he wondered if he could believe it.

"You shit me, man," he said.

"No way. His body's down in the morgue now."

"What fucker shot him? The Counts get him?" His head was spinning.

"No, not the Counts. Nobody from the barrio."

"Well what happen, man? Tell me!"

Mott turned off the freeway and began to weave his way toward the police parking area at the hospital. "You remember that some guys came by and offered Luis a job?"

"Sure, I remember."

"Now use your head, Danny. Luis had a record a yard long. He just came out of the joint a little while ago. He'd never done a day's work in his life. So who do you think would come around and hire him?"

"I dunno, man, but it was a good job. He said it was before he left."

"What kind of a good job?"

An inkling of the truth had already forced its way into Danny's mind, but he didn't want to admit the fact even to himself.

"A job, I guess, just a job."

"The only way that Luis could have gotten a job—a real one, I mean—is through his parole officer. But I talked to Luis's parole officer, and he told me that Luis was all but hopeless. He did get a job for him, in a car wash, and Luis wouldn't go near the place."

"He too big a man to wash cars," Danny said, but without much real conviction. He was still stunned by the disastrous news.

Mott wheeled his car into a parking spot and set the brake. Then he gave full attention to his charge.

"All right, Danny, I'll lay it out for you. For years you have been interested in the medical field. Your mother told me that—and you did. You even said that you would like to take care of kids. When you were in school, you did exceptionally well—I've seen your grades."

"You know a whole fuckin' lot, don't you?" Danny felt resentment, but he was also aware that most of this had been on his behalf, and he didn't know how to behave. He would have given a lot to have had the chance to ask Luis what he ought to do, but Luis was dead. He believed that now.

"That's right, I know quite a bit about you. I made it a point to find out—to find out, Danny, if you had it in you to become a doctor or not. Then I had the forms sent to you. Getting a job here is a first step."

"How did Luis die, man? You didn't tell me that."

"The job he was hired for, Danny—if you want to call it a job —was to help hold up a bank. Luis was to be one of the guns, to help keep everyone frightened while the two leaders took the cash. It didn't work out that way. The moment that the guys went into the bank, one of the tellers hit a hidden alarm. LAPD was there in force, and it was the Metro boys. They know their business where heavy crime is concerned."

Danny read the paper, because it was delivered and he didn't have a lot else to do. "Was that the holdup on the south side of L.A.?" he asked. He was so stunned, he spoke the kind of English he heard his mother use at home.

"That's the one, Danny. Two of the bandits were killed, one other wounded, the fourth is in custody. And that's a federal beef, by the way. Luis panicked and fired a shot at one of the police officers who came in. That's the last thing he ever did, except go down when he was hit. He died in the ambulance on the way to the jail ward. It's on the thirteenth floor, right here. That's an unlucky number."

"The cop, he got killed too?"

"No, he had on his protective vest. He got a slight bruise on the chest."

"How you know all this, man?"

"I read the crime reports. This one just came in this morning. When I saw that Luis Cabrera had been killed, I called LAPD and got the details. So now, Danny, it doesn't matter what Luis thought about your chance to work here. He took his own advice and now he's a cold corpse on a slab in the morgue."

Danny was shaken more than he realized. "Don't talk like that, man, he a friend of mine."

Mott softened his tone. "I know that, Danny. I'm sorry for you and more so for his family. I know about them. They're decent people—just like your family. Anyhow, the fact is that Luis is dead. He did advise you not to come here, didn't he?"

"Yeah." Danny was inside a kaleidoscope and the wildly colored patterns of his thoughts were driving him mad.

Mott got out of the car and opened the door for Danny. "Now," he said. "We're going in to meet Dr. Sanchez. He's expecting you. He's arranged a tour of the hospital for you—I think you'll like that. You'll have some lunch first. When you've finished all that, you're set up for an interview in personnel. This time fill out the forms. When you're all done, you'll be given a ride home. Meanwhile, I'll go back and let your mother know where you are and what you're doing."

As they went inside, Danny looked around him. There were many long corridors and people everywhere, some of them visitors, others in hospital whites who belonged and who were working there. Some of them had to be doctors and nurses.

Mott found the office he wanted and went inside. Waiting for him was a young man with thick glasses, black curly hair, and a solidly built body. He had on a slightly soiled white coat, and there was a thermometer tube clipped in his pocket. "Dr. Sanchez," Mott said, "this is Danny Torres."

The doctor got up and offered his hand. "Hello, Danny," he said. "I've heard a lot about you. They tell me you like hospitals."

Danny swallowed hard and looked at the man who, unaccountably, seemed to be interested in him. "That's right," he said.

Mott made a phone call to the Torres home from a public booth and then drove to the new plant to see if any progress at all had been made in cleaning up the defaced mural.

He could not believe what he saw: the black had all been removed, and underneath where it had been there were even the faint outlines of the original painting. Lorenzo was at work up near the top, and he seemed in good spirits.

That was a material lift for Mott, and God knew he needed one. On the way back from the hospital he had been thinking about Craig Russell and the many times they had spent together when they had both been in the academy. It had been a hard road. Neither of them had been a natural athlete and the physical training program had been rigorous. But they had both stuck it out, and graduation day had been one of the proudest events of their lives. Nancy, whom he had just married, had made a big fuss over them both. Now Craig, God bless him, was dead.

He forced the anger down in him. If he allowed himself to get worked up and then had to go out on a call, he wouldn't be in a position to handle it properly.

The fact that the mural had at least been cleaned up made a difference. All that had really been lost was time. An additional week's work might see the whole damaged area restored.

He was startled when someone abruptly appeared at the door

of his car. He had been paying too much attention to the mural —he should not have let someone sneak up on him like that. His reaction mellowed when he recognized Brother Julio. Where the man had materialized from, Mott did not know.

"It is quite remarkable what has been done," the Brother said. "Do you agree?"

"I certainly do. Tell me, Julio, how did you persuade the Magnolias to go to work like that?"

"It was really very simple; I merely told them that another gang had put its symbol on their turf and that we all wanted to help them get it off."

"That was astute," Mott conceded, "but wasn't it dangerous?"

"I see what you mean," the Brother agreed. "I thought of that, of course, before I spoke to them. When I first saw them, they were already enraged about it. Actually, I hope that I calmed them down a little, and the fact that the deputies were on their side helped a great deal—it gave them a little more macho."

Mott thought for a second or two. "The thing has been erased now," he said. "Which raises two questions: will it ever happen again—"

"No," the Brother interrupted him. "I will see to that."

"All right. Then, secondly, will the Magnolias hit the Lagunas in retaliation?"

It was the Brother's turn to think for a few moments. His smooth face wrinkled around the mouth. Then he came up with something totally unexpected. "Your friend Craig Russell—was he a Catholic?"

"No, he wasn't."

"It does not matter. I have spoken to Father Lopez; we will say two masses at our church for the repose of his soul."

"Thank you. I know his family will appreciate that very much." He forced himself to return to the topic they had been discussing. "You didn't answer my question," he reminded.

Brother Julio responded in a calm voice. "I pray to God that they will not. I will do my utmost to prevent it. If they do, it will be very bad, and almost surely someone else will be killed. It could come very soon, or at any time in the future."

He stopped and thought carefully before he went on.

"For us, we have the fact that the two turfs are relatively far

195

apart—that will help a little. But I must be honest with you—the Magnolias have conceded a great deal lately; they have permitted the factory to be cut out of their turf, and there was an incident in the plant that was not made public. The Magnolias have been too quiet for some time. For that reason, if for no other, I am very worried."

"If anyone can guide them, you are the man," Mott said.

"There are limits to what anyone can do," the Brother retorted. "I do not believe that the Lagunas had any idea what they were starting when they defaced that mural. I pray also to God that they never find out."

CHAPTER EIGHTEEN

JUDGE EMILIO RAMOS seemed to defy in his person every standard concept of what a jurist should look like. He was a small man with a pinched, narrow face and a nose so prominent it was an embarrassment. He was still in his thirties, and at times he displayed a touch almost of boyishness through his jaunty walk, quick abrupt movements of his arms, and a regrettable tendency to interrupt others when they were speaking. Mott had already been briefed on some of this when he met the judge at the not much better than middle class restaurant that his honor had suggested. The judge was already ensconced in a booth when Mott was ushered in. The judge shook hands without getting up and waved Mott to the opposite side of the booth.

"The onion soup is good here, if you like it," he said by way of greeting."

"I do—thanks." Mott picked up the menu. "Anything else that you recommend?"

"My lunch is usually soup and bread, but have whatever you like. It's a free country."

"Thank God for that," Mott commented. He ordered onion soup and a sandwich with iced tea—none of the heavier items on the menu appealed to him at that moment. The waitress picked up the menus and left.

"Well, how is the gang business this week?" the judge asked, principally to show that he knew the exact nature of Mott's assignment.

"At the moment, reasonably quiet, but potentially explosive. I presume that you know Brother Julio—everyone else does."

"Of course I know him," the judge snapped. He had not intended to sound as harsh as he did and followed up at once with a mollifying comment. "A remarkable man. I hold him in very high regard."

"We agree on that," Mott responded. "He and I are sitting on something right now that could blow up at any time. If we can keep the lid on for a couple of weeks, then the worst period should be over."

"It never really stops, though," the judge said.

"No, your honor. Unfortunately that's right."

"Drop the formalities. Off the bench my friends call me Sparky. That isn't my choice, but I've learned to live with it."

"Ralph."

"Good, now we can talk, and I know why you wanted to meet with me. I'm aware that some of my decisions haven't won me any brownie points across the lake at the sheriff's station. But there's something I hope you understand: we both are sworn to enforce the law as it is written. Both of us exercise some judgment in how we do that. If we didn't they wouldn't need me—they could install a computer."

"Amen to that," Mott agreed. "There isn't a day that I don't make a judgment, and usually several of them, on how I do my job. If every motorist were to be ticketed for every infraction, nobody would be able to drive anywhere."

"In general," the judge said, "people aren't accused until they have really done something to deserve it. But in adjudication there is a lot more than just a question of guilt. Civil rights, for instance."

"It's the same on our side of the lake," Mott said. "We know who was responsible for the murder of Mrs. Espinoza, but we can't bring the guilty parties before you with enough hard evidence to convict. We haven't given that one up, by the way—it's still getting a great deal of attention."

"I'm glad to hear that, Ralph. It was a terrible thing. But we agree that there is no use in bringing the guilty parties before the bar if there isn't firm and positive proof. We're not living under the Code Napoleon, where you have to prove your innocence of a charge. If the solid evidence isn't there, I won't convict."

The waitress reappeared with two servings of soup. She put down an assortment of bread, some water, and Mott's sandwich. "Will there be anything else?" she asked.

"Iced tea," Mott reminded her.

"It's coming."

"Thank you."

She left and was back with it within seconds.

"Let me ask you something," the judge said when they were alone once more. "Suppose a black defendant is in court charged, say, with burglary. Don't you feel that because he is severely disadvantaged and subject to admitted prejudice, he should be shown a little extra consideration?"

Mott had not expected the question, but he did not duck it. "No, I don't. And I don't think he had a thing coming because his ancestors were brought here in slave ships. What happened to them was heinous, but that doesn't apply to him today any more than I would arrest him as a thief because his grandfather once stole a cow."

"You don't feel sorry for him, then?"

"You didn't ask me that. You asked if he should be entitled to extra consideration during the adjudication of his case."

"I'll concede that, but I think you're like most policemen—no real feeling for the individual."

"I challenge that, Sparky," Mott responded. "Policemen are intensely concerned for the welfare of society—for the Mrs. Espinozas of this world, the decent, law-abiding citizens. It's a dedicated profession. If a black man breaks into someone's house and steals that person's possessions, I'll bust him and hope to hell I get a conviction."

"Suppose the man is hungry?"

"Then there's a huge welfare program to help him. We take care

199

of people who need help—and sometimes, I think, a lot of others who don't."

The judge buttered a piece of bread and bit off a corner. "From what I've heard of you," he said, "I expected more than that."

The conversation wasn't going at all the way Mott wanted it to, but a proposition had arisen that he could not ignore. "Let me put it to you this way, Sparky: can you give me any reason that would justify a man's raping your wife?"

The judge was not to be trapped. "We're talking now about a question of degree. Also another factor that hasn't come up at all as yet, and that is the extent to which a person can be rehabilitated. That's the main reason for the parole system. I don't believe that you can support the idea that there is anyone so completely evil that there is no possibility of his eventual normalization and return to society."

"I'm certainly not trying to pick bones with you," Mott said, "but if you ask me a question, you're going to get an honest answer. Let's say that the Romans who tortured early Christians in the arena were misguided, and that Torquemada was overzealous."

"It wouldn't happen today," the judge interjected quickly.

"Hitler wasn't so long ago—but let's bring it closer to home. How about the persons who tortured and murdered innocent Mrs. Espinoza?"

"They were angry because she had betrayed them."

"As I understand the law, Sparky, anger isn't an excuse for murder. And this was premeditated."

The judge fell silent. "Historically our nation is becoming more and more permissive," he said at last. "For example, cohabitating isn't frowned on as much any more."

Mott softened his own tone. "That's totally true," he agreed. "But we've never condoned rape, armed robbery, murder, arson— any of those—and I don't honestly believe that we ever will. We protect the rights of the accused to a fair trial and full consideration of every defense that he has, but if he's then found guilty, the law decrees that he must be punished. And in such a way that the remainder of society is protected."

"For how long? Even a murderer can reform."

"That's true, of course, but suppose that it became generally known that all you have to do is to reform and you can get out of prison immediately. We'd have a mass migration of reformed criminals back into general society. The problem is twofold: they're not too likely to stay reformed, and the penalty for murder would become meaningless."

The judge seemed interested, and entertained, but Mott was uncomfortably aware that he had been led into almost everything he had said. Clearly, despite his apparently passive role, the judge had been calling the signals all along.

At least he had expressed himself with honesty, and he didn't have to apologize to himself for that. Perhaps he had sounded too hardnosed, but the image of Mrs. Espinoza was still too strong in his mind for him to be entirely rational about it.

The rest of the luncheon was pleasant, but the general subject of law enforcement was studiously avoided.

At a little before three in the afternoon, Angel Cardozo went to the men's room. From the first day of his new employment at the Morrison and Hale plant, he had known that he could manage an extra ten- or fifteen-minute break by pretending the need to relieve himself. His foreman was well aware of what he was doing and intended to speak to him about it, but since the very recent episode of the vandalized mural, everyone had been making a massive effort to avoid any more friction of any kind. Apparently the policy was succeeding, because there had been no more incidents within the plant, and the flow of work had reached almost sixty-five percent of the projected full capacity. It was still not a paying proposition, but it was getting better week to week, and the outlook was good.

Angel was a dedicated member of the Spiders, which meant that he harbored a more or less permanent belligerency toward Los Magnolias, who held the turf rights to Belvedere Park. The park was right at the line that separated the two gang territories, but it was on the Magnolias' side. Also, the only available high school for the Spiders' members was also on the Magnolias' turf, so there was no way that the Spiders could attend even if they wanted to.

Of all of the turfs in the barrio, the Spiders had the smallest, hardly more than eight square blocks. The White Roses were on the other side, but there had been a truce for some time between

201

the two gangs. There had been some talk that the two small gangs might combine to make one much larger and stronger one, but the Spiders were a proud lot, and they bitterly resisted the idea of losing their identity.

Angel entered one of the toilet stalls and made himself comfortable. He had already received two pay checks from his new job; the next one that was coming up would provide him with enough funds to buy a set of lifters for his car. He had wanted them for some time. They would be a powerful macho symbol when installed, and his status as the owner would be materially enhanced. He did not like the job he was doing, because each day he was told what to do and that grated strongly on his nature. After the third day of that kind of humiliation, he had carried a knife securely strapped to the inside of his left leg. It was well fitted and difficult to detect, but if he were to need it, it could be in his hand in a matter of three or four seconds. Angel was not one to take unnecessary chances.

The door to the washroom opened, and two more employees came in. Through the crack between the door and the partition he caught a glimpse of them in the mirror. He did not know their names, but they were both Magnolias.

Within a few seconds Angel knew that they too were killing a little time away from their jobs. They conversed in street Spanish as they used the urinals and then went through the motions of washing their hands. Angel had almost forgotten about them, concerned as he was with his own thoughts. Then he heard his name mentioned. That galvanized him into instant attention; he almost held his breath as he listened.

The two Magnolias were laughing over something.

"Saturday he was down on Whittier with Elvira Torres—you see him?" one voice asked.

"Yeah, I see. He with her all right."

That much was true, Angel remembered vividly, because what had followed later in the evening had been some of the best sex he had ever had. Elvira could fuck like a mink, and she had milked him as if he had been a Guernsey cow. She had literally left him breathless, and after a little while the second time had been almost as good. That particular piece of merchandise he intended to keep to himself, both for his own gratification and to deny it to others who were less deserving of such excitement. He had talked to her about that and she had promised.

"You think he knows what she is?" the other voice asked.

"No, he not know she's a *puta*. But someday he find out." The speaker started to laugh, but he stopped abruptly when the door to the supposedly unoccupied stall flew open and Angel burst out, violent rage on his face and a sharp, pointed knife held edge upward in his right hand.

There was a bare moment of stark fear, then Angel lunged. His girl had been called a prostitute, and the barrio held no greater insult than that.

The Magnolias were both fighters, and they reacted with almost blinding speed. One of them ripped a container of paper towels off the wall, his hand in the slot, and he had a weapon of sorts. As he did so, his partner threw himself feet forward to kick the abdomen of his sudden enemy.

Angel sidestepped the attack with snake-like speed and ripped his knife upward. He caught the Magnolia squarely in the leg before he had time to regain his feet and a surge of blood told him he had scored. But before he could do more, the paper towel container smashed hard against the side of his head and his vision danced madly—he could not focus accurately or use his knife with maximum effect. He thrust out nevertheless, knowing that he was likely to hit somehow, somewhere. White-hot rage engulfed him and nothing but blood could mitigate it. There was no place in his consciousness for the least thought of consequences.

His thrust was empty—he hit nothing. Then he felt the paper towel container slam corner first into his body, just over his left kidney. For a second or two he wanted to be sick, but he was fighting for his life and he could not yield.

The door of the washroom burst open, and the two Magnolias ran out. He saw them through his clearing vision, and he dashed after them, blind rage transfixing him and blocking every other thought from his mind. He saw one of his enemies ahead of him and knew that he would never be able to reach him on foot—someone would intervene. The plant was full of people, and already someone was trying to grab him.

He whipped his arm back and threw the knife, desperately hoping it would inflict a mortal wound. He saw it whirl through the air and strike, point first against the back of his target. He knew that it had penetrated; wild joy engulfed him as someone tackled him just above the knees and threw him to the floor. He landed hard, but he was almost unaware of it.

The first responding patrol unit pulled up before the plant barely three minutes after Angel had been captured. The two deputies who ran inside were met by the plant manager himself, who led the way as fast as he was able to the scene of the outbreak. The plant nurse, a thin young woman with glasses and a severe hairdo, was down on her knees attempting to bandage the leg of a young man who was lying on his back and pressing his hands in harsh pain against the sides of his skull. A second victim lay on his face, the hilt of a knife protruding from just under his right shoulder. Three massive Chicano men had Angel in custody: one of them had taken off his belt and with it had strapped the young Spider's arms to his sides.

Deputy Agrivar took in the scene with swift efficiency. He reached for his belt radio and called in a quick, precise evaluation of the situation. He reported at least two casualties and requested back-up aid and paramedics. While he was doing that, his partner, Deputy Sloan, took a quick statement from one of the men re-straining Angel Cardozo. He then cuffed the suspect and returned the leather belt to the man who owned it.

Deputy Agrivar bent over the victim who was lying face down, the knife still in his back. Agrivar did not attempt to remove it— he knew better. The paramedics would be on hand within the next five minutes and they would deal with the problem. He satisfied himself that the victim was still alive and that there was nothing that he himself could do for him. The paramedics had both the equipment and the training to do whatever was necessary.

A few feet away Angel Cardozo was suddenly fighting once again. He kicked out with his right foot and caught one of his captors squarely in the groin. It was totally unexpected, and the shock of the sudden violent pain transfixed the face of the work-man. He let out a sharp, explosive scream and grabbed toward his genitals. As he did so, one of his companions seized hold of Angel and slammed him hard against a supporting post. Deputy Sloan stepped quickly forward, took charge of Angel, and forestalled any more violence. The man who had been kicked was down on his side on the hard concrete, holding his crotch and giving short, sharp cries of anguish. Two more deputies came in on the run; outside the sound of an approaching siren could be heard.

Deputy Agrivar used his radio again to report another injury—possibly two. Angel was leaning against the post holding his own head. The few plant security people were forming a rough perimeter around the scene, keeping the other workers away. Some of the office personnel were also on the work floor. All production had ceased and the spreading stains of blood on the concrete offered the reason why.

Dolores Fernandez stood by fearfully at the plant manager's side, waiting to carry out any instruction that he might have. She was a quick-witted girl, and she already knew the devastating impact this new and serious incident would undoubtedly have on the future of the plant.

George Wilkinson noted her presence and wondered if it was his duty to report what had happened to the main office immediately or if he could wait until it had been dealt with by the deputies and paramedics. He decided that it was his duty to stay right on the spot and to defer the bad news for at least a few minutes. He didn't see any possible way that he could soft-pedal this one, and there might be decisions he would have to make. The insurance people would have to be notified. That would probably bring in the lawyers, and if there was one thing that he did not want at that time, it was lawyers.

Two paramedics came in on the run, carrying their equipment with them. The plant nurse pointed at once to the Magnolia member who still lay face down on the concrete with the knife protruding obscenely from his back. The solid circle of spectators watched intently as the paramedics went to work. They took readings of vital signs, then they expertly removed the knife and literally tore the t-shirt off the victim's body. They maintained radio communication with their base hospital, reporting on the patient's condition.

Another paramedical team appeared and went to work on the victim with the slashed leg. The plant nurse, who had only limited resources available, had done a competent job of staunching the flow of blood from the wound, but the dressing she had applied was already badly soaked and losing its effectiveness. The second team of paramedics split up, one man went to work to replace the leg bandage, while the other turned his attention to the heavy-set, middle-aged man who had been so viciously kicked in the groin. After a brief examination that was necessarily incomplete, he radioed in and received permission to give the patient a pain-killing drug. Seconds later he administered a shot and stood by, waiting for it to take effect. Two ambulance men came in with a Gurney.

Deputies Sloan and Agrivar took Angel out and transported him to the sheriff's station. By that time, at least four units had responded, and a number of other deputies were on hand to control the situation. The man who had been kicked in the groin was carried out on the one available plant-owned stretcher by his friends to the front of the facility, where he was helped into the waiting ambulance. The pain-killing drug had begun to take effect, and he showed little interest in what was going on.

Two minutes later the first paramedic team came out with the Magnolia member who had been knifed in the back and saw him carefully stowed in the ambulance. One of them climbed inside and rode away with the two patients.

That left only the victim who had been badly cut in the leg. A paramedic picked the slim youth up in his arms and carried him outside. As soon as he had gone, the ring of watching workers was broken up. Gradually production resumed. The maintenance supervisor put three men to work cleaning up the spilled blood and restoring the men's washroom to usable condition. The towel container was refastened where it belonged on the wall.

Within half an hour most of the work had been done. It never occurred to the people involved that they were destroying evidence. There was no doubt in their minds as to what had happened, and they were practical men who did not think in terms of police procedures and lawsuits.

Mott learned of the incident some ten minutes after it first occurred. It shook him hard, and for a few moments he let himself give way to his emotions. He knew that as a policeman he should not allow himself that luxury, but he could not help it. He saw the whole picture too clearly, and his first reaction was an intense, surging concern for the people of the barrio.

The Morrison and Hale plant was the first big new source of employment to be opened in East Los Angeles in many years. It represented a substantial investment, and it was a pilot plant for the rest of industry. If it succeeded, then there were many places where other facilities could be built and additional employment opportunities opened up. As soon as there were enough jobs, most of the area's problems would be drastically reduced; gang activity was one of them.

All three incidents at the new plant had been gang-related. The business of running a hand truck into someone's legs had been passed off as a small accident; only a few knew the actual circumstances. But the vandalizing of the fine mural couldn't be overlooked; the quick repair being made was the only mitigating factor. Now a serious knifing had taken place, and Morrison and Hale's management could not be expected to dismiss it as an isolated incident. The barrio had been given a great opportunity, and the gang kids had already badly jeopardized it.

Those reflections consumed about ten seconds of his thinking, then he was ready to take suitable action. He jumped into a car and drove to the plant Code Two, as fast as he safely could without lights or siren. He met a deputy coming out who told him that the suspect and the victims had been taken away. A detective team was coming in. Mott thanked him for the information and went immediately to George Wilkinson's office. He had met the plant manager previously, so no time had to be spent on formalities.

The atmosphere in the small office was deadly. Wilkinson had been on the phone when Mott had been shown in. He hung up almost at once and tried to be pleasant without much success. "Well, Lieutenant," he said. "I see you know that we've had another small problem to deal with."

"Exactly what happened?" Mott asked.

Wilkinson told him all that he knew. As soon as he had finished, he sent Dolores Fernandez for the floor supervisor, who had witnessed the whole thing, apart from its start in the washroom. He gave his account carefully and precisely, knowing as he did so that he was helping, in part, to spike the future hopes for the plant.

"Let me be sure that I've got this straight," Mott said. He knew that he had everything clear in his mind, but he wanted some additional commentary. "The person who started the trouble was apparently Angel Cardozo. I know who he is—he's a member of the Spiders and a hard-core gang member."

"I know," Wilkinson added. "I wouldn't have employed him on my own, but the word we had from headquarters was to try and take on as many of the gang kids as we could consistent with getting any useful work out of them. The company has always been more socially minded than most; our retirement program is one of the best."

"So I understand. Now, we have Cardozo in custody. He's seventeen, as I recall, but I'm sure in view of his past record that we can have him declared unfit to stand trial as a juvenile. That means he'll have to face an adult rap, and it keeps him out of the control of the California Youth Authority, thank God. If I have the account straight, there's no way he's going to avoid going to prison for attempted murder."

"That's fine," Wilkinson said. "But that doesn't help us now."

"Have you talked to your top people about this yet?"

"Yes, there was no way to avoid it. It's part of my responsibility to report any serious incident immediately. Anything, that is, where we have to call the police. I've had to do that twice within the week, and this was by far the more serious matter."

"All right," Mott said. "I'm going to see that the handling of this from our standpoint is as prompt and effective as I can make it. If it will do any good, I'll talk to your management people myself."

"Can you guarantee them that nothing like this will ever reoccur? That's what they'll want to hear."

"You know the answer to that," Mott declared. "I can tell them that we'll do our best, that we'll intensify our protection of your facility, but I can't guarantee that something like this will never happen again. I couldn't no matter where you were located."

Wilkinson didn't want to talk any more, he was too visibly upset. Mott saw it and rose quickly to his feet. "I'm going to handle this myself," he said by way of thin reassurance, and left as quickly as he could.

Back at the station he checked on the detective team that was going to the plant and found out that the two deputies had already left. It was late in the day and the employees would be leaving for home within a short time. Nevertheless, some information might be gained.

From the account that Wilkinson had given him, Mott had a fairly clear picture in his mind of what had gone down—all but the first part. Angel Cardozo appeared very obviously to be the attacker, but appearances in such matters are often highly deceptive, and Mott was in no mood to run on guesswork. He wanted to pin this one down tight as fast as he could, for a very pressing reason: the future of the new plant was obviously at stake. If he could come up with a completed case quickly and take Angel or whoever else had started it out of circulation, he just might be able to persuade the plant owners to give the barrio and its great majority of honorable people another chance. He could not have felt more deeply about it if he had been a Chicano himself.

Deputy Alvarez appeared at the door of his office. He motioned her in and liked the way she sat down. It was a neat trick to be both a uniformed deputy and an appealing female simultaneously, but she managed it effortlessly. "The watch commander thought I ought to check with you before we go out on patrol. We're going to be in two eighty-one, two ninety-one, and two ninety-two."

Mott saw at once why she had been sent in—that area covered the turf of the White Roses, Spiders, and Los Magnolias. Based on what he already knew about the incident at the factory, heavy trouble could arise at any time. Then he remembered that she was fluent in Spanish.

"I'm going to the hospital to talk with the victims," he said before he thought too much about it. "I presume that they speak English, but would you care to come along?"

"I'd like to very much."

He picked up his phone and asked the watch commander to relieve Alvarez so that he could take her with him to the hospital. That was quickly attended to without trouble, after which he led the way onto the parking lot, where he picked up one of the plain cars. He could have taken his own, but under the circumstances he preferred to use an official vehicle.

As he turned from Third north onto Eastern, Elena said, "You're really up-tight about this one—it shows."

"Yes," Mott responded. "And you know why. I may be looking too hard at the dim side, but this is the second major incident at the new plant within a week; Morrison and Hale would have to be staffed with saints not to react pretty negatively to it. The main hope right now is to show an example of fast, efficient police work good enough to restore their confidence. A lot of jobs may depend on it."

"You're really concerned for the people of East Los Angeles, aren't you, Ralph."

"I am. I know how much this plant means to them. Because if it closes, then hell will freeze over before another company will take a chance on opening up here."

"I like you for that." she said.

Mott didn't respond, because there was nothing he could really say. He turned onto the San Bernardino Freeway when they reached it and gave his attention to the radio until they were at the entrance of the official parking area. If anything was going down between the Magnolias and the Spiders, he wanted to know about it immediately.

They stopped at the entrance security desk and got the directions they needed. Mott elected to go first to see Oscar Ledesma, the Magnolia member who had been slashed in the leg. He would certainly be able to talk, and he might even feel like doing so. As they went down the long corridors of the huge facility, he briefed his companion. "This kid is a hard-core gang member. He's been involved in a number of incidents, but we've never hung anything substantial on him. He's eighteen and, for a wonder, he goes to high school off and on. In any other environment he might be a pretty good kid; as it is he has three or four minor convictions. He's been in and out of the hands of the Youth Authority without any visible results. We don't have him down for a gun user."

After a right-hand turn and half of another lengthy corridor, they reached the ward that Mott had been seeking. There were eight beds inside, seven of them occupied. Oscar was in the third one down on the left-hand side. For a hospital patient, he looked moderately healthy, and there were no evidences of his injury visible.

Mott drew up two chairs to the bedside and then sat down. "Hello, Oscar," he said. "How are you feeling?"

"Not too bad. Who you, man?"

"My name's Mott. I'm with the Sheriff's Department. This is Deputy Alvarez."

"Yeah, I know about you. Hey, she your girl friend, I hear. Nice stuff." He looked at Elena. "You like him, heh?"

"Yes, of course," she answered, and then added. "Everyone does."

"Alvarez. You Chicano, right?"

"Right."

"Habla Espanol?"

"Si."

The boy in the bed grinned a little and poured out a small stream of Spanish. He seemed to know automatically that Mott couldn't understand. Elena answered him in the same language. Mott let it go on, because obviously some kind of rapport was being built, and he wanted that very much.

When the spurt of conversation was ended he looked at her and asked, "What was that all about?"

"Oscar wanted to know if we were sleeping together and how often. He thinks it is good taste on your part to choose a Chicano girl." She said that as dispassionately as if she had been reporting on the weather. "For your love making, that is."

"Yeah, man," Oscar added. "You fuck her good, right?"

"I'm married, Oscar; I've got a very nice wife."

"Good. That give you something on the side—at home."

Mott smiled and pretended to go along with the joke. He knew that he was compromising his companion just a little in doing so, but she could take care of herself. "I'll tell you this," he said, "Any man who gets to sleep with Deputy Alvarez will be very lucky."

"You right there, man. I get outta here, I take the job. Satisfaction guaranteed, like they say."

"Fine, Oscar, I haven't heard any of the girls complaining. Now, I want you to tell me what happened this afternoon. We've got Angel Cardozo in custody, and of course he's got his story. But I want you to tell me what really happened."

Oscar waited for a second or two while he shifted the position of his cut leg. As he did so, a small bulge made by the dressings could be seen under the covers that protected the lower half of his body.

"Me and Freddy Ruiz, we been working all afternoon, so we went to the crapper to take a leak, see. We don't do nothin'—we just talking. I'm washin' and Freddy, he on my right side next to the wall there. All of a sudden Angel he come out of one of the places like he gone mad. I see quick he got a knife, and I don't want no part of that, man, cause I'm standin' there with my bare hands and they's wet. I do the best I can—I jump up and try to kick him back. I think he drop Angel Dust, man, but I got no time to think about it. That's where I got cut—he comes up with that knife and he gets me good in the leg. Right away I'm all blood down there.

"Freddy, he real good man. He grab the towel holder, and he smack Angel good with it. But Angel he not quit, he still got the knife and he out of his mind, man. So when Freddy yank open the door I go outta there, like I got my ass on fire. Freddy, he come after me cause at least he got somethin' to fight with. I ain't got nothin', and already my leg ain't so good. I run to where a bunch of older guys are and then my leg goes out—I ain't goin' no place no more. I look back and I see Freddy go down. He got a knife in him, man, right in the back. Then about six guys, they jump on Angel and it's all over. Except that me and Freddy's in the stinkin' hospital. How he, anyway?"

"I haven't seen him yet, but I will. Then, if you'd like, I'll stop back and tell you how he is."

"That's O.K., man. You O.K."

"Thanks, Oscar. Now, why do you think Angel did that?"

"Like I said, man, I think he drop Angel Dust. You know what that do."

"I certainly do," Mott agreed. "Thanks, Oscar, and we'll be back."

"Give it to her once for me, O.K.?"

Mott got up. "See you later," he concluded and with Elena got safely out of range.

They were unable to talk to Freddy Ruiz; he had been in surgery and was in the recovery room. The doctor they spoke to did not think that it would be practical to try and interview him for at least twenty-four hours. The patient was believed to be in satisfactory condition, but it was too soon after the procedure to give out any definite prognosis.

Mott kept his word and called back to give Oscar Ledesma the news. He wished at the moment that he had not brought Elena with him, but the Ruiz boy, according to his card, much preferred Spanish and would talk more freely in that language.

He reclaimed the car, put his companion inside, and drove back down toward the freeway. When they were out of the hospital

212

grounds, he put a question. "You were observing everything. How much of his story did you believe?"

"Only one thing definitely," Elena answered. "The rest of it sounded all right, and a lot of what he said can be checked with reliable witnesses. But I didn't buy that part about the washroom —it sounded a little fishy to me."

"I thought the same thing," Mott agreed. "What was the part you definitely accepted?"

"When he described me as a good lay," Elena answered.

Angel Cardozo sat sullenly, slumped on the base of his spine, when he was brought from his cell for questioning. With him came a young Chicano in his late twenties. He wore an extremely full head of hair, a massive mustache, and a ready-made suit with six-inch lapels. His name was Minjarez, and he introduced himself as the accused's lawyer.

Mott shook hands with him and invited him to be seated. "Mr. Minjarez, I'm about to question your client concerning the events that took place at the Morrison and Hale plant around three this afternoon. For your information, we have talked with one of the victims in the hospital and with several reliable witnesses who saw much of what happened when it went down. So far, all of them tell substantially the same story. Now I'm inviting your client to tell me what happened from his viewpoint."

"Suppose you put the questions, Lieutenant, and I'll advise Angel whether or not he should answer each one."

Mott had been up against this kind of thing before and he knew exactly how to handle it. "Very well. To simplify matters, suppose I put the questions and Angel answers them, unless you have an objection."

Minjarez revealed some inexperience by considering that for several seconds; then he gave his consent.

Mott began slowly with routine questions concerning Angel's employment at the plant, the nature of his duties, how well he liked the work, and his opinions concerning his supervisors. In that way he laid a careful foundation of questions to which no reasonable objection could be taken. After several minutes of this he had Angel talking and his lawyer keeping still, which to him was an ideal state of affairs.

That accomplished, he began to probe into more sensitive areas.

"Angel, before today you'd never been involved in any trouble at the plant—is that right?"

"That's right, man, ask anybody."

"Good. While you were working there, did anyone ever attempt to attack you or interfere with your work."

Angel looked at his lawyer, who remained silent. "No," he responded tersely.

"Now, Angel, I want to ask you why you took a knife with you to work."

"I don't want him to answer that," Minjarez said.

"Mr. Minjarez, I don't know if you have been told this or not, but after your client was arrested, he was body searched for any weapons or other illegal possessions. That, of course, was strictly proper and routine procedure—we do it uniformly to all suspects taken into custody. During this search we discovered a knife scabbard taped to his left leg; it's now being held as evidence. Angel was seen by at least a dozen people to throw a knife which struck Frederick Ruiz in the back and inflicted a serious injury. The knife in question exactly fits the scabbard."

"But that isn't proof that it was ever kept there," the lawyer interjected.

Mott refused to be flapped. "Considering the circumstances as I have set them out for you, Mr. Minjarez, I believe that it would be next to impossible to convince any judge or jury that Angel didn't have a knife in that holder. Otherwise why would he have taped it to his leg? And, also, you might consider how you would explain his having the knife if it didn't come from that scabbard."

Minjarez was obviously uncomfortable with that, but he did not want to concede the point if he could avoid it. "Suppose you rephrase the question," he suggested.

"Certainly," Mott agreed. "Angel, did you have a good reason to take a knife with you to work?"

The young suspect looked at his attorney, who this time remained silent. "For protection, man—and I needed it!"

"All right. Now as I understand it, a little before three you left your work and went to the men's room. I'm not questioning your right to do that, I'm just asking if that's correct."

"Yeah, man, I go."

"When you entered the washroom, was anyone else in there?"

"No, nobody else there." He looked again at his attorney, but Minjarez kept still. He was smart enough to realize that that fact had already been checked out and there was no point in arguing it.

"Just to be sure, Angel, were the doors to the stalls open enough so that you could see they were empty?"

"That's right."

"Now, what did you do first when you went into the men's room?"

Angel looked around him very quickly for a moment, possibly hoping that someone would interrupt the interrogation. When no one appeared, he answered. "I gotta take a crap, so I go in a stall and shit."

"There are three stalls in that washroom, Angel. Which one did you use?"

"I don't remember—the middle one, I guess."

"While you were having your bowel movement, did anyone else come into the washroom? I mean, before you finished."

Angel squinted and appeared to think. "No, not while I was crapping."

"Now, I understand that two other men came into the washroom while you were still there, is that right?"

Again the young suspect looked at his attorney, who gave no sign. "Yeah, two guys came in."

"And where were you at the time?"

"I still in the place, man. I was still pullin' my pants back up."

Mott nodded as though he were fully satisfied with the answers he was getting. His manner was deceptively mild. It seemed as though he considered the whole thing a boring routine that had to be completed before he could go home. He appeared almost uninterested.

"What happened next, Angel?"

That was the key question, of course, but as it stood it appeared so innocent there was no basis for objection. Angel looked swiftly and hard at his attorney. Minjarez appeared about to interrupt, but didn't—there was no premise on which he could base an objection.

"Well, we got into a fight . . ."

Mott's brow furrowed as though he did not understand. "When

you were in the stall, did you have the door closed?"

"Of course, man." He answered that quickly on his own.

"Then with the door shut, the other two men couldn't see you, right?"

"Yeah. No way, man."

"And you couldn't see them."

"No."

"Now I don't understand something here. When they came in, they couldn't see you and you couldn't see them."

Minjarez spoke up. "Lieutenant, I think that I'll have to advise my client not to go along any further with this line of questioning."

Mott was not disconcerted. "As you wish, sir, but it might be easier for him to answer now, because at the preliminary hearing he will be asked these same questions, under oath, and the court will be able to direct him to answer. I want to find out if your client was attacked."

The attorney drummed his fingertips on his chair arm and then looked carefully at his client. "You may proceed on a question-to-question basis," he said.

"Fine. Thank you for your cooperation, Mr. Minjarez. Angel, I'd like to ask you what started the fight. They must have done something to you."

To Angel the question was all in his favor—it gave him the chance to prove his justification. Before his attorney had a chance to say anything, he answered with quick intensity. "I still inside the crapper stall when those guys made me blood *insulto,* like they call you cocksucker, man."

Mott was very quick with his next question. "What did they call you, Angel?"

"They say my girl, she *puta.* "

"Prostitute," Minjarez translated quickly. "Please understand, Lieutenant, that in the Chicano community such an insult is unendurable. It would provoke the most peace-loving individual to immediate retaliation. It's a cultural thing, like stripping the veil off the face of a Muslim woman on a public street."

"Thank you for the explanation, counselor, that's most helpful." Mott turned back to his now simmering subject. "I understand that you were grossly insulted while you were still in the toilet stall—is that the way it was?"

"Right on, man!"

"Then they must have seen you go into the washroom and knew that you were in there."

"Maybe, but I think they not know. They never dare say that they know I listening."

"So they were talking about you in a public place and you happened to overhear them."

"That's right."

"Angel, if they insulted you, would that mean that they had insulted the Spiders, too?"

Angel couldn't wait to answer that. "Sure, man. Our gang, we always together. You insult one, you got big trouble. Real big trouble."

"And the two guys that insulted you, what gang do they belong to?"

Minjarez raised his hand to stop the answer, but Angel was giving his full attention to Mott, teaching the stupid *gringo* what he ought to know. "They Magnolias, a lousy gang we beat up any time we like."

"Do you think they insulted you because you were a member of the Spiders?"

"Of course, man. Nobody my gang ever say anything like that. They want trouble, man. They ask big for it. They get it."

Minjarez half rose out of his chair. "I don't want to go into this gang thing any further, Lieutenant. In fact, I think that my client has been very patient. He has answered all the questions that he can at this time. You have established the fact that he was mortally insulted in a public place and he then sought to redeem his honor, as any respectable Chicano would feel compelled to do. That's the significant fact. You must understand that such a vile verbal attack is fully equivalent to a physical one in this community. Angel was therefore defending himself with remarkable courage when the incident started. Both of his opponents fled the washroom after having provoked him beyond endurance. Also, let me add, that one of them seized a weapon off the wall and struck Angel so hard with it, he was temporarily almost senseless and not responsible

217

for his actions. He was, in fact, struck twice—hard physical blows—and he defended himself as best he could. One of his attackers jumped into the air and tried to slam him into the hardware with a lethal karate kick. Then, and only then, Angel used his knife in desperate self-protection. You can see that he has very strong grounds for a civil suit. It is possible that we may not file in the interests of keeping the plant operating successfully as it is now. If we don't, it will represent a major concession by my client on behalf of the whole community. In view of all this, I strongly recommend that you release him from custody so that we can allow the whole thing to simmer down as fast as possible."

"Thank you for your opinion, counselor. I can't release Angel at this time, but I thank you for your cooperation."

He sent the prisoner back to his cell and then looked at his watch. If he was going to get any dinner, he would have to go to one of the twenty-four-hour coffee shops on Atlantic Avenue. He was just about to leave when the indefatigable Brother Julio appeared in the doorway to his office, and he knew that he was in for another long session.

CHAPTER NINETEEN

WHEN WORD of what had happened at the factory reached Brother Julio, it seemed to him for a minute that the pit of hell had opened at his feet. Furthermore he was already tottering on the brink, with no opportunity to offer a desperate prayer before he began to fall into the hideous depths. God was testing him as He had never done before. For the second time within a week, gang activity had disrupted the smooth operation of the plant, and what was critical was the fact that this second incident was far more serious than the first. Blood had been shed, three people were in the hospital, and another had been taken into custody.

He had worked for well over a year, visiting company after company, trying to interest one of them in opening the barrio plant and making use of local unemployed workers. At last it had pleased God that he succeed and Morrison and Hale had gone ahead on his assurances. The whole project was now in serious jeopardy, or worse. Something had to be done, and instantly would not be too soon.

Because he knew the barrio as few men did and understood the gang psychology with penetrating insight, he jumped into his car and drove at once to the hospital to interview Oscar Ledesma. He arrived there at about the same time that Ralph Mott was seeing George Wilkinson, the plant manager. Using the semi-Spanish street patois that all the gangs employed, he talked to Oscar with the towering authority of the Church behind him. At least he let it appear that way, with the result that within five minutes he knew almost the whole story, including the details of the insult that had provoked Angel Cardozo to such violent reaction.

Brother Julio went next to talk to the other victim, but he was in surgery and would not be able to answer questions for some time, probably not before morning at the earliest.

Brother Julio then drove as fast as he dared to the East Los Angeles sheriff's station and asked to see Angel. Normally that would not have been permitted, but Brother Julio was a different matter, and the word had long been out that he was to be given every help possible whenever he asked for it. The watch commander assented and the Brother was admitted to Angel's cell.

No one overheard the conversation that took place there, which was appropriate, because Brother Julio was acting, at least to some extent, in his religious capacity, and the interview was therefore privileged. Angel tried to make a good case for himself, but he did not succeeded in deceiving the brother for a moment. He admitted what he had done, knowing that the Brother would never take the stand against him. Angel did not regret a thing. His macho had been challenged, and he had defended it as more important than life itself.

From the sheriff's station Brother Julio drove the short distance to the turf of the Spiders. He knew where the gang regularly hung out, and as he had expected, almost all of the members were there. He wasted no time in preliminaries. He signaled them to gather around him as he stood, with his back to the wall of a convenient building. It had been observed by those who knew him best that Brother Julio's survival depended, among other things, on the fact that he never took any unnecessary chances.

"I have very bad news for you," he said, "and some urgent advice to give."

"What they do to Angel?" he was asked.

"Angel is in custody. This time he's facing a very heavy charge. He is probably going to go to prison for many years."

There was a shuffling of feet after that and some sideways looks among the various members. The Spiders were a small gang, and they could not afford to lose one of their key members.

"That is not the worst part," Brother Julio continued. "He has made a violent attack on three others at the new factory. The management will be outraged by this. They may even close the plant down for good."

That was the bad news that they had not already known. And Angel was their gang member. There was no possible way to deny it.

The Brother continued delivering the bad news, his voice and manner suggesting Judgment Day. "Angel attacked with a knife two of the members of Los Magnolias. He did this in the men's room. He cut one of them very deeply in the leg, slicing into the muscles. He is now in the hospital, and I fear for the future use of his leg. When he had done that terrible thing, Angel then threw his knife into the back of the other person he attacked. That Magnolia had to be taken to the hospital in serious condition. He is now being operated upon by the surgeons. I pray that he will live, but I am not sure. It is possible that the knife penetrated into a lung."

He was not sure himself of what the effect of that kind of injury might be, but none of his listeners seemed about to challenge him. He had their total attention.

"I tell you that Angel did this, and I know that you believe me. I do not lie."

He stopped, but no one gave any reaction at all.

"I now warn you that Los Magnolias are fearfully enraged. They may attack you at any time, for they know all about this. I am going to talk to them and try to make them understand that it is only Angel who is to blame, but I cannot promise that I will succeed."

The soberness of his words had had their effect. The Spiders knew that Los Magnolias had every right to come looking for them with guns, and that this time they were up against deep trouble that was not of their own making.

"I will now give you some advice," Brother Julio continued. "You will take it at once and do as I tell you, or I will not be responsible for the consequences. Do not stand here and wait to be attacked. Go at once to your homes and stay there. I will see what I can do, but it will be very difficult. The Magnolias have already had two other things, bad things, done to them, and for the sake of the whole barrio they have endured them."

"You mean the mural, man?" he was asked.

"Yes, the mural, and there was also something inside the plant which was passed off as an accident. And remember also that they had to give up some of their turf in order to allow the plant to open in the first place. They cannot afford to lose anything more, and now they will be bloodthirsty for vengeance."

The Brother managed to look very much like the avenging angel himself. "Now I direct that you break up immediately. Go to your homes. Stay there. Do not waste another minute."

The Spiders were a fierce and independent gang, but they knew when they had been dealt a completely bust hand. The presence of the messenger of the Church gave them the excuse they needed to stage a temporary tactical retreat. There was no further discussion—the gang members began, one by one, to drift away. In less than a minute the last of them was gone.

Then, and only then, Brother Julio got back into his car and set out once again to do the Lord's work. He drove fearlessly onto the turf of Los Magnolias. He did so with the realization that never in his experience had a gang been so patient and therefore now so almost certain to explode. From their standpoint they had suffered unendurable indignity, and the only thing that would be concerning them would be how best to wreak their vengeance.

It was the worst possible time to approach them about anything, but no other time would do. It had to be now and the Brother knew it.

The whole gang was gathered at their usual corner, the same one where Brother Julio had met them the first time that he had brought Mott to meet them. As he crossed the street to where they were, he could almost feel the extreme hostility in the air.

Although shaking inside, the Brother kept his outward appearance of calmness. When he reached the place where the Magnolias were waiting, he did not have to ask them to gather around him. They did so on their own, and they did not allow him to rest his back against the building, as he had done before.

"I came to bring you the most recent news," he said. "A few

222

minutes ago I talked with Oscar in the hospital. He is all right. He is resting comfortably and he has been given something to stop the pain. He has a bad cut in his leg, but the doctors told me he will recover without trouble."

That was received in dead silence. No one spoke and no one moved.

"I tried to see Freddy Ruiz, but he was in surgery. I have left word that I am to be notified as soon as he has begun his recovery. When I am through here, I am going to go to the church to pray for him."

When he stopped speaking, the silence was complete once more. It was deadly quiet, but Brother Julio did not allow himself to think of that.

"I have also been to the sheriff's station," he went on, apparently as calmly as before. "There I learned that there is no question who injured Oscar and Freddy—it was Angel Cardozo."

For the first time someone spoke. "We know that, man." The words were individually frozen.

"There is more that you will want to know. He is seventeen, but he will not be tried in juvenile court—he will have to stand trial as an adult. This will have only one outcome that I can see: he will be sent to prison for many years. He has a bad record and that will increase the length of his sentence."

He stopped, hoping that someone would say something, but the ominous silence remained unbroken.

"Now there is some more you should know, and I have to ask you something. Do you know who Elvira Torres is?"

For a few seconds he feared that they were not going to answer him. If they didn't, then he was in serious physical danger, and he knew it. He knew a little about fighting, but it would be utterly hopeless to try to defend himself against the whole gang. The best way would be to do nothing and simply take whatever they inflicted upon him. If he did not fight back, it might be a little less severe.

Ernesto finally answered him. "We know her."

"What is her character?" He wanted desperately to ask if she were a prostitute, but if he did, he would be putting a sin against her name that she might not merit, and he could not do that.

223

He thought he detected a very slight lessening of the tension, but he was not at all sure.

"She *puta,* man."

That did it. Now he was free to explore that avenue a little more, to try and build up to what he had to tell them. "Does she take money?"

Again a silence. Then presently another member answered him. "We said she *puta,* man. You no believe us?"

That hung things on the ragged edge again, and Julio was almost afraid to breathe. His next question could well decide his fate. He knew that he had to show complete acceptance of what they had said. "How good at it is she?"

That drew a sneer, because every member there knew that Julio had taken an oath of celibacy and that he had never had intercourse with a woman. He was the least qualified judge there could be. Ernesto could not resist the temptation to rub it in a little. "She a red hot fuck, man. She good. Another thing: she damn good cocksucker. She make you go right through the roof."

They waited to see how he would react to that.

Brother Julio would never pass gossip, but now he had to state some facts because of desperate urgency. He did so only because he knew them to be true and because they were already on the record. "Angel Cardozo has been going with Elvira. He did not knew what she was, and he thought she was his girl."

That put Angel in a ridiculous position, but the Brother knew that it could not be helped. In this instance the end was so overwhelmingly important, he could not afford all of the Christian charity that he would have liked. He was playing an intensely dangerous game, and in that situation he could not afford to put down even one of his cards.

He went on calmly. "This afternoon he went into the toilet room at the factory. He went into a booth and sat down."

He stopped, trying to sense how much of that they had already known, and could detect nothing.

"Oscar and Freddy came in. They used the urinals and then washed their hands. While they were doing that, one of them talked about Angel, and said that his girl was a *puta.* They laughed about it. Angel heard them. He did not know it was the truth."

He stopped, very careful to say no more. He had given them the reason why Angel had started the fight, a reason that they would understand completely. It did not mean that they would accept it, but it would satisfy them as to why the attack had been made. There was a good chance that they had thought the Spiders had been looking for an opportunity to start a war and that Angel, seeing two of his potential enemies at an unguarded time in the washroom, had decided to go ahead and score big in the first round.

Now they knew better. They at least knew why the attack had been launched, and they knew also that Angel had made a fool of himself. He had gone with a prostitute without knowing it and then had fought in defense of his nonexistent honor.

He had lost all of his macho, and his gang had also suffered. And macho was more important than anything else a gang could possess. Brother Julio had brought the news that Angel Cardozo had all but cut off his own balls.

The Spiders had been disgraced by one of their leading members, and every one of them had to know it—or would know it before the night was over.

Los Magnolias had been put in a superior position, for ridicule was the poison that no gang could possibly endure.

"You shit us, man?" one of the gang members asked.

Brother Julio knew instantly that the question had been asked to try to make him answer "no shit," but they could not force him to say that. "It is the truth," he said. "I do not lie."

When he had finished those few words he knew that his mission had been successful. Los Magnolias had been given some valuable ammunition, and it would be carefully spent all over the barrio. But deadly as it was, it was not the kind that explodes and kills or the kind that that cripples and maims. He was almost sure that Los Magnolias would not go out shooting after the Spiders for at least the next several days.

The air was less tense then, and Brother Julio knew that he would be allowed to leave in peace. He had given them something, and for that he would be permitted to go. He knew they had not for a moment forgotten that it had been he who had talked them into allowing the plant to open on their turf and also into permit-

225

ting members of other gangs, such as Angel, to pass to and from the facility.

Whether the plant would overlook this latest outbreak of violence, he had no way of knowing. He went back to his car with that cold fear still in his heart.

CHAPTER TWENTY

THE FORMAL announcement that Morrison and Hale had made a firm decision to abandon operations at their new East Los Angeles facility hit like a bombshell. Immediate angry protest meetings were held and racism was charged. Suddenly it appeared as if every social service agency in the barrio was up in arms. In response, the company held a news conference to explain the matter to the press.

The chairman of the board took on the distasteful job himself and succeeded in making a good impression for his company. He explained why the plant had been opened in the first place and the desire of Morrison and Hale to give employment to minority groups, particularly in areas where jobs were badly needed. The fact that that plant had been opened in East Los Angeles in the first place supported his words.

He stated truthfully that their insurance coverage had been cancelled and that they had not been able to find any carrier who would accept the risk. Without adequate insurance it was clearly impossible to continue. The decision was a costly one, but the company had not been given any choice. He answered a number of questions very reasonably and had copies of his statement handed out to the media. He did not refer to the unfortunate incidents that had caused the insurance protection to be withdrawn.

Less than a week later the job of dismantling the plant had begun. Once more a procession of trucks backed up to the loading docks, but this time they were taking equipment away. More than two hundred employees had been given termination notices carefully stating that the recipients were being released only because of "conditions beyond the ability of management to control."

A pall spread over the entire barrio, and with an intensity that was dangerous. Captain Gutierrez increased his patrol force to maximum strength. He had read the signs and knew them all too well.

During one day, three different neighborhood stores were held up by gang members. There was one knifing, fortunately not serious. Six attacks on pedestrians, principally purse snatchings, were suspected of being gang-related. Two suspects were caught; both of them were active gang members.

At the Morrison and Hale plant Lorenzo Archuleta continued to work on his mural. The damage that had been done to it had been fully repaired, and he was continuing in a new area. He knew what had happened, of course, but in his mural he had seen a vision and no matter what happened, he was determined to finish it. The new owners of the building might not like it and decide to paint it over, but that was a risk he had to take.

The face that he was working on seemed almost to leap off the wall.

Ralph Mott sat in his office trying to remember that a policeman is not supposed to get involved with the people he encounters on his job. Normally that was sound advice, but it did not apply while trucks were backing up and removing equipment from what had been a promising new plant in the barrio. What might have gone down as an almost routine street knifing had destroyed the best opportunity the barrio had seen in a decade. He was heartsick about it, not for his own sake, but for the decent, honorable people whose new hopes had been snatched away.

Elena Alvarez appeared at the door of his office. "Ralph," she began without formality, "we just came in. They're moving out all right."

"Yes, I know."

"Goddamn it to hell," she said, and Mott knew that he was not alone in his thoughts. Probably the whole station shared them.

Mike Wickman came in and laid two pieces of cardboard on Mott's desk. "The captain's compliments," he said. "Two good seats for the championship fight at the Olympic tonight. He can't make it and thought you might enjoy it." He left before he would have to say anything about what was on everyone's mind.

Elena looked over. "Sixth row ringside," she noted. "That should put you where the action is."

"Wait a minute," Mott said and picked up his phone.

"The fights?" Nancy didn't quite believe him. "Go if you'd like to, but I'd just as soon not. I don't really care for that sort of thing —I thought you knew."

He had known, but he was still disappointed. He loved his wife, but it would have been an added bonus if Nancy had shared his interest in sports. He had taken her to one baseball game, and she had pretended that she was interested, but nobody had ever taught her to appreciate the game. Football, to her, was simply senseless—she didn't understand it at all and didn't especially care to learn.

He told her that to turn down the captain's gift would definitely not be politic and then hung up. He knew what he was going to do and he deliberately didn't allow himself to think of it. "Nancy can't make it," he said. "Would you have any interest in going?"

"Would it be all right with her?" That, of course, was what she was expected to say.

Again he refused to consider the matter. "She knows that I'm going, and she certainly doesn't expect me to go alone. You heard me tell her that I have two tickets."

"In that case," Elena said. "I'd love to go. I've been following the challenger, and he looks very good. He's a boy from Mexico, you know. However it goes, it should be a damn good fight."

That made him feel a little better. When he was alone he allowed himself to realize that he had just dated up a member of his staff. Obviously he would be expected to take her to dinner; he

229

would let her decide where she would like to go. Candlelight and wine hardly went with a prefight date, and he doubted if she would ask for that. She wasn't one to take advantage.

A queer thought came to him at that moment: when he got home and was with Nancy once more, he would make it a point to make love to her, just to let her know. Then he remembered that he couldn't—she was having her period.

One of those things. He refused to chide himself for having made a date with Elena. He could visualize a bearded little man with a thick Germanic accent and eyeglasses on a black ribbon telling him that he was infused with guilt. To hell with him! He knew guilt when he saw it—it was his profession. Of course he had felt it when Mrs. Espinoza had been killed, but he had not deliberately harmed her. That would have been impossible.

Wes McBride came in. "In the mural vandalism job," he said, "I've got it pinned down. Four of the Lagunas were in on it, and I can name them. I let them know I've got them spotted. How do you want me to take it from here? Shall I come down hard and try to get someone to cop or hold it over their heads for a while?"

"Dangle it. We can't get a heavy enough conviction to mean very much. For one thing, the defense will contend that there is hardly a building in the barrio that hasn't been spray painted repeatedly. They can bring pictures of the local art work into court and make us look like monkeys."

"That's how I see it," McBride agreed. "On the Espinoza killing: we're at a temporary dead end. We've sweated Los Counts as much as the law allows—and possibly a fraction more—and no dice. They've all been through interrogation before."

Mott didn't say anything to that. He didn't want to.

"Lastly, the good part. I was up at the hospital this morning— we took in an S-3 victim for attention. Danny Torres was on hand, gathering up soiled linen. You've done something there. I spoke to him briefly, and he still can't believe his new job. It looks like he's going to stick."

That made things a helluva lot better, and Mott attacked his paper work in a somewhat improved frame of mind.

He did not know that almost at that moment Marcellino Acosta, better known to his fellow members of La Calle Verona as Chino, was being released from the hospital. The vicious stab wound that had kept him flat on his back for some time had healed and he was able to move about more or less normally. If he had had a reliable personal doctor and a home where he could have recuperated under reasonable care, he might have been released sooner. As it was, the hospital personnel in charge of his case had considered it more prudent to keep him a little longer until they were sure that he could survive on the jungle streets of gangland. They knew all about him, and they were reluctant to put him back into circulation. But they were medical people, not policemen.

Chino did not waste any time. He knew all about the disastrous shootout between his gang and Laguna Mara on the hospital parking lot, and he anticipated correctly that macho would still be at a subdued level. He went to his home, checked in briefly, and then had a substantial lunch of the kind of food he had been starved for while he had been subsisting on hospital rations. After three helpings of refried beans he went out once more and rejoined what remained of his gang.

It did not take fifteen minutes for him to be fully informed on everything that had happened while he was gone. He was told about the plant's closing and the stricken feeling that was permeating the entire barrio. That did not concern him too much—he had much more immediate matters on his mind. More than anything else, he wanted to know the identity of the four members of Los Counts who had attacked him.

Almost to his disbelief, the other members of his gang couldn't tell him. No one else had seen them, and no one at all had been talking. Unless he could identify them himself, revenge would have to be extracted on a haphazard basis, by hitting any members of the Counts that they could find off their turf and within range.

To Chino that was totally unsatisfactory. After he made sure that there was no information at all that he could get on the spot, he got into his car, started it after a little difficulty, and began to cruise. As he drove, a daring plan came into his mind.

He was still unarmed. His best weapon was the knife—he was an expert with it—but he was still troubled by his healing wound and not yet fully ready for combat. But he did have one thing going for him that he knew he could depend upon: he had an almost photographic memory. Once he had seen something he could remember it indefinitely, and there was very little that went on that escaped his attention.

The more he thought about his plan, the better he liked it. It seemed to be foolproof and there was no way that he could lose. He turned his car northward and headed toward Third Street. When he reached the sheriff's station, he drove into the visitors' parking lot, left his vehicle, and presented himself at the counter as anyone else might have done.

He was, of course, in uniform: the white t-shirt, the slashed blue jeans, and the broken-down tennis shoes that he wore almost every day of his life. The deputy behind the counter knew that he was a gang kid the moment he came into view. Gang kids never came to the station unless they were brought, either in custody or else, occasionally, when they came in with Brother Julio to try and make a deal.

"Yes, sir," the deputy said, using the standard form of address. He put his palms on the counter and waited with genuine interest to see what the gang kid wanted.

"I wanna ask somethin'," Chino said. "I born here—I citizen. So I got rights, yes?"

The deputy nodded gravely. "You certainly do," he agreed. He reserved the private thought that there were times when he probably had too many.

"I just got outta the hospital—this mornin'. Four guys, they jumped me on the street and they cut up my gut. I wanna talk to somebody about it."

The deputy could hardly believe it. It was almost a religion in gangland that the cops were never called in to settle a gang matter. However, miracles were said to be occurring all the time, and he was not one to turn down a possible gift from the gods. "Please wait a moment," he said and disappeared inside.

No one in Mott's gang control unit was in the station. The lieutenant himself was out somewhere, and so were all of the other personnel of the section. A burglary detective was in and although he was relatively new in East Los Angeles, he was willing to help. Chino was brought in and seated at the side of his desk.

Very carefully, Chino told his story. By happy coincidence he did not need to lie even once. He had been a totally innocent victim, and he made the most of it. When he reached the point of his hospital release, he made an added statement that sounded highly logical. "My gang, we been hit hard—two guys dead. We don't want no more of that. Them mothers that hit me, I wanna make a complaint. Then you go out and bust their ass, that right?"

"That's our job," the detective agreed. He picked up a pencil and held it poised over a block of yellow paper. "Give me their names."

Chino had been waiting for that. "I don' know their names, man, but I know what they look like. You wanna get an artist or somethin'?"

The detective knew, as he had to, that the station had gang books with pictures of all the known gang members. They were used from time to time to help victims identify their attackers. He did not see that the complainant in this instance was himself a gang member should make that much difference. The big shoot-out might well have put the fear of God into the youth. "Do you know what gang they come from?" he asked.

Chino knew better than to come up with too ready an answer. "I not sure," he said. "But could be the Counts. I heard talk."

That figured, so the detective got the Counts gang book. He laid it on the desk before Chino and gave instructions. "Just look at the pictures," he directed. "Look at them carefully and see if there is anyone you recognize."

Chino appeared to concentrate as he slowly turned the pages of the book. On each one there was a picture and, underneath, some data. The fourth page that he turned showed him the face of Jambo, and he recognized it instantly. But not by the slightest sign did he give any indication of his find. He glanced at the page exactly as he had looked at the others and then turned. By the time he had gone through the entire book—and it was a thick one—he looked up with a half-disappointed expression. "I ain't sure," he said.

That, of course, was a bad sign from the detective's viewpoint: an uncertain identification was of no value at all. Nevertheless he gave it one more try. "Is there any picture you would like to see again?" he asked.

Before Chino could answer, Deputy Rose came into the room. He took in the situation with a single glance and came over at once. "What's the problem?" he asked.

"This young man was attacked on the street by four apparent

gang members. He doesn't know who they are. He got out of the hospital this morning. He's here to make a complaint, but he can't identify any of his assailants."

Rose picked up the gang book and flipped the pages. "This is the wrong book," he said with authority in his voice. "See if he can give us some clear descriptions."

At that moment the detective knew he had been had. It was a charade from there on in. Chino pretended to supply descriptions —they were meaningless—then, as soon as he could, he got out of there. As he drove away he hung onto the tiny steering wheel with savage satisfaction. Engraved in his mind he had the names of the four Counts who had jumped him, and what was more, he knew exactly where they lived.

The first step in his revenge plan had gone off amazingly well. The patrol deputy had known what he was up to, of course, but the dumb pig in plain clothes had been stupid enough to let him get away with it.

He went back to his own turf and spent the rest of the afternoon inspecting it for any changes. Then he rejoined the gang and told them what he had planned.

The restaurant was a good one, away from the barrio where either of them might have been recognized. It was not a fancy place, but the food was appetizing and that was what counted. Mott noted that Elena was not one to be taken to a strictly first class establishment or be seriously unhappy. That didn't seem to concern her in the least.

They talked a little bit about the barrio, then by common consent switched to sports. The Angels had just acquired two front-line players with excellent promise. The California team's prospects seemed to be of real interest to Elena, and she talked about the subject with more than casual knowledge. Clearly, Mott recognized, she was a young woman with wide and diversified interests.

He sincerely hoped that he would be able to find at least one spectator sport that would interest Nancy. For the time being he had abandoned the hope that she would learn to play tennis with him or participate actively in some other game. He had seriously proposed scuba diving to her, but she had absolutely refused to consider trying it.

234

When the meal was over, they went to the arena. The place smelled faintly like a jail, with the combined odors of antiseptics, floor cleaners, and the essence of many thousands upon thousands of human bodies that had come and gone. It didn't seem to bother Elena, which was to be expected since she had just put in her detention time at Sybil Brand. She certainly knew the familiar clang of iron barred doors and the sharp snap of electrically released door latches that separated the administrative and confinement areas. She was an appealing female, but definitely not a helpless one.

The seats the captain had given them were squarely between the side posts and mercifully out of range of the TV cameras. There was a slight tinge of the illicit about having Elena Alvarez for a date when he had a wife at home, and Mott was subconsciously aware of it. He reminded himself once more that what he was doing was entirely aboveboard.

In the second preliminary there was a young boxer who was out to make a name for himself before a championship crowd. He was overmatched, but he bore into his opponent with total courage and fierce determination. He was a thin Latino, his more experienced opponent a muscular young black who hit with short hard blows that sometimes came in fluries.

The Latino was decked in the fourth round. When he got up, the referee stopped the fight and thereby ended his hopes. Against a more suitable opponent he might have pulled off an impressive victory.

It was then Mott realized that Elena had grabbed his arm during the high points of the action and had hung on for dear life. He had almost been unaware of it at the time; now it all came back and he realized how much he had subconsciously enjoyed their physical contact.

The main event, after the usual preliminaries, went on with the champion ceaselessly moving forward, never taking a step that did not advance him on his challenger. He was up against a clever boxer who had the ability to take a steady flow of punches and stand up under them, waiting for his moment. The rounds marched by with mechanical precision, precisely timed, the action sometimes slowing, sometimes erupting into an attempt by one fighter or the other to rally enough to finish it off.

In the eleventh round the challenger switched to a left-handed stance that momentarily confused the champion. In those few seconds he followed some flicking right leads with a solid left uppercut that landed. The champion sagged into the ropes, then came off again, not quite recovered. The challenger measured and landed one behind the champion's ear with all the speed he had left. When the champion dropped to the canvas, Elena sprang to her feet, Mott and the rest of the crowd with her.

He turned to look at her, not caring for a moment whether he missed a few counts or not. Then he looked back in time to see the referee raise the challenger's arm. Elena jumped up and down with pure animal excitement and hung on tight while the ring announcer gave the time and proclaimed the new champion.

While she went to the ladies' room on the way out, he tried to think of what he should do next: offer her a drink, take her back to the station where her car was parked, or whatever. When she came back she took his arm as though they had been close friends for years. They went outside.

While they were getting into his car, she solved his problem for him. "If it's all right, would you take me right home? It's not too far, and I've got a friend who can drop me off in the morning."

"Fine," Mott acknowledged. It was appropriate and relieved him of any appearance of trying to prolong their date unduly. He drove out of the lot and, hardly more than fifteen minutes later, pulled up before the better class apartment building where she lived. "Come on up," she invited. "Coffee and chocolate cake. I made it myself."

Strangely, that last bit made the difference. Bakery cake he could safely have declined, but something she had made herself was a little harder to refuse. He made a firm resolution not to stay too long, and to watch himself. She was abundantly attractive and she was still glowing with the excitement of the evening.

Her place was about what he had expected. She lived alone and had well-chosen, if not too expensive, furniture. No little china dolls were standing about; instead there was a Le Mans poster framed on one of the walls. The chair he sat in was comfortable. When he got up and on his own found the bathroom, it too was neat and tidy, without a lot of feminine things hanging about. No pantyhose were draped across the towel bars.

The cake was delicious and the coffee freshly brewed the right way. He stayed fifteen minutes, enjoying what he had been given, and then rose to go. She came to him, laid her hands on his shoulders without passion, and thanked him for having taken her out.

He told her honestly that he had enjoyed every minute of it. Then he realized that she was ready to be kissed, if that was his wish. To refuse would make him a prig. He took her into his arms and kissed her with just the proper amount of warmth and restraint. When he had finished she rested her head on his shoulder for a few seconds and then kissed him once again on her own. Not lavishly, just nicely. "I know you're married," she said. "I don't want to do anything to interfere with that."

"Thank you," he said.

She smiled with a warm sincerity that he could not ignore.

"Otherwise . . . ," she said, without losing an iota of her poise.

She was less than three feet from him and desperately appealing.

When he got home, Nancy was deep asleep. He was tired himself, but because of where he had been, he carefully shut the bathroom door and had a quick warm shower that took away the last vestiges of the arena and of the girl with whom he had spent such a completely fulfilling evening.

He was grateful that Nancy did not even stir when he climbed into bed. She was turned away from him, sleeping on her side, and oblivious of the fact that he was even there.

CHAPTER TWENTY-ONE

FLACO was only fifteen years old. That in itself was deceptive, because he had been an active soldier as a member of Los Counts for more than two years, and his expertise with a knife was well known. The thinness that had provided him with his street name made him appear slightly taller than he was; the beginnings of a faint mustache suggested a maturity he had yet to obtain physically. He was streetwise, and while he did not know it himself, he was already the father of a child. (The girl involved had confided her problem to Brother Julio, and he had seen to the matter. The infant, although available, had not yet been adopted; it gave evidence of retardation.)

To Flaco each day was complete in itself. He did not go to school —he had no need to, since he was secure in his gang affiliation, and that was all the social acceptance that he would ever want. He was relieved of the need to make any decisions, because the gang made up its mind collectively, and for the most part he did not participate in the process. Jambo and the other leaders largely did that, which was fine with him. He ate, slept, fornicated, and gave the rest of his life to his gang. The future, in the larger sense of the word, did not concern him in the least.

It was Tuesday morning when he ate his breakfast and then decided to go down onto Whittier Boulevard to look around. There were a lot of girls who hung around various places. When they did that, they were available. Sex was one of the few solo activities within the gang, except in the case of a gang rape, and he had been in on only two of those. He had had a disturbing dream during the night, and he was anxious for a woman.

He had not walked a half block on Whittier before Chino spotted him, wandering up the street on foot, looking around him with his basic objective in view. He did not detect that he was being stalked, which was a tribute to Chino's skill—Flaco was still young, but he had already been through a lot.

Chino knew exactly what he was going to do. He had already talked to his girl friend, Elsa, about it, and she had agreed immediately to his suggestion. She lived on the turf, and her brother was an active member of La Calle Verona. So there was no problem at all baiting the trap.

He found a dime in his jeans and spent it in a public telephone. Elsa was home and ready. He picked her up with his car a few minutes later, then drove slowly westward on Whittier, relocating Flaco. He found him within half a block of where he had expected. With a warm sense that the breaks were all with him, Chino dropped Elsa off just around the next corner and then kept out of sight.

Flaco was almost too easy, because a woman was what he was specifically trying to find. Elsa was only sixteen, but she was totally aware of her femininity and already skilled in its use. She had a chest that enticed men; one of the brief preparations she had made for her mission was to take off her brassiere.

When Flaco spotted her, walking slowly and with her breasts in subtle movement under her blouse, he almost had an erection from the sight. His approach was standardized, but one that the gang had found effective. He was so anxious to score with her that he didn't want to waste a minute in useless preliminaries.

Elsa knew all this, of course, and used it to her advantage. She teased him a little, made him buy her a *tostada,* which she took her time eating. As they sat together at one of the outside tables provided by the fast-food stand, she pretended to drop her compact by accident—that gave her a chance to bend over and pick it

239

up. As she did so, she calculated the angle carefully so that Flaco would have an enticing view down the front of her loose-fitting blouse. Chino, who saw her do it from where he was concealed, took savage pride in her technique. Flaco was solidly hooked. From that moment on he would have done anything to possess the maddening girl he had miraculously found.

He propositioned her swiftly, exactly as the gang had taught him, and there he ran into a snag: she wouldn't come onto his turf. He had a place, but she would not budge. Just when all seemed lost and Flaco was thinking desperate thoughts, Elsa mentioned that her home was empty—her father was doing thirty days in the county jail, and her mother worked. The other kids would not come into the house if she left the right sign on the window.

Every street instinct he had developed told Flaco not to go onto the turf of La Calle Verona, but this was different. He had a specific house to visit where he could go in and out in a few seconds' time. No one would disturb them during his time of ecstasy, and after it was over he could leave the bitch right there and be back on his own turf in five minutes. Once he was in his car and on the road, no one would challenge him. And the Veronas' turf was only two blocks from the neutral territory of Whittier Boulevard. He got his car, and when she got in beside him, he knew that it was a certainty. He drove slightly bent over so as to conceal the swelling in his pants.

She showed him where to park behind her house so no one would see the car. Normally Flaco would have known better than that, the gang would see everything, but he was in no mood to quibble. He drove into the ancient wooden garage that she showed him and cut the engine. He got out as quickly as he could, before something premature could spoil everything for him. Elsa stood waiting, her arms outstretched. He embraced her, and the sudden warmth of her body almost drove him crazy. He was kissing her passionately when Chino's knife entered his back and penetrated deep into his abdomen.

It was the worst shock he had ever had. He knew almost instantly that he had been trapped and betrayed; he also knew that he was badly wounded and helpless on hostile turf. The agony that was beginning to fill his body was matched by the knowledge that he had allowed himself to be killed. He was too good with a knife himself not to know how badly he had been hit.

He expected to be stabbed again and asked then only that it be over quickly, but it did not come. He slumped to the ground as Elsa, with calm deliberation, spat on his face. That meant nothing: the passion that had consumed him was totally gone; he was overwhelmed by the knowledge that he was dying. And he didn't even know why he had been hit.

Then he looked up and saw Chino. At first he did not recognize him, but Chino stood there, smiling, until he did. Then the memory came back of the time, just a little while ago, when with Jambo, Apache, and Angel, he had attacked a Verona on his own turf. This was the same enemy. It told him why he had been betrayed and that his death was certain.

His bladder had emptied itself in his pants, and he hardly noticed it. The thing that was framed in his mind at that terrible moment was the face of old blabbermouth Espinoza when he had stuck his own knife right through her right tit. It had been delicious then; now he knew complete terror, and not one member of his gang would know to come to his rescue. He would be avenged, but that knowledge was no comfort as his urine mixed with his blood on the earthen floor of the garage.

The added agony assailed him that he had allowed himself to be trapped like a total fool, something he had been taught all his life not to do. The thought burst into his mind that he was too young to die, but reality snuffed it out. Chino, standing above him, showed him his knife, then gestured unmistakably toward the crotch of his trousers.

Flaco wanted to scream. He had forced himself to accept the idea that his life was over, but he could not face torture—or the supreme indignity with which he was threatened—and with the girl who had betrayed him watching. He had loved the knife as a weapon; now his knowledge of the way that it could cut flesh had him petrified. Knives were to be used on people; the reverse thought had never before entered his mind.

As the pain in his back mounted, he wanted desperately to die, to have it over with, and to escape the mutilation that would occur within seconds. Even as a corpse, he could not stand the idea of being deprived of his genitals.

Chino bent down and, despite the sodden condition of Flaco's pants, carefully opened the zipper. He looked into Flaco's eyes and saw total terror. It was splendid, magnificent revenge, and he was about to extract even more. He handed his knife to Elsa. "Do you want to cut him off?" he asked.

To have a girl do it was more than Flaco's mind could stand. Despite the deep stab wound in his body, he arched his back and screamed. The blood burst out of his body in a renewed flow, but he was unaware of it as he screamed again, in compound agony more than he could bear.

Chino froze for an instant, then grabbed Elsa by the hand. Without a word he yanked her toward the door at the back of the garage. He had only a few seconds; he used them to race up the back steps of her house, dragging her with him, and to slam the door behind them. He sprinted to the front door, hardly more than twenty feet away, and was outside like a shot.

The gang-control black and white unit manned by Deputies Sloan and Agrivar was coming slowly down the alley. The Veronas' turf was being intensively patrolled, and that included the alleys behind the houses. Deputy Agrivar, who was driving, had his window down and heard Flaco scream.

Agrivar stopped the car and was out at once, his weapon at the ready. His partner had already spotted the garage from which the cries were coming; baton in hand he sprinted toward the rear. He arrived five seconds too late to see the door of the house being closed, and the sound that it had made had been covered by the fast closing of the patrol unit's door as he had gotten out.

When the two deputies entered the garage and saw what they had to deal with, they knew exactly what to do. Agrivar, who spoke Spanish, knelt beside the victim while his partner ran back to the patrol car to radio for medical help and backup.

Flaco lay moaning, rolling his head from side to side. He was all but out of his mind, unable for the moment to comprehend that he had somehow been granted a reprieve. Agrivar found something that he could put behind his head, giving him a modicum of comfort. "Lie perfectly still," he said in Spanish. "We are here now. The ambulance is coming."

Flaco looked up and formed words. He was not devout, but he was going over the edge, and he didn't want to risk anything more. "A priest," he said. "I want a priest."

242

To Deputy Agrivar, who was himself Catholic, that was the most sensible thing the youthful victim could have asked. The moment that his partner reappeared, he asked that a priest be summoned Code Three. Sloan ran to put it on the air—it was a common request in the barrio.

He was heard by Deputy Valdemar who was at that moment cruising a half block from St. Ynez's church. He radioed in that he would handle it, and within two minutes he had Father Lopez in the car. He hit the red lights and siren and took off at the maximum safe speed to the location he had been given.

He arrived directly behind another unit that had Brother Julio aboard. The Brother had been cruising with the deputies, largely so that they could talk. The moment that the stabbing had been reported, Deputy Rose, the driver, had made for the scene with all possible speed. He knew that Brother Julio was not a priest, but he also knew that the Brother was a mighty force among all the gang kids. He could give comfort at least.

Flaco lay very still, despite the fact that a paramedic team had already responded and he was receiving attention. Father Lopez quickly put a ribbon across his shoulders and opened a tiny box containing holy water and a sponge. He saw at a glance that Flaco was in desperate condition. With all the haste that the ritual permitted, he began to administer the last rights to the fifteen-year-old victim. The paramedics continued working; when they very carefully turned Flaco over, the Father continued his ministration without interruption. Brother Julio knelt, his hands in prayer, assisting in the sacrament.

Flaco could not see very well. He knew that something was being done to him, but his pain was so great he wanted them to let him die. He saw the priest beside him and knew then that in a few minutes, or even seconds, he would be dead. But not in a state of grace. The horror of the hell in which he believed yawned beneath him, and he knew that every one of his sins would be intoned against him. He would burn in fiery torment into all eternity unless, in some way, he could unburden himself.

Then he saw a man, another man, who was standing watching, doing nothing. He had seen him somewhere before, but he did not remember or care. He heard the words of forgiveness from the priest, the cleansing of his soul, but one black and terrible sin still

243

forced itself into his mind, and he desperately wanted to rid himself of it. He wasn't sure if the final absolution would include that or not.

The priest finished and then knelt beside him. "God will bless you," he said. "Christ will redeem you."

It was comfort, but it was still not enough. Then the man he had seen was down close beside him and in a quiet, understanding voice saying, "I'm Lieutenant Mott from the Sheriff's Department. While you can, do you want to tell us about Mrs. Espinoza?"

That was the terror he feared, the unforgivable sin that, unless confessed, could plunge him into eternal damnation and everlasting torment. He had no loyalty left and owed nothing except to God. His gang was forgotten on another galaxy. Now he had to save his own soul, and time was rapidly running out. He felt a fresh stab of violent pain as the paramedics did something to his body, but his mind blocked it out. He was about to discard his body.

He tried to look up at the man who somehow knew the awful thing he had not yet confessed. He knew that he was not a priest, but it did not matter. He gasped air into his lungs and spoke, with every word a fresh agony. "I kill her. I kill her with Angel, Apache, Jumpy, and Stick. We all kill her. We kill her hard. I sorry now."

An automatic phrase came into his mind, and he repeated it in Spanish, sensing that the painful words might contain his salvation. "Father, forgive me, for I have sinned."

Mott gave way at once to Father Lopez, who completely understood. Kneeling where Flaco could see him he forgave the already forgiven sin and gave the sign of absolution. The paramedics then lifted Flaco onto a Gurney and put him into the ambulance with great care. Brother Julio climbed in with the victim and before they could close the door, Mott got in too. With the paramedic who was giving medical care, that made three of them in back with the patient.

Deputy Agrivar knew better than to put what he had just heard on the air. Instead he got back into his unit, and with his partner drove in Code Two condition back to the sheriff's station. There he located Lieutenant Finley and gave him the information.

The lieutenant knew most the the gang kids by heart, both by their right names and by the street names they used as much as possible. Nevertheless, he doublechecked the Counts' gang book before he dispatched units to pick up the suspects named in the dying declaration. The four Counts were picked up with swift efficiency and brought into the station. They were carefully informed of their rights and booked on suspicion of 187—premeditated murder.

At the hospital Flaco was rushed into the emergency room, where a team was standing by. It is doubtful if a better or more competent unit could have been assembled anywhere to deal with a stabbing—every member was long experienced in the results of street violence. Flaco's garments were cut away deftly and rapidly, and for a moment he lay naked on the table.

He was worked on there for fifteen minutes, then he was moved swiftly up into surgery. He was still alive when the anesthetic was being administered.

Mott could not go into the surgical theater, of course, but he had seen enough to know exactly want he wanted to do. He spoke to Brother Julio and asked him to come along. Then he went directly to the office of the hospital chief of staff.

His badge got him in for an immediate conference. As the doctor rose to greet him, Mott waved him back down again. "I'll only take a minute," he said, "but this is very important—and highly confidential. I'm Ralph Mott, lieutenant at the East Los Angeles Sheriff's Station. This is Brother Julio."

"I know Brother Julio," the chief of staff responded. "What is it that you need?"

"A patient has just been brought in, stabbed. He's now in surgery. I don't know the prognosis, but I suspect that he's dying."

"We'll do our utmost to save him," the doctor said.

"Of course, I know that. What I want to ask is this: please don't release any information on the patient's condition to anyone for, say, the next few hours."

"You're asking officially, I take it."

"Right. What we have, sir, is a dying declaration which includes a confession of murder and the implication of four others in the same offense."

"Five people murdered one victim?"

"That's right. We're picking up the other four now. That's an assumption on my part, but I'm sure that it's accurate. We're going to confront them with the declaration and try to get them to confess on their own. You understand, doctor, that a dying declaration will hold up in court if there are reliable witnesses to it, but it is not valid if the patient subsequently recovers."

"I see. So you want your other suspects to believe that the patient has died."

"We're not going to tell them that unless it becomes a fact. If they jump to that conclusion, we're not going to do anything to stop them."

The chief of staff pondered for just a moment, then he had the matter thought out. "I want the name of the patient, of course," he said. "Then let's leave it this way: if the patient does die, I'll see that you're notified immediately. I presume that you'll take care of advising the family."

"We'll do that," Mott promised.

"If he survives, we won't give out any information to anyone but you until, say, early morning. I don't think we can sit on a patient's status much longer than that. Is it a juvenile?"

"Yes."

"Then certainly we have to consider the parents and other concerned people. You see my point."

"Absolutely, doctor. If we do obtain the necessary confessions, then we'll see that your people are notified promptly, and you will be free to follow your regular routine."

"On that basis, we'll be glad to help out," the doctor concluded. "Now I need the necessary information."

Brother Julio supplied it. He knew from memory the patient's home address and the names of his parents.

When he had finished, Mott used a phone to call a patrol car to pick them up. As it happened, there already was one at the emergency entrance—there had been a minor 415 fight, and two of the participants had been brought in for medical attention. As they walked out to pick up the transportation, Brother Julio had a request. "If you will allow it," he said, "I believe it would be good if we could stop for a short while at Hector's home."

"Hector?"

"Yes—Hector Rosales, who is called Flaco. I am afraid that his parents are not very bright people, but they need to be told what has happened to their son."

"Have they any other children?" Mott asked.

"Quite a few. I tell you privately that they are receiving assistance, and we have one of the girls in our school. She is, I fear, not able to learn very much, as her mind is weak."

At Mott's direction, the patrol car took them to one of the humblest houses on the Counts' turf, a very small wooden affair that was in desperate need of repair in almost every particular. It had once been white, but it was so covered with gang graffiti it would probably never be repainted that color. The tiny porch slanted dangerously to one side, and half of one of the wooden steps was missing.

As they walked up to the door Mott asked, "How many children live here?"

"The last that I knew it was fourteen, but I am not sure now." Brother Julio raised his hand and knocked.

The short conversation that followed was entirely in Spanish, Mott was introduced, and he nodded an acknowledgement. Then he returned his attention to the one completely broken-down sofa and the scraps of cloth on the floor that made up the rest of the furnishings—with one exception. A late-model color TV stood in one corner. At least six or seven rag-clad youngsters were crowded in front of the screen watching a cartoon program. They included one baby that had been parked on a thin cushion close enough to the set for its nose to have touched the glass.

The couple that presided over this forelorn scene received the news that Brother Julio was delivering without any visible shock. They listened as though to an account of something that had happened to some other people whom they knew only vaguely. If anything, they seemed to be almost embarrassed. By the time that the brief interview was over, a number of other children had come into the room, teenagers among them. One of the very young girls appeared to be pregnant, but her figure could have been the result of inadequate and badly balanced diet. Mott was relieved to get out of the house and off the premises.

He was acutely uncomfortable seeing anyone living like that, but the hoard of children told its own story. He knew the religious strictures that probably pertained, and once again he reminded himself not to get personally involved.

As soon as they were back at the sheriff's station, Mott went directly to his office, checked his desk, and then phoned to ask if the suspects named by Flaco had been picked up. He had a quick surge of satisfaction when he was told that all four were in custody, booked on murder one. They were about to be transported to Central Jail, the mammoth sheriff's facility that held a normal population of about 5,000 inmates, eighty-five percent of whom were repeaters. C.J. was a vast concrete and steel cavern with many floors, a large infirmary area, and long modules of cell blocks many tiers high. It was the largest such facility in the world. Gang kids were sent there regularly, and none of them liked it.

Brother Julio excused himself. He had pressing duties to attend to, and he didn't require any transportation. Mott was privately glad that he had not asked to talk with any of the suspects in custody—he had his own program laid out for dealing with those four young men.

Captain Gutierrez appeared at the door and sat down without an invitation. "Ralph," he said. "I've heard about the knifing this afternoon, and I certainly approve of the way you handled it."

"Thank you," Mott responded.

"While you've been busy, we've dug up another witness, a sixteen-year-old called Elsa Gallegos. Her story is that the victim picked her up on Whittier, fed her, and then offered to drive her home. She accepted the ride and had him come down the alley because she only had the key to the back door. When he began to make passes, she ran inside and locked the door. She claims that she didn't see the actual attack and has no idea who was responsible."

"How much of that do you believe?" Mott asked.

"Very little. It does explain how a member of the Counts got onto the Veronas' turf, and we checked out her statement that the kid bought her something to eat. Beyond that . . ." He shrugged his shoulders.

Mott leaned back in his own chair to relax for a moment. "First of all, I'd like to know what a fifteen-year-old was doing driving a car. Secondly, if little Elsa was fighting off unwelcome advances, she was quite something if she could run to her back door, get out her key, let herself in, and then lock the door behind her—all before Flaco could catch up with her. I'm in favor of bringing her in for further questioning."

248

"I won't oppose that," the captain said. "What I wanted to say was: if you can get one or more of the Espinoza murder suspects to cop, it would lessen the load considerably. Another thing: a member of the Veronas was released from the hospital recently. He's the kid you interviewed—Marcellino Acosta. I get it from Rodzinski that Elsa Gallegos is his girl, and also that Acosta is known to be good with a knife."

"He didn't waste much time, did he," Mott commented.

"Not if he's the one, and right now I consider him a good lead. But we're shy any real evidence. Perhaps you can get some."

"Thanks, Mike, I'll see what I can do."

The captain went back to his office in a relieved frame of mind. He particularly liked the fact that Mott hadn't made any rash promises. He was working out well, but he had a major test right in front of him. The verdict would probably be in before morning.

As a first step, Mott called together all of the members of his staff who were on duty and briefed them on exactly what they had. There was general elation. No one appeared to have any doubt that the long looked-for break in the Espinoza case had come. Even the units going out on patrol showed fresh enthusiasm. The fact that Mott had been on hand to hear the confession himself added a little luster to his position. It appeared to be a double-edged triumph coming up—the solution of the Espinoza murder and the elimination for some time of five of the most active members of Los Counts. Mott was so totally involved he completely forgot to call Nancy and tell her the usual news that he would be home when she saw him, and not before.

Shortly after the briefing concluded, he was told he had a telephone call. He had asked not to be disturbed with routine matters if they could be handled by the desk, but this one had been put through. He picked up the instrument and gave his name.

"Ralph," came over the wire, "Sparky. This is a strictly unofficial call, but I'd appreciate some information."

"Anything I can do." The last thing he wanted to do was to rile the judge who might be sitting for the preliminary hearing.

"I've been getting bombarded over here," Ramos continued. "The story I hear is that your people went out and seized four juveniles without provocation and that you are working them over

249

to try to get them to admit something about the Espinoza killing. I don't necessarily buy all that, but I would appreciate knowing what this is all about."

"I'm glad you called," Mott said truthfully. "I'll give it to you exactly as we have it here. Incidentally, only two of the suspects are juveniles, and in my opinion, they're unfit to be tried in juvenile court."

"They have records, then."

"Yes, impressive ones."

"Thanks for that information. Now what's happened?"

Mott gave the judge a full rundown without wasting any words. He concluded by saying that he didn't know as of that moment if Flaco was still alive, but his death was expected.

"All right, Ralph," the judge said. "Based on what you've told me, I'm going to go along with you over here, and I won't take any action until this thing has developed a little more. If the Rosales boy does pass away, it might be well to let me know."

"I'll do that, Sparky."

"Thank you. Repeating, this is all totally unofficial."

"Understood."

Mott hung up with a certain grim satisfaction; the breaks were beginning to go his way. His opinion of Judge Ramos went up a little—obviously he would not be a soft touch for the defense attorneys when they got on the job. Let Ramos be fair, that was all he asked.

McBride came in. "We've got a lot of people to deal with," the sergeant reported. "Parents of the suspects, some press personnel, and representatives of two different Chicano organizations. I expect that the lawyers will be descending at any time."

"All right," Mott said. "Get them together in the conference room, and I'll meet with them there. Say in ten minutes."

McBride nodded his approval of that and left to make the arrangement. Mott picked up his phone and called the duty sergeant. "Has anyone talked to the suspects since they were brought in?" he asked.

"Only what was necessary while they were being booked. I had their rights read to them again in both English and Spanish with two witnesses present—they won't be able to get away with that one again. Then they were told that they were being charged with the murder of Mrs. Espinoza. No one has talked to them since."

"Good. I want as little contact with them as possible. Of course, you'll have to allow attorneys in. Otherwise keep everyone out."

"How about spiritual advisers?"

"Yes, of course. You're right about that—I'd forgotten."

"That would include Brother Julio."

"Is he there now?"

"Yes, he is."

"Invite him to attend the meeting I'm going to have in the conference room in about ten minutes."

"Will do." The sergeant hung up.

Mott left his office and went into the report writing room to see who was there. To his surprise Elena Alvarez was among others. He hadn't seen her all day and had unconsciously assumed that she was off duty.

He realized at that moment that he could make a mistake, and he wanted to avoid it, since there were several others present. He looked around the room and then spoke in a normal voice. "I'm going into a meeting with some parents, Chicano reps, and some media. I need a Spanish-speaking deputy, just in case."

A tall black deputy put up his hand; so did Agrivar and Elena Alvarez.

The duty sergeant was in the doorway, checking if he would be needed. "Take Alvarez," he advised. "It may help the women to feel more comfortable."

That made excellent sense, of course, and spared Mott the need to pick her out himself. Since he had had her out for an evening, he had been particularly careful in the way he handled himself when she was present. He assumed that everyone knew he had taken her to the fights, with a ninety percent chance that he was right.

Eight minutes later he walked into the conference room with Deputy Alvarez, in uniform, at his side. There were almost twenty people waiting for him, so the room was already crowded. As he took his place at the head of the long table, he saw some familiar faces from the Citizens' Council and many that he did not know. A strong sense of foreboding hung in the air, and he could feel it as if it were a living thing.

"Ladies and gentlemen," he began, deliberately somewhat formal, "my name is Lieutenant Mott. This is Deputy Alvarez, who is fluent in Spanish. She will be glad to translate anything I have to say for anyone who might wish it, or to answer questions. Does everyone here understand me now?"

There was a general nodding of heads. As far as he could see, it was a hundred percent.

"Here is the situation," he continued, looking carefully up and down the table as he spoke. "Not long ago an elderly widow who resided in East Los Angeles was brutally murdered. She was alone in her home at the time of the attack. I very much regret to have to say this, but she was sexually abused and quite obviously tortured before she finally died. A number of stab wounds had been inflicted on her body, some of them clearly intended only to cause pain. This is the opinion of the coroner's office, and they are experts in such matters."

"Was robbery a possible motive?"

The question came so quickly and unexpectedly that Mott did not see who had asked it. Nevertheless he answered. "No, definitely it was not. The victim, Mrs. Consuelo Espinoza, was poor; her little home was about all she had. The few dollars she had in her purse were not taken. The only object in her house of any value at all was her television set, and it was a ten-year-old black and white model that would hardly bring ten dollars on the street."

"She might have had some savings hidden away."

Mott saw now that the speaker came from one of the more militant Chicano organizations. Opening the folder he had brought with him, he carefully removed a picture without letting the others see any of the contents. "This will answer your question, I believe, sir. It is a photograph taken at the scene of Mrs. Espinoza's death shortly after we arrived there. The other pictures we took are frankly too grisly to be shown—they are among the most horrible I have ever seen, and I have been a policeman for a long time." He handed an eight-by-ten enlargement to the person on his right for circulation. It showed the spray-painted wall with the vindictive word in Spanish that told its own grim story. The picture passed down the table rapidly, delivering its message as it went. Mott deliberately waited until it had been handed all

252

of the way down one side and back up the other. No one asked to have the word translated.

"Since this particularly vicious crime was discovered, we have been conducting an intensive investigation. Earlier today, a young man who is a known member of Los Counts gang was found in a private garage south of Whittier Boulevard. One of our patrol cars came past, apparently immediately after he had been deeply stabbed from the back in the area of the kidneys. The deputies who made the discovery at once radioed for medical help and backup. A paramedic unit responded and was on the scene in approximately five minutes. By that time more deputies had arrived, myself among them."

He had their complete attention then, and what was more, he sensed that they believed him.

"The victim, who was in great pain and bleeding badly, asked for a priest. His request was put on the air, and one of our patrol cars rushed Father Lopez from St. Ynez's Church to his side. Father Lopez, on seeing the condition of the victim, administered to him the last rites of the Catholic Church. While he was doing that, the paramedics were working desperately to save the victim's life. Because he is only fifteen years old, his name is being withheld."

"Was it Hector Rosales?" That was in a different voice.

"No comment," Mott responded. "To continue: after the victim had received the last rites, I asked him if he wished to tell us anything about Mrs. Espinoza. That was all. Brother Julio, who is here now and who was present then, will confirm that he was asked if he would like to unburden himself while he was still alive and conscious."

He looked toward the Brother who nodded. "It is as the lieutenant has said. The question was asked only; there were no threats or any shouting. The boy was asked quietly and properly if he would like to make his peace and unburden his conscience. His sins had already all been forgiven, and he knew that."

"Thank you, Brother," Mott said. "The victim then, in the presence of seven reliable witnesses, including Brother Julio and Father Lopez, confessed to the murder of Mrs. Espinoza and, without being asked, gave the names of four others, all members of his gang, who he said had taken an active part in the murder. He was

253

put into an ambulance almost immediately after that and rushed to the hospital. I rode with him in back. A paramedic was also there to care for him, and Brother Julio to give him comfort. Halfway to the hospital the paramedic indicated to me that the victim was probably dying. At the hospital he was given emergency treatment and then taken immediately to surgery. I have had no report on his condition since then."

A question was voiced in Spanish and Elena answered. Mott understood that it was a clarification of what he had just said, and went on.

"I would now like to explain a point of law to you, in case you are not already aware of it. Whenever a person who is about to die makes a statement or a confession, the law assumes that he is speaking the truth. This is known as a dying declaration. It has long been held by the courts that a person who is unburdening himself just before meeting his Maker will not lie. Therefore a dying declaration is one of the most powerful pieces of evidence that can be laid before a court or a jury."

"What happens if the person recovers?"

That was a reasonable question, and it was put in a reasonable tone of voice.

"Oddly enough," Mott answered, "if the person eventually recovers, then the dying declaration does not have the same force, even though it was made in the immediate expectation of death. I most earnestly hope that the victim now in the hospital will recover—we all do. I suggest that we all pray for him."

He had not intended that, but once the words were out, he was glad that he had said them. They were no less sincere for having been unpremeditated.

"As soon as we had done all that we could for the victim," he continued, making his voice factual again, "we acted on the information he had given us and took the four persons he had named into custody on a charge of P.C. one eighty-seven—premeditated murder. I should advise you further that there is no bail for this offense. The suspects will therefore be held in custody, unless otherwise ordered by the court, until the preliminary hearing. The investigation is continuing. That is all the information I have for you now."

"How about the names of the suspects," a reporter asked.

"Two of them are technically juveniles, so their names will be withheld by us, at least for the time being. I would like to confer with the Hall of Justice before releasing the names of the other two."

There were no more questions for a few seconds, which gave Mott a chance to escape. Elena remained behind, talking in Spanish with a very upset woman who apparently still did not understand what was going on.

Mott was intercepted on his way back to his office with the news the Hector Rosales had died five minutes before without recovering consciousness following surgery. The news hit him hard, because he had believed that Flaco's recovery was possible. He returned to the meeting room, which no one else had left, and made the announcement. After that there was nothing else he could do. The watch commander would make the necessary calls, and two deputies would go to the Rosales home. News of that kind was never given to the next of kin over the telephone.

When he got back to his office, the telephone was ringing. He picked it up and gave his name sharply—he was in no mood to talk to anyone. An instant later he regretted it. Nancy was on the line, and of all the people in the world, she deserved his first consideration.

"What's the matter?" she asked. "I just called to find out—"

"I'm very sorry," Mott interrupted her. "I didn't mean to speak that way, especially to you. We've just had another gang murder. We cleared one up and got another right on top of it."

"You didn't call, and I've had dinner waiting for hours."

"My fault, I should have found a minute. I'm sorry."

"Ralph, is there something else you're not telling me? You don't sound at all like yourself."

"I don't feel like it either," he admitted.

"It's the barrio. Please, can't you get out of there? I want you back again—the way you were."

He forced himself to be calm and patient. "Right now I've got a dead fifteen-year-old on my hands, and the investigation has to be set up right away."

"Yes, but there must be other people there!"

"There are, but I command the unit, and I have the responsibility."

255

Nancy's voice rose enough to warn him that she was losing control. "Ralph, please. I'm entitled to some consideration, too."

It was getting dangerous, and he closed it off as quickly as he could. "Nancy, please go ahead and eat. I should be able to leave here in an hour or so, and I'll come directly home. Save something for me, and forgive me, please."

"All right," she answered, but there was no conviction in her voice.

He wanted to say something more, to speak words of comfort to her, but while the thought was still in his mind the dial tone came on. For a moment or two he contemplated calling her back, then he thought better of it. Hopefully, he would see her in a little while, and words over a telephone were never very good anyway.

He hung up the instrument and then forced himself to turn his mind back to the urgent work that he had to do. For the next ten minutes he kept remembering what she had said about the barrio and tried his best to deny that she might have been right.

CHAPTER TWENTY-TWO

THE INVESTIGATION into the murder of Hector Rosales, known on the street as Flaco, did not go well. Two detective teams combed the neighborhood where he had been attacked without turning up a single witness who had seen a thing. Most of the people were probably telling the truth, but whether they were or not made little difference. The only witness available was Elsa Gallegos, and her story, while highly improbable, could not be shaken. For a sixteen-year-old she was case-hardened, and the more she was questioned, the more she stuck to her account.

She admitted to having been Marcellino Acosta's girl friend, but she claimed that they had had a fight and that she had gone down to Whittier Boulevard looking for a new boy friend. There she had met Flaco. He had been nice to her, he had bought her something to eat, and she had invited him to her home. She had suggested that he leave his car in the garage where it would attract less notice. He was a member of Los Counts and the turf belonged to La Calle Verona.

Just as he was parking, she claimed, she felt the beginning of her period. It was unexpected, so she had excused herself and had gone as quickly as she could into the house to take care of herself.

She had been in the bathroom for some time, she said, and when she had come out, a police car had already stopped behind her house in the alley. She swore that that was all she knew. Later, under questioning, she admitted that she had patched up her quarrel with Marcellino, better known as Chino, and that they were together once more.

Mott had no doubt in his mind who had killed Flaco or how it had been done. Chino had recently come out of the hospital, and the odds were good that Flaco had been one of those who had put him there. Obviously Chino was set on revenge, which explained his unusual visit to the sheriff's station for a look at the Counts' gang book. It had been a daring move, and he had gotten away with it. Furthermore, Chino was a known knife expert. It was clear to everyone concerned at the sheriff's station that Elsa had been used to trap Flaco into going to her home, and no one had any doubt that Chino had delivered the fatal thrust. At that point the case passed into a too familiar category: the guilty person was known, but there was no way, barring a miracle, that enough evidence could be gathered to put him on trial.

It was frustrating, but it had happened before. The only way to resolve the matter was to keep a very close eye on Chino and nab him the next time he tried anything. In that way he might be taken out of circulation for a while.

After that there was a two-week period of near quiet in the barrio. Each day there were two or three gang-related incidents, but they were widely scattered, and most of them were relatively minor. Most of the calls were classified 415, which could be almost any sort of disturbance of the peace. Often they were fights or arrests for the illegal use of narcotics, principally marijuana, but increasingly for PCP, the deadly Angel Dust that literally drove its users out of their minds. Most of the PCP addicts had to be taken to the hospital, sometimes in comatose condition, sometimes in a state of wild frenzy that took several people to control. On the emergency treatment tables, PCP users sometimes fought so madly they broke the restraints. One injured himself badly by springing from a prone position into the air and then landing hard on the floor. When he was finally brought under control, he had a compound fracture of his right arm, but was oblivious to it.

But the guns were not in evidence. The Veronas had been badly hurt, both by the shoot-out on the hospital lot and by arrest. The Lagunas had suffered similarly and were still laying low. Los Counts had lost Flaco, and four more members were in custody. They had expected to be set free at the preliminary hearing, but the damning indictment of the dying declaration caused them to be bound over for trial. Furthermore, all four had been set up to be tried as adults—the two underage suspects had been found unfit to stand trial in Juvenile Court. It was a severe blow to them, and Assistant District Attorney Mendoza was confident that one or more of the defendants would cop out in the hope of a lighter sentence.

Three days later his wish came true. Emilio and Arturo Lucera, known as Jumpy and Stick, pleaded guilty and asked for the mercy of the court. That left Angel and Apache with no possible defense remaining. Finally they offered to plead guilty if it could be with the notation that they had been under the influence of narcotics and therefore were not fully responsible for their actions. That plea was rejected. They tried two more with complete lack of success. At the preliminary hearing, an attempt to prove that Flaco had been out of his mind at the time of his declaration was balked by the two paramedics, who gave expert testimony that their patient had been fully conscious and in his right mind at the time of his confession. Father Lopez and Brother Julio were both present, but neither of them was asked to take the stand.

Finally, at the end of their legal rope, and on the advice of their attorney, they confessed and also asked for mercy.

That closed the Espinoza case and got four of the more dangerous gang members off the street. Montaña Mara still showed signs of coming activity, but the death of Luis Cabrera had deflated the gang to some degree.

Mott put in a call to the hospital and talked with Dr. Sanchez. Danny Torres was still working at the hospital, and what was more, he was showing unexpected progress.

"I think you picked a winner in that young man," Sanchez reported. "He has a great deal of catching up to do on his education, but the ability is clearly there. He learns very rapidly, and so far he's shown a gratifying sense of responsibility. We're allowing him to do some simple things in patient care, and he's a natural.

In particular, we have a nine-year-old patient who needs a great deal of body massage. Danny has been learning to do this, and now he takes his turn."

"You've made my day," Mott said. "And I started out with a fight with my wife this morning."

"Does she want you to quit?"

"No, transfer. She wants me to get out of the barrio and away from all this gang activity. It's relatively quiet now, but I've been warned that it won't last."

As soon as he spoke he wondered why he had told Sanchez that. They were acquainted, but the doctor was by no means an intimate friend. He had better watch himself—he was beginning to talk too much.

He did not have time to chide himself further, because the indefatigable Brother Julio had made an appointment to see him and was due at any moment. He got up to go to the men's room and met the Brother in the hallway.

Five minutes later the two men sat together in the day room, having coffee, which Mott had been glad to buy.

Brother Julio was in a remarkably serious mood and his manner showed it. "As you know, I spent a great deal of time convincing the Morrison and Hale people to open up the plant in the barrio. I all but promised them that if they would do so, they would not have any trouble with our youth gangs. They took me at my word and spent a great deal of money putting in their equipment and setting up operations. You know what happened. As a result, I am discredited with them, and now they will not listen to me with any degree of confidence."

"It isn't your fault," Mott said. "You certainly did your best. How in the hell you ever got the Spiders and Los Magnolias to bury the hatchet I'll never know. That was a major achievement."

Brother Julio appeared to ignore that. "Are you aware of how things stand at the plant now?"

"Not since it stopped operations."

"Then I'll bring you up to date. Some things were moved out, mostly work in progress. The greater part of the equipment is still there, waiting for some decisions to be made."

That was genuinely interesting. "Do you think that they may open up again?"

"More people, including myself, are praying for that than you can imagine. But it is doubtful. However, some of the former employees of the plant, the good and responsible people, want to have a meeting. They have some proposals to make and want to talk with the Morrison and Hale management people, as I have done in the past."

"That sounds like a good idea."

"I am glad that you agree, because they wish to have you extend the invitation. You are asked to be present, of course, but they feel that if you would ask them to come, stating your position here, they might be encouraged to accept."

Mott thought about that for a good half minute without saying anything. Obviously, he wanted to do anything he could to help the people who had so unexpectedly lost their new jobs. At the same time, he didn't want to sell a bill of goods to the firm, which had already taken a big chance and lost.

Brother Julio once again displayed his disconcerting ability to know what others were thinking. "Remember, you are not asking them to reopen the plant," he pointed out. "You are only asking them to come to a meeting."

"Whom do you want me to call?"

"Mr. Frank Hale, Jr. He is the chairman of the board. He is asked to bring with him the president and the treasurer."

"The treasurer is likely to be against you," Mott warned.

"That is true, which is why we especially want him to come. We hope to convert him. Other officers are also invited—as many as wish to come."

"Where is the meeting to be? And when?"

"At the parish hall of St. Ynez's Church, next Tuesday morning at eleven. Lunch will be served. If they cannot come at that time, we will change the date to suit them."

"I'll be glad to make the call," Mott said.

Brother Julio handed him a slip of paper. On it was the telephone number.

As Jambo walked slowly down the street, automatically looking about him, he was in a dark and bitter mood. His gang had turned up a traitor, and as a result four of his best soldiers would be going to the joint for a year, possibly two. There were still many mem-

261

bers of Los Counts, but the whole barrio knew that a Count had chickened out, and the loss of macho was almost more than could be endured.

When he reached the meeting place, most of the Counts were already there, talking about what had been going on. As Jambo gathered the principal members around him, the rest of the gang stayed within hearing range, because this concerned them all. Little Benjie Morales knew that there were now vacancies in the upper structure, and despite the fact that he was only thirteen, he was ready to earn a promotion. He would be fifteen in two years, if he survived, and Flaco had been fifteen. Before he'd been killed, Flaco had been a mainstay of the gang, one of the best switchblade men they had. Benjie resolved to get hold of a weapon and practice.

Jambo dropped into the street language that was almost impossible for an outsider to understand. "We ain't so bad off," he began. "Flaco, he dead, but the other guys, they come back pretty soon. They gotta new law now, they get out sooner. So when Angel, Apache, Stick, and Jumpy come back, we make 'em proud."

No one argued that.

"The Veronas, they get their ass kicked bad, they hurtin'. Chino, he kill Flaco, so we get him. His girl, she fuck Flaco so he got his back up when Chino stab him. We get her, too." He squatted down, picked up a stick, and began to trace a pattern in the dirt. That meant only one thing: what he was about to say would be a gang secret it could mean death to betray any part of it. He was listened to intently.

"Montaña Mara, they know we lose five guys. We kick their ass when they come down to shoot up my house—they not forget that. They lose Luis Cabrera—the cops shoot him. So they gonna come for us. They shit on us, they look real good. But nobody shit on us—we too Goddamned tough. They gotta guy, he workin' at the hospital. Every day he go back and forth—same time."

"Why he work hospital?"

Jambo didn't even look up to see who had asked the question. "He fuckin' the nurses." That was a completely satisfactory explanation that wouldn't be questioned—true or not.

Jambo continued to draw with the stick. "Montaña, they come

after us now they think we sick." He looked up for the first time. "We not sick!"

The rest of the Counts emphatically agreed. More than thirty of them were at the meeting, and without exception they were thirsting to reverse the bad luck that had plagued them.

Jambo continued. "We go up on the Heights—four cars from different directions, same time. They no know what we gonna' do. We shoot up their cars; they shit in their pants."

That was understood to be the opening for a discussion. It took almost an hour to argue all the pros and cons of the plan before it was discarded. There weren't enough guns for one thing, and the cops could foul it up. They often had a car cruising around the Heights, and they could radio for more in a hurry.

Out of the argument came a new plan. That was the way Jambo wanted it. If they thought of it themselves, they would be much more anxious to carry it out. They were like brothers, and when they had established themselves as the toughest and most feared gang in the barrio, they would have sky high macho and they would run everything. Montaña had a big reputation, but that was because they had the advantage of the high ground. Once Montaña had been dethroned, it would be Los Counts all the way. And they all remembered that they still owed two murders to the hill gang. Shooting up their attack car had helped, but it didn't really count in the score. It had been more luck than anything else, and the Montañas knew it.

Carefully, and with much discussion back and forth, a detailed plan was worked out.

On the turf of Montaña Mara, another meeting was going on. Gaucho had at last accepted that his brother Kiko could never come back, but his burning passion for complete revenge had grown until he could not contain it much longer. Once again he was feverishly pleading that they hit Los Counts and wipe out the only one of Kiko's killers who was still on the street. He had a powerful argument: five of the Counts had been taken out, one by death and four by the cops. That had to be a major blow for the only gang that had dared to challenge the supreme position of Montaña Mara. Once the Counts had been put down, no one would ever again question which gang was the boss.

Jin-Jin hung back and listened. Without his balls he was considered a vegetable, but he had not lost his skill with a shotgun, and he could not wait to prove that fact. Maybe then the girls would stop laughing at him, and he would be a full member of Montaña Mara once again. For that he would have sold ten years of his life without ever looking back.

As he listened, what he heard made his heart begin to pound faster, and he almost felt as though he had become a full man again.

CHAPTER TWENTY-THREE

AT FIVE minutes to ten on Tuesday morning, Frank Hale, Jr., laid his card on the counter at the East Los Angeles Sheriff's Station and asked to see Lieutenant Mott. He carried the Junior on his name only because he was the son of a founder—he was a fully mature man who had left the office of president of his firm to become the chairman of the board. Because his executive judgments were seldom questioned, he still largely ran the company, and no one had as yet suggested that he step aside.

When Ralph Mott appeared, he liked the lieutenant at once. Normally Hale did not deal extensively with policemen, but this one had executive calibre written all over him. Mott shook hands first with Hale, then with William Waters, the treasurer of Morrison and Hale, and lastly with Robert MacKay, the titular president.

"It's very kind of you to come here," Mott said. "A great many people will appreciate it."

"It's no trouble," Hale answered, and then regretted his words at once, because any intelligent person would know that they weren't true. The lieutenant was obviously in that category.

Mott let it pass. "The captain would like very much to meet

you," he advised. "He's waiting in his office now."

Robert MacKay glanced at Hale. The two men communicated without exchanging a word. Obviously the sheriff's station was not set up to entertain distinguished visitors, but it was about to give of its best. Someone would be standing by, no doubt, to bring in coffee that had come out of a machine.

After an electric door latch clicked, Mott led the way down a short corridor and into an open-doored office. A sergeant seated there got to his feet. His uniform was sharply creased, his shoes were immaculate, and the remainder of his grooming was faultless. Hale was impressed, without knowing that Sergeant Cook had been taking special pains ever since his son had been gunned down during a traffic stop. Cadet Cook was still officially enrolled in the academy and was scheduled to graduate with his class if he could catch up with academics in time. For that Mike Cook was profoundly grateful to God.

Captain Gutierrez came out through the connecting doorway to greet his guests. He invited them in, said the proper things about their being welcome, and asked Sergeant Cook to serve some coffee. On the window ledge an automatic coffee maker had just completed its cycle.

"Gentlemen," the captain began as soon as everyone had been made comfortable, "you know, of course, why you have been invited down here today, so there's no point in playing any games. There is a citizens' committee set up to meet with you concerning your plant here in East Los Angeles. I have discussed this with Sheriff Pitchess personally, and he is most interested in the outcome."

"That was very kind of you," Hale said, hiding the lower half of his face in his coffee cup.

"The sheriff asked me to assure you that if you decide to resume operations, our department will make a maximum effort to see that your facility is protected. I admit that our patrol unit on duty in the area on the night that your mural was defaced didn't spot the vandals at work."

"Your car couldn't be everywhere at once," MacKay commented.

"That's right, sir, and we suspect that there was a lookout to note when the unit had just passed. You might be interested to know that we have identified the vandals and have interviewed them. We don't have a witness, so we can't go beyond that point, but I feel safe in assuring you that it won't reoccur."

"Nice to know," Waters contributed. He was not a man given much to conversation.

"Anyhow, gentlemen, please consider that we are very much in favor of your resuming operations, and when you do, you can count on us to give you all the support that we can."

Five minutes later they were out of the captain's office and getting into an official car that Mott had provided. It was neither as large or as comfortable as the one that had brought them to the barrio, and the back seat cushion kept sliding forward, but no one complained. As he started the engine, Mott felt that he knew exactly where his guests stood: they had no intention of reopening the barrio plant, but they were willing to take the better part of a business day to show their fairness and good will. After that they would regretfully cite insurmountable obstacles and politely close the door.

He glanced at his watch as he drove out of the lot onto Third and saw that he was right on schedule. He had planned his route carefully, so that he would approach the plant from the proper direction, and he had carefully put Hale in the front seat where he would have the best view.

When he turned the last corner there was no other traffic to impede him, so he let the car drift to the left before turning into the parking lot. In that way the panoramic effect of the huge, now completed mural had the maximum impact. He stopped, set the brake, and got out of the car.

Viewed from a short distance away, the giant painting was even more impressive. The remarkable faces could be seen to best advantage, as could the intricate work that maintained the unity and flow of the design. In the lower left-hand corner, two massive pieces of equipment were pictured supported by ironwork in the shape of the letters *M* and *H.* It was so subtly done that Hale himself did not see it for almost fifteen seconds.

A young Chicano who had been standing patiently waiting came up on a signal from Mott, who performed the introductions.

"Gentlemen," he said. "I'd like to present the artist who conceived and executed this mural. This is Lorenzo Archuleta, who lives in East Los Angeles."

There was no doubt that the compelling mural had made an impact. Even Mott, who had watched its development from day to day, was almost overwhelmed by the finished splendor of the work. No matter what happened to the plant, the Morrison and Hale people had to see it as they were seeing it now. And, somehow, it had to be protected and preserved, no matter who took over the building on which it had been painted.

"I can't see any signs of the vandalism," Hale remarked, still looking up at the magnetic piece of mural art.

"It was quite easy to remove, sir," Lorenzo said, "and I repainted the damaged part. I did not charge for that—it was not your fault."

"How much were you paid for this?" Hale asked.

"Four dollars an hour, sir. The whole thing, without the repair, came to about eight hundred dollars. That includes the materials. I hope that you are pleased with it."

"Bob," Hale said to his president, "I had the idea of using this for the cover of our next annual report. Let's do that. In addition, I think it would be a good idea to offer some enlarged prints, say about eighteen-by-thirty, to our customers, framed, for a Christmas gift."

William Waters put a question. "Is there any practical way that this could be taken off the wall and moved to another location?"

"No, sir," Lorenzo answered. "But I could repaint it somewhere else if you wished. However . . ." He paused and then dared to say what was on his mind. ". . . I would rather do a new one. Possibly better."

Waters revealed an unexpected facet. "Better than this?" he asked. "I'm no artist, but I think that Diego Rivera would have been proud to sign this work."

That was the ultimate compliment, and Lorenzo Archuleta, who was only nineteen, flushed visibly. He could not remember a prouder moment in his life. He knew perfectly well that the new owners of the building might not like his work. If they didn't, they would be under no obligation to preserve it. The last few days had been both lonely and unhappy, but he had been driven by the determination to finish his finest effort—he had to complete what he had begun.

Frank Hale stood a little to one side and continued to study the mural while he thought. He was a director of several other companies, and in his mind he was reviewing the interior walls of their lobbies. At the same time he was nagged by the thought that paying the artist who had done such an extraordinary piece of work only four dollars an hour was inequitable.

He turned to the young Chicano. "Lorenzo, could you come and see me in my office tomorrow morning about ten?"

"Of course, sir, if you wish."

"That's a definite appointment then. I may be able to work something out for you. And you should also receive a royalty on the reproductions we plan to make."

"That isn't necessary, sir."

"I think that it is. We have a scholarship program we've maintained for some years. It might be an idea to send you to art school under that. I'd like to think it over." He turned to his colleagues. "To be honest about it, I'm not sure that they could teach him very much."

"I can look into it," Waters said.

That concluded the conversation for the time being. Mott intentionally stood by himself, immensely gratified by what the last five minutes had brought. Lorenzo's mural was by far the outstanding thing that had been accomplished since he had come to the barrio. It was there, a concrete piece of evidence that showed what the citizens of East Los Angeles could do. Granted, Lorenzo was a remarkably talented young man, but there were many other mural painters in the barrio, and their work could be seen everywhere.

As far as impact went, it had scored even more heavily than he had hoped. It was time to take his guests to the assembled meeting, and he would be able to do so with the knowledge that they had been at least softened up by Lorenzo's achievement. After seeing that mural, they could never again think of East Los Angeles as only a jungle, or of its citizens as less than gifted. Some of them anyway. One thing he knew for sure: Lorenzo had a brilliant future, and when this plant business had been settled, he was going to try and do something about it. The first step, of course, would be to bring his artist friend to see the mural. After that, a number of doors might open.

On the way to St. Ynez's Church, Mott briefed his passengers on what to expect. "I don't have to tell you that the committee has been organized to try and save your plant here. There have been several meetings, and a lot of ideas have been exchanged. A lunch is going to be served in a little while—I hope you like Mexican food."

"It's not my odds-on favorite," Hale admitted. "I've got a tender stomach, and things that are very strongly seasoned put me in orbit. I'd appreciate it if you'd steer me toward the milder dishes, if that's possible."

"I think that's been taken care of," Mott told him. "The Chicanos know that most other Americans don't care for food that's been seasoned with a flame thrower. The menu was planned very carefully, and I think you'll enjoy it."

"Who's footing the bill for all this?" Waters asked. "The church?"

"No, the individual committee members all chipped in. Incidentally, that includes me."

That statement seemed to upset Hale a little, and he responded to it. "Frankly, I'm a little uncomfortable. Right now I don't see any way that we can avoid turning them down, and under the circumstances, it won't be easy."

"If you'll allow me," Mott answered, "I'd like to suggest that you suspend judgment until you hear what they have to say."

There was no more conversation during the rest of the short ride to the church.

The parish hall had been prepared in the best way that was possible with the resources that were available. At one end of the hall some tables had been set up and covered with long strips of white paper to conceal the scars of hard usage. Steel folding chairs had been carefully placed around them in front of place settings made of ordinary metal. Where the invited guests were to sit, someone's precious sterling had been meticulously arranged.

At the other end of the room, more of the utility chairs had been set up, to accomodate some thirty people as a sort of audience. A speakers' table had been provided, and there was even a pitcher of fresh water and some glasses.

270

The room was already comfortably filled with people. Thirty or more were there and quietly waiting when Mott ushered in the guests from Morrison and Hale. Some of the men were wearing business suits, but the majority had on freshly laundered work clothes. The few women in the group largely wore blouses and skirts. Only Dolores Fernandez had chosen a dress. From the kitchen area there was a warm aroma of food being prepared. Two or three women were still busying themselves around the lunch tables.

Once in the room, Mott was acutely aware of the atmosphere that permeated the whole place. There was a visible hospitality that had been carefully planned, and behind it a deep-set desperation of the kind the early Christians must have known the night before they were to be herded into the arena to face the lions.

A strongly built, middle-aged man dressed in his obvious Sunday best came forward to greet the visitors. What he might have lacked in polish he made up in dignity. "My name is Reuben Estrada," he introduced himself. "I am chairman of our committee. I wish to thank you for us all for coming to our meeting."

Frank Hale at once knew that he was dealing with a sincere and responsible person. "We're glad to be here, Mr. Estrada," he responded. As soon as further introductions had been made and the necessary handshakes had been exchanged, the visitors were escorted to the speaker's table and invited to sit down.

"Have we got to be this formal?" Hale asked.

It did not take Estrada a second to realize that an error of judgment had been made. He at once corrected it with an efficiency that Hale had to admire—the man was a born executive himself.

"I would like to have the chairs arranged in a circle," Estrada announced. "In this way our guests can get to know us better, and it will be easier to speak back and forth."

While the rearrangement was being done, Hale slipped a folded-over piece of paper out of his breast pocket and consulted it. It was a list George Wilkinson had prepared of the best employees of the closed plant. Reuben Estrada's name was on it, and it was marked with a star, a recommendation that the employee be retained and transferred to another facility. Hale approved. Wilkinson had known a good man when he saw one.

It was quite remarkable how rapidly the rearrangement was

done. The people on the committee obviously wanted to please their guests in any way possible, and in their eagerness they almost overdid it. Everyone wanted to help so that no precious time would be wasted and so that the visitors would have the best possible impression of the efficiency of the group. At first two different rings were started, one within the other. As soon as the mistake was detected a fresh, hurried scramble corrected it. Several of the chairs were positioned four or five times before the final arrangement was worked out. To Frank Hale it was a prime example of too many cooks in the kitchen, but he saw beyond that and understood that the comparatively simple task became complicated because of excess anxiety. And he noted that despite the preliminary confusion, it was all worked out quickly and with intelligence.

When everyone had been seated in the new arrangement, Reuben Estrada, with unruffled dignity, once more took over as spokesman. "Gentlemen," he said, just a little stiffly, as though the term were unfamiliar to him, "we have invited you here in the hope that together we may be able to save you a great deal of money."

Frank Hale at once chalked up a plus for the man who had the insight to offer a benefit to his listeners in his opening salvo. Reuben Estrada was definitely going to be kept on the payroll.

"You have invested much money in the establishment of your factory here," Estrada continued. "To take everything away again and to install it all somewhere else would be very costly. So we suggest to you that the plant remain where it is."

"We'd very much like to do that," MacKay told him, "but you know some of the problems we have encountered here."

"Of course we do," Estrada agreed. "And we propose, perhaps through this meeting, to remove them. We have some proposals for you."

"We're certainly listening," MacKay said.

Frank Hale noted that the whole circle of listeners at that moment became tense—hardly anyone dared to move. They had picked their spokesman well, now his every word could mean their collective futures. He sensed fully how they felt and he empathized with them.

"Most of the young people of our community are very good

people," Estrada continued. "Only a small percentage of them belong to the gangs. Most are attending school, and they are good students. Someday they may work for you. But we admit that the gang members themselves are trouble makers, and they have given us a bad name."

He waited to see if there was any response to that, but everyone remained quiet. The other thirty-odd members of the committee were content to sit perfectly still and let him speak on their behalf.

"So we now propose to you that the active gang members, of the kind that started the fight in your washroom, not be hired any longer. If you are in doubt, we can tell you who they are. Without the gang members in the plant, we are sure that order will be maintained. We all promise this to you."

The committee members were quick to give nods of reassurance and approval, as though each one felt obligated to make a personal commitment.

Frank Hale took on the distasteful task of responding to that. "Mr. Estrada, that is a very sound suggestion, and I wish that we could adopt it. Unfortunately we can't, because by law we may not discriminate against anyone by reason of race, religion, national origin, or affiliations—unless they are subversive. I don't think that informal gang membership would qualify as subversive, therefore we have to give equal consideration to every qualified applicant."

If he had thought that that would throw Estrada off stride, he was happily mistaken.

"This we know, Mr. Hale, sir. May I explain that because of the gang activity and what they call the turf rules, many of the gang members have not been long enough at school. Many of them cannot even write their own names. Because of this, they are not qualified applicants."

"I'll think about that," Hale said.

"Now another thing, sir. We have had much discussion, and we have formed a plan. We know from our committee member, Miss Fernandez, that many of the people who applied to work for you could not fill out their own applications. From this we have an idea. We propose to you that we will form a committee to decide who may apply to work for you. In this way we will prevent any people who may cause trouble or not do their work well from applying. This will protect you from any unsuitable people you might have to hire because of the law."

"Mr. Estrada," Frank Hale answered, "I'm sure you appreciate why we can't permit that. It would be improper to allow any outside organization, no matter how well intended, to block the way into our employment office, so to speak. Everyone has to be given an equal opportunity, as I said."

When he saw the pleasant smile dawning on Estrada's face, he knew at once that somehow he had been outmaneuvered.

"With greatest respect, Mr. Hale—and Mr. MacKay and Mr. Waters—it is done all the time. By unions. In many places employers are not allowed to hire anyone except members of certain unions. So what we plan is this: we wish to form a union. But it is not to give you trouble—not to go on strike and then throw rocks through your windows. In our union, we will only allow good workers who are also dependable people. Then we will sign a contract with your company that only our members can work at your plant This is legal, we think."

"I presume that it is," Hale said, "but technically we would have to hold an election."

"It would be good if you do that. We will form our own union, the employees of Morrison and Hale. Then we will elect ourselves, and no one else will be allowed to work. Of course if there is anyone you wish to hire, we will take him right away into our union."

"You mean a closed shop," Waters interjected.

"It will be that, yes, but this time it will be for your benefit, as well as ours. We wish very much to have our jobs back. You wish very much not to lose any more money because of bad people. I can tell you that of all your good employees, everyone will vote for this union. If the contract is signed, then we can keep the bad people out of our union, and you will not have to hire them."

"I'll say one thing, Mr. Estrada," Frank Hale responded. "That's an idea that never occurred to me. I'll do this: I'll talk to our legal department and see what they have to say about such a contract."

Estrada showed his approval of that and then continued. "We have already such a contract prepared, Mr. Hale, for you to show to your legal people. We think that it is all right. We have consulted a good lawyer." He passed over a large, legal-sized brown envelope. "In this contract you will see that we have allowed Mr. Wilkinson to fire anyone at any time if they are not satisfactory. We will make no wage demands. All that we ask is that you please reopen your plant and give us our jobs back. We all need them very much."

Frank Hale was not comfortable. He knew that he could not reopen the plant—that decision had been dictated by many considerations—and he found it very difficult to tell that to these earnest and sincere people. At the same time, he could not allow them to go on paying legal fees and other expenses, in the hope of reviving their lost opportunities.

There was nothing for it except to be frank with them. Anything else would be cruel. "Mr. Estrada," he began cautiously, "I deeply appreciate all that you and the other members of your committee have done. I am grateful to you all. We have already announced that we will keep as many employees as possible from the plant here. That is to say, they will be offered jobs at whatever location we choose to open, and we hope that they will take them. But we have much more serious problems with the East Los Angeles plant that we have not been able to solve."

"The building, is it all right?"

"Yes, the building is, but—"

"And the location for shipping in and out? That is also all right?"

"That part is all right."

"But you have trouble with insurance."

"Yes," Hale admitted. "Among other things."

"We have one question, Mr. Hale: if our committee can find a good and reliable insurance company to protect your plant here at a good rate, will you then consider opening our factory once more?"

Since he had more or less decided by himself that the East Los Angeles experiment was a failure, Frank Hale had stuck to the principle of not sending good money after bad. He had determined to cut his losses and avoid what seemed to be inevitable future headaches. It was a sound principle, also, to make a decision and then to stick to it—every business school in the country taught that.

However, to some degree he had received new data. Also there were human considerations involved, and he was sensitive to them. He had served on too many public commissions of various sorts not to understand some basic human needs. And the answer to most of them was gainful employment under satisfactory circumstances. But he was not about to send his long-established company down the drain if he could help it.

It was while he was in that frame of mind that he saw Estrada patiently waiting for another opportunity to speak. "What is it?" he asked, a little more abruptly than he had intended.

"We only wish to tell you that we have called on many insurance companies to tell them of our plans. I must tell you that we were always turned down—until yesterday. We have now found a company that has listened to us. They have said that they would like to talk to you."

Frank Hale was immediately cautious. "It would have to be a thoroughly sound company," he began.

That damned smile came onto Estrada's face again. "It is, sir. It is the same one that insured you before. We were able to convince them that things will be much better now."

At that moment a portly, perspiring, but agreeable woman presented herself. "Lunch, it is now ready," she announced.

CHAPTER TWENTY-FOUR

IT WAS unusually hot in East Los Angeles. A strong and steady Santa Ana wind had been bringing in warm air from the desert for several days, until the whole area was saturated with it. The normal cool evenings did not come, so the tens of thousands of home-owners in the greater Los Angeles basin who had private swimming pools used them to good advantage.

There were few if any pools in the barrio. Instead the people came out of their small houses onto their front porches, if they had them, or onto the streets, where at least there was a fair breeze. Both the supermarkets and the small grocery stores sold greater quantities of soft drinks and beer. Eight times in one day various store owners were forced to part with a cold sixpack because the point of a knife was aimed at their abdomens. For the price involved they were not about to risk their lives. In one case an arrest was made.

Ralph Mott was returning to the barrio from a conference held in the downtown Hall of Justice. As he turned off the freeway and back onto the surface streets he automatically resumed his habit of noting everything that was in sight. He checked the gang graffiti to be sure that no new challenges had been spray painted across a wall or a window. He watched the traffic to see if there was any unusual movement of gang cars. And he watched the sidewalks to see if anything was happening there that might forecast possible trouble.

Back at the station he got himself a cold drink out of the machine. Then he sat down in his office to catch up on the overnight reports. Deputy Morse appeared in his doorway. For a police officer, he was a relatively small man, but no one questioned his capabilities.

"What have you got?" Mott asked.

Morse was direct. "The word is out that you want to know if we see anything unusual on the street," he said.

"That's right. Anything at all, I want to know about it."

"There's no hard evidence, but Sanchez and I have been cruising on the Heights, and neither of us felt quite right while we were up there. I can't cite anything specific—it's simply the feeling we have."

He did not need to add to that, Mott understood him perfectly. In court, hard and concrete evidence had to be presented, but crime prevention was another matter. Sometimes even the vaguest hint would provide enough information to forestall something of a serious nature. If both Morse and his partner felt that all was not right on the Heights, the chances of their being right was strong.

"I think I'll go take a look," Mott said. "Is anyone in and free at the moment?"

"Vetrovec just finished a booking."

"Ask him if he'll go out with me."

Five minutes later Mott wheeled a black-and-white out of the station, with the dependable Vetrovec beside him in the front seat. "What's your feeling?" he asked.

"I've been a little uneasy for the past two days. It's too hot for one thing—that makes the kids restless. And . . . full moon."

Let's see what we can pick up," Mott said. "We can do some field interviews."

Vetrovec pointed to a small pile of forms beside him on the seat. "I'll be surprised if we don't come back with something," he declared.

As soon as they reached the Montaña Mara turf, Mott sensed the thing Morse had noted. Everything apparently looked orderly, but something he could not define challenged his senses. He drove back and forth through the short, winding streets, seeking to pin down what it was that was not right.

Then Vetrovec spoke. "I know that kid. Let's pull over."

Mott swung the car over to the edge of the roadway and stopped close to an obvious gang member, who seemed slightly amused at his maneuver. Vetrovec got out of the car, a field interview card in his hand, and beckoned the youth over. As Mott got out, the boy sauntered over, taking all the time he could. Vetrovec let him, filling in one or two blanks on the card in the meantime. When the subject was close enough, he looked up and asked, "What's your name?"

"Bosco, man."

"Your real name is Verdugo, isn't it?"

The kid shrugged his shoulders.

Vetrovec continued to write on the card. "Verdugo, Gabriel. Member of—"

"Montaña Mara, man! Don' you know where you are? This our turf man. Everybody else they scared come near this place."

"I'm not scared," Vetrovec said. "My partner isn't scared."

"Sure—you got shotgun in the car. You got another gun right there. Me, I'm helpless."

That was a familiar gambit, which Vetrovec ignored. Instead he became even more informal, as though he were simply killing time. For six or seven minutes he talked with the Montaña Mara member, asking meaningless questions. He filled in the address on the card, added the phone number, and put down details of the physical description. "Have we got a picture of you, Bosco?" he asked.

"How I know that, man? Maybe yes, maybe no."

Almost languidly Vetrovec went back to the car and returned with a Polaroid camera. "Somebody from the Counts, they say you belong down there."

"They full o' crap, man!"

"Since you're Montaña Mara, I better take you off the Counts' list and put you up here."

"Damn right."

Vetrovec raised the camera and took a picture. It was all over before his subject was fully aware of his intention. "Hey, I don' like that, man," Bosco protested. "I din' say you could do that."

At the end of a few seconds Vetrovec peeled off the backing and showed the print. "That's not too bad," he said. "Want one for your girl?"

"I get my choice?"

"Why not."

Vetrovec shot another picture which, when ready, was very much like the first. Bosco took his choice and pushed the print into his pocket. During the whole procedure Mott was careful to keep himself in the background. Vetrovec had everything under control, and he needed no help.

Then the atmosphere changed. It was a subtle thing, but Mott caught it at once. "Hey," Vetrovec said. "You better watch out for your ass tonight. I hear that something heavy is going to go down."

Bosco looked at him, his head cocked slightly to one side. He was bigger than most of the gang kids—a little taller and already somewhat heavyset, despite that in appearance he could not have been more than nineteen or twenty. He had a well-developed mustache, but in dress and manner he was very much like all the others. "Nothin' go down I don' know it," he said. "Everybody, they scared of us now. The Counts, they just got four guys go prison. They never no good anyway."

Vetrovec slowly shook his head. "Something's going to happen. I'm surprised you haven't heard yet."

Bosco let his contempt show. "You crazy, man. Tonight we got big party, fuck girls. Nobody gonna miss that."

Vetrovec didn't comment. Instead he went back to the car and climbed in while Mott took the driver's seat. When they drove away Bosco was still standing at the same place, laughing at them.

"What do you think?" Vetrovec asked.

"That bit about the party was a little thick and too convenient. I didn't buy it."

"Same here," Vetrovec agreed.

"Fill me in on Bosco, I haven't seen him before."

"He's nineteen. He's been picked up for burglary two or three times, once for a minor two-eleven, and two counts of rape. The only time he's done is one very short term with the C.Y.A. We don't have him made as a gunman, but he's hard-core Montaña Mara, and I wouldn't trust him an inch. He's got a wife and two kids."

"Legally married?"

"I doubt it. We've had to take his wife to the hospital several times after he beat her up, usually on Saturday nights. The last time it was pretty bloody."

"Why don't we do something about that?"

"She won't sign a complaint. We took him to court once for wife-beating and she refused to testify. It's the macho thing again, although she could simply be scared of him. But I don't think so."

Two more field interviews on the Heights yielded very little. After that Mott cruised the Counts' turf, but hardly anyone connected with the gang was in sight. When another gang control car came up the street in the opposite direction, they stopped for a conference.

"What are you getting on the Counts?" Mott asked.

"They're having a big meeting," the deputy driving the other car answered. "There most be forty of them there."

"How do you read it?"

"Trouble. Montaña Mara has a couple of lookouts stationed on the street—Jin-Jin and Bosco—but the bulk of the gang is out of sight."

"How about the rest?"

"The Locos are out cruising. Apparently they're expecting the Veronas to hit them. Chino is out of the hospital, and he wants blood. The Sapos are cooking up something, but right now we don't know what it is."

"How about the Spiders and the Magnolias?"

"That's cool. They're having a peace meeting right now."

Mott pulled away and drove to the small facility where Brother Julio lived and worked. If anyone knew what was in the wind it would be Brother Julio, and he would be equally anxious to see it forestalled.

One of the sisters on duty met them. "Brother Julio is out," she said. "We do not know where he is."

"One question, Sister." Mott was careful to speak casually. "Is

281

it usual for Brother Julio to go off like this?"

The nun, who was simply dressed in plain street attire, blinked twice before she answered. "I have not known him to do it before. He is often gone, but he always calls in. We have not heard from him, and we are just a little concerned."

CHAPTER TWENTY-FIVE

AS DANNY TORRES drove the short distance home from the hospital, his mind was in a torment. Up to that time the one focal point in his life had been his gang, and to it he had pledged his total loyalty. During the past three years Montaña Mara had eclipsed all other considerations, even his own family. In a sense the gang had become his family, and he had felt the powerful macho of being one of its leading members.

Now something new had intruded and seized hold of him. He had discovered his work at the hospital to be almost endlessly fascinating. Every day he saw all kinds of people, brought in with every sort of accident and injury. Some of them died, but others came out of the emergency rooms with the death that had been in them exorcized and their injuries repaired. They were not yet well, of course, but he had seen what he considered to be near miracles. He had not been allowed in the actual treatment rooms when they were in use, but he had cleaned up after emergency procedures, and he had seen the patients before and after they had received medical attention.

Now he wanted to become a doctor more than ever before in his life. He saw himself as a skilled emergency surgeon in command of an operating team. With his gifted hands he too would cure the sick and bring back life when it was ebbing away. He knew that it was a remote dream, but it was sharp and clear because he saw such things happening every day. If others could do it, it was not too fantastic that he could learn the same skills and acquire the same knowledge. He already had a strong sense of being part of it all, even though his duties were humble and he had as yet no real responsibility.

On top of it all, he was getting paid. He had a fresh crisp check in his pocket made out for almost more money than he had ever possessed at one time in his life. Before too long there would be another such check, and Dr. Sanchez had hinted that in the near future he might be assigned to some kind of study program.

All of this meant that for the first time Montaña Mara had a powerful rival. In the past he had given almost blind obedience to the wills and dictates of the gang. Now that might be open to question. He was still a completely loyal member, but he had glimpsed the fact that there were other things in the world that he had never really known existed before he had begun his new job.

Lastly, of late his mother had shown signs of being proud of him. That was an entirely new side of her that he had not seen since he had first been jumped into his gang. And now he no longer had to lie to her about what he was doing.

He turned off the freeway at Eastern Avenue and headed his car up onto the Heights. His euphoria and his new job did not rob him of his street sense; when he saw Bosco wave to him he knew immediately that something important was about to happen. He would not be able to sit down and tell his mother about what he had seen and done that day. He was needed, and as soon as he had changed into his regular clothes he would have to go and find out what it was. He was not afraid, but he allowed himself to hope that he wouldn't have to do anything that would interfere with his job. At that moment he remembered that he was due to be taught how to give emergency treatment to the victim of a sudden heart attack. Everyone at the hospital had to learn that, but to him it would be the first giant step that would forever separate him from the laymen.

When he was ready he went out on the street and, by cutting through the intricate passageways of the Heights, he reached his gang's meeting place within two or three minutes.

When he learned there what was being planned, his thoughts about the hospital and the possible future that it held for him were effectively blocked out of his mind.

The very warm weather and the bright promise of the full moon that would be in the sky by nightfall had their combined effect in many parts and corners of the barrio. On the turf of La Calle Verona, Chino and the other members of the gang had been gathering every day until they once more felt like a tightly organized, potent fighting unit. Several new members had been jumped in so that the lost strength had been recovered. Chino was not the nominal leader of the gang, but he had gained much stature for the successful way that he had brought disaster to Los Counts. One dead and three in the slammer had more than avenged the Counts' attack on him in the street and the insult to the gang. Now the time had come to settle old scores with the Sixth Street Locos; after that had been done La Calle Verona would once more emerge into full gang glory, something that it had not enjoyed since the freeway had taken so much of its turf many years before.

The Machetes and White Roses for the moment had no quarrel with anyone. Most of their activity centered around burglary, purse snatching, and other similar actions. North of Montaña Mara, on the other side of the extensive railroad tracks, Los Lobos were more concerned with the gangs in Hollenbeck territory. West of Montaña Mara, Los Marengo Chicos were also spilling over into the Hollenbeck gang-infested area. If they got into trouble over there, it would be the Los Angeles Police Department's headache, but the CRASH program there was well equipped to handle it.

Mott had that whole picture very clearly in his mind as he drove back to the station. His immediate problems centered around five gangs, and he intended to keep a very sharp eye on them for the next two or three days. If that amount of time passed without any serious incident, it would be beyond his expectations.

He had a talk with the watch commander coming on duty and learned that he was in complete agreement as to what to expect. The regular patrol units would maintain their established schedules covering the whole barrio; the gang control units would be concentrated in those areas where trouble, if there was to be any, was most likely. When that had been done, Mott put in a call to Brother Julio, but he was still out and no message from him had been received. That was not any real cause for concern, but he put out the word to the units in the field that if they saw Brother Julio to please ask him to call the station. Since the concentration of sheriff's cars in the barrio was approximately three times normal coverage, that was likely to get results fairly quickly. Mott called Nancy and then went out for a bite to eat. He took a walkie-talkie with him and kept it on in the booth on the table while he ate, but nothing significant was reported.

By the time he was back, the sun had reddened considerably and hung with majestic dignity in the western sky. The Santa Ana was still blowing, bringing in the desert air, hot and dry, off the vast Mohave. The moon was not yet up, but when it came it would be huge and yellow, and charged with a potency that could inspire romance in some and deadly violence in others. By midnight it would wash the streets with enough light to purge the blackness and only the deepest shadows would remain inviolate.

Only a few official cars were left on the lot—most of the available units were out. If a real crisis came, the Special Enforcement Bureau had all its own equipment and could pour strong reinforcements into the street, but normally the SWAT personnel would not be called upon unless there was something critical for them to handle.

After that it became a waiting game. There was nothing concrete that Mott could focus on, yet he was uncomfortably close to certain that before the watch ended, something in the nature of a serious incident would be recorded. He took strength from the fact that others, with the instinct that policemen develop, felt as he did. There was comfort in not being alone.

He talked to the duty sergeant and then went in to spend a few minutes with the watch commander. The calls were beginning to come in—from Whittier Boulevard, from Eastern Avenue, from the other streets and structures of the barrio. Within a half hour four different 415s were put on the air, the official code for a disturbance of the peace. Two of them were family altercations, one was a fight in a parking lot that took three units to handle. That early in the evening it was a bad sign.

The stores were still open, which left the way for shoplifting and other incidents on business premises. The few places that sold guns were kept under special watch. Not all of the people who attempted to hold up gun stores came from the barrio—they gravitated in from all parts of the basin. Guns were legitimate articles of merchandise, but they were also killing machines, and some of them could be very easily concealed.

A field unit called for backup. It had found two unconscious juveniles in an alley, apparently stoned on PCP. Every patrol deputy knew that when on that drug, subjects could change from catatonic to hyperactive and violent within a second or two.

As the calls continued, the cars began to roll into the yard with prisoners in the back. They were faced against the wall in the small jail section and carefully searched before being booked. The females were taken directly to Sybil Brand Institute for Women, which was only a short distance away, and turned over to the custody people there. Although it had already been done in the field, Miranda rights were read in English and Spanish before the male prisoners were booked and stored away in the cell block to await transportation to Central Jail.

Soon the report writing room was almost full with deputies doing the necessary paper work connected with each arrest. It was an essential routine, but while it was going on, a number of needed units were being kept off the street.

A 211 at a small grocery store came in—three juveniles armed with knives. This time they had not just taken beer, they had emptied the cash register and cut the owner badly in the arm, despite the fact that he had offered no resistance. The young bandits had not been satisfied with what they had taken and had slashed the owner to show their disappointment.

That triggered a major response, and six units rolled, some to the scene, some to the vicinity to look for the suspects. Mott was tempted to respond to that one himself, but he had made a firm decision not to interfere in the regular patrol work. He could add little there. It was more important for him to stand by in cases of any outbreak of intergang violence.

He remembered a promise he had made to Nancy, one that made very good sense. He went back to his office, took his protective vest out of the bottom drawer of his desk, and put it on under his shirt. It was a little uncomfortable, but it gave good protection against anything up to and including a forty-five. If he was called into the field, it would be best to go prepared. There was no percentage at all in being foolhardy.

He went back to see the duty sergeant. "What's the volume like?" he asked.

"Heavy," the sergeant answered. "We just got an OD and a wife-beating, both in Sapos turf."

"Any signs of gang activity?"

The sergeant knew what he meant. "Not yet, but I wouldn't be surprised."

That reminded Mott. He picked up a phone and dialed Brother Julio's number. No answer.

The duty sergeant raised a hand. Mott stopped to listen. One of the field gang control units had switched to another frequency. That meant a semiprivate communication less likely to be overheard.

"La Calle Verona is out in force," the deputy reported. "We've just come from the Lagunos' turf, and they seem to be relatively quiet, so it isn't between them. It doesn't look good."

Mott gave swift orders to send two more of his gang control units into the vicinity: it was just possible that a show of force would be enough to deter any hastily made plans. No one wanted to get busted even for a short time, if it could be avoided.

Still unsettled in his mind, he went out onto the parking lot to have a look and a feel of the weather. As he had expected, the daylight was gone. It was still very warm, and the brilliant moon had just cleared the eastern horizon. He went inside, a tight sensation building in his gut. He thought of a cup of coffee and rejected the idea. The way he was feeling, it might just give him an acid stomach.

The door banged open and four more deputies came in, bringing three prisoners with them. Two were placid, the third was struggling hard, and it took two strong men to restrain him. He was kicking, yelling, and swinging his head hard, trying to bite. When he ceased screaming, he poured out vituperation, repeating the same short obscene phrases over and over. The deputies paid no attention. He was turned toward the wall and the searching procedure began. The prisoner tried to stomp on a deputy's foot and

288

almost succeeded. Unfortunately, it was a familiar scene.

The report room became even more crowded. The radio calls were almost continuous, while the corridors saw a steady flow of deputies going back and forth. Mott tried once more for Brother Julio, and again there was no answer.

Quite suddenly he knew that he could not endure his static role any longer. If the sword of Damocles was over his head, there was no need for him to remain under it. He picked up the keys to the unit assigned to him and headed for the parking lot.

As the hot night air met him once again, he told himself sharply that as a policeman he should remain dispassionate, maintain law and order exactly according to the book, and under no circumstances allow himself to get personally involved. But he could not live that way. Despite all of his experience and the excellent record that he had built within the department, he *was* involved with the barrio and dedicated to the fight against the blight of juvenile gang warfare that had been ripping it to pieces for more than forty years.

He got into the car, hoping that Brother Julio was O.K. He wondered how a man could give up his whole life, as Julio had done, and be content to serve in a restricted capacity without any of the authority and powers of a priest or the prestige that went with the office. The work that he did was unquestionably important, but he was a man of much greater capacity.

Getting to know Brother Julio had been one of the unexpected rewards of his new post. There were others: Reuben Estrada, his colleagues at the station—and Elena Alvarez. By the standards of the Department he was a man of good moral character, but Elena was more woman in one package than he had ever encountered before.

He snapped on the radio, checked that the shotgun was locked in place, and ran through the other equipment. He touched the electronic siren for a second, checked the roof lights, and verified the status of his own weapon. By rights he should shake down the back as well, but he knew that had been thoroughly done by the last user of the car. He had his seat belt already fastened. Besides, in all the years of faithfully checking the rear seats of the units he used, he had never found anything. There had been things after prisoners had been transported—many kinds of evidence discovered by himself and other deputies—but no car gassed and ready to go out had ever held a thing.

He played the odds and drove smoothly down onto Third Street. After putting out a radio call advising that he was in the field, he turned westward, toward the turf of the Counts, Montaña Mara, the Lobos, and the Veronas. Their various areas were lined up in a row at the formal boundary that separated East Los Angeles from the city itself. He was reminded of the time that a troublesome drunk had been picked up by one of his cars close to the dividing line. Since no LAPD units had been in evidence, the unwanted prisoner had been transported a block or so inside the city limits and left there for the LAPD to find.

A half an hour later another sheriff's unit found the same drunk three blocks inside its patrol area. He was picked up and brought in before someone could be charged with littering.

The radio kept going. The feminine voices from the hilltop Communications Center never displayed any excitement or emotion. Mott knew that the women were remarkable at their job; the consoles they operated were like the controls of a space ship. Repeatedly he heard the same code, 415, and there was also an unusual number of traffic reports. Two pursuits went down at almost the same time, and the frequency he was listening to was only one of nineteen actively used by the Sheriff's Department.

He wondered what it would be like to be a policeman in a smaller, far less complex department. He decided that he wouldn't like it. There was a point of professional pride in belonging to the largest organization of its kind in the world, and the sheriff himself was one of the best-qualified and most respected top lawmen around. The whole department knew that. Apparently the citizens knew it, too, because he had been reelected six times by large majorities.

Mott cruised slowly through the turf of the Counts, then turned south across Third and into the territory of the Locos. He saw many things, but nothing that touched a responsive chord in his brain. He continued on down into La Calle Verona territory and met two of his units in that small area. He exchanged a few words with each one, then drove on.

The words "Officer needs assistance, shots fired" jumped into his consciousness. He caught the location—East Whittier Boulevard—as he snapped on the roof lights and rammed down on the gas pedal. Within a half minute he heard the siren of the unit going Code Three. There would only be one, because two units coming with sirens on could not hear each other, and because they would be traveling at high speed, disaster could follow. Code Two was nearly as fast, and much safer.

Because of his rank he rolled directly to the location, ready to take command if necessary. Patrol units would respond to the scene while others would take up a perimeter, positioned to intercept any fleeing suspects.

When he heard the sharp sound of two more shots, he was glad that he had remembered to put his vest on. It only protected a part of his body, but that included most of the vital areas. Whatever it did or did not do, it was a comfort to know that it was there.

Just as he rolled up, a Code Four came over the radio—no further assistance required. He glanced at the graffiti visible on a side wall and knew that he was on the turf of Los Sapos.

Again his attention was riveted by the radio. "A four-fifteen fight, Rowan and Princeton, several juveniles."

That was squarely in the territory of the Sixth Street Lobos. It had to be them and La Calle Verona—he had foreseen that possibility before he had left the station.

The call was on the other side of the barrio. He had plenty of units in that area, and there was no need for him to go there unless it became more serious. A sergeant would be well equipped to handle it. He radioed to call him if he were needed.

He continued westward, but began to work his way north toward the Heights. That was where trouble was brewing and on such a night two things could well go down at the same time.

Jambo was the last to slip through the loose board that allowed entry into the garage where Los Counts planned most of their campaigns. It could not hold the whole gang, but it was large enough for the chosen warriors and provided a well-concealed meeting place. As far as any of them knew, it was also completely secret.

Although it was night and he was inside, Jambo kept his eyes slightly squinted, as though it aided him in his thinking. It did make him look quite fierce, and for that reason it was admired.

"Tonight," he said, "them mothers from Montaña, they plannin' to get us. You look, you see they not goin' down Eastern, 'cause they loadin' up for us. Last time they come to get us, we fix them good. One guy up there, he got no balls anymore. 'Nother guy, we get his brother, so he pee in his pants to get us."

He stopped and let that sink in.

"He called Gaucho. He swear he kill us all. His brother was Kiko and we got him. It's tonight."

Jambo didn't go beyond that. If they couldn't figure it out from there, they didn't deserve the high honor of belonging to the deadliest gang in the entire barrio.

"So we gonna' hit 'em just before they ready to hit us. If they come lookin', we not here. We go up back way an' hit their houses. We make 'em hurt where they live—on their turf."

He paused again and squinted his eyes even more. "They got their guns, we know. They come to hit us here. We go hit them there instead."

There was a silent ripple. They all knew that the Heights had natural defenses that gave the gang up there an advantage on its own ground. But if Los Counts were ever to show their greater macho and their skill in combat, they would have to invade the enemy territory.

Even though they were inside the garage, they sensed and felt the warm night, and they all knew that the moon was full. The combination was compelling. The very air seemed to be telling them that this was the time that could not be passed by.

Jambo looked down at little Benjie Morales, who was four inches shorter than himself. "Benjie, he been good since we jump him in. He fourteen now and we been trainin' him. He got no rap sheet, so they can't bust him hard no way. Tonight, Benjie, he gonna carry a gun."

Benjie tried his best to look very proud and not at all scared.

Jambo, like a skilled advocate, had kept his best argument for the last. "We got no choice. We wait here, they come kick our ass. We go hide, we got no macho no more—we cut off our own balls. So now we go."

He had not told them anything new, but he had given them the feeling of a need to take action. They were all ready. The guns had been brought from the places they had been concealed.

The time for talking was over.

Mott was half way toward the turf of Montaña Mara when he got a call to change frequencies. He did and met the car that wanted him on the new band. Deputy Rose came through calmly and clearly. "On the turf of the Counts. Nothing definite, but suspicious circumstances."

That was enough. A deputy of Rose's experience would not report that without good reason.

Mott picked up his own microphone. "Stay and cover it. I'm sending backup. I'm going on the Heights."

"Right. Any sign of Brother Julio?"

"No. Let me know if you contact him."

Mott switched frequencies and check with his station dispatcher. He received the news that the 415 on the Lobos turf was apparently quite heavy and that no Code Four had as yet been put out. Sergeant McBride was on the scene.

For a moment he considered backing up Rose himself; then he decided to stick to his original decision. Rose had nothing definite, and another car could handle it. Every bit of policeman's instinct he had developed in the barrio told him that the Heights was where he should be.

He turned off Eastern and began the climb up onto the turf of Montaña Mara. Halfway up he met another unit coming down. He directed the other car to back up Rose and to advise if any more help was needed. Then he continued up the hill. The area above him was limited, and now that he knew it by heart, he could cover all of the few streets in not much more than five minutes. He had all four of his windows down, but the only real sounds that he heard were those of his own vehicle.

He passed the Torres house and wondered how Danny was making out. The last he had heard, he was doing well at the hospital and seemed to like the work very much. He continued on, weaving slowly through the short, twisting streets, watching and listening. He was breathing a congratulatory sigh that everything was so quiet when the truth hit him with the impact of a blow. Montaña Mara was nowhere in sight. On such a hot night, with the moon out full, the gang members should have been everywhere. They should have been gathered in small groups around their cars or in the other places where they were usually found, but a strange silent absence hung over the Heights, and the very thought of it make Mott break out in a mild sweat. For a brief moment he wondered if he might be in personal danger, because it had all the earmarks of an ambush.

He called Rose on channel two and asked him what he had. Rose reported that the Counts, and their cars, were largely gone.

He thought immediately of Hazard Park, just below the Heights, but part of Montaña Mara's turf. He sped up his car's pace and rolled down to the small park that in times past had been a battleground. Some of the lights were on; there were people about, but no signs of gang activity at that moment. He got out of his car and checked the clubhouse. The steel-edged door that protected the few pieces of sports equipment provided by the county had been pried open again; the three-inch metal hasp had been broken. All that was left inside was a deflated basketball torn open on one side.

The radio he held in his hand jerked his attention away from everything else. "Twenty-three boy nine, four-seventeen—shots fired. Twelve hundred block of Dwiggins."

Dwiggins Street was almost directly in the center of the Heights.

He ran to his car, jerked the door open, and threw himself behind the wheel. He revved up the engine and burned rubber as he spun out into the street and accelerated toward the nearest intersection that would take him up onto the high ground. He turned the corner with screaming tires and floored the gas pedal as much as he dared, forcing the patrol car to climb at its maximum performance.

He snapped on the colored roof lights, then made a near U turn onto another street by skidding the second half of the way around on the dry pavement. He had to slow down then, because the streets on the Heights were all short and winding. As fast as he dared, he reached Dwiggins Street and looked for the signs of trouble. He traveled around the loop at the east end of the street without seeing or hearing anything. Then, just as he straightened out, he heard the clear sharp explosion of an unmistakable shot. At the same instant the windshield before him erupted into a maze of cracks.

He grabbed the mike. "Twenty-three boy nine, four-seventeen —just hit. Possible ambush twelve hundred block Dwiggins Street. Request assistance and ARGUS."

A second shot hit something in his vehicle, and the engine stopped—he was trapped where he was. Backup would be coming fast, but he was a visible target in his immobile unit. He made an instant decision and acted on it. He cut the lights, sprang out of his car and squatted behind the engine hood, using it as a shield until he could determine the direction from which the shots had come.

Two more guns, of different calibres, split the night air. He saw the flash of one of them coming from a figure crouching between two close-together houses. Then the figure was gone.

His service weapon in hand, Mott circled away from his car on the dead run, heading toward the place where the phantom figure with the gun had been. As he sprinted on a long curve across the narrow street, he heard another two shots and knew that all hell was breaking loose. He didn't have a moment to think. He reached the place where the gunman had been and almost threw himself down the passageway between the houses. His own weapon was still in his hand, but he was not equipped with speed loaders, and he knew that he might have critical need of them.

He could have fired ahead of him, but he did not dare—he could not see his target and he would not shoot blindly. There would be two or three hundred innocent people on the Heights, and the hot night would tend to bring them out of their tiny houses. Running dangerously fast in the blackness of the passageway, he reached the next street and saw a body lying in the middle of the roadway.

He made an instant decision: even if it was an ambush, he had to take the chance. Crouching low, he ran to the victim and dropped to one knee, trying to make a diagnosis of his condition.

The bright moon lit the face enough for the victim to be identifiable. The build and the mustache confirmed it—Bosco. Mott listened a scant moment and heard no car coming. "How bad are you?" he snapped. "Quick!"

Bosco's mouth opened in a wide, almost horrifying grin, and blood appeared at the corners. He could barely speak, but he did not seem to care. "I fool you good, pig. You not know a Goddamn thing!" Then he went limp.

295

Mott thrust his gun into its holster, hooked Bosco under his armpits, and dragged him off the roadway onto the dried earth at one side. The moment that he had his hands free once more, he reached quickly for his weapon and looked for the best place to take cover. He heard another shot, saw the figure ahead of him, and felt the hard thud as the bullet hammered into his protective vest just below the breastbone. He dropped prone, aimed, and fired. It was the first time in twelve years that he had discharged his weapon in anger, but he did it without hesitation. He saw a figure turn and fall, face down.

The siren of a car coming Code Three bit into his consciousness, and he knew that within a minute at the most he would have help. He needed it desperately. He had to get back to his car, to the radio, and to the place where his support could find him. He turned back down the narrow passageway and ran, more carefully this time, toward his unit. As he emerged once again onto Dwiggins Street he heard more shots. The siren was very close; then it shut down abruptly, indicating that it had reached the top of the plateau.

He made it back to his car on the dead run. He yanked the door open, lay face down on the seat, and used the mike. "Twenty-three boy, Dwiggins Street. Nine ninety-eight—possible one eighty-seven victim."

That would do it—everything would roll on that call. He would have been a casualty himself if it had not been for the blessed vest, and as it was, a pain was steadily growing just under his rib cage.

He had already requested ARGUS; the 998 "officer needs help" call would insure it. The turbine-powered Hughes 500s that were the regular patrol vehicles could respond at close to 180 miles per hour, if they weren't already tied up elsewhere. It was a hell of a big county.

There was no point calling in any more. They would know to send paramedics and ambulances—and to keep their heads down. It was the first moment he had had to think, but before he could use it a gang car with smoking tires almost screamed past him in second gear and was gone before he could make out the license plate.

He got back behind the wheel in four seconds, put on the headlights, and found that he could see enough through the windshield to drive. He kicked the engine over without much hope. To his surprise it caught and held. He hit the roof lights again to identify himself to incoming units and started down the street the way that the gang car had gone.

Overhead a brilliant light split the sky; the sound of a helicopter was suddenly sharp and clear. Mott drove ahead, toward the point where the light was aimed, a possible two blocks away. He had to turn two corners to get there, and he still did not see the unit that he had heard coming Code Three. It had to be somewhere close by, looking for him. It could have found the two victims that he knew were down.

Another gunshot barked, and immediately after it came the thunder of a shotgun. It was war, and he knew he was on the battlefield. The intense light from the helicopter shifted to a point two hundred feet away and fixed there. There was no fast way to drive. He jumped out of his car once more and raced across bare ground, his gun again in his hand.

He had his ID clipped to his coat pocket, but he was not in uniform, and it was not very visible, especially at night. The other deputies would see it, but the warring factions might not.

He took shelter behind the corner of a small wooden house and looked out cautiously to see as much as he could.

Poochie knew that this was the biggest gunfight Montaña Mara had ever had, and for the gang that had been almost his whole life, he was ready to take even desperate chances. They had been hit, attacked by Los Counts, who had sneaked up the back way from City Terrace and caught them before they were ready to fight. He was panting hard, but his heart was pounding more from the excitement and the danger than from the running he had done. No one knew the complex geography of the Heights any better than he did, which was why he was such a valuable member of the gang. And he was a good shot.

He was Poochie now, all other identity erased. He could not even think of himself as Danny Torres. That had been another time, in another world—to the gang he was Poochie, and the gun in his hand was part of his gang's front line of defense.

When the light from the helicopter burst down from the sky, it instantly changed the strategy, because darkness in that area was

297

crucial. The withering light was a plague. Poochie knew at once that no one would stay in its stark glare. He dove into the protecting darkness of deep shadow and, almost like a ghost, worked his way toward the place where he knew his enemies would be hiding. As he ran he saw a white car ahead that had been stopped by shotgun fire. One blast had put it out of commission. The doors on the left side were both open, and two people lay in the street. One of them was still; the other, a smaller one, was crying—not the agony of a wounded soldier, but the cry of something younger and more terrified.

Poochie was on his own. He did not know where the others were, but he knew better than to approach the unknown car. Someone inside could be waiting with a cocked gun. The snap of a small caliber shot came from somewhere opposite him, and he sensed an enemy. He had a much more powerful gun in his right hand, a thirty-eight, and he had only fired one round. He crouched, concealed, and strained his eyes trying to detect his unseen adversary. He had no way of being sure that the shot had been aimed at him—he had been well out of sight, and he hadn't heard the bullet go by.

The helicopter light was not coming closer, it was moving away. The darkness deepened until only the moonlight was left. He knew then that he had the advantage of knowing every twist and turn of the terrain as no one but a Montaña Mara could.

The desperate crying in front of him kept up and even seemed to grow stronger. Then it came to Poochie that it had to be coming from a child. He had heard that exact kind of sound before, in the hospital. With that recognition the instant projector in his mind showed him the emergency rooms he had serviced, the stricken patients coming in. He froze in indecision and there was silence— blessed, deadly silence.

Then a scream of anguish tore at his soul and whipped the mask of Poochie from his face. Danny Torres ran forward, bent over the pitifully small frame that was Benjie Morales. He knew at once what he had to do. He dropped his gun, sank to his knees, and lifted his patient into his arms.

Standing up he heard sirens, the sirens just like those that the paramedics use on their Code Three runs coming into the hospital. Benjie's small hands grabbed hold of him in agony, pleading for help. In sudden desperate hope Danny turned, ignoring the dead form of Jambo ten feet away, and walked quickly back toward the shadows and the short passage that would take him to the place where the flashing red and blue lights were waiting.

He was three steps from the safety of the shadows when the bullet hit him.

The hilltop was alive with police cars and emergency vehicles. The first call of "shots fired" had triggered a substantial response; the backup call of "officer needs help" had made it close to an all-out effort. Only the seldom-heard call of "nine ninety-nine"—"officer in danger of his life"—would have produced a greater reaction, sweeping aside all jurisdictional boundaries. There was no need for outside help. The SEB had responded in its own black and white cars, and the whole area was perimetered. Three obvious gang cars had been stopped trying to escape from the Heights and their occupants detained for questioning. A number of weapons had been recovered.

On the plateau itself regular black-and-whites, gang control units, and SEB cars saturated the place where the principal fighting had taken place. Two red paramedic units were on hand with two supporting county ambulances.

Aided by the ARGUS helicopter, which kept a brilliant light concentrated on the scene as it circled, the western section of the Heights was rapidly searched and defused. Eleven gang suspects were taken into custody as the paramedic teams looked after the casualties. The battle was over. The heavy sheriff's response on the ground and in the air had purged all thought of anything but possible escape. Many of Montaña Mara tried to slip down the hillside through passageways and by hidden trails in the steeper areas, but the deputies pursuing them knew the ground almost as well, and at the bottom of the hill more cars were waiting, keeping the whole territory sealed off.

A van came up the hill to handle the considerable number of juveniles in custody. As it did so the SEB commander on the scene put out a Code Four, no further assistance needed. To the best of his knowledge the situation was contained and the mop-up was well under way.

Two short blocks away Gaucho was crouching in a patch of

299

almost total darkness, breathing hard and obsessed with the idea that at last he was avenging his brother Kiko. Half out of his mind, the presence of so many police vehicles not far away told him only that the enemy was out in force. He was oblivious to it. He had a gun in his hand, and it had become part of him. With it he would kill and kill, and if enough of the enemy were destroyed, then Kiko would come back to him.

In front of him, in the street, was a Counts car that one of his gang brothers had blasted with his shotgun. When the driver had tried to get out, Gaucho had shot him; he lay still now in the street. When another enemy had picked up the screaming kid that had been beside him, Gaucho had shot him too, and the score for Kiko had gone higher. A hot red mist seemed to engulf Gaucho, making him a superman, the very embodiment of vengeance that nothing could destroy or deter.

His breath came faster and faster as he waited, praying desperately for another target, perhaps the one that would release Kiko from his bonds. At any moment more of Montaña Mara would join him, coming out of the blackness to form with him an invincible wall of ruthless firepower, and their oneness would dominate the earth.

Half a block away, Mott pressed himself against a wall, his weapon in his hand, trying to fight down the knowledge that he had shot and possibly killed a teenaged boy. He knew he had had no choice—when he had been fired upon he had had to return fire to protect himself and any others that the juvenile gunman might otherwise get in his sights. He had always known that the time could come when he would have to use ultimate force. When it had finally happened he had not had a second in which to make his decision. He had aimed for the center of his target and had seen his opponent fall. The image persisted until he heard, to his right, the cries of a child in agony.

He ran toward the point the sounds came from his radio in his left hand. As soon as he determined the situation he would be able to call for medical assistance. A half second later he heard the sound of another shot.

For a bare moment it startled him, because he had thought that the shooting was all over; now it was breaking out again. Three more strides took him to where he could see the street and a car standing still. Near it was movement. A figure was falling to its knees almost in front of him while holding something in its arms. He froze, taking the one second necessary to discover what was happening. An anguished cry that began just in front of him was blanketed by a sharp, short-range shot. This time he saw the flash and knew where the gunman was concealed. He tried to raise his arm to return the fire, but it would not move. He tried harder and still his muscles refused to react.

Then a stab of pain told him that he had been hit somewhere near his right shoulder. Too late he realized that he was in the open. He tried to throw himself down, but his body was stunned and did not respond as fast as it should. He tried again, desperately, to raise his arm and fire, but his gun hung uselessly in his frozen right hand.

He heard movement, looked, and saw a crazed figure jump into full view. He saw a gun being leveled at him and knew that careful aim was being taken. A deputy in a flat-out sprint burst into view, letting out a wild yell. Like a cornered wildcat the figure whirled to shoot as the deputy hurled himself into the air and came down on the gunman in a flying tackle that froze his arms against his sides. They both went down hard and rolled over, still locked together.

His body recharged, Mott ran to help, his temporarily useless arm hanging at his side. He was beside them in six seconds—by then the gunman was face down, screaming incoherently. The deputy who had downed him was spread prone across his back. Mott dropped beside them and let his radio go to free his good hand. He saw the suspect's gun lying at his feet and grabbed it a little awkwardly in his left hand, ready to use it if he must. The deputy on the ground threw him one quick glance. He was startled to see Elena Alvarez.

More running feet told him that he need do no more. Almost at once two more uniformed deputies were beside him, but it was Alvarez who locked on the cuffs and got her prisoner to his feet.

Mott handed the gun over and recovered his radio. With it he called for medical help at the location. Seconds later the brilliant overhead light reached him, and he saw the still body lying beside the car. He went closer and saw that it was Jambo. The medics would take care of him.

There were crying sounds almost like those of a small child in his ears, and he remembered the figure he had seen sinking to the ground. A bright red light caught his attention—a paramedic van was coming. He flagged it down and pointed to where the sounds were coming from. He was dimly aware that he was in pain himself, but he had no time to think about that.

Two paramedics ran to the place he had indicated, carrying their equipment. SEB deputies took the prisoner to the van. That left him virtually alone, still standing in the bright bath of light from overhead. It was strong enough to show the pattern of blood that stained most of the right side of his shirt.

Alvarez came to him, still breathing hard from her all-out sprint. "You've been hit," she said, almost as if he didn't know it. "Let's go. I'll drive you to the hospital."

"I want to go back to my car first," Mott answered.

"Are you able to?" she asked.

"My right arm isn't functioning, but otherwise I'm O.K.," he replied. She understood—he was a lieutenant and the ranking officer in the field. He would want to check on the status of the operation and delegate someone to take his car back to the station. If he could hold out long enough to do it, he should. And it was only a short distance.

Since the shooting had stopped and the mop-up operation was in full swing, he did not hesitate to take a slightly shorter route between two buildings and up a small gully. The helicopter was still overhead, lighting most of the area.

It was in the narrow bottom of the gully that he and Alvarez found Brother Julio. He was lying quietly on his side, as though he were asleep. The moment Mott made the discovery he was grateful to God that he had come that way, but a dangerous, blood-red anger took command of him as he dropped to his knees to see if Julio were alive or not.

Alvarez had her flashlight; by its beam Mott could see that the Brother had been stabbed in the side and, what was worse, that it had happened some time ago. The blood that had run out had hardened around the wound.

Mott did not waste a second. "Shine your flashlight so they can see it," he barked. He twisted the tiny knobs on the top of his radio and raised it to his mouth with his left hand. On the frequency he had tuned he was in direct contact with units a short block from where he stood. "This is Mott," he said. "In the gully . . . look for the flashlight. We need a Code Three run to UCMC."

Barely thirty seconds later two paramedics came running as fast as they could, closely followed by two deputies bringing a Gurney. He waited while Brother Julio's body was loaded onto the Gurney, then he climbed the short distance to see it put into an ambulance that took off immediately, red lights flashing in the night.

An SEB sergeant was beside him. "Go in," he said. "I'll handle the cleanup."

Mott fought to keep the image of what he had just seen out of his mind. He turned to Elena and saw that her face was a picture of anguish. "I'm ready now," he said.

They went Code Three, but as he let his head lean back against the seat his shoulder began to hurt so much he didn't even notice.

CHAPTER TWENTY-SIX

SHERIFF PETER PITCHESS stood at the podium, his hands resting on its edges, and flashed the famous smile that had insured him tens of thousands of votes he would have gotten anyway. His particular manner of informal dignity invited the confidence of his colleagues, who were well aware that he headed the largest law enforcement agency of its kind in the world.

As he waited for the large gathering to quiet down, he knew perfectly well why he had been invited to preside over this key session of the national conference of police executives. He was a headliner, and the work of his department was literally known throughout the world.

His smile vanished when he began to speak. "Gentlemen," he started, and then noting some feminine members of the press group he added, "and ladies. One of the most critical problems we are currently facing is juvenile gang violence. It has developed in many forms in different areas, but certain patterns of lawlessness have emerged and they are terrifying. Most large urban areas are affected, particularly those where ethnic minorities and cultures are prominent."

He turned and smiled at Mott who sat patiently behind him on a plain folding chair.

"In East Los Angeles, which is very strongly Mexican-American, we have been faced with this critical problem for some time. To tell you how we are dealing with it, I would like to introduce Lieutenant Ralph Mott, the commander of the gang control unit at our East Los Angeles Station.

"As you can see, Lieutenant Mott has his arm in a sling. I can tell you also that he is well taped-up underneath as a result of a recent encounter between two rival gangs. Perhaps in our academy we should put more emphasis on learning how to duck. At least it will prove to you that Ralph Mott is not a chairborne peace officer, but a very active one who has acquired a great deal of experience first hand. The only thing I have ever known really to intimidate him was the prospect of having to address you today.

"I invite you to listen to Lieutenant Ralph Mott."

Mott rose and took his position at the podium as soon as the sheriff had stepped aside. He put down his notes and then looked at his audience.

"Gentlemen," he began, "Some of you may remember those short films that were called 'Our Gang Comedies.' They featured a group of loveable kids whose harmless pranks did nothing more serious than splatter the milkman's white uniform with nice fresh mud. It was all a lot of fun. A gang at that time was a group of playmates and nothing more.

"Those innocent times are gone forever, at least insofar as the word *gang* is concerned. Gangs are now deadly terror organizations, and new ones are being formed, somewhere, while I am speaking to you now. For example: in the Casablanca area of Los Angeles County, which is about four or five square miles in area, eight new gangs were recently formed in less than four months, all in emulation of the gangs of East Los Angeles.

"The dangerous gang activities we know today started about forty years ago among the Chicano youths of what is commonly known as the barrio. From the beginning, participation was limited. At present we have between forty and fifty-five thousand young people under twenty residing in East Los Angeles. Of these, only fourteen hundred can be described as hard-core gang members. But I assure you that they are quite enough to account for the startling crime statistics that we are piling up every month.

"In the whole of Los Angeles County there are at present one hundred and eighteen known gangs that carry on an almost continuous program of theft and violence. In addition to the Chicanos, there are gangs made up of blacks, Samoans, Chinese, and Anglos. There are also outlaw motorcycle gangs and car clubs, most of which are ethnically mixed. They are almost all heavily involved in narcotics, weapons sales, extortion, robbery, forced sodomy, rape, and murder.

"Within East Los Angeles, the gangs are made up principally of juveniles from eleven years old on up, but there are also members who are twenty-five and more. The eleven-to-fourteen age group is called peewees; those from seventeen to twenty are heavies; above twenty-one they are known as *veteranos.*

"Sex is a substantial part of Chicano gang activity. In the barrio, the 'old culture girls,' who are in the strong majority, refrain from sex until they are married. The gang girls, who go with the gang members, are sexually very active. Within the gangs boys start sex at an average age of twelve or thirteen, but sexually active children as young as ten and eleven have been reported. The girls also often begin their sexual activities at a very early age—one study devoted to this subject notes that they often appear much more mature than they are. The birth rate in the barrio is very high.

"The problem is intensified by the very high percentage of illegal aliens, most of whom are by conviction totally loyal to Mexico. They have crowded into the area in such numbers that housing has become extremely critical, particularly in the Hollenbeck section of Los Angeles proper, which directly adjoins our jurisdiction. Under these living conditions, crime has spawned. In cooperation with Mexican authorities, we have developed information that juveniles are being trained in burglary in Tiajuana and then smuggled into the United States to join gangs specializing in that crime. They pay for their trips across the border by breaking into American homes and sending their loot back to their teachers. This is a continuous traffic that has not been abated.

"The most serious offense we have constantly to deal with is murder. It is a fallacy to believe that our juvenile gang murderers restrict themselves to killing each other. As an example, an ice cream vendor pedaling a tricycle was murdered in broad daylight by two gang youths for the sake of the small amount of money he had on his person.

"At present we are recording several serious incidents of gang-related violence daily. Gang members have boarded public transportation vehicles and robbed the passengers. One driver was forced by gang juveniles to drive six miles away from his route while they held an ice pick to his throat. The use of drugs, particularly marijuana and PCP, commonly known as Angel Dust, is commonplace.

"Let me summarize some incidents for you, all of which involved gangs or gang members in East Los Angeles. Two suspects were arrested driving a stolen car. Two more suspects were caught stealing a teacher's paycheck from her mailbox. A citizen's home was fired upon several times by shotguns. Two gang members threatened an off-duty deputy sheriff with a knife across the street from the sheriff's station. When he arrested one of them, the other committed battery on him while he was taking his prisoner in custody across the public highway. Two suspects were arrested after a high-speed chase through the streets of the city: the charges were reckless and drunken driving, and just prior to the chase, attempted murder. Three suspects, also gang members, walked up to a member of another gang and blasted him with a concealed shotgun, inflicting serious injuries. As the suspects fled, they shot another gang member who happened to be driving past in his car. A young woman with no gang affiliation had her car shot at several times, all in the same incident. From the suspects' car we recovered a twelve-gauge, sawed-off shotgun, a twenty-two calibre rifle, and a large quantity of ammunition.

"All of these events took place within *one day*, a day I selected at random from our monthly gang-activity reports."

Mott paused for a moment and took time to drink from a glass of water. Then, in almost complete silence, he continued.

"You may now be congratulating yourselves that East Los Angeles does not lie in your jurisdiction. I cannot offer you any comfort in that thought. According to our current intelligence reports, there are now approximately a hundred and fifty gang-related murders per annum in Chicago. In New York City, the gangs have developed to the point where they are terrorizing whole neighborhoods. They are made up principally of Puerto Ricans, Irish, and blacks. They usually work at night. One of their prime activities is burning down the houses of witnesses who have testified, or who possibly might testify against them.

"Also in New York, a gang invaded an apartment house and tried to evict the tenants from all thirty-two units so they could take over the building as a headquarters and clubhouse.

"In Detroit the gang situation has reached the level of intolerability. Philadelphia is not far behind. Throughout every part of the country, urban areas are being invaded and taken over by gangs, and law enforcement agencies have an almost impossible task in attempting to eradicate them. If two bandits hold up a liquor store, there is a good chance that they will be caught. But if fifteen juveniles invade the same store, terrify or kill the personnel, and then flee in fifteen different directions, apprehension of all of the suspects, identifying those who can be charged, and then gathering enough hard evidence to bring about a conviction in court are extremely difficult tasks.

"Even if all that is successfully done, there are some agencies, including some in our own state, who will release them after only minor periods of detention."

Mott stopped and looked up from his notes. He had detected a certain reaction from the area set aside for the press. It was subtle, but definite. He looked that way and spoke almost informally.

"There may be some of you who feel that the root of this problem lies in the citizens themselves and that the gang members are, in actuality, simply victims of their environment. Perhaps you feel that being disadvantaged, they are taking a certain revenge on society, perhaps even an understandable one. That is equivalent to describing a wildcat as a misplaced family pet.

"Cities have existed for centuries, and as a broad general rule they have offered more opportunity to the gifted and capable, or to the ordinary honest workman, than the rural areas ever have. Thirty years ago Central Park in New York was a recreational area for all the people of that city and it was widely used for that purpose. Now it is definitely unsafe by day and totally dangerous at night.

"It's altogether too easy to blame the cities themselves, or their law enforcement agencies. I offer the opinion, a purely personal

308

one, that those who advocate excessive leniency and who do not believe that a fifteen-year-old will regularly commit rape, are themselves in part responsible for some of the acute situations we face in the line of duty almost every day."

He didn't know if he had reached them or not, but at least he had tried. He had recognized one TV commentator whose antipathy to the police was well known. He went back to his notes.

"In another decade, most of the juvenile gang members, who are already skilled and hardened in criminal activity, will be mature adults. It is too much to hope that they will have taken up normal life-styles and occupations. Instead the tens of thousands of them comprise a massive criminal complex on a scale to rival the Mafia. In fact, they have already formed their own adult criminal organizations, and I can name them. Every law enforcement agency will have a greatly increased burden to bear, and the taxpayers will have to meet the cost.

"If the streets of our cities are unsafe now, it is deadly to forecast what they may be like ten years hence. Before we retire to our beds tonight, several people will be murdered by this new class of criminals; hundred of others will be robbed, stabbed, beaten up, raped, or mutilated. All of this will be done by the graduates of juvenile street gangs and by the gangs themselves.

"One final word. The gangs are no longer content to stay on their own turfs—they are beginning to be more mobile. They are coming out of the dense urban areas to hit other communities and to spawn new branches. Even quiet suburban areas are being invaded, and on a steadily increasing scale."

He looked again toward the media people. "You may feel that the particular place where you live is fairly safe from this kind of criminal activity because no such thing has ever invaded your decent privacy. Then you will open your door some day, step outside, and find that someone has defaced your property. On your front porch, on the side of the building, even on a window, you will discover black initials sprayed haphazardly for everyone to see. That will mean that your property has been claimed as gang turf, and your own time of terror will have begun.

"In summary I can put it simply: juvenile street gangs are the deadliest growing criminal virus we have to contend with today. And unless some existing laws are drastically revised, we will all find ourselves waging a losing fight against their kinds of violence. As of this moment it is an epidemic condition, and it is spreading. Thank you."

He stood there for several seconds in near silence. Then as he turned away from the podium, a thin ripple of applause at last began. Sheriff Pitchess stilled it by taking the rostrum once more.

"Every word you have just heard is true," he said. "If we can assist any other law enforcement agencies by detailing the techniques we have developed to deal with the youth gangs, please call on us."

At the break Mott made his escape and went out into the lobby. Elena Alvarez was there, neat and trim in a freshly laundered uniform, presiding over a table stocked with reports on gang violence and antigang programs. "That was a good speech," she said. "I listened."

"Any recent word from the hospital?"

"Danny is improved a little—he's ambulatory now. Next week they're going to let him sit in on some elementary training classes in the paramedic program. He asked after you."

Mott drew a deep breath and let it out. "One blessing, anyway. Anything else?"

"I'm on the committee for the Brother Julio Memorial Benefit."

"You told me that. Homicide just advised that they have his murder pretty well tied up. Montaña Mara had been planning their big operation for days. Julio stumbled onto it, and they felt he had to be silenced or he would betray them. Some of the gang members were sure that he had. It doesn't make any difference now. He was the best friend they could possibly have had, but at the showdown the gang came first."

Elena looked toward the meeting room. "How much did they believe of what you told them?" she asked.

"Some of it, perhaps. It's hard for some of them to accept what's going on without first-hand experience. Not all of them have that yet."

His side began to itch again under the tape, and it annoyed him more than it should. He tried to twist his body enough to relieve it, but it didn't work. If anything, it made it a little worse.

"Elena, I'm going home," he said. "Make my excuses, will you?"

"Of course. Take a good rest."

"I'll try to."

When he finally located his own car on the huge, crowded parking lot he unlocked it and got behind the wheel without too much trouble. He had pretty well mastered the art of one-armed driving, and if he had to use his right hand, he could. He started up and threaded his way out onto the street.

After a few blocks he was impatient to be within his own four walls, where Nancy could look after him. Whatever her other limitations, she did that superbly well. He got onto the freeway eventually and then settled down in the right-hand slow lane, partly to keep his injured arm out of sight. The less people knew about it, the better.

Forty minutes later he was in front of his apartment. He turned off the street down into the garage area and maneuvered his car into its designated stall. Thank God, that was the last thing he would have to do.

He walked up the ramp and felt the slightly cooler air of Santa Monica. He was hungry for every amenity he could have, for every fragment of peace and quiet. The talk was at last behind him and finally he could truly unwind.

He turned gratefully toward his own door—and then saw the sprawling black design that had been starkly spray painted all across the entrance wall.

www.ingramcontent.com/pod-product-compliance
Lightning Source LLC
Chambersburg PA
CBHW05055260626
47157CB00002B/569